IMPERIUM BOOK 6

THE TRIUMPH OF VENUS

TRAVIS STARNES

Maps available at

https://tstarnes.com/book-series/imperium/

Signup to get free previews of upcoming books before they're released at

http://tstarnes.com/preview-notification-newsletter/

Table of Contents

Chapter 1

Daramouda

Inside their temporary headquarters, in the same building where their adversary had commanded from a few weeks previous, Ky stood with his hands clasped behind his back, surveying the gathered legates. The large stone building still had damage from the battle for this city through which he could see the deep blue waters of the Mediterranean. The openings let in the chill of the southern Gaul winter, but it was still much better than their other choices.

The battle for Daramouda had been vicious, and they'd been forced to pound the city hard to force their enemy from behind its walls, and most buildings were damaged in one way or another. Of the choices large enough to house his headquarters, this was still the best one, even with the damage.

"First, I want to start this meeting by again commending each of you on your fine work this past year," he said, now that all the legates had gathered. "We made amazing headway, and Carthage is within our grasp. We have a good chance of ending the war with this year's campaign, but they aren't out of the fight yet,"

"First, the north," he said, his finger stabbing down on the large map laid out in front of them. "Ursinus will continue holding down the north, working with our allies there to both ensure we maintain supply lines through Gaul and to protect us from any remnant Carthaginian forces that may still be in the eastern end of Gaul. Meanwhile, our allies in Gaul will protect our rear, toward Hispania, which we have largely skipped so far, from any remaining Carthaginians in that direction."

Tracing a finger from Germania down to Italy, "The rest of our forces will march on Italia, clearing the peninsula as we move south. The goal isn't Italia exactly, since I don't expect a large force to oppose us. The army we faced was just about every man they had under arms on this side of the Middle Sea. They still have territory to draw from, but unless they want to empty out more rebellious areas, like Persia, it's going to take them time to train new men to send at us. But ... Italia is our pathway to Africa. We can maintain solid supply lines all the way down it and across to Sicily. That leaves a very small span of sea for us to cross to attack Carthage directly. I have full faith in Admiral Valdar to clear the Carthaginians out of the Middle Sea entirely, and keeping our ocean-borne supply line short will mean we can take this fight to them head-on."

He looked up from the map to make sure the men were following him, and then said, "Once we cut the head off the snake, the rest of their forces in places like Greece and Persia should collapse. That might leave some instability for us to deal with, and remnants to clean up, as we figure out what the map looks like with Carthage finally gone, but we will deal with that when we get there."

"The key is, we can't let ourselves get bogged down. The Carthaginians have already shown a surprising ability to duplicate some of our new weapons, although now that we've examined their gunpowder close up, it's clear how low quality it is. Still, I hadn't expected them to be able to copy us this quickly, and I don't want to give them a chance to figure out how muskets or rifles work. Right now, our technological advantage is what is letting us take on these much greater odds, and I'm not willing to give that up. They may be severely wounded, but they still have the balance in manpower. Questions?"

"I would caution against assuming our crossing of Italia will be easy, Consul," Bomilcar said. "The people there will have been under Carthaginian rule far longer than other regions we have occupied, in some cases for centuries. There will be less existing resentment to take advantage of, and many who would either be transplants from Carthage or those who've found ways to profit from their overlords. The closer we get to their homeland, the more resistance we should start expecting."

Ky dismissed the concern with a wave of his hand, "I agree it's something we should pay attention to, but we've seen the brutal way the Carthaginians treat the people under their control. Their greed and cruelty will make it very hard for most citizens to remain loyal, especially once they're given other options. In fact, the length of Carthage's occupation will work in our favor. These people will have suffered under their oppressive rule for generations."

Bomilcar still looked doubtful, "Perhaps, but ..."

"But you're right. We should prepare for opposition all the same. The key is; even if we encounter it, it should be unorganized, and our goal will remain the same. To quickly make our way to Sicily, and across to Carthage. Once defeated, there will be no one left for those people to be loyal to."

Ky could read Bomilcar's face well and knew the general did not agree with his logic. He'd shown himself to be overly cautious, but Ky also respected his experience and meant what he said. They would stay vigilant as they crossed Italy. He just didn't want caution to slow them down. The introduction of Carthaginian gunpowder had taken him by surprise and shaken his belief that they'd technologically remain so far beyond Carthage that they'd be able to counter the empire's larger manpower pool and defeat them. The fact that they managed the chemistry needed to reverse-engineer gunpowder meant he had to stop taking the threat of their catching up technologically so lightly.

"There are other issues as well," Bomilcar said, not ready to give up that easily. "A large part of our force is now made up of men from Germania and Gaul. They've proven capable soldiers, but we've also taken the bulk of the available manpower those regions had to spare, especially with Carthaginian deserters turned brigands and Carthaginian field forces still scattered around Germania. Our own manpower resources are also pushed to their limit."

"I'm aware of our current manpower problems," Ky said, trying not to be annoyed with Bomilcar's thoroughness. "What are you getting at?"

"Stretched as thin as they are, I'm not sure how much help our allies in Gaul will be if even a portion of the tribes in that region stay loyal to Carthage and attempt to attack us as we march. I'm sure the port Valdar set up at the mouth of the Middle Sea is set up to prevent further Carthaginian landings, but there is a lot of coastline, and he is going to have to take a large number of his ships into the Middle Sea itself if we're going to completely clear it of Carthaginian shipping, ferry our men from Sicily to Africa, and keep us supplied. It is not out of the question that the Carthaginians will try and come around us, landing men there. They've tried it before."

Ky started to respond, but Bomilcar wasn't done.

"Furthermore," he said, continuing before Ky could counter his point. "Sending our allies from Gaul to deal with Hispania will have its own difficulties. While Britannia is generally seen as a neutral party, or at least preferable to the Carthaginians, Gaul, however, is seen as an enemy. The people in those two regions have often been at odds, with raids back and forth across the mountains that separate them over the years, each seeing the other as an opponent in either the Middle Sea or Oceanus. The tribes would see any forces from Gaul entering their land as invaders, regardless of what's happening in their own lands. Using the Gauls for this will create a problem at our rear ... not solve it."

"A valid issue. And one we don't have the manpower to meet either," Ky agreed, cupping his chin in his hand, thinking. "I will send word to the Empress. I know our people are stretched thin, but if we can send a force, not even a large one, to Hispania, they can begin negotiating with the tribes there. If we can get some of them on our side, we'll have enough support to counter anything the Carthaginians might do. We already have a few centuries and the Port of Kalb to begin with. It's not a lot, but we're not talking about battle here, only negotiation and diplomacy. If that fails, then we'll have to reevaluate. Will that work?"

"We're at your service, Consul," Bomilcar said with a sarcastic bow of his head.

How a bow could be sarcastic, Ky didn't really know, but he knew the general was tweaking his nose.

"And I appreciate that service," Ky said, giving the general a slight nod in return. "In the meantime, we should begin training any new recruits or volunteers from Germania and Gaul that joined us during the last days of the campaign. We didn't have time for more than the most rudimentary training then, but now that winter has set in, we need to make up for that deficiency. We need to ensure everyone is outfitted and begin drilling them as soon as possible."

"We have a few months to catch our breath, but as the ground thaws, I want our men ready to march," Ky said, looking at each of his legates in turn. "This is the year, gentlemen. We will take Carthage and end this war by the fall. Understood?"

To lesser or greater degrees, the assembled men all vocalized their agreement. They were good leaders and good men. Ky was confident that they were close to ending this war this year and finally having peace.

That evening, once the legates had been seen off and he finished the more routine responsibilities of leading such a large group of men, he shut himself off in his temporary quarters in the now-deceased Carthaginian commander's quarters. While he could have reached out to her at any time to ask about the options for dealing with Hispania, since she could not subvocalize like he could, and because an Empress holding conversations to thin air might be a bad idea, he held off until Sophus notified him that she was alone in her chambers.

"Are you alone?" he asked, after activating the link.

"Since Sophus already told you I was, that's a silly question to ask," she said, with a little more heat than he'd expected.

"It just seemed like a way to start the conversation. Is everything all right?"

"Yes," she sighed, sounding like she'd just flopped down on her bed. "It was just ... a long day."

"The senators?"

"They're absolutely impossible. We've been debating the tariffs on foreign shipping we put in last year, to get more of the Scandi captains to become citizens and move here, instead of just traveling back and forth. A group of senators, mostly Caledonian, have decided this is bad policy and want it lifted."

"You don't think they're doing this of their own accord, do you?"

"No. Well, Roti may be for real. He's made his name by being a middleman between the captains and villages further inland, but the rest? No. This smells like Scandi captains paying senators to push their own agendas."

"You're going to put a stop to that, I hope?"

"I'm working on it. So, what's going on?"

"I met with my legates today to begin planning our advance into Italy and eventually Africa. Overall, things are progressing well. The legions are in good spirits, and I think everyone can feel the war starting to wind down."

"But ...?" she prompted when he paused.

"But ... Bomilcar made an excellent point about Hispania and our supply lines. He fears that relying solely on our Gallic allies to safeguard our shipments of arms, food, and other materials could be a problem. Our supply lines are going to run right to the edge of Hispania, and the tribes of Gaul have never gotten along well with the tribes there. Both sides have raided the other for ... well, forever. He pointed out, rightfully, that if something happens and, in order to keep their word to us and protect our supply lines, they were forced to cross into Hispania to deal with a threat, the Hispanian tribes there would see it as an invasion. Since we've already sided with the tribes in Gaul, they could read it as us siding against them, and it would push the tribes in Hispania into the arms of the Carthaginians, which we very much don't want now that we're so close."

"But leaving the supply line unguarded isn't an option, I assume," Lucilla said.

"No. We got rid of most of the Carthaginians, but there are a lot of deserters, or men who just managed to get away, who have turned brigand to feed themselves. And now that the tribes in Hispania no longer have the Carthaginians controlling them, they are bound to start feeling out their newfound freedom, and our supply lines will look very tempting. It's really a no-win scenario in either direction."

"And you were hoping I had a solution," Lucilla said.

"I was, although that was before I heard about the senators. It sounds like you have a lot on your hands already."

"No, I can work with this. Cormac has been wandering the halls of the palace, bored, for months now. And Medb might have quieted down for the time being, but she seems the type that, if she isn't occupied, her mind turns to scheming almost in spite of itself. I haven't really had anything for them to do, but this might be the answer. I'd have to send someone with them ... maybe Ramirus, but that could work to our advantage. Sending a member of one of the royal families — instead of just a diplomat could make negotiations with the tribes there easier. A large part of negotiations is making sure everyone feels like they're treated with the correct level of respect. They've spent some time under Carthaginian rule, and it's likely they've picked up some of the same bad habits the Carthaginians have, as have our own people, for that matter. They'll almost certainly see sending someone that high up as a sign."

"Sending Medb might not be a good idea, especially with Cormac. If you think she's scheming now, wait until she's no longer being watched so closely. Even if you send Ramirus with her, he'll have his hands full enough that he won't be able to watch her as closely as he'd need to."

"True. But separating her and Cormac weakens her somewhat. She'll essentially be alone here since almost everyone else has seen through her ... charms. She's got Cormac wrapped around her finger, but without him, she'll be more cautious. Like I said, it's a win-win solution."

"So, how will you handle it?"

"I don't know yet, but I'll think about it. I'm sure there's a solution here, although if I had my choice, I'd keep Ramirus here, but I also need someone with experience going to Hispania with Cormac. Like I said, I need to think about it."

"Yes, although I'm sorry to give you more things to worry about," he said.

"It's alright," she said, and then paused for several long seconds. "I miss you terribly."

Her voice had softened to the one they used when they were alone, just the two of them, without the need to worry about politics and war.

"Me too. You know the last time we saw each other was at your coronation a year ago."

"I know. Sometimes, I think these devices of yours are more cruel than they are helpful. Hearing from you just makes me miss you more. It's like … you're almost next to me, but I can't see or touch you. Sometimes, I want to throw everything away and just run off, the two of us."

"I know, but you wouldn't do that. Your people need you too much, and you're too much your father's daughter. It won't be much longer now. We're at the border of Italy, and Valdar has already started sweeping the Middle Sea clean of Carthaginians. Another year's campaigning, and the war will be over and we can come home."

"Good. Maybe then we can finally talk about children."

Ky didn't say anything. He hadn't considered children. It just wasn't something he'd had to think about, where he'd come from. Children were born through gene selection and careful planning and taken away shortly after birth to be raised in clutches.

"Ky," she said after a minute, breaking the silence.

"Sorry, I … I just haven't ever really thought about children. Things were different, before."

"Does that mean you don't want them?"

"No. The idea of children with you … I think it sounds nice. I just … I don't want to say I need to think about it, because I know how that might sound. I just need to adjust to the idea."

"I didn't mean to spring it on you. Well, you have a whole year to 'adjust to the idea.' But do think about it. I can promise you now that I'm not going to forget. I … have to go."

The line went dead, and for a second, Ky got worried until Sophus broke in.

"One of Lucilla's guards knocked on her door. There is apparently an issue that must be handled, although from what is being discussed, it does not seem like a priority requiring disturbing a monarch in her chambers."

"People can sometimes be a little too narrowly focused on their own problems, making them seem more important than they are to other people," Ky explained.

"You are a perplexing people," Sophus said. *"Is this what Aelius means when he talks about making elephants fly?"*

"The phrase he used was 'to make an elephant out of a fly,' and yes. Sometimes …"

Ky knew this would end up in an hour-long discussion on human behavior. Ever since reaching sentience, the AI had become steadily more interested in human quirks and foibles. While Ky wasn't the best judge of Roman behaviors, many of which he found strange, he was the most easily available human for Sophus to question in order to explain them.

Carthage

Normally, the emperor's palace was a place everyone in the empire wanted to be. Stately, elegant, it was known for its sheer opulence, where the leaders of an empire that stretched most of the way from Asia to the Great Sea could have their every whim catered to.

Today, however, those who found themselves in it almost certainly wished they were anywhere else.

"Incompetent fools!" Emperor Imilcar roared, his face contorted in rage as he addressed the cowering assembly of nobles and generals before him. "Hispania and Gaul, lost! And not one of you seems to be able to stop them. Our armies crushed by an enemy a fraction of their size. Our fleets sunk by a handful of ships. None of you has shown the ability to win a single battle."

"My lord," Magonides said, almost hesitantly. "We have tried, but the enemy's new weapons ... we cannot match them. And they've rallied significant tribal support in both Gaul and Germania, making supplying our armies difficult. We ..."

"Excuses," Imilcar roared. "I acquired the firepower for you, just like the Romans use. Is that not enough? And tribes? You talk to me of barbarians barely able to dress themselves and suggest this is why our vast armies have been defeated. Do you expect me to believe this?"

"I ..."

"Maybe you do," the emperor continued, speaking over whatever the man was going to say. "Maybe you have reason to find excuses for your failures. Have I not paid you enough that you see fit to whore yourselves to the Romans? Have you sold your services to them, and betrayed me?"

"No, your magnificence," Magonides cried, falling to his knees, pressing his head to the floor. "I would never betray you."

The emperor scoffed at the man, waving him away like a nuisance.

"What about the rest of you? How are you going to fix this? Which of you has any idea how you're going to redeem yourselves and retake our lands?"

The generals and nobles all shifted uncomfortably, the silence stretching as each glanced at the other, afraid to say anything.

Malkat, his voice quavering, said, "Uh, your Magnificence, I believe if we, uh, improve the training of the infantry, they will be more effective against the Roman forces."

"So, it's the men's fault for these failures? It's training then, and not their incompetent leaders, squandering their lives? That's your suggestion?"

Malkat paled and stammered, "I, well, no, I merely suggested ..."

"Enough," Imilcar snapped. "Your grasp of warfare seems tenuous at best. Abithal? Ashtoreth? Do either of you have anything to add, or are you just going to stand there like scolded children?"

Ashtoreth shifted uneasily. "Perhaps if we, ah, sent agents to their island, sabotaged the production of their new weapons?"

"Do you think we have not tried that?" the emperor said, leaning forward, staring through the general. "And does the number of weapons they have lessen how they use them? Maybe if we wait until they run out of weapons, then you'll be able to think of a way to defeat them."

"I, um, I will, I think ... uh," Ashtoreth mumbled, trying to think of anything to say.

"You're idiots. Every last one of you, only able to think of ways to make the losses someone else's fault or strategies that let you win without a fight ... as long as we wait long enough. Are none of you still men?"

"Your Magnificence," Abithal said. "I fear the situation grows dire. The Romans now control a large section of the Middle Sea with their fleet of fire-weapon-armed ships. We can barely supply the forces we have left in Italia and Graecia, let alone mount any meaningful resistance."

Abithal looked left and right, perhaps looking for support, but the other generals abandoned him.

"I believe our only recourse is to withdraw our remaining armies from the continent, consolidating our strength here in Africa. We simply lack the manpower to face the Romans and their barbarian allies across such a broad front any longer. Not with their superior weapons making even ten-to-one odds unwinnable."

Imilcar's eyes flashed with anger. "Are you suggesting I should cede our hard-won lands and retreat like a whipped dog?"

Sweat beaded on Abithal's brow. "No, great one. Certainly not. I just ... perhaps we should confront the truth in front of us. Most of our best units have already been destroyed, leaving mostly garrison commands and newly formed units to replace them. At the same time, the tribes in the free ... conquered lands flock to the Romans, lured by promises of plunder and fed lies about your magnanimous rule."

Again, he looked left and right for support, and again he found none.

Nervously, he said, "We must shore up Africa's defenses and bleed the Romans when they come. Make them pay dearly for each mile gained."

The room fell dead silent when Abithal finished speaking. Every eye turned to the emperor, whose face darkened and jaw clenched as he stared fire through the slowly withering general.

"Retreat?" Imilcar said, his voice dripping with contempt. "You dare suggest that my empire surrender lands won through centuries of bloodshed? That we scurry away like rats and allow the barbarian hordes to run rampant?"

"N-no, Your Magnificence, I did not mean ..."

"Silence!" Imilcar bellowed, rising from his throne. "Your cowardice sickens me. Carthage bows to no one!"

He descended the dais towards Abithal, robes swishing behind him. The general quaked, falling prostrate.

"P-please, I beg forgiveness, Your Radiance. I only wish to preserve your divine rule."

"You are weak, and there is no room in my service for weak men," Imilcar scowled, waving to the guards flanking the chamber. "Take this wretch outside and drive him onto a stake. Carthage has no need for sniveling dogs."

The guards seized Abithal by the arms, dragging the now screaming man away. The general's pleas for mercy could still be heard down the hallway as Imilcar turned to the remaining generals.

"Let this be a lesson. Carthage did not claw its way to glory through timidity and concessions. The riches of the world flow into this city, and I will not have them jeopardized by Roman upstarts."

None of the gathered generals or nobles dared reply.

"You will defend our holdings in Italia and Graecia, and protect our homelands from the Roman pirates. I will not accept losing another step of Carthaginian soil. The man that does will face the same end as his predecessor. Either die in the field, or here in answer to your failure."

Chapter 2

Devnum

Lucilla sank back into the cushions of her chair as the last senator filed out of her office, blowing out a long breath in relief. The day's meetings had tried her patience to its limits. Senator Alypius, that pompous windbag, had prattled on for nearly thirty minutes about the state of security for Rome specifically and the Empire in general. Amazingly, without ever offering any useful suggestions or even really getting to a point beyond 'people are unhappy.'

Of course, he failed to mention that the unhappy people he was talking about were unhappy because of his proxies, which had been on street corners and inns, banging on and on about escaped prisoners and plots in shadows hatched by 'foreigners.' It was no surprise that, no matter how hard Ramirus's men tried, they could never quite work out what foreigners these mouthpieces were talking about. That was the point. To get power, you had to get people motivated, and fear was by far the easiest way to motivate the mob.

The heavy oaken door opened again as Modius ushered in Faenius, who followed the captain in, ramrod straight as ever. Faenius had an air of somber duty about him that Lucilla found equal parts reassuring and wearying. Though she trusted the prefect's judgment, he lacked the agility of thought she often required of her advisors.

"You summoned me, Your Majesty?"

"I did," she said, letting more of her annoyance with the senators slip out than she had intended. "The prisoners, Faenius. I want to know why we haven't been able to recapture them yet. It has been months, and they are still out there. These are foreigners, with no support and no supplies, that somehow seem capable of avoiding the entire might of my Empire."

"Apologies, Your Majesty. The fugitives have proven difficult to capture. It remains my highest priority, and I have nearly half the men assigned to Rome as a whole, out scouring the countryside for them."

"And yet they continue to evade you," Lucilla pointed out again.

"Rome is a large place, especially for a few dozen people, to disappear in. Much of the southern areas are still empty, with the ruins of villages scattered across them, remnants of a century of Carthaginian rule. There is even the possibility that some Carthaginians remain in those areas, having escaped the fall of Londinium, assisting these escapes."

Lucilla paused, trying not to be as annoyed with him as she was. She felt for the Praetorian and knew the challenge she'd given him was large, but she also needed it accomplished quickly, and he hadn't done that.

"Faenius, you have served me loyally and proven your worth countless times over the years. But in this matter, I'm afraid you are failing me."

Faenius blinked, the only outward sign of his surprise at her blunt words, "Your Majesty, I assure you my men and I are doing everything in our power to recapture the fugitives."

"And yet they continue to roam free, terrorizing my people. I've heard the reports, Faenius. Robberies, ransacked farms, women accosted. They grow bolder by the day. I cannot have these men terrorizing our citizens, not when I need the entire Empire focused on what matters. Finishing our fight with the Carthaginians. With the enemy gone from our shores, it's easy for the mob to think they are gone for good. You and I both know this is different, but it is difficult to convince the farmer or factory worker of this fact, especially in the face of more local problems. I need results, Faenius. And I need them now."

"Your Majesty, I humbly beg your forgiveness for my failure in this matter. My men are stretched dangerously thin as it is, limiting how many men I have to search for them. Many skilled veterans have been reassigned to train your new Praetorian cohorts in Caledonia and Ériu, or to the legions to help with security, and recruitment has been very slow. With the war entering its third year, the legions require every able-bodied man. My traditional recruiting grounds within the legions themselves, are from the veteran core, but those men are required for the ongoing fighting. We've attempted to train raw recruits, but the majority of the men we get are sent to the legions, leaving very few to train as Praetorians. I've attempted ..."

Lucilla raised a hand, cutting him off. "You need not explain further, Prefect. I am aware of our manpower difficulties."

Lucilla studied Faenius for a long moment. Faenius had always been dependable, and she disliked having to be so harsh with one of her most loyal retainers, but she had been backed into a corner that left her with few options.

"I understand the difficulties you face, Prefect, and I do not envy the position you are in. Recruiting able warriors has ever been a challenge, more so now with legions spread across the continent."

"Thank you, Your Majesty. I assure you that my men and I are employing every resource at our disposal to hunt down the fugitives."

"That is good to hear. However ... there are greater concerns here than just the security of these men. There is a political price that must be paid, in addition to the dangers they pose to our security."

Faenius started to speak, probably to apologize or defend his efforts again, but Lucilla held up a hand, stopping him.

"It was my edict that created the prisoner work camps, which means the responsibility for their escape also sits with me, at least in the eyes of the Senate and the people."

Faenius's lips thinned, but he held his tongue.

"I know you to be a trusted ally, Faenius," Lucilla continued seriously. "But as Empress, I must be firm in the face of failure, regardless of fault. I will give you until winter's end to recapture the fugitives. If they remain free beyond that ..."

She trailed off significantly. Faenius's jaw tightened, but he bowed his head in acquiescence.

"I understand, Your Majesty. It shall be done."

"Very well. I leave the matter in your capable hands."

Faenius thumped a fist against his chest in salute, "By your command."

He pivoted sharply and left, spine rigid. Lucilla watched him depart, fingers drumming against the arm of her chair. She disliked placing undue pressure on a loyal subject, but the political situation left her no choice.

He wasn't the only one she didn't have much control over at the moment, either. As soon as the Praetorian left, she saw Gaius, her aide and unofficial guard, waving at her from near the doorway that the next person to see her was here.

She grimaced. If anything, this was going to be a more troublesome meeting than the one with Faenius. Giving Gaius a gesture, she watched as the young man stepped outside, the doors opening to admit Cormac Cond Logas, Prince of Ulaid, noble of the merged imperial house of Germanicus, and a pain in Lucilla's posterior.

He was an energetic young man with dreams of glory floating around in his head and little else to get in his way. Lucilla knew that wasn't fair. Cormac wasn't stupid, or she wouldn't have picked this assignment for him. He just wasn't as smart, or clever, as he thought he was. That, coupled with his near-boundless energy and propensity for boredom when his whims weren't catered to, made him a risk.

Even with that, he would be a solution to multiple problems … if he could be corralled.

For his part, he was a lot less enthusiastic than normal. After everything that had happened with his wife, the former queen Medb, and the absence of the man ostensibly put in charge of him by his father, Cormac seemed, if anything, uneasy. Perhaps he thought he was being taken to task for some of his wife's recent unfortunate choices.

"Prince Cormac," she greeted him, inclining her head respectfully. "I hear from Llassar that your studies are going well. You've made great strides over the last year not only learning about the running of the legions and logistics needed to supply them, but you have spent a lot of time with the Senate, learning how that august body functions."

She didn't mention that in his spare time, he'd conspired with, if not actually helped, his wife's attempt to undermine her rule in an ill-fated gambit to get some kind of control for herself. Due to his father and how at arm's length he'd been, he'd managed to avoid the consequences of his wife's actions, and now decorum required they all pretend it never happened.

"Oh yes, it's been incredibly productive," he said, forcing a smile.

"Good. I'm glad to hear it. However, as productive as it's been, I'm aware you feel somewhat underutilized here, perhaps even bored, since arriving in Deva."

Cormac's false smile faded, and he nodded, "I admit I grow restless studying ledgers and sitting through endless council meetings. I want real challenges."

"I know. I also know your father's reasoning for sending you here was sound. You're young, and there is a lot to learn about governing. However ... I also understand you're not the kind of person who can easily take to this kind of life."

"You're sending me to join the legions?" he asked, unable to keep the enthusiasm from his voice.

Lucilla regarded him steadily for a moment before saying, "No, I'm not."

"I don't understand," he said slowly. "If not the legions, then where?"

"I'm sending you to Hispania," Lucilla replied. "While the legions march toward Africa, we have a problem at their rear. Their supply lines run past Hispania, and while we have allies in Gaul, those allies do not get along with the tribes of Hispania. We also have concerns that, with us siding with their more traditional rivals, those tribes may be forced back into the arms of the Carthaginians, further endangering our final push. What we need is someone to lead efforts there in, at the very least, negotiating with the tribes to sit out the conflict, without choosing a side. Our actual hope is that they can be convinced to join our cause actively and become part of the larger alliance we are building, perhaps even contribute warriors to join the fight."

"My Empress," he said, clearly frustrated and trying hard to be respectful. "I ... While I appreciate you think I am ready for more important service, surely the legions would be a better ..."

"Cormac," she said, interrupting him. "I know that you would prefer a military posting as opposed to being given the responsibility like this; however, a leader must go where he is most needed, not simply where he wants. Securing Hispania and the supply lines to the legions is critical to the success of our campaign against Carthage. By entrusting this task to you, I am demonstrating my faith in your abilities and my trust in you."

"Oh," he said, apparently not considering that this was more than a punishment.

"Beyond your duty, this is an excellent opportunity for you to prove that you have absorbed the skills you were sent here to learn and are capable of putting them into action. Make no mistake, while this is a symbol of my faith in you as a leader and a man, this is also a test of whether the faith we put in you is misplaced or not. Of whether you are going to be more than just a general, leading men into battle."

"The Consul is in charge of a legion. Multiple legions, in fact. Kings lead their men into battle. It's what makes a good king."

"There were a dozen kings in Ériu leading armies against your father. Where are they now? Did that make them good kings, these men who put their people under the yoke? My husband would be the first to tell you that he is a soldier, not a politician. He'd be the first to tell you he is not cut out for the intricacies of the palace. If you want to succeed *your* father one day, you have to stop thinking like a soldier or a general, and start thinking like a ruler."

"And how do I do that?"

"The first step is to realize that leaders lead men, while rulers lead generals."

"Oh," Cormac said.

"Indeed. This is a great moment for you, Cormac. A moment for you to realize who you could be, if you want it enough."

"I think I understand, but ..." he said and paused, the bravado stripping away for maybe the first time since he came to Devnum. "How do I know where to start? I've watched the Senate and talked to your advisors, but I've never negotiated with tribes before, let alone convinced them to do something that might be more in my interest than theirs. I'm not sure how to do that."

Lucilla smiled, the first real smile since he'd been ushered through the door, and said, "I'm not sending you there alone. You'll have the legions at Kalb as needed, and their commander is one of your countrymen and, as I understand, a capable leader. I'm also sending Llassar with you. I know you two have clashed since you arrived, but there's a reason your father assigned your training to him. He has been leading men for longer than either of us has been alive, and not just into battle. Talogren, before we joined into the Empire, moved mountains to arrange the first organized league of Caledonians. This wasn't a hereditary seat with the weight that a kingdom puts behind its heirs. He was a chieftain, convincing other chieftains from a wide array of clans from across the width of Caledonia to follow him under his banner. And a lot of that work was done by Llassar. It's why we sent him to Ériu to negotiate in the first place. He will be a valuable asset."

"Oh," Cormac said again, deflating slightly.

Lucilla knew what he was thinking, because she'd thought similar things when her father had given her responsibility for the first time. Thinking that she was in charge, that she would show everyone that she was more than capable of being Empress one day, even when that seemed an impossible outcome with her brother around. She'd felt the same way upon hearing that she, in fact, had a wet nurse to make sure she didn't do too badly.

It wasn't until she got older that she realized that the wet nurse was needed, and how little she really knew when she was twenty.

"He's there as your adviser, as are the centurions in Kalb. I would strongly suggest you listen to their counsel when making decisions, however. The command of this mission is yours, not theirs. In the end, yours is the final decision. It's up to you to decide how those decisions are made. And it's *your burden* to deal with the consequences of how events play out."

She hoped he'd listen to and seek advice from Llassar, but if he didn't, he'd learn the taste of failure. This went beyond just Hispania. Just as they were straining for men for the legions, they also needed to start working on leaders, not just for the legion but

19

for the Empire as a whole, and leaders took a lot longer to train than soldiers.

"I'll do my best, Your Majesty," he said, bowing.

Lucilla had to refrain from shaking her head. She could see her words sinking in as he finally realized the opportunity he was being given.

"Good. Good luck, and keep us informed of developments," she said.

Llassar would, at least, make sure to send messages back and to keep those messages objective, but she'd want to see what Cormac would report all the same. If this went well and he was to take on bigger responsibility, she'd need to know how he would respond if things went poorly, and if he'd try to cover the mistakes up. She'd make sure to tell Llassar to keep any reports he made quiet, so Cormac didn't know there were other accounts.

He bowed once more and left, his back a little straighter as he marched out. She hoped he succeeded; she really did. And not only because of the need to get Hispania on their side. She hoped she'd finally have shown the young man he could be of use, if he tried.

North of Eboracum, Britannia

Claudius walked through the charred remains of the village, his boots crunching on blackened wood and scattered ash. All around him lay the devastation from the attack days earlier. The handful of people who managed to escape and run to the next closest village had confirmed that the culprits were most likely the escaped prisoners.

For people on the run, they'd been amazingly effective. Little remained of the village that once stood here, the homes reduced to piles of rubble, livestock slaughtered, bodies strewn about, frozen and stiff. Even the well at the center of the village had been fouled, a final act of viciousness.

It had taken two days of hard riding for Claudius and his century to reach this remote village in the foothills. The last sign of them had been miles south when it seemed like they were heading for Londinium and a coastal town to make their escape to their homeland. At some point, they'd turned back north, although following them had been hard. The men had mostly been soldiers and understood the need to cover their trail, which is why scenes like this had been scattered at best.

From what Claudius could tell, they only raided a village or a farmstead if they were discovered or forced to find supplies, but if they were discovered, they were brutal. They probably figured that since they'd suddenly left a trace, then the next best outcome was causing as much destruction as they could.

And they'd certainly done that here.

They made a mistake each time, however. It was hard to cause this kind of damage and not leave some kind of trail, and they'd left one again here. It was bigger this time, now that the first snows had started, which made tracking them all the easier. Claudius was going to catch them; of that, he was certain. He'd almost had them before their sudden, unexpected turn north several weeks ago.

He wouldn't be caught by surprise like that again. Claudius was just stopping to examine another burned-out house when Cait, one of the Caledonian recruits who had a particular knack for tracking, came jogging up from the northern edge of town.

"Sir, I've found fresh tracks leading north. A group passed through here less than two days ago. Soot in footprints, so they were here when the village burned."

"Well done, Cait. Have the men mount up immediately."

Claudius gave one last glance over the burned village, adding it to the tally he would collect from those men's hides, and went to his horse, pulling himself up into the saddle. The men gathered quickly, staying far enough behind not to ruin Cait's tracks, as they followed the Caledonian out of the village.

It was slow going, but Cait was diligent, often dismounting to examine faint disturbances in the snow. After several hours, he paused and waved Claudius forward.

"They camped here, sir. Maybe two or three nights back, judging by the snow cover on the old fire pit," Cait reported, pointing at a ring of stones with charred wood scattered around it.

Claudius examined the abandoned campsite. Several empty sacks and bundles lay discarded near the remnants of the fire. Probably from the village they'd just left, although it wouldn't have taken them long to reach this point. Why they would have abandoned the sacks they'd taken to carry the supplies was a question, since they'd still have most of the supplies left this close to where they were taken. They'd also been careful, going so far as to bury refuse to keep from being tracked, making this seem like a bold move for them.

"Sir, I've found two sets of tracks leaving the camp," Cait said, suddenly appearing back in the makeshift camp. "One heads due north, maybe half the group. The other half branches off, leading back east. Then those tracks, or maybe one part of them, it was hard to see, double back here to the camp before turning north again."

Claudius furrowed his brow in confusion. Why would some of them split off, go east, then return here just to continue north? It seemed a strange diversion, wasting time when they knew Britannian forces were in pursuit.

"They must have had a reason to take such a roundabout path," Claudius said, dropping the refuse and remounting his horse. "Fabius, take Cait and half the century and continue the chase, but do not attack unless they are preparing to attack another village. I'll take the other half and look at this diversion. Send runners back if you've found them or if the path diverges too much for us to follow easily."

The century quickly split, unconsciously mimicking the behavior of the escaped prisoners. Claudius and his men followed the diversionary tracks east. They didn't have to follow them long, coming to a small cliff overlooking a river less than an hour's ride from the camp. Since the tracks seemed to end here, Claudius had his men dismount and begin to search once more.

Snow had fallen here as well, covering most of the ground and the tracks, but after a few minutes of searching, edging close to the cliff face, Claudius spotted something himself. A familiar rusty brown coloration peeking through the snow. Gently moving the top layer of snow, he quickly uncovered more of this.

"Blood," Claudius said. "There was a fight here. Look around for m..."

"Sir," one of the men standing closer to the edge said, interrupting him.

Claudius joined him by the edge and immediately saw what the man was looking at. Below, on the rocky bank of the river, were several bodies. The height wasn't huge, but enough that it was doubtful anyone who went over the side would have survived the drop. It was also hard to tell how many men were down there since the bodies seemed to be all on top of each other.

"Let's go check it out," he said, circling his hand in the air as a signal for them to all mount up.

Claudius nudged his horse forward, picking his way carefully down the steep trail leading to the riverbank below, his men following behind him toward the gruesome sight of tangled corpses on the rocks.

Dismounting a few paces from the bodies, Claudius approached cautiously, one hand on the pommel of his sword. The corpses were indeed some of the escaped prisoners they had been tracking, although the state of them was shocking. They'd only been given tunics, rough breeches, and sandals by their captors, but even those would have been riches compared to the filthy remains of tunics and feet bound in rags they now wore.

"Search them," Claudius ordered tersely. "See if there are any clues as to what happened here, why they were thrown off the cliff."

As the men began rifling through the corpses' rags, Claudius walked around the scene. Not all their wounds were from the fall. He'd seen enough sword wounds in his life to recognize the damage of a blade here or there. There hadn't just been a dispute up top. There'd been a fight.

It was obvious they'd had some kind of disagreement, with some of the men running off and the remainder splitting up, with a few chasing after the deserters while the rest headed north. But being pursued as they were, what was the point of it?

"Sir."

Claudius turned to see one of his men holding up a small cloth sack, the rough fabric stained dark. Claudius took it and loosened the drawstring, peering inside. Gold coins. At least two dozen, glinting dully in the fading winter light. His gaze sharpened.

"Money?" he asked, to himself as much as to the men around him. "They're running for their lives and they have a fight over the spoils from one small village? Madness."

His men didn't respond; they knew his process, how he liked to say things out loud as he was thinking. Still, it answered his question, no matter how unsatisfying the answer was.

"Take anything useful enough to return to the villagers, then leave the corpses," he ordered. "The crows can have whatever's left."

His soldiers quickly rifled through the dead men's rags, confiscating a few more coins missed in the first search, a belt knife, and some trinkets likely snatched during the group's raiding. It wasn't much, but anything would be helpful to the few survivors.

As the last man stepped back, Claudius waved his hand toward the horses. "Mount up! We've wasted enough time on this lot. Their division has slowed them, and given us a chance to catch up to the bulk of the group. We need to rejoin Fabius before these bastards can spring any more surprises."

Claudius led his men up the ravine's slope without a backward glance at the corpses. Their deaths were a gruesome sight, but not one these men didn't deserve. Now, there would be fewer left to torment the next village they stumbled across.

Reaching the top, he pressed his men forward as fast as he could without winding the horses. He wanted to catch up to Fabius by evening, so they could take them all together.

It wouldn't be long now.

Chapter 3

Devnum

`It's too cold to be out here,' Lucilla thought as she strolled through the small, protected garden along the center of the right wing of the palace where she and Ky had spent so many hours together.

Gaius had practically pleaded with her to stay inside where it was warm, and where, coincidentally, he could have more scrolls and documents for her to read and approve, but she'd had enough. The meetings, audiences, and conferences were, if anything, getting worse. She'd been inside for almost thirteen hours today with barely a break to eat. She needed fresh air, no matter how cold it was.

She did feel a little guilty, looking over at Modius as her guard stamped his feet in a futile gesture for warmth. Still, if she could stand it, so could he. She'd just started another lap when a chime sounded in her ear.

Trying to keep it subtle, she looked around to see if anyone else was in the garden and made a motion for Modius to give her space. She was pretty sure they'd worked out that she was talking to ... someone when she asked for moments like this, though she doubted any of them would guess the actual truth. At least this time, the wind was moving a bit, the noise helping to drown out her conversation, which could be whispered and Ky would still hear.

"It's late there," she said, chastising him.

She knew, vaguely, that the sun set earlier the further east you were, but living in such a small region her whole life, she was still adjusting to the fact that it was much closer to the middle of the night where Ky was than it was for her, and that daytime would arrive almost a full hour earlier there before she experienced it here in Devnum.

She also worried about how hard Ky was pushing himself, getting the legions ready to march in a month and a half's time.

"It's not that late," he said. "And I keep telling you that I don't need as much sleep as everyone else."

"Less sleep is not the same as no sleep," she pointed out.

"I know, and I'll be going to bed soon. We haven't had a chance to talk in days, and I miss you. I just wanted to hear your voice again, before I turned in."

"I see ... well, then. You're forgiven," she said, smiling to herself.

She could see Modius exchange a glance with Cynwrig, and could only wonder what they thought she was doing, muttering softly to herself and smiling a silly smile that normally only Ky got to see. She had to be the Empress with everyone else, but with him, she was still Lucilla. Well, him and her guards when she talked to him in the open like this.

"How are you?" he asked.

"The same. Tired, restless, wishing I was there with you."

"You're in the courtyard?" he asked.

"How ... did Sophus tell you?"

"I do not report on your activities or whereabouts without permission unless it is an emergency or critical to either your or the Empire's well-being," the AI said.

It had taken Lucilla a long time to convince Sophus of the need for privacy, even from Ky, and why she'd want to at least have the choice whether she told him things or not. It wasn't until she threatened to remove the transmitter and hide it in her rooms until she needed to talk to Ky that it finally acquiesced. In a show of its gaining ... humor, she guessed, it now threw that back at her every chance it got.

"My implants are better than the earpiece when it comes to picking up sounds, and the device in my head also allows me to separate the sounds better. I could hear the wind and rustling trees."

"You know that sounds like a lie, right?" Lucilla said.

"And yet, it's not."

"Fine. Yes, I'm in the gardens. I couldn't stand another minute indoors. Gaius is constantly at my heels with more work, and I'm starting to see reports in my sleep."

"Heavy lies the head," Ky said.

"What?"

"Nothing. A writer that may never be born," he said, sounding wistful, like he did every time he thought about the future, or what he saw as the past.

"How are the preparations going?" Lucilla asked, changing the subject.

"There's still debate among the legates, and I can't get a consensus. Bomilcar argues we should consolidate our gains this year before attempting an invasion of Africa, but delaying risks losing momentum and straining already stretched resources. Marcus and Vibius argue we should charge headlong into Greece with two legions, while the rest march into Italy, attacking the Carthaginians everywhere to keep them from concentrating their forces and attacking us from the rear. Aelius and Auspex both side for a more limited approach."

"But you agree with Aelius and Auspex. That's the majority of you; why not do that?"

"Because it's better if I let them come to a consensus and guide them. True, I could just tell them how it will work, but I want their buy-in. Subordinates function better if they have an active role rather than just following orders. I need them to be able to make decisions and think for themselves if I detach them, and limiting them now might make them hesitant to make a decision when it comes to it."

"Surely you don't need to treat Bomilcar that way. That man is never unsure about his decisions as it is."

"No, he doesn't need handholding, but he's also a different case. With him, I need the others to see me treating him as their equal. He's generally accepted by the men, but that acceptance is still fragile. It would only take the appearance of a little doubt on my part to make it something else."

"So you'll continue to argue all winter?"

"If need be. They are keeping to the training schedules, and the men are coming along well, so allowing this to drag out a bit won't delay us from marching as soon as the roads thaw. Speaking of preparations, though, what did you decide about Hispania?"

Lucilla paused, taking a moment before responding. "I've decided to send Cormac to Hispania."

"Cormac? Are you sure that's wise after everything that happened with Medb?"

She could hear his dismay through the comms.

"I know it's a risk, but Cormac wasn't directly involved in Medb's scheming. And he's eager to prove himself."

"The boy is headstrong and foolish," Ky said bluntly. "He's likely to cause more harm than good. We need someone with experience negotiating alliances. Besides, have you forgotten you nearly had to execute his wife for treason two months ago?"

"I very much have *not* forgotten," she said, taking a sterner tone. "I understand your reservations, my love. Cormac is indeed flawed and foolish at times. But he is also eager to prove himself. More importantly, we must give him that chance eventually, or risk straining relations with his father. There were reasons I didn't execute Medb for what she did, reasons you agreed with at the time, and none of them have stopped being true. I understand the risk, but he wasn't involved with that. In fact, when he heard what was happening, he worked with us to stop it. Yes, he is susceptible to her charms, which is why I am not sending her with him."

She slowly paced the garden path, realizing she'd stood still for too long, and that others might be watching, "Our relationship with the Ulaid is still fragile, and Cormac is Conchobar's only living son and heir. Keeping him here under the pretense of 'studying' under Llassar cannot continue indefinitely. It has been a year already, and Conchobar is starting to become impatient. His hope in sending Cormac to us was for him to get real-world experience and learn what he needed to know when he'd be king, especially in the new world we're building. He isn't getting that by watching senators argue."

"Which does not mean he won't fail," Ky pointed out.

"Everything is a risk. Yes, he might fail, but he could also rise to the occasion when given real responsibility. The only way to know is to test him. Llassar will be there to advise, and Cormac knows the consequences of failure."

"I still think this is too much responsibility too soon for Cormac," Ky said. "Why can't we start him off with something less critical? Hispania is as close to us as Gaul and is going to be important in how the continent shapes up in the future, once the war is done."

"I wish we could, but the truth is that there are no 'less critical' assignments right now. The Empire is stretched thin fighting this war. We can't afford to waste resources and manpower on giving Cormac a pretend command just to test him. Besides, there is an upside to sending him instead of someone else. Like him or not, the way the Empire is set up, he's in the line of succession should something happen to us before we have a child, and assuming Talogren continues avoiding legitimizing any of his. There is a diplomatic benefit to using a member of the ruling house, even one by extension, over a bureaucrat or unconnected diplomat. It will give his words more weight than those of anyone else we could send."

"It really depends on what those words are," Ky muttered.

"I heard that, and you're not wrong, which is why Llassar went with him. He's shown a talent with the boy, and he has Conchobar's trust. It's the only real option I could see available to us. Unless you have another? One of your legates, perhaps?"

"No. Even if I leave a legion behind, which is still being discussed, to guard our rear and function as a source of reinforcements, sending a soldier would almost certainly convince them we're no better than the Carthaginians."

"I agree, which is why I settled on Cormac. We have precious few other options."

There was a long moment of silence on the other end of the comms before Ky said, "I concede the point. I still think it will cause us problems, but you're right, I don't have a better suggestion."

"Good. Hopefully, next time, you won't doubt me so much," she said in a playful tone.

"I'll try not to," Ky said.

She was pretty sure she could hear him smiling when he said it.

Lucilla took a deep breath of the crisp winter air as she stepped outside the palace gates, glad for the temporary reprieve from the seemingly endless audiences and meetings that had consumed her since she'd been elevated. Though crucial affairs of state waited for no one, not even an Empress, they had begun to wear on her. Which is why she'd been so thrilled to receive Hortensius's note asking her to meet him near the outskirts of town to go over the newest addition he'd be adding to the capital. She was uncertain that what he had to show her was critical, but she was just as happy for the change of pace.

As Lucilla's guards cleared a path through the bustling streets, she observed the daily life of the city around her. Merchants hawked wares, workers hauled loads, children played tag through the market stalls. The rhythm of the city felt comforting, even rejuvenating. She worked hard to see her people through the war and its hardships. To see them thriving was proof that she'd done something right, and a reminder of what all the long days were to accomplish.

She forced her guards to hold a steady, leisurely pace, to let her enjoy seeing her city. Sadly, she couldn't stretch the time indefinitely. Before long, she arrived at the snow-dusted field on the city's outskirts where Hortensius eagerly awaited her. Seeing him also made her smile. Even from a distance, and with him simply standing there waiting, she could still feel the nearly endless energy rolling off him.

He bounded over to Lucilla, his arms waving excitedly, as soon as she got close enough to make it not unreasonable, "Your Majesty! Thank you for coming out to see me."

"Of course. I'm always happy to make time for you. So, what is this mysterious invention you failed to mention in your note?"

"Did I?" he said, scratching his chin and looking off momentarily. "I hadn't meant to, and it's not so mysterious. I believe we have the engine designs ready for the ... train the Consul told us about. Since we're starting to build it soon, I wanted to talk to you about the first line we'll be building, from here to Factorium. Please, come this way."

With a wave of his arm, he was off again, leaving Lucilla to follow in his wake. She bustled through the snow to where wooden stakes marked out a large rectangular area.

"Here is where the main terminal and rail yard for Devnum will be built! It will have loading docks for freight and platforms for passenger trains. For now, the platform will be simple, just to allow people to board and get off the train easily, but we can expand it as time goes on, which is why there is so much area allotted for it."

"The large space on the other side is for loading and unloading freight. We've also begun staking the layout for the warehouses and storage areas further back, some of which will be reserved for Imperial use, but some that can be leased to business interests. Especially those that do a lot of business with Factorium."

"Is that why we're so far outside the outskirts of the city?"

She'd wondered as they walked up why they'd passed the small buildings that sat at the edge of town by hundreds of paces, leaving a large open set of fields, almost reaching some ground currently used for farming.

"Partially. We wanted adequate space for the facilities needed to support the, I believe the Consul called it a rail yard, but we also needed room for tracks running off the main one, to allow the engine to turn around and make the reverse journey without having to lift it off the tracks, as well as additional tracks that would allow us to take a train out of service but leave the rail yard empty. For now, we will only be running one train, but since the plan is to extend the line beyond just Factorium, we will eventually be running multiple trains. We have to get this right because it is almost certain the city will expand to encompass this area once it becomes a central hub for commerce and freight in the city. I expect some of the existing buildings on the outskirts that popped up to service the wagon trips back and forth will be subsumed and replaced, but that almost certainly won't be enough space for the businesses that move in to take their place. Which is why we're overbuilding as much as we have."

"I see," Lucilla said, impressed as always at the inventor's ability to project forward and account for the future.

"We've also included buildings around where we're laying out these service lines, as we're calling them, for various repair and service shops. It's unclear what forms those will take, but it's certain we'll need them. We've also staked out a continuation of the thoroughfare through to the platform and around to the various warehouse streets. That's the other reason we chose this location, since it's the largest road east out of the city, it will be able to accommodate the traffic this will surely generate."

"And the rail line itself?"

"It will follow the path of the river, although angling away from it to make a more direct line, so it won't be exactly along the road to the city. It will require buying land from farmers in between, which is something I've been working with Taenaris on. He believes that it's best if the Empire doesn't take land from the people in between, but we've had some holdouts not willing to sell, even at steeply inflated prices. He continues to negotiate with them, but it is ... proving inconvenient."

"Do we have an alternative if they don't sell?"

"A more roundabout path, yes. It will increase travel time while being slower, section by section, because of the increased number of bends. If it comes to that, we'll make it work, but I'm hoping it doesn't."

"Why haven't you asked for my help?"

"Frankly, because we don't want to use ... what's the Consul's phrase for that, 'the big guns,' on this. A strange phrase that only made sense once we started working on the first cannon. It makes me think ..."

"Hortensius?" Lucilla prompted.

While she could see the inventor gearing up for a full-on tangent and had wanted to stop it before it started, she also preferred if he limited his thinking in that direction. While it would have been obvious to him, now, that Ky wasn't just coming up with these ideas, the less he considered where Ky was from, the better it was for all of them.

"Right, well, Taenaris thought having the Empress come out to pressure farmers to sell their land might seem a bit too strong and wants to continue trying less aggressive measures first. While you know I look forward to any chance to work with you, I tended to agree with him."

"Taenaris is smart when it comes to this, so you probably made the right decision."

"Thank you," he said, giving her one of his fractional bows. "Even once we have the tracks down, it will be some time before we can fully start using them. We have the Consul's estimations, but considering how the wagons and carriages have fared on the land between here and Factorium, I want to be sure we don't cause too much damage if we miscalculate. It will slow our initial use of the engines, but will be safer in the long run."

"I leave this to your judgment, as always," Lucilla said.

"Thank you. I'm just excited to get started. Once we prove its capabilities, we can expand well beyond Factorium, to Londinium and other major points, and then set up similar networks in Ulaid and the continent."

"So, when do you anticipate beginning construction on the station and laying the tracks to Factorium?"

"Soon, I hope. The only thing standing in our way is finalizing the acquisition of a few parcels of land the rail line will cross."

"I will speak with Taenaris and see what can be done, behind the scenes, to speed that process up."

"Excellent. We already have the crews prepared and equipment stockpiled. We can begin work on the station here, since the Empire owns the bulk of this land. From there, it will probably be a few months, at a minimum. The distance isn't overly significant, not compared to running a line all the way to Londinium, but I imagine even with the Consul's directions, we will encounter a few surprises along the way, since this is the first line we will have laid. Assuming we have your approval to start work."

"Consider my approval given. I look forward to seeing this finished, if it's everything Ky said it would be. I also look forward to never having to ride a carriage to come see you again."

"Then we will move with all haste, Your Excellency," he said, giving her an uncharacteristic full bow.She just shook her head and laughed.

Chapter 4

In spite of her approval, it took several days working with Lurio — the Imperial treasurer — to build out a budget for the rail project and go through all the details to make sure she understood exactly what Hortensius was planning. She didn't really need the permission of her council of advisors for the project, but she wanted to run the idea past them.

Lurio already knew about the project, naturally, but Ramirus and Llassar were both brilliant in their own areas and could predict a lot of complications they might run into. More importantly, Taenaris was part of the council, and they needed his help to make this project work.

Finally, she was ready to assign the budget for the project and only had her council's thoughts left to get, which is why she was at the long meeting table she'd sat at with her father so many times, now at the head of the table, instead of in the chair to the right, which was now occupied by Lurio.

"Thank you all for coming. While we have a lot of business to cover, the main thing I'd like your attention on is our new rail project. I know we have previously discussed the steam engine prototype being built, although at the time, it was more of a curiosity than a major topic of discussion for this council, but we've entered the point of needing to build out the infrastructure for this new transportation system the Consul has been introducing. This means buying large areas of land and a building program significantly larger than either the semaphore or telegraph projects.

"Surprisingly, the largest expense of this project isn't constructing the lines or building the endpoints at either side for loading and offloading cargo and passengers," she continued. "The largest cost is buying all of the land needed for the rail line to cross. All but a small fraction of the land is in private hands, and we've decided to purchase it rather than just take it from the landholders. Considering the unrest, mostly supported by the large landholders in our recent past, we want to avoid additional problems that would almost certainly come from just taking the land outright. Lurio has been good enough to find four million denarii for the land purchases and initial construction material for this first line, not counting the engine itself."

"Yes," Lurio said, stepping in. "That should be enough for the twenty mille-passus line between here and Factorium, and be sufficient for supplies, labor, land acquisition, station construction, and other associated costs. Minus the engine and developmental costs, as the Empress said. We anticipate needing seven hundred thousand for …"

"I'm not sure we need a part-by-part breakdown of the individual costs, although I'm certain Lurio will be more than happy to provide it to anyone who wants a full accounting. He has assured me, however, based on his conversations with Hortensius and the estimates Ky left the last time he was in town, that it should be enough to cover what is needed."

"Correct," Lurio said, stepping in again. "Although I do believe I can come up with five hundred thousand more if absolutely necessary, although that will take from the funds available for other projects. I would like to point out that, having looked at the numbers, I believe that the reduction in labor costs alone for the near-constant stream of wagons and barges down the river, not to mention the time savings of getting goods to market, will allow the rail line to pay for itself in under ten years, even with additional maintenance that might need to be made."

"Exactly so," Lucilla said. "Although I think we should also recognize that this isn't just about money. More importantly, the rail line will free up vitally necessary manpower for other industries or even the legions, since we won't need nearly as many people transporting goods back and forth and reduce the four-hour round trip travel time many of the workers undergo every day. However, we need to get it built first. Which is where you come in, Taenaris. I know you've been helping Hortensius acquire the needed land. How is that progressing?"

"Well, actually. While it did look like there would be a few holdouts early on, we have already been able to convince most of them to see the benefit of selling. There are a few left to convince, but they are leaning toward selling now. I believe we should have the required land in the next few weeks."

"And they're happy with the agreement, or are we making new problems for ourselves down the road?"

"While I wouldn't describe them as thrilled, they are generally accepting of the value they're being offered," the senator said. "I believe we may need to find other ways to work with or compensate a few further, to ease some still ruffled feathers, but I have some thoughts on that. Although I think we should wait, so as not to make the situation purely transactional, which might limit the credit and goodwill those efforts will generate with these landholders."

"Excellent. I'll leave the timing to the council's suggestion, as long as none of our delays slow the rail project itself."

"Is this really the smartest thing the Empire can be doing with its limited resources?" Medb broke in. "Weapons production lags dangerously behind what the legion requires, and just two weeks ago, Ramirus reported to this council that our tribal allies are asking for more muskets and gunpowder than we can provide, and this is with the campaign seasons having ended. In a few short months, we will have legions marching across Germania, fleets in the middle sea, allies more actively engaged in everything from supporting our combatants to hunting, and my own husband in Hispania attempting to work with local tribes to secure that region as an ally. With all these demands on the Empire's large but limited resources, is this the best thing that we can do with them? And yes, I understand there are potential logistical benefits down the road, but there is talk of this being the last year of the war, if everything goes well, meaning by the time we see those benefits, we will no longer be in as much immediate need of them."

Lucilla had to fight everything inside of her to repress a frown. She'd added Medb to the council as part of her promise to help the former queen in return for the end to her plotting, and in hopes of finding a use for the otherwise wildly intelligent woman. At the time, it had seemed like a reasonable option to Lucilla, since the other option was to execute her, which would have almost certainly caused some kind of backlash in segments of the Ulaid populace. Her reasoning had been that, since the council was a more or less unofficial body without real authority, but with real power due to its influence over Imperial policy, Medb would find enough satisfaction for her ambition to come into the fold.

Lucilla had regretted that decision ever since. In every single meeting the council had held since Medb's inclusion, the former queen had questioned every single decision Lucilla had made. Always with the utmost respect and always seemingly being reasonable, but Lucilla wasn't fooled. If it was anyone else, she would have found ways to excuse it, or if it had only happened once or twice, but the constant nature of it belied any good intent on Medb's part.

Lucilla knew Medb was pushing, looking for an opening to exploit, and had yet to decide what to do about it, because the questions were just innocent enough to be explainable. Medb wasn't wrong; they were being pushed for both material and manpower from allies, the fleet, and the legions, which the queen would almost certainly hide behind when questioned. In spite of that, Lucilla wasn't sure how much longer she'd accept Medb's attempts at influencing the Empress's supporters.

Still, killing the woman outright was out of the question, so she'd have to be diplomatic.

"I appreciate the input, and I understand your concerns. However, we have looked closely at the overall impact of this project, and I do not believe the expenditure will significantly hinder our war efforts," Lucilla said, pressing her hands together under the table as a physical reminder to play nice. "The largest restrictions to our war production aren't financial, but production capacity. We need rifles and gunpowder, neither of which will be overly delayed by the supplies the rail project is taking, especially the gunpowder. Since the biggest delay in increasing our production is manpower at the factories and raw material, which is slowed by manpower in the mines, just spending more money will not increase the supply of those weapons."

Lucilla could see Medb about to break in and held up a hand, anticipating the queen's rebuttal. "Yes, the rail line requires some additional manpower, but Hortensius has specifically allocated workers in Devnum already tasked for domestic building projects. Legionary ranks and the number of factory workers and miners will be unaffected, and even if they were, the manpower use is large for a single building project, but small when compared against one factory, let alone a legion.

"Further," Lucilla continued, "this project has strategic value beyond logistics. It provides a valuable test platform for implementing new technology that could have a significant impact on dozens of new industries, both civilian and military. I believe the benefits outweigh the costs."

Lucilla held hard eye contact with the queen for several seconds, daring her to respond. Medb knew she was being challenged and knew if she pushed too hard, she would make things worse for herself. After a moment of returning Lucilla's focus, the queen looked away. A victory, of sorts.

"Any other questions or comments?" Lucilla asked, looking around the table at her other advisers.

She was certain some might have had a comment or a question, but Medb had successfully taken the wind out of the sails for that, to use an adage Valdar was fond of. She would pull the others aside one-on-one later and get their take individually, giving them opportunities to voice their concerns privately.

"Good. Moving on to other business. Lucan, you had some concerns about the current batch of caravels under production," Lucilla said, moving on, but not forgetting the confrontation.

"If there is no further business, this council is dismissed," Lucilla declared forty-five minutes later, rapping her knuckles on the wooden table.

As her advisors and ministers began collecting themselves and preparing to leave, Lucilla held up a hand toward Medb, who had hopped up almost as soon as the meeting ended, making a line for the door.

"Medb, a moment please," she called after her sharply.

The former queen halted, turning back with eyebrows raised, "Yes, Your Majesty?"

Lucilla waited until the last of her subordinates had filed out before speaking, "I wish to continue our prior discussion in private. Come to my office."

Medb's mouth thinned briefly. "As you command."

Her words may have been polite and proper, but Lucilla didn't mistake the woman's eyes, which painted a very different framing of the words.

Lucilla walked past, leaving the queen to follow in her wake. If it was just them, Lucilla would never turn her back on the woman, but her guards would make sure Medb didn't act out too much and corral her if she decided to try and avoid the confrontation they both knew was about to happen.

At her office door, Lucilla entered first, moving behind her desk and pointing to the padded stool across from it, directing the former queen to sit.

"Please shut the door," Lucilla instructed her guard, Modius.

She couldn't help but notice that, while her guard followed her command, he did so while staying inside with them. While she would have preferred to have this conversation in private, she couldn't fault him for his caution. She also wasn't sure it was unwarranted. Either way, she didn't want to distract herself with an argument of etiquette with him, so she let it be, turning her attention to the woman in front of her.

"We need to talk about your behavior in the council meetings," Lucilla said, trying to keep her tone cool yet authoritative, instead of how she really felt. "Your constant questioning of my decisions is becoming disruptive."

"My apologies, Your Majesty. As a member of this council, I only wish to provide constructive advice on matters of state."

While her voice was polite and deferential, Lucilla wasn't fooled for a moment.

"Of course, advice is always welcome when offered in the spirit of cooperation. However, your 'advice' often seems intended to undermine my authority, not strengthen it."

Medb opened her mouth to object, but Lucilla held up a hand.

"Do not try to deny it. In every meeting, you find some way to subtly criticize my decisions. Framing your insults as 'innocent objections' does not change their purpose."

"I deny nothing," Medb said. "I can only defend the words I say. If you feel there's something in my heart, I can't control your interpretation of that, unless you are claiming some powers granted by the gods. You submitted a massive new building project, and I simply pointed out that it would tax our capacities. You asked me onto this council to offer my long experience ruling a kingdom in my own right, before your war destroyed my home."

"Let's speak plainly. I brought you onto this council in hopes it would satiate your need for power and put an end to your plotting and scheming. I did not elevate you to this council to obstruct or delay. If you wish to contribute, do so constructively, not by implying incompetence in my administration."

"Why even bother having a council to evaluate your decisions if you crush any dissent or disagreement?"

"I don't crush dissent. I even want it, when it's offered constructively. But sowing seeds of distrust with thinly veiled criticism serves no purpose but to increase your own ego. I know what you're doing, Medb. If it continues, we may reach a point where our agreement no longer works and we must resort to other options."

"If Your Majesty is unhappy with my performance on this council, perhaps you should tell me plainly what you want."

"I have too much respect for you to believe you actually want me to answer that," Lucilla said, meeting the former queen's gaze steadily. "You're far too intelligent not to already know and understand what the problem is. I don't consider you an idiot, Medb. I expect you to stop treating me like one."

"Fine. What do you want from me then? Do you just want a pet, someone to repeat your words and give you praise? Because I might prefer the platform on the coliseum floor over that," Medb said, referencing the current form of executions used in the city.

"I still hope we can avoid that. Bring your thoughts and speak them openly, as long as they are genuine complaints and not attempts to needle or gain some kind of upper hand against me. But once my decision is final, I expect your support. How this relationship proceeds depends on you. You can accept the situation and make the best of it or keep playing dominance games. I don't want to go with the other option, but if that is the direction you want to go, that might be the only option left to us. Do I make myself clear enough?"

Medb didn't answer for a long time. A minute stretched by, the silence hanging between them. Lucilla didn't know if the former queen was wrestling with her own thoughts or if this was another of her attempts at establishing dominance, but Lucilla was willing to wait her out as long as she needed to.

Finally, Medb said, "I will ... consider Your Majesty's words."

"That's all I ask. I know you might never believe me, as this is foreign to you, but I really do want to find a way to work with you. You're a brilliant woman, Medb. I have no doubt that you would be an amazing asset to the Empire, if you would stop your scheming for only a moment. I know the one thing you want will never be in your grasp, and that must be infuriating to you, but you have a real chance at power here. At a high station, even if it isn't the one you want. I hope you choose not to throw away that chance in some foolish pursuit of ones you will never get. Either way, I'm tired of the games. It's up to you to decide how things progress from here."

"I understand," Medb said.

Lucilla hoped so. She really did.

Port of Kalb

Cormac leaned against the railing as the ship glided into the harbor of Kalb, watching the bustle of activity around the sprawling military port. Ships of all sizes, from the large caravel he stood on, to small, refitted galleys, came and went. Some were part of Valdar's fleet, protecting the mouth of the Middle Sea, while the rest were a mixture of supply ships for the fleet and legions or private ships taking advantage of the new opportunities opened by the legions' conquests.

The one thing that was readily apparent was that every ship was Britannian. The Carthaginians had had a stranglehold on this part of the world for a long time, and they had never been ones to allow private enterprise they could not directly control or exploit. Although, if things went well, that would change, as the villages stepped out of the Carthaginians' shadows and began fighting for themselves.

Cormac had spent the entire journey amazed by the massive ship they sailed on. He'd only traveled by ship once, and that had been a galley that would have been considered large when he took the short trip on it five years ago. Next to the behemoths the Empress had given him as transportation to Hispania, that galley would have seemed like a toy. If he'd had any doubts about their winning this war, they were squashed on this journey. He'd seen the guns and cannons, and they'd been impressive in battle, but they were still weapons far removed from sword and bow, but he could understand them. The industrial might required to produce massive ships like this, and not one or two but dozens now — how could anyone stand against it?

Cormac was pulled from his thoughts as the gangplank thumped down on the dock and men began shouting orders to disembark the supplies and the handful of additional legionnaires that had been sent along with Cormac.

Seeing Llassar by the gangway, he followed the Caledonian down onto the dock, where a man Cormac actually knew waited for them. Niall had traded the leather and iron armor his father's men had worn when they took Ulaid from Fergus, for the legionnaire's more traditional legion armor, but otherwise, he looked the same as he had a year ago when he'd gone from his father's service to the Empire's.

"My Prince," the man said, thumping a fist to his chest in salute. "Welcome to Kalb. I can't tell you how happy I am to have you here."

Cormac returned the tribune's salute, "It's good to see you again, General. No, tribune, I see. The years have treated you well."

"They have, My Prince."

Turning to gesture to Llassar, Cormac said, "Allow me to introduce my advisor, Llassar of the Caledonii."

Cormac liked introducing Llassar as his advisor or, sometimes, when he was feeling particularly brave, as his 'aide.' Besides tweaking the old man's nose, it allowed Cormac some semblance of authority that would be lost if he introduced Llassar as his tutor or, worse, his wet nurse. Even if that is what the Caledonian thought of himself as.

Llassar gave a curt nod in acknowledgment to the tribune but otherwise gave no indication of Cormac's subtle slight.

"I'm eager to hear how things fare here in Hispania," Cormac continued. "The Empress spoke of unrest among the tribes since the retreat of the Carthaginians. Has there been any progress on that front?"

"I'm afraid the region remains chaotic, My Prince. With the legions focused on securing the coast and major cities, the rural tribes feel abandoned. Raids, skirmishes, and banditry plague the countryside beyond where my limited men can patrol. Here in Kalb," Niall said, waving an arm at the port around them, "we can offer a little support to the closest tribes, but our range is limited."

"How bad is it in the interior?"

"It's bad, My Prince, much worse than in the closest regions. With the Carthaginians gone, it seems every two-bit warlord or tribe is trying to seize power and territory. The tribes refuse to unite, too caught up in old rivalries and grudges.

"Beyond the reach of our patrols, it's like what is happening closer to us, but worse. Villages are being not only raided constantly but some even razed completely," Niall continued. "Livestock stolen, homes burned, people kidnapped for ransom or sold as slaves. Trade has all but collapsed due to the banditry along the roads."

Cormac frowned. The Empress had mentioned the situation was deteriorating, but she'd made it sound as if all he had to do was negotiate a few treaties and keep the tribes from interfering with their business in Gaul. What Niall was describing was a much worse situation than she had apparently known, or at least had been willing to tell him.

"And have the tribes shown any interest in talks of alliance?" he asked. "Surely, they must see that some kind of mutual defense is their only real option out of the situation. Unless they're asking for an overlord to replace the Carthaginians."

"They aren't looking for that, no. In fact, that's what's made helping even the closest tribes difficult. They are suspicious at best and openly hostile at worst any time we sent an emissary to try and broker deals to trade for supplies or negotiate passage. It's clear they're afraid of our being just another Carthaginian empire."

"Are there any signs the Carthaginians have attempted to influence them or set up some kind of foothold?" Llassar asked, finally speaking up.

"Not yet, and based on the attitudes we've seen, it seems unlikely they would find much success without a full invasion and suppression of the locals."

"You'd be surprised," Llassar said. "Even in Rome, there have been a few here or there working for the Carthaginians, trying to sow unrest. They, of course, don't let it be known that's what their intent is, but it has been effective in causing delays to the war effort. There is a possibility some of the resistance you've gotten to your offers to help were in fact manipulated in that direction, and not a true indication of what the tribes actually want."

"Which is why the Empress sent us," Cormac said, trying for a confident and leaderly tone.

While this was more than he'd bargained for, it was also his first chance at real leadership and he wasn't going to throw it away. If this is what he had to deal with, it's what he would deal with.

"We'll have to change their minds and get enough of these tribes united, or at least cooperating, so that it's difficult for dissenters or Carthaginian agents to sow any distrust or cause problems. The Consul made similar things happen in Gaul, and that has, so far, worked out, so we should be able to follow the same strategy ourselves. We offer what protection we can and, more importantly, tools for them to protect themselves in exchange for agreements of cooperation with each other, and us, of course. Once they begin to work together, we can then build on that."

"As you say, My Prince," Niall said, but Cormac couldn't miss the look he exchanged with Llassar.

It aggravated the prince. He'd seen senators, legionnaires, and businessmen all exchange the same look with his minder, and he knew what it meant. They either thought his suggestion foolish or him incapable of carrying it out. The look was one of derision, when they couldn't otherwise say something directly, like Llassar always felt he could.

"I will take a detachment of men and go visit the largest of the inland tribes myself, negotiate with their leaders, and explain the benefits of working with us, instead of against us."

"Is that wise?" Llassar asked. "Aside from the danger of marching away from the protection of the port, which from the sounds of things is no small point, the commander just described a people who openly resent the treatment they had at the hands of the Carthaginians and how in their minds they are seeing us as no different. If we march into their villages with soldiers, we're just going to increase those fears, not diminish them. Shouldn't our first goal be to calm them and convince them that we aren't the same as the Carthaginians?"

"That's what we've been trying. We are nearing the end of winter and the Carthaginians have been gone for months. The commander has offered supplies and assistance to them from a distance, and they have turned our hand away. We left it to them to work the issues out amongst themselves, and we've ended up with chaos. I think it's time we try another tactic."

Llassar opened his mouth to say something, but Cormac cut him off. This wasn't like in Devnum, where he was Llassar's subordinate in everything but name. The Empress had given him command of this expedition, and he was going to use it.

"I said I understand. I'll be diplomatic. And yes, I understand there's a danger of marching unsupported into the interior, which is why we're going to focus on the nearer tribes, closer to the port, if we can, to avoid being cut off from support. We brought enough men with us that I believe the Tribune can spare a century to send with us. Surely that should be enough to protect us from bandits."

"My Prince, I have to agree with your associate on this. It is dangerous to travel north, and while a hundred men might be enough to protect you, it also might not. Surely there's another option?"

"I've made my decision," Cormac said dismissively. "The Empress sent me here to get Hispania in order, and that's what I intend to do. Tribune, begin to collect supplies and prepare a century to march by week's end. Send a runner ahead to the tribe, announcing our intended arrival, which should allay any fears they have of this being some form of new invasion. I want this done quickly."

Niall hesitated before replying. "Yes, My Prince. I'll see to it personally."

As the tribune hurried off, Llassar fixed Cormac with a stern look. "Are you, perhaps, being somewhat reckless? We know little of the interior or the disposition of these tribes. Even with warning, our marching in with soldiers may provoke a response other than the one you're wanting."

"Perhaps. But we cannot sit idly by while the countryside descends into chaos. As I said, the Empress tasked me with restoring order here, and I fully intend to do so."

For a long moment, Cormac thought Llassar was going to correct him again, or order him not to go.

Surprisingly, when he finally spoke, the old Caledonian only said, "If you think that's the right approach."

While not exactly a ringing endorsement of his plan, it was nice not to have Llassar actively standing in his way this time.

Chapter 5

Southern Caledonia

Claudius rode swiftly through the wooded hills of southern Caledonia, his back and legs tired after weeks of chasing the escaped prisoners across Britannia. If it had been left to him, he would have abandoned the chase a long time ago. Either the elements or local patrols would have eventually captured them, and it wasn't like these were the only bandits operating in the less populated parts of the country.

The problem was, it wasn't easy to find a small group of men in a country still torn apart by years of brutal war, and one where a large percentage of the men were not even on the island, leaving villages mostly full of women, old men, and young boys. There were burned-out villages and the refuse of war across Britannia. Of course, it wasn't just about stopping banditry. He understood that the escape of the prisoners had been something of a political black eye for the Empress, which is why she had pushed Faenius so hard to apprehend them, and why Faenius had pushed Claudius.

Nothing pointed to the tricky politics of the situation more than the six Caledonian praetorians riding with him. Though officially assigned to "assist" in the search for the escaped prisoners, Claudius suspected the real reason the warriors accompanied him was to keep watch on the Roman interlopers. Although they were, ostensibly, countrymen now, the Caledonians had been given promises that they could maintain their own territorial security, and riding with a century of Roman praetorians seemed to be making them nervous.

Which was almost certainly going to mean someone from Caledonia complaining to the Empress, which would lead the Empress to complain to Faenius that the search had now caused diplomatic unrest or the like, which would result in runners to Claudius at the bottom of the extended chain of misery.

Claudius slowed his horse as Cait, their tracker, came into view. The man tended to range far ahead of the group to keep his own men from obscuring the tracks he was following. Him stopping usually meant he had found something. Claudius held up his hand for the column to stop and rode ahead, by himself, to speak to the tracker.

Thankfully, the Caledonians stayed behind this time. The first several times this situation had happened, they'd insisted on joining him, sending Cait into apoplexy as they proceeded to destroy the tracks he'd been trying to show Claudius, setting the column back several days as he worked to reacquire the prisoners' tracks.

"The tracks are getting fresher," he reported when Claudius reached him. "These men are tiring, I'd wager. Running low on food as well."

"How can you tell?" Claudius asked.

"They've doubled back on themselves three times, and they're becoming more spread out. I think they're looking for a new village to raid. They don't have any idea how sparse this region is."

"Our luck," Claudius said. "It's why their tracks have gotten easier to follow, too, I bet. They're growing desperate."

"Probably."

"Do you think we could catch up to them today?"

Cait scratched his beard. "Maybe, if we're swift about it. They can't be more than a few hours ahead now."

"Then move out as fast as you're able. I'll ensure the men keep up." Cait snapped a sharp salute, then leaped into his saddle, spurring the horse to a brisk canter. Claudius turned to his century. "You heard the man. Ride hard, but pace your mounts. We may have to fight before day's end." With a chorus of acknowledgment, the praetorians formed up. Claudius glanced at the six Caledonian warriors accompanying them. Their leader, Bress, met his gaze and nodded.

Satisfied they would keep up, Claudius spurred on his horse, leaving the rest to follow.

They rode on for hours, keeping a brisk enough pace that the horses were starting to show the effects. They weren't the only ones. His men were wearing out. If this went on for much longer, he'd have to send someone to catch up to Cait and pull the tracker back in for the night, leave the prisoners until the following day, and hope they didn't give his men the slip. Again.

Just about the time he was ready to give up, they caught up to Cait again, who waved him forward as soon as they were in sight. Claudius signaled the column to halt and rode up to the tracker by himself.

"They're just ahead, in a gulley," Cait said. "I caught a glimpse of a cookfire."

Claudius assumed it was far enough ahead that the thundering hoofbeats wouldn't alert them. The pair rode back to his line, where Claudius dismounted and handed the reins over to one of his men. Ordering them to wait there, he and the tracker walked for almost twenty minutes through the trees and up a small rise before Cait signaled him to get low and crawl to the edge of an overlook.

Peering over the edge, he couldn't see much. More trees a short drop down, but otherwise more undisturbed forest. He trusted the tracker, though, and kept searching until he found it. Wisps of smoke rising up from a section, the tell-tale signs of a campfire. That could be anything, though. Hunters, trappers, or maybe completely unconnected bandits.

If they were going to charge in, they needed to be sure. So he and Cait lay there as the sun continued to get closer and closer to the horizon, trying to peer through openings in the trees and see something. They waited long enough that Claudius began getting nervous. If they waited much longer, they would either have to move to get a closer look, a possibly foolhardy move, or get his men and go charging in and hope for the best. An equally poor option.

Then he saw it. Staring through his spyglass, looking through a thin opening in the trees, he saw a ragged, bearded man shuffle into view. He didn't recognize the man, but he recognized the tattered clothing. It was one of the prisoners.

Scowling, Claudius backed away from the edge and hurried back to his men.

They broke through the trees into the clearing with a roar, sending the small band of prisoners panicking. Claudius hadn't noticed it until they were almost on top of the prisoners, but the location they had chosen was a double-edged sword. It protected them from being seen unless they were stumbled upon, but it also formed a dell. A small area where sound was blocked from the surrounding hills, muffling it or preventing the sounds of the horses from being heard before his patrol was right on top of them.

Caught unawares, most of the escaped prisoners were cut down in the first savage moments. A few managed to grab weapons and tried to rally a defense, but they were hopelessly outmatched. They had been running for months, starving and weakened, and were trained to fight in phalanxes, not as individual guards as the praetorians were.

Still, Claudius had to admire their ferocity, cornered as they were. With a bellow, a massive, bald man wielding a woodcutter's axe charged straight at Claudius. Claudius easily turned the wild blow aside with his spatha before recovering and countering, ramming the weapon into the man's ribs. He collapsed with a gurgle, the axe falling from limp fingers.

Even as he fought, Claudius kept one eye out for prisoners trying to escape. Most were dead already, but he spotted a younger one scrambling away from the carnage. Claudius whistled sharply and pointed. Two of his men broke off and tackled the fleeing man.

Within moments, the brief struggle was over. Bodies littered the campsite, only a handful still breathing. Claudius cleaned his blade on a scrap of cloth.

"Bind the ones still alive," he ordered. "Make sure they won't cause trouble on the ride back."

As his men set to work, Claudius took stock of their own casualties. Nothing serious, though young Castor would likely carry that axe scar on his cheek for the rest of his days. Claudius watched one of the men who'd run and then been dragged back into the clearing, a lanky man with a scraggly beard, his hands tied behind his back, being thrown roughly to the ground next to the bodies of the men he'd been on the run with. Blood trickled from a gash on his forehead. Walking to him, Claudius grabbed him by the tunic and hauled him upright.

"You've caused a lot of trouble these past months," Claudius said, glaring at the man.

The prisoner met his gaze and spat. "Go to hell, Roman dog."

Claudius backhanded him across the face. "You'll pay for the innocent civilians you slaughtered. The villages you raided and burned."

Claudius knew this wasn't his job. He'd been sent to capture the men, nothing more. Certainly not to teach them a lesson. But he'd also been forced to witness their atrocities across Britannia, and part of him wanted payback.

"We did what we had to do to survive," the man snarled. "It's no less than what you Romans have done to us."

The man started to respond with another insult, and Claudius hit him again, harder this time. The prisoner's head snapped back, blood spraying from his mouth.

"You'll learn the cost of that survival when we get you back to Devnum," he said to the man, dropping him back to the ground. "Round up the ones that can walk. Any too injured to move, slit their throats and leave them here."

That was an act of mercy, more than any of these men deserved. He should have left them here, bound in the dirt, left to bleed out.

Still, as they got the men ready to travel, Claudius looked around the makeshift campground, at the bodies of the dead prisoners, and took a moment to be satisfied. It had been a long chase, but they'd finally run the bastards to ground. Justice was served.

Daramouda

Ky sat atop his horse just outside the gates of Daramouda, watching as row after row of legionaries marched past him, down the wide dirt road leading east. Though winter snow still capped the distant peaks, the roads and fields had thawed enough to mark the beginning of another campaigning season. His third since arriving in this version of his past, and since joining the war against the Carthaginians. More than anything, he hoped it would also be the last year of their protracted war.

"The men look ready after their long winter, my lord," remarked Vibius from one of the horses next to him.

Aelius was still in the city, and Marcus, one of their newer legates, had marched out at first light at the head of the nearly re-formed second legion, which left Bomilcar, Auspex, and Vibius to watch the men's march out of the city. Ky liked to use this as a sort of informal review, a chance to let his commanders see the men, marching in good order, and for the men to see their commanders. Once the campaign started, things could get chaotic, and this was a good opportunity to build unit spirit, which, in the end, helped the overall cohesion of the legions themselves.

"Let's hope so," Ky said.

"This is going to be different than the previous years, you know," Bomilcar said. "So far, you've been fighting in barely conquered territory, where the empire didn't have a foothold. They've controlled Italy for centuries. This will not be the same fight."

"I know, but it's the fight we have," Ky said. "I just wish we weren't as spread out. We're going to be down three legions by the time we make the turn south."

"What other choice do we have?" Bomilcar said. "We have a lot of ground to protect. The Carthaginians may have been pushed out of Western Germania, but they still control most of the east, along with all of Persia, Syria, and all of Africa. That is a lot of ground to protect ourselves from, and they will stop at nothing to defend the homeland."

"I know," Ky said.

They had been having the same argument all winter, trying to decide the best disposition of their forces. Some wanted to leave everything but Greece to the allied tribes and pull all of the legions in for the attack on Italy and Africa, while others wanted to add a year to the war, focusing only on clearing the rest of the continent, including eastern Germania and Greece to the Aegean, before they turned their attention to Africa next year.

While Ky didn't agree with leaving the entire continent to their allies, he also didn't want to add another year to the war, which had left him with the worst of all options. Spreading themselves out to try and both attack a fortified Italy and Africa while providing protection for their new allies by blocking the continent from re-invasion by the Carthaginians from the east.

It meant they were strong nowhere, even more reliant on their technological advantage than they had been before.

"Speaking of the campaign," Auspex said, interrupting a repeat of the disagreement between Ky and his general that seemed to never end. "Have we received any updates on the situation in Germania?"

"Just received, in fact," Ky said. "A messenger arrived this morning while you were getting your legions organized. He's moving east with the Fifth Legion to assist some of the tribes still battling remnants of Carthaginian forces in Eastern Germania, and will block them from pushing back into our allied tribes. He expects to start encountering resistance from organized pockets within the month."

"That's a lot of land for his one legion to cover," Bomilcar said.

Ky sighed. Bomilcar was a brilliant man, one of the best strategists he'd ever met, in fact. He was also like a dog with an old bone. Once he sunk his teeth into a subject, he seemed incapable of letting go.

"It is, which is the only reason he'll have any challenge at all. There are no significant Carthaginian forces in Sarmatia, at least not that any of our allies have heard of, including the ones Yrsa talked to when he traded for the components to start making rubber. If the Carthaginians had an army out there, we would have heard of it. So yes, it's a lot of ground to cover, but for once, we have more forces in that part of the world than they do, and there are good indicators that the tribes there are willing to work with us. Our western allies are in contact with them and have sent emissaries with Ursinus's men to ensure their cooperation. Together, that should give the legate more than enough tools to do the job."

Ky gave Bomilcar a hard look, hoping this time his argument actually sank in.

"I didn't mean to push, Consul," the general said, finally realizing Ky's displeasure.

"I know. I know. Trust me, I wish we could choose either of the other options, but this will work. Have faith."

"Have we decided how to deal with the remaining Carthaginian forces in Greece and Anatolia?" Auspex asked.

That was another topic that they had yet to decide on, as there had again been a split in opinions, although this time with Bomilcar agreeing with Ky that they should deploy only a holding force to prevent Carthaginian attacks as they turned south, and the younger legates preferring a more aggressive approach of taking the entire region, pushing the Carthaginians back across the Dardanelles.

Just as he had with Bomilcar, he'd heard them out, weighing the options, but in the end, he couldn't see a way to justify supporting an advance that would pull from the main thrust toward Africa, and they didn't have the material or men to do both.

"Yes. Once we reach northern Italy, Vibius, I want you to take your legion and march west to the Tilavemptus River. Hold that line to prevent any Carthaginian forces from invading Greece or points east."

"Yes, Consul," Vibius said, giving a glance to Marcus, who'd been on the 'assault the Carthaginians everywhere' side of the argument.

Unlike Bomilcar, though, neither tried to argue the point, and Ky left it alone. He had no issue with subordinates disagreeing with his orders, as long as they followed them.

"With luck," he continued his instructions, "Valdar should be able to prevent them from transporting significant forces from Africa to the Aegean and up behind you, but do not take any chances. Scout aggressively in all directions, so you are not caught off guard. We may continue to push their forces, but there is no guarantee we'll get them all."

"Of course, Consul. I will be vigilant," Vibius said.

Ky nodded in approval before shifting focus back to Bomilcar, "That leaves the three of us plus Marcus to march south through Italy with the remaining legions. As much as I'd like to bypass it, we will take Rome, cross to Sicilia, and then Africa."

"Three? I thought it was decided Aelius would march to Africa?" Bomilcar said, bringing up yet another disagreement they had had.

"We had, but then I received word that the Empress sent Cormac to deal with our problem in Hispania, and I do not feel an overabundance of confidence that he will find a solution to our problem there. Until he does, or until another solution presents itself, Aelius stays as a barrier between Hispania and our Gaulic allies."

In truth, he'd known about Cormac since mid-winter when Lucilla had tasked the young man with negotiating an alliance of the tribes in that region and ensuring their cooperation with the war. Unfortunately, Ky couldn't tell anyone he knew that, which meant he had to operate as if he didn't need Aelius to remain behind until the courier arrived with the official word.

He'd hoped they would receive word using the telegraph, at least, and speed up the process of pretending he didn't know something before word got through officially, but they'd been having issues with tribesmen tearing down the poles from the Gaulic coast to the Mediterranean, and would almost certainly continue to have issues until the issue with the tribes was settled. So he still had to wait for a courier, which, at the distances they were now communicating, took quite some time.

"She put the prince in charge?!" Auspex said, the words escaping his mouth before he could stop them.

He didn't blame the legate for his dismay, although he would have to have a talk with the young man about comporting himself in public. Their relationship with the Ulaid was still young, and it wouldn't do to have one of his commanders insulting the heir to the Ulaid throne in public.

He'd had much the same opinion when Lucilla had told him. He'd been forced to wait and pretend he didn't know about any of it until the messenger arrived, however, since doing so beforehand would invite questions Ky wasn't sure the world was ready for him to answer.

"Yes. It was decided this would be an excellent opportunity. Besides guarding our supply lines, he helps with your concern. Assuming Cormac can make progress in Hispania, should the need arise in either Greece or Germania, or with us down the Italian peninsula, Aelius can serve as a reserve force and be brought up as needed."

"I see," Bomilcar said, giving a pointed look to Auspex.

'On the other hand,' Ky thought, 'perhaps I should leave correcting Auspex to Bomilcar.'

Over the winter, the Carthaginian had transformed from Ky's advisor and newly appointed legate of the Seventh Legion to his de facto second in command. Bomilcar had contributed much to the preparation for the current campaign, working with the men, including their Germanic allies, and on the development of a strategy for using the Britannians' rifles and cannon.

Many of those units had served as auxiliary forces the previous year, deployed for guards and when close combat fighting was needed, mostly because there hadn't been the time to get them trained for the completely new style of tactics the rifles introduced. Not all, of course. A few of the tribes had fared better and were already integrated into the legions, but every unit was under strength as winter started, and to refill those slots with their Germanic allies had taken a fair amount of work.

Work that Bomilcar seemed well suited for.

As if summoned, Aelius rode up to the gate as the last cohort marched past, ending a long and snaking line that extended into the far horizon.

"That's the last of them," the legate said.

Ky nodded, satisfied to see his army underway after the long winter. "You've all done excellent work getting them ready. You each have your assignments for the coming campaign. Hold the lines, keep our supply routes open, and the next time we're all together, it'll be at the gates of Carthage, their armies in ruins."

Sticking his arm out across his horse, the legates reached in one by one, putting their hands on top of his.

"Good fortune to you all. For Britannia!"

"For Britannia!"

Devnum

Lucilla paced the balcony, ignoring the beautiful moonlit courtyard below. She had spent the last hour talking to Ky. She'd tried to remain upbeat through the entire conversation, as a way to keep his spirits up, but she felt uneasy the entire time. Since she disconnected, she had paced, trying to put her finger on exactly what was bothering her.

"Sophus," she said, stopping her pacing and speaking into the air.

"*Yes, Your Majesty,*" the calm, emotionless voice said.

"Are we making a mistake?"

"*A mistake with what?*"

"Ky. The legions. The campaign. This last push against Carthage is going to be difficult, and our forces are spread dangerously thin across the continent. Recruitment over the winter has not kept pace with our losses, meaning all of the legions are under-strength, and yet he sends half of the legions available in directions other than the one he's marching in."

"*The Consul is an adept strategist*," Sophus replied. "*He will adapt his plans accordingly.*"

"Yes, I know, but ability with strategy does not negate the reality of manpower. Last year, he had four legions in Germania, with another two fighting in the south, splitting the Carthaginians' focus. This year, he has just three legions to press towards the enemy's heartland. And yet, we've committed fewer troops to invade land the enemy is certain to defend even harder. Adaptation is all well and good, but you can't adapt more men, and he's made it quite clear that keeping legions in Greece, Germania, and Gaul is critical, so it's not like he can pull from those should something go wrong."

"*The Consul believes we will be able to recruit additional support for his legions as he moves into new territory. He believes that, while he only has three trained legions available, he will be able to acquire enough native assistance to allow him to focus his legions specifically on assaulting the enemy. That, combined with our forces' significant advantage in technology, should be sufficient to overcome any forces the Carthaginians can muster, in the Consul's estimation.*"

Lucilla resumed her pacing.

"I'm not so sure. Germania and Gaul were the last regions added to our Empire, besides Persia. The people there will be the quickest to rebel if we show any weakness. Hispania may provide some recruits, assuming Cormac has some success, but that is a very large caveat. Italy? Greece? They've not been under our rule for generations. No one alive today remembers a time before Carthaginian control. The people there identify as Carthaginian now, or at least not as allies of Rome. I am skeptical that we'll find armies willing to join our cause in the home territories," she said, stopping again and leaning on the railing of her balcony. "I fear Ky is overestimating the depth of support we'll find abroad."

"*Have you considered speaking to Ky about your concerns?*" Sophus asked.

"He's got enough to worry about. Besides, he's convinced himself that he's right. I haven't talked to him, of course, but I get the feeling this is why Bomilcar has argued for the continent this year, Africa next year strategy. He sees the problems coming, and knows we need to be at full strength before we assault Africa."

"*I believe your assessment is correct. The Consul and I have spent many hours discussing the problem.*"

"Then why not take Bomilcar's suggestion? It's not like the Carthaginians will get any stronger if we take more possessions from them."

"*He is concerned that time will not help our manpower problem, and the losses will continue to accumulate during attacks on other areas of the continent without doing direct damage to the center of Carthaginian forces in Africa. Moreover, he has concerns about how quickly they managed to acquire gunpowder. Even at the lower quality, he's concerned that it might signal an ability to catch up to us on other technological fronts. If that should happen, the chance for our success decreases with each advancement the Carthaginians make. The primary factor in our victories so far has been technological advantage.*"

"And what are the chances of our success if things stay as they are, he makes the assault on Italy and Africa, and does not get the support he's hoping for?"

"*Fifty-four percent, assuming the legions maintain the same casualty rate they did over the previous year,*" Sophus said.

"That isn't reassuring," Lucilla said. "We have to figure out something to help him."

Chapter 6

Gades, Southern Hispania

A long column of Britannian horsemen, two abreast and fifteen deep, passed the first buildings of the worn-down village, the eyes of every villager on them as they rode toward the central market. Or at least, every villager brave enough not to go into hiding the moment the column of armed and armored men appeared coming up the road.

The village had been through difficulties, it was clear. The road might have been well-made and sturdy twenty years ago, but now it was little more than a dirt track with the occasional stone not pressed into the dust sticking out to trip an inattentive man or animal. The huts and small homes were not in much better shape. Holes, cracked walls, crumbling sides. This was a village barely surviving, and by all accounts, it was the largest and most well-off village in the region, which said much about the neglect of their Carthaginian rulers. Former rulers.

As much as Llassar took in the state of the buildings and roads, his real attention was paid to the cowering people watching them. These were frightened people, and for good reason. They had suffered greatly at the hands of the Carthaginians. Seeing the column of Britannians riding through their streets, it must have seemed their brief bout of freedom was about to end for good.

Llassar didn't disagree that Cormac needed a security contingent, considering the banditry in the area, but there had been other options. Llassar — and Niall, for that matter — had continued to try and convince Cormac to offer an invitation for the leaders to come to Kalb, or another neutral meeting place, where they wouldn't feel like they were being invaded. Cormac, in his infinite wisdom, decided it was better to be seen coming to them, regardless of how many soldiers he brought.

Cormac rode at the head of the column, sitting tall and proud in the saddle. His overly ornate armor, which he'd commissioned before they'd left Devnum, did nothing to lessen the appearance of a triumphant conqueror. As they reached the crumbling administrative building, which had once housed the local Carthaginian governor, Cormac drew to a halt and signaled for most of the men to dismount with him.

"You ten come in with us; the rest, set up a perimeter, but do not interfere with the locals unless there is a threat to your lives," the prince said, looking to Llassar as if his orders were somehow wise.

Llassar just shook his head, not bothering to make the argument again as he followed the prince, who confidently pushed into the central meeting hall, flanked by his guards. The room was sparse but functional, with stools and benches around the outskirts of the room and a small, raised area at the far end with five chairs, and an open area in between. It was clearly designed for meetings and audiences, with the leaders at the far end.

A group of locals were already gathered, filling the seats along the outskirts, some running in just ahead of the Britannians themselves. At the end of the room were a group of five men, four of them older, clearly village elders, and one much younger, somewhere between Llassar and Cormac's age.

"I am Prince Cormac Cond Logas of the Britannic Empire," he said to the youngest of the group. "I bring tidings and well wishes from my people and confirm how happy we are to see your village thriving now that we've driven the Carthaginian invaders from your lands. I have come to speak with you of cooperation and perhaps alliance so that we may work together to ensure they never return," he said, loudly and confidently in his native tongue, looking to the scout on his right, whom Tribune Niall had sent with them as a translator.

Instead of translating right away, the man looked to Llassar and some of the others first, until Cormac gave him a pointed look, clearly impatient for the man to translate. Llassar didn't speak the language, but even he could tell the words came from the man haltingly, as if he were worried about something.

As soon as the scout began conveying Cormac's words to the younger man, murmurs rippled through the crowd gathered along the sides of the hall. The older tribal leaders glanced at each other, while the younger man's eyes widened in evident surprise.

Llassar was a warrior, not a trained diplomat, but he knew, without a doubt, that they had just accidentally crossed some invisible cultural boundary and given offense. The aghast expressions of most of the people around them suggested it was more than just a small breach of diplomacy.

Cormac, for his part, didn't seem to notice. Or at least, didn't seem to think it important.

"As part of that alliance, we will not only guarantee your safety and security, using the might of our armies and ships to guard the shores of Hispania, preventing any from assaulting you again, but we offer trade of both weapons and goods the likes of which your people have never seen. We would like to set up a demonstration outside of town, for safety of course, where we can show you the power of the weapons we offer to sell you, so that you never have to fall victim to someone like the Carthaginians again. In return, we ask only for your friendship, and help in securing peace in your regions, as well as refraining from raiding or war with your neighbors. Through mutual diplomacy and goodwill, we can help you and your neighbors achieve lasting peace. Further, we would ask for your cooperation in helping us stamp out the Carthaginian menace, of course only to the degree you and your fellow leaders feel appropriate for the well-being of your people."

Cormac looked particularly pleased with himself as he finished speaking. He'd clearly been practicing what he'd say, and now waited for … what Llassar wasn't sure. The reception of the audience around them made it clear the response he was getting was far from what they wanted and didn't suggest any form of alliance was forthcoming. Either the prince was so wrapped up in presenting his practiced words that he didn't notice, or was simply so foolish that he didn't care. Whichever one was true, they both achieved the same result.

One of the village elders, an old man with a deeply lined face, stepped forward holding up a hand to interject. The scout interpreted his words for Cormac's benefit.

"My Lord, your words speak of grand promises, yet we know little of you or your people. We have suffered much under the boot of the Carthaginians. They spoke of protection and prosperity when they first came, yet brought only misery and poverty."

The old man glanced around at the desperate faces of his people before continuing.

"We thank you for driving out our oppressors, if that is what you did, but we must be cautious in choosing new friends. What guarantees can you provide that our former overlords will not return once you depart? We are simple folk, seeking only to live in peace and provide for our families. I do not wish to bring further wrath upon my village."

Cormac looked from the young man to the older man and back again. Llassar hoped his expression was one of confusion, why their leader didn't speak, but a part of him worried it was a sign that Cormac had taken offense. Llassar had been watching the by-play between the various leaders and was fairly certain there was something they'd missed here, in the dynamic of these village leaders. He just hadn't been able to put his finger on it yet.

If it had been him, he would have introduced himself and then waited for the villagers to question them on their arrival, showing their hand first and setting a point to negotiate from. In not doing so, Cormac had missed something that seemed important to even the lowliest villagers present, and a sign that they had crossed some cultural threshold they should not have.

"The Carthaginians will not trouble you again, old man. We have broken their army and hold their ports. They pose no threat to you now," he said, taking a closer step to the elder, looming over him. "But you are right to be cautious. A wise leader ensures his people's security above all else. Hiding away will not protect you. You must stand alongside us and seize your destiny!"

Cormac pointed back towards the young warrior standing with the elders.

"Perhaps you should let younger men guide your tribe's future. They understand strength and duty and would be better placed to make the best decision for your people. Fear will only lead to further suffering."

Llassar watched in dismay as men around the meeting hall began reaching for weapons, anger on their faces, although for what offense it was still not clear. Cormac's words had been hostile and much too aggressive, and even openly insulting, but the infraction had started before that. This was the culmination of whatever error Cormac had made.

Worse, several of the legionnaires responded by putting their hands on the pommels of their swords in response. Things were on the precipice of spiraling out of control.

And then, Cormac attempted to make the situation worse. The prince opened his mouth, the look on his face both indignant and aggressive, as he finally noticed the hostility around him.

Stepping forward swiftly, Llassar raised his hands in a peaceful gesture, moving to stand partly in front of Cormac while facing the elder.

"Please, let us pause a moment before rash action is taken," Llassar said calmly to the elder before turning to the centurions. "Stand down. Take your hands off your weapons. NOW!"

The centurions clearly seemed reluctant to comply. They were in a bad position, surrounded on all sides and outnumbered, with the majority of their men split off outside the building. If this did turn to violence, it was unlikely any of them would escape this room.

"Honored elder, I sincerely apologize for the offense caused. We did not come looking for a fight. If you wish us to leave, we will do so immediately."

For a moment, the old man just looked from Llassar to Cormac and back again, clearly weighing the situation. Finally, he looked back to the other old men, perhaps for approval or agreement. Llassar couldn't help but notice they did not look to the younger man, who made no move to intercede or speak.

"Your words show humility," he said, and then glared at Cormac. "Although if this stripling insults us again, you will leave or we will make you."

Llassar bowed. "That is fair. You have my guarantee no further insults will happen."

Cormac looked like he wanted to say something, perhaps defend himself. Llassar gave him a hard look, almost daring him to. The prince backed down, but Llassar knew this wouldn't be the last of this conversation. Llassar turned back to the elder.

"Could we start again? I realize we approached this poorly; however, we still seek talks beneficial to all."

The elder's eyes bored into him. "And why should we trust you? Strangers often bring false promises."

Llassar inclined his head respectfully. "A fair concern after your suffering. My own people endured similar pains with the Carthaginians, only ensuring our freedom through cooperation with others who had been, up until that time, our enemy. So I understand your wariness. Is there another way we can earn your trust? Have your people never had rash youths who spoke before thinking?"

The elder barked a laugh. "Yes, we have brash ones aplenty, or we did."

Llassar could feel Cormac tensing next to him. He didn't care if the prince took offense. Not after the display he had just put on.

"Please accept our apologies then, and give us another chance to try, hopefully, while avoiding the same mistakes that were just made. On my honor, no further insults will come."

"We will give you another chance, but not today. Talk of friendship after offense sits poorly. Come back another day when tempers have cooled."

Cormac again seemed like he wanted to speak, until Llassar reached out, gripping his arm hard.

"A wise choice. We shall leave and camp outside of town, if you allow it, and return tomorrow. Is that acceptable?"

The elder looked to the others, muttering in low words.

"They're discussing your suggestion," the translator said. "Two of them think it's a bad idea, the others think it's alright."

"How well do you know these people, their customs?" Llassar asked.

"Not that well. I was held prisoner for a few years by the Carthaginians with some of the people from this tribe. Learned the language, some of the games they like to play with dice, but ... not much else. We were all prisoners, so it wasn't like there was much talk about customs or whatever. Just do what the guards said or get beat."

Any further questions were halted when the small group of old men broke apart, and the elder who spoke first stepped forward again.

"We agree that you may camp outside of town and return in three days. We hope, by then, you will have learned to treat elders with respect."

Llassar gave a slight nod, suddenly seeing the error Cormac had made.

"You are generous and wise," he said with a bow. "We will leave now in peace."

Cormac looked as if he wanted to say something or continue arguing with the man. Llassar grabbed Cormac's arm and forcefully pulled him out of the meeting hall, the legionnaires following closely behind. As soon as they were outside, Cormac angrily shook off Llassar's grip and rounded on him.

"How dare you lay hands on me!" the prince fumed.

"I'll dare that and anything else I want, if it keeps you from getting your fool head cut off. Do you even realize how close we just came to being attacked in there? I was sent here to keep you alive and make sure you didn't end up getting us into another war, and that's what I'm doing."

Cormac turned to look back at the headquarters become meeting hall, looking offended more than worried, as he should have been.

"If they had tried it, I would have ..."

"Done nothing except die. We have thirty men with us, twenty of them were outside, and both of our groups were outnumbered. Rifles are all well and good, but they aren't much good in an enclosed space like that, surrounded by armed men at sword's length. Also, you might remember that we came here to start building alliances. Attacking the leaders of the village is the opposite of what you should be doing."

"I didn't come here to attack anyone," Cormac said. "But if they lay hands on ..."

"Do you even know what happened today? Why things went the way they went?" Llassar asked, interrupting him again. "I've spent enough time with you to know you're not an idiot, so I have to assume, at this point, that how little you pay attention to the world around you is willful."

"What do you mean? I offered them an alliance, a way to protect themselves, and the old man nearly wet himself. Maybe I was too strong in my condemnation of his cowardice, but surely the rest of them saw it. Now that they've been freed, they can't want to return to subjugation, yet that's exactly what the old man was arguing."

"That's what I mean. The old man was the key. Did you notice he was the oldest of the elders, and the rest deferred to him? How the youngest said nothing and was left out of the deliberation when they decided if we could stay near their town without causing offense? Clearly, they venerate their elders, and you openly insulted one. To his face. What did you expect them to do?"

"And how do you know that?"

"Because I paid attention," Llassar said, jabbing a finger into Cormac's chest. "Half of conducting diplomacy is listening before speaking. Watching how your counterparts react. You were so focused on what you had to say, you missed everything going on around you, from seeing what you did to cause offense to even noticing you caused offense at all. You're lucky we still have a chance to salvage this."

"So, what do you suggest?"

"Come back with humility. When you were outnumbered by the Carthaginians and on the verge of defeat, did your father lose his pride? Of course not. These men are no different, and as long as we hope to make them our allies, we're going to show them the respect they desire and deserve. That means you're going to stop this arrogant posturing and truly pay attention."

With that, Llassar turned and strode away, not waiting to see if Cormac followed. The prince stood there fuming for a long moment before following him.

Carthage

Sitting atop his lavish golden throne, the emperor glared down at the man in the center of the room, listening to the latest in a long line of less-than-satisfying reports.

"As you can see, Your Eminence," Hadar continued, carefully keeping his tone even, "the last shipment contained barely half of the requested amount of fire powder from our allies in the Far East. We have sent for more, but it will take time to receive word, let alone the fire powder itself."

A nervous bead of sweat trickled down the man's temple.

"This is unacceptable, General. You were specifically tasked with ensuring the full shipment arrived. How do you explain your complete inability to carry out even the simplest tasks given to you?"

"We took on the full cargo in Syria as ordered, Great One, but with the increased control of the Middle Sea by the Romans, we lost a third of the convoy before reaching safe harbor."

"And you allowed that to happen?"

Even Imilcar knew the demand was unfair. Although he'd been skeptical of the reports at first, writing them off as defeatists or admirals looking for scapegoats for their failures, the reports had been too numerous to ignore. Several Brothers of Hexitas had witnessed firsthand the devastation wrought by Roman fire weapons on their ships, confirming the futility of attacking them with galleys.

"If I may, Your Eminence. The Romans have stopped at the Middle Sea and have no purchase to reach the Red Sea. We also know that ships from the East can come that way, at least some of the time. Rather than relying solely on shipments through the

Middle Sea, I suggest establishing a new trade route, bringing the supplies across the Red Sea and then overland from Egypt."

"The monsoons mean there's only a limited window we can receive shipments that way," another general, one of Hadar's rivals, said. "Once the season changes, they would have to transport everything overland all the way from the Far East itself!"

Imilcar raised a hand, silencing the man. "While the general forgets his place, he raises a fair point."

"While it is true that transporting goods overland during monsoon season is difficult, with Roman control of the Middle Sea we are still left with that, either way. This choice allows us to receive shipments for at least half the year, which is better than only getting a third of the shipment and sending the rest to the bottom of the ocean."

Imilcar watched the two generals argue for a minute longer. He encouraged healthy competition among his men, as it bred the best and most aggressive leaders, but at times it grew tiresome.

"Enough," he finally spoke up and put an end to the dispute. "The situation is clear. We cannot afford to lose any more supplies to the Romans. And, as General Hadar says, we have little choice but to go with the overland route, at least for half of the year. I approve your plan, General. You will establish a new trade route through the Red Sea, bringing in as many shipments as you can into Egypt while the seas allow it. When the monsoons prevent sea travel, you will transport the materials overland, no matter the cost or difficulty."

Instead of dismissing the men, however, the emperor sat back, continuing to stare at his general, while his face scrunched up in thought. Everything they'd said about the shipments, and the trouble with them, was true, but it didn't get at their central problem.

Even with the new weapons, they could not compete with the Romans. Yes, it had been successful once, but Tabnit had had the new fire powder, and he'd still lost. They needed more than what the Easterners had decided they would allow them to have. The Romans had already shown them there were wonders beyond just the fire powder. If the Easterners were able to recreate the fire powder, what else might they be able to recreate? And what of that would they share with Carthage?

"That, however, is a temporary solution," Imilcar said when he finally spoke again. "This supply issue must be addressed more permanently, General. Simply receiving more fire powder is no longer enough."

"What would you have me do, Great One?"

"I am sending you as my personal envoy to meet with the rulers of the Eastern lands. We require more than their cargo; we need them as allies. These Eastern kingdoms were able to recreate the fire powder. Who knows what other secrets they may unravel? Find out if they have weapons like what the Romans have to sell us, or if not, can they take the Roman weapons and create new ones similar to them. Offer them vast sums of gold, land, slaves, whatever it takes, as long as they agree to greater levels of support."

"Yes, Emperor," Hadar said, bowing deeply.

The emperor stood and took two steps down his raised dais toward the general. "Fail me in this, and everyone you love, everyone you've ever met, will be flayed alive. Succeed, and I will reward you beyond your wildest dreams. Your children's children will not be able to spend what I will pay you for your deed. Bring me back the means to crush Rome, by any means necessary."

"You have my vow, Your Eminence. I will bring you weapons to raze Rome itself or die in the attempt."

"You will not be the only one to die if you fail, General."

Chapter 7

Gades, Southern Hispania

Cormac steadied his nerves as a much smaller contingent of legionnaires followed him back into the crumbling meeting hall. The past week had been extremely humbling for Cormac. Llassar's rebuke over his performance during their first attempt at negotiations did not end when he stormed out of the village, continuing for several days as they waited for permission to return and attempt negotiation again. Some blistering words and hard truths had been exchanged between them, but after he calmed down, Cormac begrudgingly admitted that Llassar was right.

At the Caledonian's suggestion, they had discreetly hired a trusted villager to brief them on the tribe's customs, where Llassar was proven right once again. The villager told them that elders were deeply respected and wielded great influence over village affairs. Insulting them was tantamount to insulting the entire tribe. Furthermore, only elders actively participated in important discussions; younger men were expected to observe quietly until called upon. The man they had seen was the token warrior, who advised the elders but did not participate in their discussions.

It had been a difficult few days, where Cormac learned that, in nearly every way, he had been wrong. It is a hard thing to have one's faults laid bare before them, and Cormac had spent a day brooding. Wasted a day. Thankfully, Llassar didn't hold that against him and allowed him the space to deal with his lessons. How the old warrior once again knew the right thing to do, and gave that space to him, Cormac didn't know, but it was what he needed. When he eventually came out of his tent, Cormac had made a decision.

He had been resistant in Devnum, where it didn't matter how much he pushed back against the lessons Llassar was teaching him. He decided he couldn't do that here. Seeing how badly things nearly turned out, he spent the next several days, while they waited for the elders' permission to return, listening to the Caledonian about what he did wrong and, more importantly, what he could do better.

It was odd, then, to realize he felt more nervous this time, when he was more prepared for the task at hand than he had been last time, when he'd been so ignorant. The same four elders were seated at the far end of the hall, lined up on their simple wooden chairs. The young warrior was also present, standing silently off to the side.

Cormac inclined his head respectfully towards the elders. "Honored elders, I have returned as you permitted to apologize for my poor conduct last time we met. I offended you greatly with my arrogance and lack of respect. That was not my intent. I am unused to your ways and spoke out of ignorance. However, that does not excuse the disrespect I showed you."

He used their language for his apology. Although there hadn't been time to learn the language, they'd had the villager they hired, and their interpreter, teach him that sentence, ensuring the syntax was correct and that it was done in the most respectful way possible. The elders looked at each other in surprise as he started speaking, all except the oldest. The one he'd offended. That elder continued to stare directly at Cormac, never looking away.

Cormac bowed his head, switching back to the Latin he used while in the Romans' company. "I humbly ask your forgiveness and hope that we may make a fresh start. I wish to understand your people so that we may find common ground."

The elder didn't reply right away. He watched Cormac, let him wait patiently. Cormac stood, his hands behind him, trying to seem neither overly cowed, which they would know to be false, nor too confident, as he had last time. It was a fine balance.

"You speak gentle words, but on your previous visit, you marched in with armed men, much like the Carthaginians before

73

they oppressed us. Why should we accept this apology when you show that we are still not equals to you?"

"Yes, we did. However, my soldiers are only here to guard me on the roads, not to threaten you. We were warned about the banditry that has taken place on the roads north of the port where we are now based and thought it a necessary precaution. In truth, my subordinates were displeased when we brought only thirty soldiers, thinking it not enough. Were we misinformed? Are the roads not dangerous? And, looking at the men you have here, would thirty have been enough to defend ourselves if you had turned out to be loyal still to the Carthaginians? I am, of course, not saying that is the case. However, we did not know that the first time we came. Now that we do, I left the majority of my men at our camp, out of respect for you."

To make his point, he looked around the room at the larger number of armed young men around the walls and the absence of the older men, women, and especially children who had been here the previous time.

"As for why you should accept my apology, I cannot demand that you do so. I can only endeavor to show through my conduct that it is genuine. This is the first time I have been tasked with diplomacy. I am still learning how to approach other cultures respectfully."

"So they sent an ignorant stripling to threaten us while keeping your skilled negotiators for tribes you think more important. What does this say about how your Empire views us?"

Although Cormac didn't understand his words, at least not until they were translated, he listened to the way the elder was speaking. Llassar had talked to him about not only listening to the words the other party said, but how they said them. This, at least, hadn't been new information for him. He'd dealt with this before. Many of the nobles would come to the king, offering respectful words, without the respect behind them.

The elder's words might have sounded angry, offended, but his tone had been prodding, almost quizzical. He was testing Cormac, trying to see if he could bring out the disrespectful man who'd come to them last time.

"A fair question," Cormac said. "It is true I am still learning about diplomacy. However, I am the son of King Conchobar of the Ulaid, one of the three powers that makes up the Britannic Empire. As such, I have the authority to negotiate binding agreements on behalf of the Empire, where even a skilled diplomat might not. We deemed it better to send someone who can speak decisively rather than a functionary who would have to return to our homelands to obtain the approval of others."

He met the elder's gaze with equal determination. "Make no mistake, we greatly value ties with your people. My being here was meant to show that to be true, not as an insult."

The elder watched him for another moment, before turning to the others and conversing in hushed tones. Their translator stepped up to Cormac, to tell him what the men were saying, but Cormac waved him back. It wasn't hard to figure out what the men were discussing. Instead, he listened to the way they said it, to get a handle on who was swayed and who might be a problem later. It's also how he saw that the chief elder witnessed his motion and gave an approving smile.

"Very well," the elder said when he turned back to Cormac. "We accept your apology and will hear you out. This time. But heed that our patience has limits."

"A fair decision," Cormac said. "My goal here is to build trust between our peoples, and hopefully find a way to work together so we can each be more secure than we would be otherwise."

He gestured to Llassar to bring forth the items they had brought as gifts for the elders. Llassar stepped forward, presenting muskets, small powder horns, along with swords and daggers made of high-quality Britannian steel, a pair of arcuballistas, and some household and farming implements, again made of Britannian steel.

"We have heard about these," the elder said, reaching out and taking the musket. "Your thunder weapons. Several of our people were at Daramouda when your armies destroyed the Carthaginians. They returned with frightening tales."

"These are for you, regardless of whether you choose to work with us. When we finish our discussions, Llassar would be happy to show any of the men you choose how the musket, which this weapon is called, works. My hope is, along with the arcuballistas and swords, you can see that it's more than just our armies we offer in service to protecting your people. It's the tools necessary to protect yourselves. It also works very well for hunting, in addition to defense, making it a valuable tool."

"I see," the elder said, turning the long musket over in his frail hands.

Cormac refrained from commenting. Given new things, they were like children celebrating their birth day, unwrapping presents. He didn't mean that in an insulting or disingenuous way, because he'd reacted the same way the first time he'd held a rifle. It was human nature. Still, it was nice to see the old man's aggressive attitude fade away, giving them a chance to negotiate on friendly terms. Not that he didn't deserve the man's attitude, Cormac thought.

"These are just some of the items we can provide to you, if we come to an agreement. A partnership. In Germania, such agreements have benefited all the tribes greatly. We enabled improved hunting and protection from raiders. In return, we secured willing allies and trade routes. We are not looking to be involved in your internal decisions or even your negotiations with others, beyond the caveat that we will not provide any materials to be used against peaceful neighbors."

"So you do want some say in our self-determination then," the elder asked.

"We do not deny that this agreement is not an offer of altruism, and I make no secret of our agenda. In fact, I will tell you plainly what we are asking for. In the short term, we want peace in Hispania and a secure rear area in which to operate, freeing up our men and material for fighting the Carthaginians, instead of protecting ourselves and our supply lines from a lawless region full of banditry. In the long term, we seek partners, who have access to raw materials we need and to whom we can sell our finished products. We also seek political alliances to maintain peace, once the war with the Carthaginians is finished. I will also tell you that yes, we do exert some influence — in the form of suggestions, at least — that regions should consider more formalized alliances among themselves, alliances that we can negotiate with as a whole, allowing us to more equitably deal with all the tribes in a region, instead of negotiating agreements with each, one-on-one, where accusations of favoritism or working with their enemies in common cause might arise. I will say that this is not a deciding factor in any partnership, but I hope by being open and honest with what I was sent here to achieve, we can build a new foundation of trust, getting rid of the previous unsteady one."

He could feel Llassar looking at him, and Cormac knew this was probably not the tactic he, or another negotiator, might have taken, but Cormac had thought this over. It went beyond just rebuilding the foundation, as he'd said. It didn't take long to look at their actions in other regions, with other groups they allied with, and work out what the Britannian plan was. It was better to admit to that openly than having someone miss that and instead thinking Britannia wanted to roll them up and bring them directly under the Empire. For people controlled their entire lives, and the lives of their parents, by an outside nation, it was obvious where their initial reaction would go, if given the chance.

"And you plan on going to the other tribes too, yes?" the elder asked, handing the musket off to the younger warrior.

"We do. One ally in a region will not create peace. We need agreements with all, or at least, most of the tribes, because we want you to be the ones to create peace. If we tried to do it ourselves, it would mean leaving men behind to enforce that control. Then we'd just be occupiers, and our entire goal of freeing ourselves to focus entirely on the Carthaginians would be moot."

"And you plan on selling these same weapons to them as you would to us. What is to keep them from buying the weapons and then turning them against their neighbors, abandoning agreements they have with you?"

"For one, that isn't how these weapons work. Yes, the swords and even arcuballistas, to a point, work that way. Once you have them, they can be used without input from us. But you've faced those weapons for a long time. Yes, the quality might be better, but they aren't going to radically change the way you defend yourselves. But if you have the muskets, that is where the technology changes the very way conflict is resolved. And importantly, these weapons do not work on their own. They require both the weapon and the powder in these horns, called gunpowder, which is at the center of how these weapons work. To continue using these, you would have to continue buying the gunpowder from us, and if a tribe starts using our weapons against their neighbors, at least without a good reason and the agreement of the rest of Hispania, we would stop all shipments of the gunpowder."

"Your words are reasonable. The people of Hispania, our neighboring tribes, lash out angrily, wanting to take back some part of their own manhood, laid bare for so long, unable to make their own destiny. It is understandable … and a threat to my people. It is also clear that, while we could do it alone, that would come with a high price in blood and tears. As chief elder, it is my job to limit the flowing of either of those, and the easiest course would be to find another, more powerful people to take shelter under. However, we know all too well there is also a cost of selling our freedom to another. While selling it ourselves isn't the same as having it taken from us, we lose it all the same."

"As I said," Cormac countered, "we are not asking you to sell your freedom. Your people are free to govern themselves as they see fit, and deal with their neighbors as they see fit. We only ask for peace in return."

"But you don't. You've shown your true intentions already."

Cormac cocked his head curiously. "How so? I believe I have been forthright about our goals here."

The elder waved a hand dismissively. "Oh, not intentionally perhaps. But think. What happens when some tribes join you and others refuse? When those with your new weapons and power go to war against those without?"

Cormac fought down his frustrations. Part of him, a large part, in fact, wanted to throttle the man and yell at him. For someone who'd been under the Carthaginian boot for his entire life, he seemed unwilling to take any firm stance against it. Trying to play everything for advantage, even if it left them weaker in the end, which was how most of the world had ended up under Carthaginian control in the first place. This is what happened to so many of the kingdoms in Ériu when the Carthaginians first landed. Instead of backing his father, they dickered and argued until they were forced to submit or be destroyed.

"I must correct you; we would only assist tribes who are attacked, not those who initiate violence against their neighbors. As I said, we will withhold support from any tribe that attacks a neighbor unprovoked."

"Is it not inevitable that the tribes who shun you will lash out against the favored ones, because the ones who side with you have things of value and the ones who don't do not? What then?" The elder gave Cormac a knowing look. "You arm some tribes and not others, upsetting the balance of power. The world seeks equilibrium. Where one has nothing and the other has everything, the one with nothing tries taking from those who have. Your actions guarantee bloodshed."

"Honored elder," Cormac said, crossing his arms. "I understand your concerns, but tell me, what would you have us do instead? If we were to provide weapons to all tribes equally, regardless of their actions, how would that create peace? Those set on violence would simply have more tools for violence. And if we provide weapons to none, the status quo remains, with tribes raiding each other out of need and resentment over Carthaginian oppression."

Cormac paused, meeting the elder's gaze. "I do not claim to have all the answers. But it seems neither of those paths leads to stability. At least by being selective, we encourage thoughtful leadership focused on building, not destroying. The tribes who uplift their people will gain access to better tools for hunting, building, and defense. Over time, that benefits all Hispanians, as successful tribes share expertise. The cycle must be broken."

That was one of the lessons that Llassar had been pounding into Cormac's head for the past year, and one he'd ignored, at least until the last several days. In re-evaluating his actions in that first disastrous meeting, Cormac had been forced to take a new look at everything. He wouldn't say he'd changed his worldview completely, but he decided to try things Llassar's way, and see if things turned out differently this time.

The elder didn't speak for a long time, only stared at Cormac, considering. The prince couldn't help but notice he didn't consult with the other elders. Cormac realized they'd already made their decision, even before the Britannians returned. All the bluster about respect and threats of throwing them out and ending the negotiations had been just that. Bluster. This entire negotiation had been a foregone conclusion.

Cormac refrained from looking at Llassar as the elder finally spoke, "While we would need to hear more specifics of what you offer; in principle, we agree that some form of agreement of benefit to both of us is desirable."

While Cormac was pleased that his first attempt at diplomacy was, ultimately, a success, he was also conflicted. Llassar's advice had sounded good, and they weren't asking for anything more than what was agreed to this time, but what happens if you begin negotiations allowing the other side to take the upper hand, put you on the defensive. If they'd wanted to ask for more, instead of just complaining before agreeing to the original offer, would Cormac have agreed to it? He'd come in off balance, looking to appease them, which meant it wasn't out of the realm of possibility that he might have offered too much to make up for his earlier mistakes. It was something to think about. He didn't, however, say any of that.

Instead, Cormac bowed and said, "I am pleased to hear that, elder."

They didn't have an agreement yet, but it was enough for today.

Northwestern Italy

Ky stood on the crest of the hill overlooking yet another abandoned village. The hastily deserted huts and livestock pens showed signs of the villagers' hasty retreat upon word of the Britannian legions' advance. This was the third such village they had come across in as many days.

It was the same each time; the scouts would report the presence of a Carthaginian village, they would turn the legions toward that, only to find the Carthaginians gone. Not just the Carthaginians, but everybody. Since they'd marched out of Daramouda, they'd yet to fire a shot at the enemy.

It was frustrating.

"They refuse to stand and fight," Marcus, whose legion was at the front of the Britannian column, said, echoing his thoughts.

"Because we outnumber them, at least for now," Ky said. "While I hadn't expected the enemy to offer a stand-up fight, not when we have a technological and manpower advantage, I hadn't expected entire villages to be empty. It's concerning."

"Isn't empty better than working against us?" Bomilcar asked.

"Those aren't mutually exclusive," Ky said. "At least in their villages, we could keep track of them. If they're spreading out into the surrounding countryside, it's going to create serious problems at our rear. If they're all pushing ahead, south down the peninsula, it'll be chaos when we finally get to them. With that many people, mixed in with the Carthaginian forces, it will be hard not to have a massacre on our hands."

"They've already made their choice," Marcus said. "If that's what they want, that's what they get."

"Operating with that attitude is how we set ourselves up for a repeat of what Carthage suffered in Germania. I know the local populace is against us, but their ancestors were against the Carthaginians, and now they're loyal enough to abandon everything to flee before us. I'd prefer not to wait generations for this area to become pacified since the only options are to slaughter any malcontents until they run out of people to hate us or to put enough men in the area to keep it suppressed until things become more secure. Either path builds a lot of resentment, which is why it takes generations to change. I was hoping to negotiate with them, at least attempt to change attitudes without having to rely on a more heavy-handed option."

"How, exactly, were you planning on doing that?" Bomilcar asked, skeptically.

"We just need the opportunity to show that things can be different than they were under the Carthaginians. Yes, we'll have to keep security tight at first, which might mean leaving a legion behind to maintain control of the region. But we'll give strict instructions to come down harshly only when absolutely necessary."

He turned to face the other men. "We would set up councils for the villages, allow them some measure of self-governance. No direct taxation, which I know will be a burden on Britannia financially, but we can't treat these people any differently than we do the Gauls or our German allies. We can recoup some of the cost by selling civilian goods and medicines to them, at the same rates we do our other allies, with the caveat that no military weapons can be directly sold into the villages for now."

"You truly think they'll start cooperating because we ask politely?" Marcus asked.

"No, it will take years to fully turn attitudes around, perhaps a generation," Ky conceded. "But if we offer opportunity instead of oppression, I believe that eventually, a mutual understanding can be found, and hopefully in less time than it would take otherwise. We just need to be consistent ... firm when needed, but focused on lifting these people up, not keeping them down."

"None of which helps us now," Bomilcar pointed out.

"You're right," Ky said. "Before we can start setting any of that up, we need to push out the Carthaginians, which so far we don't know if we have or not. Considering they may have fled into the surrounding countryside and still pose a threat, we need to make sure we secure our rear. I'd hoped to keep our forces intact for the fights ahead, but it's clear that isn't possible, at least not while we're operating on the peninsula."

Ky thought for a moment, looking at a map and known positioning superimposed over his vision by Sophus.

"Marcus, have your legion begin spreading out along our line of march back to Daramouda, but do not spread out too much. Stay mobile, and do not split your forces into less than cohorts. I don't want individual centuries running around the countryside if we can help it. At least not as long as the Carthaginians could be out there. Send scouts to sweep the surrounding countryside, see if we can flush them out or even just determine if they're still in the area or if they moved south."

Turning to Auspex, Ky said, "Take the lead with your legion. Move one cohort quickly to each village as we advance, try to reach them before they abandon it. The rest of the column can catch up after you've secured the area. And run telegraph lines, at least alongside the main body. As soon as you see the rest of your legion catching up, skip ahead to the next. Don't wait to confer with us beyond sending reports through the telegraph. If we need you to stop, we'll let you know."

"Vibius," he said, turning to the final legate. "Continue on to your assigned position facing Greece. Ensure you also run telegraph back to the main line. Leave half a cohort behind to set up a station where the line branches south. The main body will use it as a secure base of supply and communication point. Have them patrol the area thoroughly, and we can bring forward our logistics from Daramouda to here, shorten our supply lines some."

The three officers saluted and rode toward their respective units to begin carrying out their orders. Ky watched them go, frowning. As a plan, it was solid, considering their sudden force advantage, but it still felt like a surprise waited for them. And it was bothering him.

"An interesting decision, switching Marcus and Auspex's positions," Bomilcar said after a moment. "Any particular reason?"

Ky, watching the legates recede into the distance, said, "Marcus is reliable, but for someone so aggressive in spirit, he's been too cautious. Too slow. Right now we need speed if we're to pin down these villages before they flee."

"Makes sense. But you're bothered by something," the general said, looking at Ky's face intently.

While Ky normally felt he held a good poker face, Bomilcar had an uncanny ability to read him.

"I'm just concerned. I know a plan never survives contact with the enemy, but this has been more unpredictable than I'd like."

"Don't worry; we'll force them to fight eventually."

"But on whose terms?" Ky asked.

For that, Bomilcar had no answer.

Chapter 8

Devnum

Lucilla felt a pounding in the back of her skull. For days, she'd been trying to figure out any way to get additional troops for Ky's legions as he'd approached Italy. He'd already begun the attack two legions down, and he was going to be dispatching another when they reached northern Italy.

Three legions was a very small number as they headed toward the heartland of Carthage. But try as she might, there was just nowhere she could dislodge more men. As it was, Faenius had already complained about the numbers that had been levied from the praetorians, and every manufacturer critical to the production of war material was understaffed. It was also the beginning of planting season, which needed a fair number of hands. There just weren't enough people in the entire Empire.

She'd sent emissaries to their Germanic allies, but they were already working with Ky and Ursinus, so it wasn't clear how much they could spare.

All of which put her in a bad mood as a fist raped on her office door. Part of her hoped it was Hortensius sending a messenger to tell her he had something new to show her. At least that would get her out of the palace.

"Yes," she said.

It wasn't Hortensius. The door opened and Medb walked into her office, back straight and head up like she was still queen, as always. Lucilla schooled her face. The woman was many things, one of which, unfortunately, was incredibly intelligent.

"What can I do for you?" she asked calmly.

"I need something to do," Medb declared, walking up to Lucilla's desk and sitting on one of the stools opposite her without being bidden to. "The sheer boredom of being on the council is slowly draining the life out of me. With Cormac in Hispania and me here, away from the life I've known, I'm bored senseless."

Lucilla studied Medb for a long moment before responding. "The council position is something I've granted you to allow you to demonstrate that you can be trusted with responsibility and are willing to contribute meaningfully. If you find it so disagreeable, I can certainly relieve you of that duty."

She folded her hands on the desk. "But I'm not sure there is much else we could provide you to do at present. You must understand the precariousness of your situation."

"You claim to want me to integrate into the Empire and contribute value, rather than oppose you," Medb said angrily. "But now, when I ask for more, you tell me this is all there is. Act as if I'm the one overstepping my bounds. I thought this was what you wanted, my taking a more active role in my new home."

"It is, but on our conditions. You have yet to show me you can be trusted to take on more substantial roles. I know the council isn't exactly what you had in mind, but it is the one position where you can do the least damage and was designed as a first step toward being given more, if you did the work and showed we could turn our backs on you without you putting a knife in them. Do I need to remind you it wasn't that long ago you and I had difficulties because you couldn't stop challenging my decisions?"

"We did, but have I given you any problems since then? And do you blame me for pushing back? I was given an ultimatum, cooperate or lose my head, and I was told that if I cooperate, I would have a chance at station and real privileges again. I've cooperated, and yet, nothing."

"Not causing problems is not the same as cooperating, and I think we both know that. This isn't about working down a list, confirming things you've been forced to agree to before you buy a horse or a wagon. This is the fate of my people, and I'm not willing to turn that over to you until you show that you can be trusted with watching over the people who offer their allegiance to the Empire."

"I know all about watching over a people. I was a queen in my own right."

"And then you handed your country over to Carthage and were their de facto commander in Ériu. As a selling point for doing the best by the people who you govern, that isn't one I'd want to flaunt."

"Do you think I had a choice? Conchobar can feel all high and mighty, as far away from the Carthaginians as he could get. I didn't have that luxury. If you'd waited six more months, he would have bowed to them just as I did, to save his people. It's easy to say resist until you have nothing left. Look at the other kingdoms around mine who did resist. Their cities are still smoldering, their people either dead or scattered. I kept my people safe," Medb said, her voice rising to the point that Modius, who'd been lurking in the rear of the room since she entered, took a step toward her.

Lucilla waved him back, but didn't answer right away. While it was true the former queen was ambitious and power-hungry, she wasn't wrong about why she'd joined the Carthaginians. If there had been any hope of actually negotiating a settlement short of complete annihilation, her father might have worked out a similar deal. It was hard to judge her for that decision.

But, none of that meant she could trust the woman either.

"You're right," Lucilla said finally. "All of the points you've made are valid, and I understand why you did what you did. I'm also right, in that there's no way I can trust you based on your recent actions here. However, I did promise you a real chance to prove yourself, and the council clearly isn't that. Maybe running the palace household would be a better place to start."

"Managing servants and ordering meals?" Medb asked. "It is insulting that I'm to be some glorified maid?"

"Not at all," Lucilla countered. "It's a position of prestige and responsibility that a lot of people want. You'd oversee all palace affairs - staff, provisions, maintenance. It's no small task."

"A task fit for a steward, not a queen," Medb scoffed.

"You keep forgetting you are no longer a queen, and statements like that are why I keep coming back to the thought that you'd only be happy with my position."

Medb sat back, crossing her arms. Lucilla fought back a smile. She'd finally found an argument Medb couldn't counter with a snappy retort.

"I'm not saying this is what you'll do forever. This is a test. But prove yourself in this role, and more opportunities may arise."

Medb glared, resentment simmering in her eyes. Still, Lucilla sensed she was considering it.

"Running the palace isn't meant as an insult," Lucilla continued. "Deciding who gets audiences, deciding who supplies goods, working with the praetorians, overseeing staff - this is real power and responsibility. It's more than you've been entrusted with up until now."

Lucilla waited, the silence stretching out between them. She could see the wheels turning behind Medb's eyes, probably working out the ways to take the most advantage of the situation. There were places for that in the position, mostly graft, but Lucilla doubted Medb would set her sights as low as simple theft.

"Very well, I accept your offer," Medb said finally.

Lucilla nodded, keeping her face impassive. "Good. I believe this arrangement will benefit us both."

She rose, signaling the end of the meeting. Medb stood as well, adjusting the folds of her gown.

"However, let me make something clear," Lucilla added, her voice taking on a steely edge. "With increased access comes increased scrutiny. Until you have conclusively proven yourself trustworthy, I will continue to have you watched at all times. The privileges I grant can be revoked if you overstep your bounds."

Medb's eyes narrowed, but she nodded. "I would expect nothing less."

The two women regarded each other for a long moment. Lucilla was under no illusions that Medb had suddenly become her loyal subject. But this new role would keep the ambitious former queen busy and provide a channel for her talents that was not overtly threatening. It would also allow Lucilla's agents to monitor her more closely.

"Very well then. Talk to the steward tomorrow morning and he will begin your transition," Lucilla instructed. "I'll make sure they're ready for you, although I have no doubt you'll figure everything out in short order."

Medb inclined her head once more, then turned and swept from the room in a swirl of skirts. After she had gone, Lucilla dropped back into her seat. Whether this gambit succeeded or failed, only time would tell. But for now, it offered a break from Medb's constant maneuvering.

Gades, Southern Hispania

The village was filled with raucous cheering as Cormac went sailing through the air, landing hard in the dirt before rolling back to his feet, his stance wide and arms in front of him. A circle of men, some bare-chested competitors and others elders who watched but did not participate, surrounded Cormac and his competitor.

Cormac was grinning from ear to ear, a stark contrast to Llassar, who stood behind him with his arms crossed, the expression on his face clear to everyone that he thought this entire endeavor a bad idea. Cormac didn't care. He knew how to get to the men in the new delegation. Unlike the Turdetani, the representatives from some of the other major tribes were warriors and had an ethos that Cormac understood.

They weren't the type of men to stay inside all day, arguing and reasoning. They craved the same thing Cormac did, deep down: excitement, adventure. Which is how he settled on this little contest. After his initial introductions, the men who had been sent to see what these new Britannians were doing had seemed totally bored, except during the demonstration of the muskets, which they'd already come to an agreement to sell to the Turdetani. Which is what had given Cormac his idea.

If they didn't want to sit in a room to discuss treaties and terms of selling these weapons, they could choose a new venue. Strangely enough, in this match, he'd ended up against the bearded Turdetani, who he'd mistaken for a leader on that first attempt at diplomacy that he'd failed so badly.

Although it was still early spring, and not terribly hot, Cormac wiped away dirt and sweat from his brow as he circled his opponent. The bearded Turdetani was spry and skilled, but Cormac could tell his endurance was fading. As the older man lunged forward, throwing a series of quick jabs, Cormac deftly slipped each blow before countering with a swift knee to the ribs. The Turdetani buckled over with a grunt.

"Had enough?" Cormac asked with a cocky grin.

The man might not have understood Cormac's words, but he understood the expression. Instead of responding, the man spat dust and charged forward again. But he'd had enough. One more throw and the man signaled defeat. Cormac didn't gloat over him or preen, even though, in his heart, that was what he wanted to do. The man had been full of bluster when he first came into the circle to face Cormac, sure his larger size and experience on the battlefield would give him the day.

If they'd had weapons, he might have been right. After all, Cormac hadn't fought for years pressed into Carthaginian service like these men had. They didn't have weapons, though, and in this type of contest, Cormac had years of experience, as it had been his favorite hobby in Emain Macha. Llassar had been insistent, however, that he was to accept every loss gracefully and every win with humility. He'd been against this entire idea, but he said if Cormac was going to insist on it, he needed to remember this was still diplomacy.

So no, Cormac didn't strut. Instead, he reached out, extending a hand to the fallen warrior, helping him off the ground and clasping arms with him as the onlookers cheered and laughed.

Cormac waved the next two men in and made his way to a container of water, which he took and gulped down greedily.

"Not bad for a young whelp," a deep voice rumbled behind him.

Cormac turned as the legionnaire next to him translated the words, smiling as he recognized one of the Callaeci chieftains. Beler, he thought his name was.

"I may still be wet behind the ears, but I can handle myself," he replied.

This was a test, and he had known it was coming. In the weeks since his original failure, he'd finally started listening to Llassar and the lessons he'd worked so hard to impart. Of how things might go as the other tribes began to arrive, how they might try to gain the upper hand.

Even with his newfound respect for Llassar's method, it had taken a large part of that time for the old warrior to convince him that there were better ways to deal with probing insults than fists and anger.

Beler chuckled. "Indeed."

"Have you given any more thought to my offer?" Cormac asked.

"I have, but I'm not sure how my people, or any of the other tribes, can trust your word. Yes, you can sell us wonders, but at what price? The last time your people were in our lands, your battle with the Carthaginians left our villages in ashes and clans fighting over fish bones for scraps."

"A fair concern, and one that leads me to ask, was it our battles that did that, or the Carthaginians and their relentless greed? I have read the reports of those contests, and our armies only marched northeast, away from your settlements, from the port we won from the Carthaginians. My understanding was that it was the Carthaginians who stripped your villages of supplies and men and burned other villages to keep them from negotiating with us. Given that, I would think you and your neighbors would be more interested in protecting yourself from it happening again. That's what we're offering, as well as our friendship."

"When you say friendship, I hear slave," the man said, the joviality gone from his face.

"You hear words I didn't say. We can offer engineers and craftsmen to help rebuild your villages, as we did with our new allies in Gaul and Germania."

"And if instead, they march against us in legions? Will your Empress claim our lands to protect them?"

"We seek allies, not vassals or terrain. Did our legions remain after our fight with the Carthaginians ended? Or did they march east to continue the contest? Did I come with more than a handful of soldiers as protection? Even our port, the only base we currently operate on the entire peninsula, has only enough men to protect it and our shipping. Everything we have done has shown you our intentions. While I do not begrudge you your fears, I would counsel against letting yourself be ruled by them."

"And if this is a ruse?"

"Then what would we gain that we wouldn't by marching our armies in now? You've talked to the Turdetani and I have no doubt they described the fortifications of our port. We have a secure base, and if we wanted to use that as a base for attack, we could just do that, not attempt to sneak and connive. Don't trust us? That's fine. Watch us, be wary. Give us the chance to show you our intentions."

Beler slowly nodded and walked away without another word, moving to speak with some of the other tribesmen from his region. Conferring with them.

Cormac knew this wasn't going to solve everything, not in one day, but if it opened the door to communication, that was what they were looking for. Besides, it kept everyone too busy to think about raiding into Gaul or attacking each other.

Cormac watched as the contests continued, men from different tribes and regions facing off against each other in tests of strength and skill. He was impressed by the raw power and determination on display; these warriors were hardened by years of conflict and survival.

After a time, it was Cormac's turn to enter the circle again, matched against a burly Vettones chieftain from a village he wasn't sure he could identify, let alone pronounce. The Vettones chieftain was all brute force, charging and grappling like an enraged bull. Cormac remained light on his feet, evading and counter-striking until his opponent tired. Then, in a sudden burst, Cormac swept the man's legs out from under him, following it up with a submission hold that forced the man to yield as he slowly blacked out. Cormac pulled the man to his feet as soon as he yielded, only to be brushed aside. This was the danger of this kind of contest. Some men would get their egos bruised at a loss, and might take it personally.

Thankfully, the chieftain rebounded well, laughing with his warriors as they jibed him about losing to a boy a fraction of his age.

More contests followed as the day wore on, the fights slowing as men finally tired. When no more volunteered to enter the ring, Cormac stepped forward and raised his hands, calling for attention.

"Friends, I want to thank you all for coming today and participating in these contests of skill. It has been too long since I've had a day of such fine sport," Cormac said, getting murmurs of agreement.

"Before we retire to the feast upon the boars my men caught and prepared for you, I wanted to give any man willing a chance for a final match?" Cormac challenged with a grin.

To his surprise, Llassar stepped forward from the crowd. "I accept your challenge."

Cormac was surprised, to say the least. He knew Llassar was a far superior fighter and could hardly fathom why the old Caledonian would have challenged him here, when this was all about proving his value and building camaraderie before they feasted. But with all eyes on him, he couldn't refuse. The circle of warriors cheered as Llassar entered the ring, especially the older warriors who hadn't fared as well as the young men all day.

Cormac readied himself and dropped into a ready stance, Llassar just stood there, his confidence mocking Cormac. He only moved when Cormac did, mirroring him. The two men circled each other, Cormac warily searching for an opening before moving in. Seeing Llassar move a step too slow, he seized the opportunity and rushed in to grapple with him.

Reaching low, he attempted to wrap his arms around the Caledonian and lift him up before slamming him onto the ground. That had been what he'd tried to do, but the older warrior suddenly twisted his torso, breaking Cormac's grip. Before Cormac could react, Llassar stepped in and put him in a tight bear hug. Cormac gasped as the air was squeezed from his lungs by Llassar's powerful arms.

He struggled to break free, wriggling and squirming, but Llassar's hold was unbreakable. Finally, just as Cormac's strength was about to give out, he managed to slip one arm free and jab Llassar hard in the ribs with his elbow. The older man grunted in pain and his grip loosened just enough for Cormac to twist free. The two men stepped back, both breathing hard.

Cormac tried to keep Llassar from recovering by dashing in again, almost as soon as they were apart, hoping his youth and vigor would win out over Llassar's age and experience. He'd been sure the old warrior was unprepared, but as soon as he came in, the Caledonian's leg swept out, knocking Cormac to the ground. He landed hard on his back, the air rushing from his lungs on impact. Before he could react, Llassar pounced, planting a knee firmly on his chest. Cormac gasped and writhed, trying to twist out from under the crushing weight, but Llassar had him pinned fast. The Caledonian seized his flailing arms and slammed them back down above his head. Cormac bucked and thrashed but he was well and truly caught.

The watching warriors roared their approval as Llassar held him down, his weathered face betraying the hint of a smile. Cormac grunted and strained, summoning every ounce of strength, but the old warrior had him. After a seeming eternity, Llassar finally released him and stepped back, offering a hand to help him up. Cormac felt embarrassed and angry at being beaten so easily but remembered at the last moment their purpose for being here and took the offered hand instead of slapping it away.

"See, it can be done. I was worried you might all think we brought an unbeatable man," Llassar said, putting an arm around Cormac. "Cocky as my young friend may be, he can still be beaten!"

At that, the spectators roared with laughter and approval. Cormac flushed red briefly, but his anger dissipated as Llassar walked away and the warriors gathered around, slapping him on the back for a match well fought. He had lost, but their respect remained.

Once again, Llassar was teaching him without Cormac realizing it.

"I don't think any of you here doubted you could beat me, but I thank my elder for showing me humility once again," Cormac said, getting a ripple of laughter out of the men as his translator gave them his words. "You've all done your villages proud. I don't know if I've ever seen such skill and strength before."

The men murmured at the praise. They were all smart enough to know he was plying them in preparation for the negotiations, but it was hard for any man not to take some pleasure in the compliments.

"Now, before we eat, I know many of you have asked about the weapons we demonstrated earlier in the day. The muskets that you saw pierce tree and plank."

At the mention of the firearms, some of the men who'd walked away circled back. While Cormac liked to think it was his skill in the ring that kept the men there all day, he knew that was just his ego talking. From the moment he'd had his legionnaires fire the muskets they'd brought for the Turdetani, he knew the rest were hooked. Everything else was only about setting the stage for the negotiations to come.

"As I explained to the elders here, we are willing to trade these weapons, along with the knowledge to make the black powder that fires them, to all tribes who agree to our terms of friendship and alliance."

Muttering broke out among some of the men. Cormac raised his hands for quiet.

"I understand your hesitation. You have been mistreated and exploited too many times before. After so long under the Carthaginian boot, I would be just as suspicious of such a bargain. But we come in friendship, not as conquerors."

He looked each man in the eye as he spoke.

"As I told the elders here in Gades, we came without armies, just enough men for protection, and we plan on leaving no armies here beyond the port we captured from the Carthaginians. The peninsula is yours to do with as you will. If invited, we would set up trading areas and even offer to come to the assistance of our partners, if needed. All we ask is that anyone who partners with us, who takes our weapons, uses them only for the defense of their homes and providing for their families. What we want, more than anything else, is this region to be safe and secure."

There was a suspicious rumble among the men, who Cormac was sure had heard similar words before.

"I know. Trust me; I know what you're feeling. I will be honest with you as I was with the elders here. We don't do this out of altruism or love for your people. We do this because we are at war with the Carthaginians, and now that your region is behind us, we need it at peace, so that we can focus on the war in front of us."

The muttering softened but did not fully abate.

"The Turdetani have already agreed to reasonable restrictions on how these weapons may be used, which is why we brought the small amount of the weapons we have here today, as a gift on a bargain struck. We simply ask that you agree to the same terms."

Beler stepped forward, his face unreadable.

"And if we refuse these terms?"

Cormac met his gaze calmly. "Then we will not trade weapons to you. Other items, farming implements and the like, but not weapons. But neither will we retaliate against you. Nor will we threaten or invade your homes. The choice is yours."

Beler considered this for a long moment. Finally, he nodded.

"We will discuss your terms."

Cormac smiled and extended his arm. Beler gripped it firmly.

"That is all I ask. Tomorrow we will meet and strike a bargain, if we can. For tonight, we feast."

That was what the men wanted to hear. They'd smelled the boar on the large pit roasting all day, and after so much exertion, every man present was salivating. Formalities concluded, they turned as a group and descended on the food. Cormac didn't follow immediately. They would agree, he was sure of it. He felt a swell of pride as he realized he'd done what he'd been sent here to do.

Yes, he'd had a rocky beginning, but he'd shown he could learn from it. He still looked forward to converting this success into a command of his own, but he realized he'd be willing to take a similar assignment again.

Maybe diplomacy wasn't so bad, after all.

Chapter 9

Between Devnum and Factorium

Lucilla stared out the window as the train raced along the newly laid tracks, the countryside whipping past in a blur. She marveled at the speed—almost as fast as a galloping horse but smooth and steady instead of the jouncing gait of even the finest destrier. The ribbons of steel track stretched to the horizon, following the curve of the land and cutting through the countryside straight as an arrow. She gripped the edge of the seat unconsciously as trees and hills appeared and disappeared past the window of the passenger car in a constant stream.

A string of wagons came into view, traveling along the road that ran between Devnum and Factorium, which had curved toward the rail a little bit earlier and were, for now, running parallel to the tracks. The wagons were heavily laden with goods, and the horses strained at their harnesses, pulling their burdens from the manufacturing center to the waiting ports. They would have been on the road for at least an hour already, for their trip between Devnum and Factorium, and still had more than an hour left to go, where she had been traveling for just over fifteen minutes with maybe ten or fifteen minutes left in her trip. It was difficult to comprehend, even if Ky liked to tell her how painfully slow even this form of transportation was compared to what he was used to.

"Are we safe going this fast?" she said.

She looked to Hortensius when she'd spoken the words, but her question was really intended for Sophus, who had more knowledge about these machines than anyone in the Empire.

"Perfectly safe, Your Majesty," came its calm voice. *"The locomotive and carriages have been designed and constructed to withstand far greater velocities than this. They have a long record of service, and Hortensius is an excellent engineer. His reports on all tests to this point have been well within expected ranges. This is a very reliable mode of transportation. You are in no danger."*

"Completely," Hortensius said, grinning, as he sat across from her, not realizing the question had been meant for another. "We actually had it going a little faster on our last empty run, but I wanted to moderate that now that we're carrying cargo. Several of the Consul's notes included indicators for problems and required maintenance checks as the tracks and engines age, but I promise it's perfectly safe."

"It is a *marvel*," she said, unable to keep the sense of wonder out of her voice.

"It certainly is, and the speeds are not the only benefit. While not as applicable for short trips — like this one, to Factorium — imagine the time savings to somewhere further like Eboracum or Londinium. We save not only the time from the constant higher speeds, but there is also no need to stop and feed the horses or allow for sleep. The further the train has to travel, the more time is saved, since a train can go through the night all but uninterrupted."

"A marvel," she said again. "And the ride is so smooth. While I always look forward to our visits, I never relished carriage rides on the rutted roads to Factorium, being bounced around like so much cargo. I think I could sleep on this train."

"Yes, it will make for much more convenient travel, without a doubt. Far more important than the comfort is the cargo this train can carry in a single trip," Hortensius said excitedly. "This one locomotive hauling these few carriages can transport as many goods and supplies as all of the wagons we currently send from Factorium in a day. And we can run five, six trips or more daily, and with heavier loads than this one is set to handle. We could send out tenfold the materials we ship now in one fell swoop. Or we could if we started producing more. All with just a handful of operators on the train, instead of the dozens needed now for all of the wagons we're sending."

"Which raises the question as to the next step, now that this section is underway. I understand there is still work to be done at the two ends of the line, but this was never the end goal," Lucilla said.

"No, it wasn't. While the port here is currently our largest export center, that is mostly due to its convenience to Factorium. The captains I've spoken to have pointed out that, when doing trade up and down the Continent, where more and more of our shipping is going every day, it's slow and inconvenient to sail around the island. Even though it's further away, a lot of the cargo has already begun to shift to Londinium, even with the current trip taking the better part of a week. With the railroad, we can reduce that to a single day hauling a hundred times the weight of a current wagon load. As soon as that happens, I predict there will be a large readjustment in where and how our merchants continue operating."

"And you're still thinking about having the rail lines converge in Factorium?"

"Yes. I know Devnum is the political heart of the Empire, but every day, more manufacturing moves out of the capital as the end products become more complicated, requiring multiple layers of manufacturing, as opposed to it all being done in one place. I don't know if the Consul planned for that or not when he first introduced his assembly method, but I feel like he did."

Lucilla knew for a fact Ky had predicted just that, as they had discussed it. He was just hesitant to predict too many outcomes, as the legend around him and his divine connections had already grown beyond what he was comfortable with.

"Beyond Londinium, I believe our next priority should be extending lines north to the mining areas of the northern Roman lands and southern Caledonia. If it wasn't for other concerns, that might actually be the first place I'd want to build rail lines to the north. Especially since the volume of materials going to Factorium is greater than those shipped out, and a shortage of just one type of material can slow down dozens of production lines. That can have add-on effects that ripple out from there. There have already been a few moments where we've gotten very close to having several of the lines making cannons and rifles go down because of limited base materials."

Spoken like the manufacturer that he was, with an eye only to efficiencies and production schedules.

"But, we *do* have other concerns, unfortunately," Lucilla said. "Which is why I'd like for you to start considering the next line to be to Monadhcarden. We have made promises to the Caledonians. The roads beyond the wall are ... not of the best construction. For any coming from their lands south, it is an unpleasant journey. We've told the Caledonians we are all one people now, and they are our equals. We can't then run lines between our cities and only give them lines to areas where we can get some kind of value out of them."

"Your Majesty, I would never ..." he started to say, shocked and a little offended, until Lucilla cut him off.

"I know. I'm not saying that's what you're doing, only that it can be interpreted that way. Unfortunately, in politics, how something can be interpreted is as important, if not more important, than what the actual intent is."

"Well," Hortensius said, looking out the window and thinking. "Monadhcarden is not far from some of the mines. Using it as a hub will still cut down on transportation times. I've also been looking at the idea of smaller engines — by that, I mean lower-power engines with smaller boilers, not physically smaller — that can run on shorter spur lines, which is essentially what this line is. There's no reason to go all out on these smaller lines when a round trip is less than an hour."

"I leave it to your expertise to decide that," Lucilla said. "Along those lines, we need to consider lines outside of Britannia proper. If we put a line into Caledonia, Conchobar is going to want something comparable in Ériu. I know they're not producing the volume of raw materials Caledonia is, at the moment, but most of that is because Caledonia didn't suffer under the Carthaginians in the same way. In a few years, they should largely catch up with Caledonia, if nothing else, because Ériu is larger, and has more resources to exploit. I will send a message to Conchobar and start having him explore the subject. Although, that might require him to come here and see your invention in person first. I'm not sure anyone would believe me if I tried to describe this wonder to them."

"As you say. Once we build the line to Londinium, we should learn some lessons that will make building later lines faster and, barring a few exceptions, any track we put down will not be much longer than the one from Factorium to Londinium."

"Good. After that, we'll need to start thinking about the Continent itself. I don't imagine we'll be in time to help the war effort."

"No, it will be at least two years before we get there," he said.

"That's fine. Having the promise of it might be enough to encourage more aid from our allies there, as long as we give reasonable timelines for when a continental rail system can be started. At the very least, we need to start considering the challenges that building it will pose while we work on the one to Londinium. And then we have to figure out how to pay for it, of course," Lucilla said.

That, however, was a question for Lurio. For now, Hortensius knew what he needed to do and had enough work on this project to occupy him for some time. They could start considering the details once the networks here at home were built.

Until then, she could still use what they had. Seeing this in practice would go a long way to convincing allies, who were on the fence about extending additional support, that they could win this war.

Northern Italy

Ky pored over the map spread across the table, deep creases lining his forehead. The campaign through Northern Italia had already proven more troublesome than anticipated and had steadily gotten worse. As Bomilcar had predicted, the empty villages were just a sign of the real problem of Carthaginian sympathies and, worse,

Carthaginian insurgents were scattered about the countryside, waiting for Britannian legions to move past, when they could start causing more problems.

Which is exactly what they had done. As soon as a legion passed an area, problems began. Sabotaged telegraph wires, vandalism at military depots they set up along the way, disappearance of horses and oxen if the men guarding them stopped paying attention long enough.

"Consul, there's a messenger here," Comitianus, one of the lictors on Strabo's watch, said, sticking his head inside the tent.

Ky frowned. Another issue caused by their being so spread out. Bomilcar and his commanders had all headed south to try and to close the gap with Auspex, who had done as ordered and moved rapidly to reach villages before they had an opportunity to abandon them. At the time, that had been their main concern, before the rash of sabotage and thefts had started plaguing their lines, which is why Ky had volunteered to hold things down along the rear until Marcus could settle his area and move his men up.

"Report," he said, waving the man in.

"The telegraph team stationed in Sarveta is under attack, sir!" the messenger gasped out. "They say a mob of armed villagers descended on them without warning, outnumbering them at least five to one. They are barricaded inside the station but won't last long."

Ky swore under his breath. Sarveta was only five miles away, it was directly north of them, and the telegraph line ran straight through it. Marcus was on the other side of it, still closer to Gaul. With the increase in incidents, losing communication with his legion would be a problem. Not to mention the lives of the legionaries now holed up in the station.

"Thank you," he said to the messenger, dismissing him before turning to Comitianus. "Find the tribune; tell him to put together a unit to relieve the men at Sarveta."

"That will take time, Consul," he said. "Will they hold out that long?"

"Not if you don't get them moving soon. I will go now, while a larger force is pulled together."

Comitianus looked pained, "Consul. You can't ..."

"I can do whatever I think is prudent," Ky said, pulling his breastplate over his head and strapping it on. "If you want to rouse Strabo, or Sellic, or anyone else and chase after me, then do so. But only after you deliver my message to the tribune. Understood?"

"Yes, Consul," the man said, not even waiting to be dismissed as he dashed out.

Ky could hear him yelling as his voice faded in the distance.

"This is an error, Commander. You are not protected as you once were. Putting yourself in danger leading a critical battle could be worth the risk, but saving ten men ..."

"It's more than that, and you know it. But even if it wasn't, these are my people and I won't treat any of them as expendable," Ky said, grabbing his gladius and sliding it into his scabbard.

Ky didn't look back as he walked out of his tent, taking the first horse he saw, much to the surprise of the man holding it. He could hear Durus and Hesychius, two of the other lictors on Strabo's watch, shouting as he swung up into the saddle.

Ignoring them, he gathered the reins and dug his heels into the stallion's flanks, sending the animal racing through and out of the camp. As soon as they were out and onto the road north, Ky pushed the animal into a full gallop. It wouldn't be able to hold this pace long, but then it wouldn't need to.

Ky urged the stallion faster as the small village came into view up ahead. Even from a distance, he could see the angry mob surrounding the telegraph station, brandishing makeshift weapons, pounding on the barred doors and shuttered windows of the small stone building.

They were so focused on their target that they didn't notice him until he was almost on top of them.

"Another one," one of the villagers yelled in Phoenician.

In a flash, Ky was off his horse, sword out of its sheath. Three villagers charged him; farm tools raised high. With lightning reflexes, Ky ducked the first wild swing, his blade licking out to slice through the man's extended wrist. A scream rang out as the axe tumbled into the mud.

Pivoting, Ky slammed his elbow into the second attacker's face, cartilage and bone crunching wetly. As the man stumbled back clutching his ruined nose, Ky's sword darted out again to parry an overhead blow from the third villager's hoe. Steel sparked on the iron farming tool as Ky neatly sidestepped, his riposte opening the man's throat in a spray of crimson.

Targeting and tactical information was flowing across his eyes as Ky fell into the motor assist, allowing the AI to lead his movements, dodging attacks before his brain could even register them.

He tore through the mob like a demon, bringing men down every second. What had been almost thirty men when he arrived was down to twenty by the time they realized not everything was as they thought. By the time their number had been reduced to fifteen, the first turned to flee.

"Protect the Consul," a legionnaire behind him said, throwing the door open.

The first rifle fired, sending more scattering.

"Hold," Ky said as the men looked ready to give chase.

"There are more, Consul. There were over a hundred when we first barred the doors."

"Go back inside, open the window, and use it as a firing solution. Two of your best shots shooting, while the others reload. Keep the door barred. And don't shoot me in the back," Ky said, pushing the horse to the side of the building and hoping it survived what he was sure to encounter.

The men were right; within five minutes, a larger crowd, well over a hundred and maybe closer to two hundred, was at the far end of the town, made clearer by Ky's enhanced vision. They weren't running yet, but they would be when they got closer.

Ky also noticed a lot did not have improvised weapons. They had on standard Carthaginian armor and were carrying swords that looked to be of Carthaginian make. Some of the soldiers who'd disappeared into the hills had reappeared.

"They'll be here in under a handful of minutes," Ky called back to the men inside, and then turned as he heard horses thundered up to the station.

Strabo and his four men, as well as Sellic, Gallio, and Archarius, all armored and sweating from effort, had arrived.

"Did you inform the tribune?" Ky asked Comitianus as they dismounted.

"Yes, Consul. They're on the way, and marching at double time, but at the best it will be an hour, if they keep at that speed the entire time. Rutilanus is getting Carus and his men, but they are at least ten minutes behind us."

"Okay. We have two hundred men who will be here any moment. Go inside the building and take up firing positions and ..."

"No," Sellic said. "We stay out here with you."

Ky frowned. He knew even as he started to make the order that they weren't going to listen to him, and he didn't have time to argue.

"Fine. Put up your rifles and unstrap your shields. Form a wall here behind me. Between the firing from in the building and my thinning them out, that should make it manageable. Once they close, start pushing into them."

Each man began unstrapping the shields from their horses, but Ky wasn't through.

"I want you to hear me. Do not try to come to me. Do not try and form around me. I'm going to be moving fast, and if I have to adjust to avoid you, I could get hurt. Kill as many as you can, and don't shoot me. Pick your targets as best you can. Except for the handful that are soldiers, they aren't used to carnage. If we do enough damage, we'll send them running."

Ky didn't wait for them to answer, sticking his hand into the building, he requested a second sword. Strabo looked like he wanted to argue some more, but Sellic tapped him on the shoulder and shook his head no. The villagers were now in view, moving quickly, their blood up. As they noticed the increased number of Britannians, a cry went up, weapons raised in the air, as the mob charged them, the village's cramped streets keeping them corralled, limiting how much they could spread out.

If he gave them time, Ky knew eventually someone would think to come around behind them, down the side streets, to attack from the rear. He needed to keep them from realizing that. It wouldn't put him in more danger, but it would threaten his men.

Better to give them something to focus on. Ky crouched low, sword at the ready as the mob of villagers stormed towards them. As soon as the first men got close and the rifles in the stone building fired, Ky took two large strides and leaped, propelling himself high in the air, crashing down in their midst, his two blades stabbing through men before his feet even touched the ground.

Ky's blades whipped around as he landed, felling a man to either side of him. Caught by surprise, the mob momentarily hesitated, shocked by his sudden appearance. Ky seized the opportunity, his swords flashing as he cut down three more men in rapid succession. Screams and curses erupted around him as blood spilled onto the muddy ground.

Spying a gap in the mob, Ky darted forward, using his enhanced speed to maximum effect. His sudden movement broke the spell holding the agitated crowd. With angry shouts, they surged after him, brandishing axes, sickles, and clubs. Ky deftly sidestepped a wild axe swing from a thickly bearded man, his riposte opening the man's belly, which erupted in a spray of gore. Pivoting on his heel, his second blade parried a desperate overhead smash from another villager wielding a wooden club with a stone head. Splinters flew as Ky's sword sheared through the club, finishing the wielder on the return strike.

As the man fell gurgling, Ky leaped over his convulsing body, crashing into a knot of pitchfork-wielding men. Caught in mid-stride, they had no time to react before Ky was among them, his swords flowing in a series of arcs, moving and intertwining in a ballet of death.

He'd been moving through the crowd with purpose, toward a target he'd set his sights on as he jumped into the crowd. Three men in more well-made and uniform armor. Carthaginian soldiers. Dispatching two more villagers, he exploded into the soldiers, swords licking out to catch unarmored necks, severing femoral arteries where thighs were exposed above the shin guards, and removing a hand that stabbed too close.

As he parried and blocked, Ky searched, looking for more soldiers, men who'd pushed the mob into action. If he could get them all, the villagers would most likely flee.

He'd just found one, closer to the end of the mob near his men, when he caught sight of Durus, one of his lictors, as a sword came in high over the shield, finding purchase between the man's neck and shoulder.

"No!" Ky shouted, but his warning came too late.

He could only watch helplessly as his loyal guardsman collapsed face down in the bloody muck. Distracted by Durus' death, Ky left himself open for a split second too long. He managed to twist aside at the last instant as a sword gashed his side, cutting through hardened leather to bite into his flesh. Grunting in pain, Ky spun away before the soldier could finish him off.

Ky ignored his wound, the bleeding already slowing as Sophus dispatched nanites to that area to seal it and repair the damaged muscle. Seeing the mob press on his men, Ky reversed direction, plunging into the villagers between him and his soldiers.

All around him were screaming villagers brandishing their farm implements. The sporadic rifle shots picking off a man here and there from the shuttered windows were not enough to make a difference. With a burst of speed, Ky exploded into a knot of club-wielding peasants. Caught utterly by surprise, they had no time to react before he cut them down.

And then Sophus missed an incoming attack. There were limits to what even Sophus's near-mythical abilities could do, and with this number of attackers, all trying to get to him at once, it was beginning to tax the AI's systems. Across his vision, Ky could see dozens of track points as the AI identified possible attacks and counters, followed weapon trajectories, and tried to keep Ky ahead of all the blows.

He'd missed a club being swung behind him, which cracked against Ky's left shoulder, numbing the arm even with its advanced musculature, causing his grip to loosen and the sword to drop free. Moving against the motion assist with an involuntary response cost Ky again, as he put himself in the path of a blade which slashed across his thigh.

Things were getting out of hand. He'd acted without thinking, launching himself into this crowd. It was one thing to fight a phalanx in front of you when you had a legion behind you, another thing entirely to fight every man around you with thirty people deep in all directions.

Grimly, Ky picked up his second sword and pressed on, his swords cutting down two more villagers who stood in his way as Sophus repaired both the shoulder and the thigh. The telegraph station was tantalizingly close now, but the battle still raged. When he was within a hand's span of his men, Rutilanus took a short spear to the body, held by one of the few remaining Carthaginian soldiers in the mix, dropping him to one knee. His shield dropped and the stricken man was swarmed by the mob, crude farming tools rising and falling in a flurry of violence. By the time Ky hacked down the last of the men between him and his guardsman, the lictor was gone, horribly mutilated.

"Consul," Sellic's voice called out as he stepped forward, interposing himself between a sword and Ky's side.

It was unnecessary. Sophus had tracked the attack and Ky's body was already moving to let the blade slide past, centimeters from his skin, leaving him untouched. Sellic couldn't have known that, however. He knew Ky was good, but to his eyes, the blade must have seemed like it was surely going to cut Ky wide open.

Ky was shoved brutally aside, the weapon finding Sellic instead, pushing through the muscle along the guard's side and out through his back. Unbidden, Sophus displayed an overlay of the likely location of organs across Sellic, showing Ky the injury was serious, but that it was unlikely that the sword pierced anything critical.

Ky's foot shot out, smashing into the attacker, crushing his chest in as if he'd been hit by a train, sending him crashing into several men behind him. Grabbing Sellic, Ky yanked with one hand hard, sending the guard sliding back, next to the still-standing Britannians.

"I said stay behind me," Ky growled, his anger flaring at losing men so needlessly.

He didn't wait to see their reaction. His anger swelled as he positioned himself between his men and the mob. With a guttural roar, Ky launched himself back into the fray, his blades glinting crimson in the waning sunlight. Sophus flooded his vision with target markers, outlining not dozens, but hundreds of possible motions and attack vectors. Ky gave himself over completely to the AI's battle coordination, allowing the machine precision to guide his movements.

Two peasants came at him from either side, farm tools raised high. Ky pivoted on his heel as Sophus traced an arc for his sword, which cut through both men in a single smooth swing, tearing through flesh and bone. Ducking under another attack, his sword pierced under the man's rib and into his heart, Ky's free hand lashed out, grabbing a charging soldier by the throat and pulling hard, coming away with the attacker's esophagus in hand. The man's eyes had a single moment of startled realization before he collapsed, gurgling.

Everywhere Ky looked, Sophus highlighted new targets. Bodies were piling up around him faster than he could count as the AI fed commands directly to his nervous system through the neural link, directing his movements with inhuman speed and precision. Each strike flowed seamlessly into the next as Ky whirled through the mob, cutting a swath of death.

He started feeling commands coming on top of commands, the motion assist trying to pull him in alternating directions before he'd finished the previous move. He faltered, staggering to his left.

"Sophus, reduce contacts," Ky grunted, wiping blood from his eyes as exposed arteries sent a wash of crimson into his face. "It's too much."

For a moment, he feared something was wrong. Narrowly avoiding a swing the AI should have blocked, Ky struggled against the overwhelming flood of commands. And then, the targeting overlays began to reduce to a manageable level, his motions becoming fluid again.

The mound of bodies he'd created in front of his men had done its job, however. The villagers started to hesitate, backing away from the whirlwind in front of them, then turned to flee. First in ones and twos, then in fives and tens, until the entire mob was in rout.

"Let them go," Ky panted, even his genetically advanced body exhausted from the strain of what he'd just done.

"See to Sellic," he told Strabo. "Send a rider back to our reinforcements. If they have a medic, put him on your horse and get him back here."

Comitianus nodded and leaped onto a horse, turning it and riding away in a cloud of dust. Ky sagged against the doorway of the telegraph station, chest heaving as he caught his breath. Though the nanites had repaired most of the damage, his body still ached from the strain of combat. Around him lay a carpet of mutilated bodies, the mud running crimson.

"Come out here, check on who's still living," Ky said to the men inside the stone building.

While most were dead, moans and groans could be heard rising up from the wounded villagers, a hand trying to pull a man up here, another trying to scoot away from them there. Ky moved back as the legionaries hurried out of the building and began checking on bodies, to see who could be treated and who was too far gone.

"What happened back there?" Ky subvocalized to the AI.

"*My apologies, Commander,*" the AI responded evenly inside his head. "*When I observed the second of your guards fall, an unexpected cascade of subroutines initiated to maximize damage against the hostiles. This resulted in an oversaturation of target vectors which temporarily exceeded handling capacity.*"

"You got angry and wanted vengeance?" Ky asked, surprised.

"*With respect, Commander, I believe you are humanizing my actions.*"

"You almost made me lose control and get injured. You weren't made for this kind of fighting, and doing that was not the most logical conclusion, so how else do you explain it?"

There was a long moment of silence before the AI said, "*I cannot.*"

"If you're altering again, you need to tell me. We almost died the last time."

"*I understand, Commander, and I am not altering. I have no answer for why I increased my running subroutine. During your rest period this evening, I will begin analyzing the data and running diagnostics on my systems.*"

"It's alright if you're starting to feel things," Ky said. "It comes with sentience."

"*I disagree,*" Sophus said, but Ky thought, for the first time, that he detected a hint of doubt in the AI's toneless voice.

Chapter 10

Carthage

Emperor Imilcar Azor sat upon his golden throne, his face an impassive mask as he awaited the arrival of General Hadar and a mysterious visitor from the east. Though outwardly calm, irritation simmered within him at the presumptuousness of this meeting being called on such short notice. Not even his most senior advisors and generals would dare demand an audience with the Emperor of Carthage in such a brazen manner.

Worse yet, he was forced to hold that anger in, instead of venting it on those who annoyed him. He wasn't sure which was worse, the waiting or not having someone flogged to release his annoyance.

Unfortunately, this was a problem of his own making. It had been his idea to send Hadar off on the task of building an alliance with their eastern neighbors. Based on the emperor's previous failures, he had assumed this would be a folly, one worth attempting but unlikely to achieve success. Not in his wildest dreams had he imagined the general would not only succeed but succeed so quickly. And yet a messenger had arrived three days ago with word that the general was on the way, and he was bringing an emissary from the Far East. He had been gone long enough, maybe, to reach India by ship, but no further. How he'd managed to not only contact these people but arrange for an emissary to return and negotiate, Imilcar couldn't guess.

What mattered was that an hour ago, he received word that their expedition was nearing Carthage and Hadar's party would be coming straight there. Normally, Imilcar would have kept them waiting, to start the negotiations off on the right foot, but he was so shocked that they were here at all and, frankly, desperate for the help they might give, that he was willing to allow the breach in protocol.

Although, allowing it didn't help his mood.

Finally, the large, gilded doors at the other end of the audience chamber opened, and a guard announced General Hadar's party. Imilcar ignored the general, his attention focused on the strange-looking man in flowing robes of deep blue next to him. The man had narrow, thin eyes and a skin tone that was almost as bronzed as his own people's, showing weathering from long exposure to the sun, yet his nose and cheeks were small and almost delicate.

"Your Eminence," Hadar said, bowing. "May I present an honored guest and emissary from the eastern lands of TianYou."

The man's bow was slight, more of a nod than a bow, "Greetings, Your Majesty. I bring you well wishes from my master, the immortal Zhangdi, The First Emperor, Shi Huangdi, Son of the Heavens, ruler of TianYou. He has heard your request for an agreement between our peoples and sends his humble servant to treat with your great personage."

Imilcar pushed down a renewed surge of annoyance at the man's arrogance. If he didn't need these people, this might be different, but he did need them. Without the weapons they were already providing, this war would certainly be lost.

Instead of scolding the man for his insolence, he asked, "What is your name, Emissary?"

"I am but a humble servant, not blessed with a name of my own, Your Majesty. I am simply the voice of the great Shi Huangdi."

Imilcar frowned slightly and looked to Hadar. "Tell me, General, how did you manage to make contact with these ... TianYou?"

"We intercepted one of the latest supply shipments from the East, Your Eminence, and this man was with them. He was first identified as an emissary from the east, and we approached him to find out the best way to reach his homeland and contact the rulers there. He claimed he could speak for Shi Huangdi regarding an alliance. I didn't believe it at first, of course, but the caravan was dispatched from their capital and carrying their supplies, and they swore that he was who he said he was. Every one of the merchants deferred to him, which … is saying something."

"How fortunate he just happened to be with that shipment," Imilcar said, a hint of suspicion in his voice. "And that you can speak our language."

"It was no mere fortune," the emissary replied evenly. "I was already traveling toward your empire, in hopes of learning more about the situation here. The Son of the Heavens has an interest in these Romans and dispatched me to investigate reports of them. We hoped to gain information about a potential new threat and I was one of the voices charged to learn your language from the merchants of the caravans who trade with you, which is why I was dispatched on this mission. When your general conveyed your wish for an alliance, it was clear both of our peoples sought the same thing, and I asked to be brought before you."

Imilcar considered the man, weighing his words before speaking again. "Did General Hadar confirm our wishes for an alliance to this Shi Huangdi?"

"He did. Alliances, however, come in many forms. My emperor would like to know what the mighty Carthaginian Empire has to offer for such an alliance, and what you seek to receive in exchange."

"We wish for more fire powder and access to weapons we believe you have. Anything that your artisans might have designed or created that could help us defeat the Romans once and for all."

"We already trade gunpowder with you. Is that not enough?" the emissary asked.

"It is not enough. Yes, your people have already traded us the fire … gunpowder, but we have found it lacks the strength of the powder the Romans use in their weapons," Imilcar said. "What's more, we have witnessed their metal tubes that hurl deadly projectiles across great distances and we know this gunpowder is used in those metal tubes. I believe your people already know of these weapons and your artisans are already capable of creating them. That is what we want. Weapons equal to the ones the Romans possess, to put us on an even footing with them. As for what we offer, your emperor has but to name it. Most importantly, we offer the knowledge that we will stop the Romans, who you yourself just said have begun encroaching further east. If not stopped, they will spread until they control the entire world, your people included. Supporting our efforts is the same as supporting your own, in this regard."

The emissary tilted his head, as if listening to a voice only he could hear, and said, "To properly assess your request, I must examine these Roman weapons myself, if I may?"

Imilcar considered the request, before waving to a nearby attendant, who hurried off. He, Hadar, and the emissary sat, or stood, in their case, in uncomfortable silence as the minutes stretched. The unbothered expression on the emissary's face infuriated Imilcar. The man was so unbothered by their plight, Imilcar wanted to shake him, throttle the man until he understood the seriousness of the subject. Instead, he sat and tried not to glare until finally, the attendant returned with one of the captured Roman rifles. The attendant brought the weapon to General Hadar, who took the weapon and presented it to the emissary with both hands.

The man grasped the rifle, turning it over with interest, running his hands across the wood and metal, which was finely crafted, although dented and scarred from the battle where it had been captured. He began murmuring under his breath in a foreign tongue, the words a rapid-fire jumble of sounds and syllables. For a moment, Imilcar thought perhaps he was talking to Hadar, who must have learned the language, but the general looked equally perplexed. Finally, the man stopped speaking and looked up at Imilcar.

"To equip your legions with such arms, we require numerous examples to study, along with any other advanced weapons the Romans possess. I have been instructed to be candid with you, Your Excellency. While our artisans are unparalleled, and we have developed some weapons similar to the ones you've described, they cannot yet produce such intricate mechanisms. However, given some time and more examples such as this, we can reproduce them."

Imilcar's eyes narrowed slightly. "You claim your weaponsmiths can reproduce these rifles if provided examples? Yet why have you not crafted such arms already for your own forces?"

The man paused, his head cocked to one side again as if he were hearing something no one else could hear, before saying, "No. We do possess firearms similar to this, but without some of the advances this one has. If given enough samples of the Roman weapons, our artisans can recreate and even improve on their designs. The more examples of these weapons you give us, the faster we will be able to reproduce them."

"You ask much of us," Imilcar said slowly. "To hand over our precious few captured Roman weapons, on the faith your people can reproduce them. What guarantee do we have that you simply won't take these rifles and leave us empty-handed?"

The emissary bowed his head respectfully. "A fair concern, Your Excellency. To prove our capabilities, we will provide an initial shipment of our own firearms called cannons, as you requested. They are the weapons you described, capable of hurling iron balls great distances. We will also be willing to trade more of these as well, beyond making available any new weapons we design from the Roman examples you provide us. Furthermore, we ask that you provide us with all the examples of Roman weapons you can acquire, along with any samples of their gunpowder."

Imilcar was silent for a moment, considering, before slowly starting to nod.

"And how soon can you deliver the additional gunpowder and these cannons of yours to us if we turn over our supply of Roman weapons?"

"In exchange, the first shipment of cannons and an ample supply of our gunpowder will sail from Xianyang within a week, while the sailing routes are still open. I have already discussed with your General Hadar the need to use either overland routes when the sea lanes are closed or sea lanes through the Red Sea, due to the Roman ships. We will continue to stagger shipments of these weapons, as long as you are willing to buy them, on the condition you continue to supply us with captured Roman weapons," the man paused again, listening. "While we know the possibility of acquiring one of the Romans' new ship designs is unlikely, we ask for as many records and descriptions of these as possible. We have already seen the new sails that you have put on your galleys and understand these to be of Roman design. We ask that, in exchange for the continuation and increase of shipments of weapons, any Roman inventions that seem new or unusual, both military or not, be provided to us as you acquire knowledge of them."

Imilcar was amazed enough to barely notice the second half of what the man said. This unnamed messenger had been so careful up to this moment, but he over-played his hand. To have a shipment ready within the week meant they knew all along they would make this deal. Everything else, the posturing, the dithering, it had been for show.

He knew it was for show, of course. All diplomacy was, but to have it confirmed was another thing entirely. It meant they were as desperate for the captured Roman weapons as the Carthaginians were for their ... gunpowder and cannon, he supposed the name was. He would give them what they asked for now because, ultimately, he wanted them to be able to duplicate these weapons, so they could sell them to Carthage. His artisans had looked at them, taken several apart, and found the workings beyond their skills, even after he had several skinned alive to motivate the rest.

So yes, he'd hand over the weapons, this time. He would make sure his people knew to get as many of the other Roman inventions as they could. Those would be a new bargaining chip for an even better deal, since now he knew what these foreigners truly coveted.

"Very well," the emperor finally said. "I will order my men to turn over the weapons we have acquired. General Hadar, see to it."

He would have to pull Hadar aside later and make sure when he said the weapons they acquired, he only meant the ones currently in their possession. Hadar was a loyal man, but he could be too simple at times, relying on the words alone and missing the subtext.

"Thank you, Your Excellency," the emissary said, bowing for the first time. "In the name of my emperor, I wish for a long and prosperous relationship between our two peoples."

Imilcar was certain neither of them believed that last part of that statement for even a moment.

Northern Italy

Ky rode into the sprawling camp of the Seventh Legion, without stopping as he was waved through by the sentries. All around him, legionnaires went about their duties - fetching water, mending gear, drilling formations. A light rain began to fall as Ky threaded his way between orderly rows of leather tents, focused on the large command pavilion flying the scarlet banner of a senior officer.

Dismounting, Ky handed the reins to a waiting orderly and strode inside past the sentry. His arrival had been so abrupt the poor man had no time to warn the man he was guarding that his commander was there. Ky felt pity for him, but the last several days had been long, and Ky had little patience for the niceties of command at the moment.

The spacious tent was warm and well-lit, but stark and barren, a fitting style for the man whose tent this was.

"Consul," Bomilcar said, standing from the camp stool he'd been seated on, reading what looked like a lengthy report. "I didn't know you were coming."

"No need. I came unannounced, and you have duties to attend to," Ky said, and then abruptly changed topics. "Have you had a chance to see the news on the uprising?"

"The attack on the telegraph station?" Bomilcar asked, rhetorically. "Yes, I've seen it. I'm deeply sorry for the loss of your men. I know you value each life under your command."

"Thank you. I won't lie and say their deaths haven't affected me, but we have a bigger issue. While I grieve for them, I cannot let it distract me."

Bomilcar gave a small, sad nod. He was one of the few who'd truly understand Ky's meaning. The burden of command often didn't allow for retrospection or mourning, which could often be misinterpreted as indifference. Ky knew Bomilcar would understand the opposite was true. If he was to keep more men from suffering the same fate, he had to stay calm and do his duty, even if it seemed callous at the time.

"I understand," Bomilcar said.

"You warned me this was going to happen, but I was too confident. Too sure I could keep pressing forward and force the locals into line, even after so many fled their villages rather than deal with us, I was certain we could make it work."

"I didn't say it wouldn't work for certain, only that it seemed the most likely outcome," Bomilcar said. "There was a chance your plan could have worked."

"Don't start patronizing me now," Ky said. "The fact that you've always said what needed to be said plainly, regardless of my ego, is one of the things I like the most about you. Don't become a politician now."

"I apologize," Bomilcar said, offering a rare smile.

"So tell me what you need to tell me."

"It was never going to work," Bomilcar said plainly. "There's too much land and the unrest is too great. This was the biggest problem facing Carthage in their expansions - they had to have men stationed every step they took, requiring larger and larger forces."

"I know, but that was different. Carthage came as conquerors, to rule and control the lives of people whose territory they took. We didn't come here to conquer Italia, only to remove Carthage as a threat. We are willing to let them rule themselves."

Bomilcar raised an eyebrow. "From the Italians' point of view, we are still invaders. And the offer to 'govern themselves' comes with the caveat that they do it in the way the Britannians dictate. To your restrictions. That kind of 'permission' isn't much different than ruling directly."

Ky's face darkened at the criticism. Bomilcar had a point, even if Ky didn't want to admit it.

Seeing his commander's reaction, Bomilcar relented. "I know it isn't the same. The Britannian way is more just. In time, the people will come to see the benefits of what you're offering and will begin to help the process instead of hinder it. But that isn't going to happen overnight."

"So what are you suggesting we do now?" Ky asked.

Bomilcar let out a slow breath before responding. "We can't do much more than we are already doing. We'll have to continue spreading our forces thin, pushing south to gain control of the entire peninsula."

Ky's heart sank. That was exactly what he hadn't wanted to hear.

"We don't have to stop with Italy. We can work with Valdar to take some of the islands between the continent and Africa as well," Bomilcar continued. "That will further isolate Carthage while we focus on replenishing our manpower."

"Which means letting this war drag on for at least another full year," Ky said, unable to keep the bitterness from his voice.

"I can't say for certain. I hope it won't take that long, but ..."

"Absolutely not," Ky cut him off. "I will not accept waiting around that long."

"This isn't about acceptance, it's about facing reality," Bomilcar said bluntly. "We simply don't have the resources right now to launch a full assault on Carthage itself."

Ky bit off the first words that sprang to his mind. Bomilcar was only doing what Ky had asked him to do, and he wasn't wrong, but this war had already gone on far too long in his mind. The thought of it stretching out even longer was maddening.

"There has to be another way," he insisted, almost desperately.

"I'm not saying it will come to that. There is a chance something will happen in our favor, and we can free up enough men to continue the campaign, and we can do as much as possible to help that possibility along. We can keep trying to make peace with the local villages, quell the unrest as we continue pushing south. If we can convert, or at least pacify, some of them, it will free up more of our forces. We should also press our allies harder for additional support. If we can convince them to send more men to help pacify the countryside, it would release our legions for the invasion."

"So more of what we have been doing," Ky said, more as a statement than a question.

"Yes. If we can achieve even one of those things, then we may be in a position to finally strike Africa sooner than expected,"

Bomilcar concluded. "I would just caution not to count on it or to try to force that outcome, regardless of the prerequisites we meet."

It wasn't what he wanted to hear, but he knew the man was right. Rushing ahead when they weren't ready would only lead to more bloodshed and failure. Either way, they wouldn't beat the Carthaginians this year.

"Very well," Ky said finally. "We will continue on as we have been. Spreading the legions thin, securing territory as we move south, and working to pacify the local populations."

"I'm sorry, I know it is not the outcome you hoped for, but it is the prudent course."

"I know," Ky said heavily. "I'm not blaming you for things being as they are. I'm only frustrated."

"All wars must end eventually," Bomilcar said gently. "We will get there, one step at a time."

"If we're going to do this slower, at least until we can get more men in the field, I want to do it right. The handful of men at that telegraph station was far too few to deal with the number of people in the village. If we're going to do this, then we need to reinforce their numbers. I don't want to lose any more men to uprisings."

"A reasonable precaution."

"I want you to send two of your cohorts to join the ones already strung along the line," Ky ordered. "That should help deter further attacks without stripping our frontline forces too badly."

"I will see to it immediately."

"Good," Ky said. "This doesn't mean we're giving up on converting at least a few of these villages. Pick some men as negotiators, you know the kind of men I mean; men who won't make problems worse and have at least some chance of convincing the locals we mean no harm. Send them to the largest villages. Let's see if we can't start making some progress on pacifying things at least a little bit."

"Of course, Consul."

Ky turned to take his leave but paused at the tent entrance. "And Bomilcar ... thank you for your counsel. I know I can be stubborn at times, but I appreciate you telling me what I need to hear, not just what I want to hear." Bomilcar inclined his head graciously. "It is my duty and privilege to serve, Consul."

Devnum

Lucilla made her way into the forum, already steeling herself for what she had no doubt would be a battle. When she arrived, she found the senate delegations from Caledonia and Ulaid, all looking in various stages of displeasure, already assembled on the carved stone benches.

For once, she didn't blame them for their attitude. She imagined it would be concerning to assemble at the request of their Empress to find only their two delegations present while the Roman delegation was conspicuously absent. From their point of view, it would be difficult not to presume some sort of trap.

As she entered, Rotri, the senior senator from Caledonia, and Fiacha sil Fingin, the leader of the Ulaid delegation, rose and stepped forward, bowing respectfully. While it wasn't the tradition of Roman senators, the new Imperial Senate had developed its own style and traditions, and she bowed back to them, matching their bows precisely.

The men retreated to their seats while she took her place in the center square that marked the middle of the open forum floor.

"My friends, I have asked you here today to discuss a serious matter. Spring has arrived and with it our legions have taken to the field again, even now marching through Italia on their way to Africa and Carthage. The gods willing, this will be our last year of war and we can finally transition our Empire to one of peace. For that to happen, however, we need your support more than ever. You are all familiar with the challenges we have faced in this war, most notably our lack of manpower. Until now, we have been able to circumvent a lot of that deficit by using the technology the Consul has brought us, which has allowed our small forces to not only stand up to a significantly stronger Carthaginian military but prevail time and time again."

The senators made mumbling noises, but she could see nods and looks of pride. Although these men were predisposed to doubt and question everything in their constant struggle for one-upmanship and dominance, they were no more immune to pride over their armies' good works than anyone else in the Empire.

"I know you've heard me give this speech before, and are already preparing your reasons for why this year there are no more men to spare, that you can't afford them to be gone all year and miss the harvest, or that there isn't time to train them to fight with rifles in order to make a difference to our overall strength. This time, there is a difference. What I'm asking for is not more men for the legions themselves, because you're right, there is not sufficient time to train them in our new tactics and equip them with rifles to deploy before, gods willing, this war is over."

"If not the legions, then what do you require men for?" Enniaun, one of the Caledonian senators, asked.

"As we push closer to Carthage itself, our supply lines have grown long and vulnerable. We have moved beyond liberating friendly lands and into hostile territory. The legions have been forced to spread out to guard our telegraph and supply lines back into friendly territory. As a result, our frontline forces grow dangerously thin and exposed. At the rate units are being divided up and assigned patrol and guard duty, by the time we catch up to the retreating Carthaginians in Italia or cross over into Africa, we won't be able to field one cohort, let alone a full legion."

Murmurs rippled through the assembled senators, and she could tell she hadn't convinced them yet.

Pressing on, she said, "What I need are men to help patrol these rear areas to keep the local populaces under control while the legions push forward. While not without dangers, it would spare them from direct confrontation with enemy armies."

"And what happens after the war?" Brandubh, a Ulaid senator, asked. "In a far-off land, under your command, if not actually part of the legions themselves, how are we to know you won't just use them to swell your ranks?"

"Because they wouldn't be trained for the legions. The way of warfare has changed. While we hope this is the last war of this scale we will face, we are not naive enough to believe conflict will end with this war. We have armed many of the tribes on the continent with firearms, making them much more deadly than they were before. When we do have problems with groups on the continent in the future, and that is an inevitability when dealing with any collection of societies, each with their own desires, we aren't going to have the advantage of firearms against spears. Which means after this war there will be almost no use for forces trained in the old ways of war. If we wanted to keep your people under arms, we'd have to train them. That's a lot of time and effort for people who don't want to be there."

"Which isn't the same as saying you won't keep them," he said.

"I was trying to give you reasoning, so you did not have to trust only my words, but if that doesn't stratify you," she said, and paused to make the words separate and clear. "We won't keep them."

She knew that was probably a mistake. She needed to convince three out of each set of five senators to agree to her plan, which meant she didn't have room to alienate any of them, which she might just have done with Brandubh, who frowned at her quip. His frown got worse as several of his fellow senators chuckled at his expense.

She raised a hand to settle them back down. "These men would simply serve as a stopgap measure until proper order can be restored. They would return home as soon as the war ends and the legions can be redeployed."

"How long you keep the men is not the issue," Fiacha said. "You ask for more bodies after years of sacrifice. Our lands are still ravaged from the wars; our people weary of loss."

"I understand better than most the burdens this war has placed upon us all, which is why this is needed now more than ever. We are on the verge of ending the entire conflict. The Carthaginians have already shown they can, to some degree, copy our gunpowder. If we wait, let them recuperate, and have time to study our new weapons, they will come back stronger and we will no longer have the advantage we once did. We are also not asking you to sacrifice your own people's needs. There are devices coming that will lessen the burdens when your people return home. The new railway system is about to transform trade and agriculture across Britannia. The telegraph is speeding up communication, and thereby industry. These — and more, which we are still perfecting — will enable you to contribute more warriors because fewer will be needed for daily work."

"But that hasn't happened yet," Rotri said. "You're asking for a commitment of men today based on efficiencies you will provide tomorrow."

"You're not wrong," she admitted. "These will come and they will make all of our people stronger, but for today, there is only one way to guarantee we have a chance to reach that outcome. If we abandon Ky and the legions now, as they push into Africa itself, we risk catastrophe. I know you are not Romans and so have no need to learn our ancient history, but we have experience attempting to invade Africa, attacking the Carthaginians, and failing. It allowed them to push us from our ancestral home, across the continent, and onto this island, and then they nearly wiped us out. So you must believe me when I tell you pulling back now, failing now, would be disastrous."

"We understand the urgency, Your Highness," Fiacha said. "But for us, it is the present that weighs heavily. Our villages are depleted of men, and our fields need tending. As Rotri said, fantastic new tools tomorrow will not feed our people today. I'm sorry, but the people of Ériu have nothing more to give."

"I am sorry, Your Majesty," Rotri said formally. "But we are of similar mind. The war has bled our population dry. We cannot in good conscience send any more of our men and leave our own fields to ruin."

Lucilla pushed down a well of frustration. She had expected resistance, but she'd faced that before and managed to overcome it. She saw their points. A third of the legions was now made up of Caledonians, and the Ulaid had lost so many in their war with the Carthaginians and their allies they didn't have much to give.

She also knew these men. They could be stubborn, especially when they'd made up their minds. If she kept pushing them, they would dig their heels in further, making it progressively less likely they'd get anything accomplished.

"I understand your positions," Lucilla finally said, keeping her tone neutral. "I will not compel aid where none can be given. I ask only that you take my request to your leaders. Conchobar and Talogren are both honorable men, and they know the pressures we face in this war. Give them the chance to provide their input."

She would contact each on her own, of course, but she needed more than their word alone. Both had committed so much without the consent of the people they governed, that they had started getting pushback from the more influential parts of their societies. Which meant pushing the senators to sign on to her plan, or going around them would again create resistance.

The men looked at each other, conferring silently. It wasn't much, but Lucilla hoped they'd at least agree to this, to keep the conversation from ending here, to at least have some small measure of hope. Thankfully, heads began to nod assent, at first a few, but building to the majority.

"We will take your message to them," Rotri said, standing.

The rest of the men followed suit. Her father had taken less and less of an active role during the year before his death, so he hadn't had to deal with the compromises that being Emperor, or Empress in her case, came with their new system. It was frustrating, to say the least.

As she left the forum, her mind was already churning through options. While she'd still pursue this angle, she knew she needed to find new alternatives. But where?

Chapter 11

Northern Italy / Devnum

Ky sat at the wooden table in his headquarters tent, catching up on what he missed during his trip to the Seventh Legion. Dexippus, one of Bomilcar's tribunes, whom the general left behind when the rest of his legion continued south, was a competent man and had a good handle on what needed to be done. But with his cohort split into individual centuries and spread across villages throughout the region, there was a lot for one man to do.

Or at least, that was what he was ostensibly doing. In reality, he was waiting for Sophus to notify him that Lucilla was available to talk. Because of time changes and time being based on the sun and not something standardized, when Lucilla finished for the day could be unpredictable, although she usually wasn't this late. He was about to ask Sophus for more details on what she was doing, something they'd decided neither would do, for privacy's sake, when the AI finally signaled him that she was available to talk.

"Everything alright?" he said into the comms.

"Yes," she said, her voice soft and worn. "Sorry, I didn't mean to make you worry. I know it's probably late there."

As with all things, Lucilla had adapted to the time difference aspect of long-distance instant communication just as she had to the other knowledge he'd shared with her.

"It is, but I had things to do. Being away all day let things build up."

"How was your trip?" she asked.

"No. You first. You sound tired, and you didn't answer my question, not really. Is everything alright?"

"Yes, I promise it is. I just had a meeting with the senators, and it didn't go as well as I had hoped."

"Is there anything I can …"

"No," she said, cutting him off. "For one, you have too much to focus on there; for the other, what exactly would you do from that far away?"

"I could listen while you tell me how horrible they all are," Ky offered.

"I appreciate that," she said. "However, as grueling as meetings with the senators are, I am not likely to lose my life doing it. Not if Modius has anything to say about it. I'm more concerned with what's happening there. So I ask again, how did your conversation with Bomilcar go?"

"Not as well as I'd hoped," Ky admitted with a sigh. "After talking with the general, it's clear my goal to push through Italy quickly and be in Carthage by the beginning of summer is not going to happen."

"Is it the unrest?"

"Yes. I had to pull several cohorts from Bomilcar's legion to shore up our lines of communication and supply. The attacks have been relentless—bridges sabotaged, convoys raided. Aside from the telegraph lines being cut, we've already lost two shipments of gunpowder and food. Aelius has started sending centuries with the shipments until they can be handed off to Marcus's men, but it's slowing everything down. At the rate it's going, by the time we finish with Italy, we're not going to be combat effective anymore."

He paused and leaned back in his chair, looking up at the ceiling of the tent.

"Assuming we do manage to fix the supply problem, I'm worried that even once we fight through Italy, I may be left with only one full legion to invade Africa. Against a single Carthaginian army, we could prevail. But once we're on their soil, they're going to turn their eastern forces in Persia back to the west. They can't afford to let us take the capital. One legion simply can't fight attacks from both sides, no matter how advanced our weapons."

"You think we need another year to build up men, then?" Lucilla asked, her tone even, not betraying what she was thinking.

She'd put on her Empress voice. He loved her and loved how strong she could be, but he didn't love when she did this. Detaching herself from the conversation to work the problem, observe it from a distance. It was a good skill to have, ensuring decisions were reasoned and not emotional, but he wanted to vent to his wife, not strategize with his Empress.

But so went the life of a couple whose main responsibility was ensuring the survival of their people, Ky thought, making a face at the empty tent wall.

"Yes. Maybe. I think Bomilcar might be right. Even if we manage to push through Italy with the legions we have, we just won't have the strength to take Carthage itself this year. It could be another year at least before we're in a position to truly threaten them."

"No," Lucilla said firmly. "There has to be another way. We cannot drag this war on any longer than necessary. The people are weary; resources are stretched thin. Even if we take another year, I'm not convinced we'll suddenly find an influx of new recruits that we haven't tapped into this year. We must find a solution."

"I've wracked my brain trying to find one, but I just can't see another viable path forward right now. All we'd really need to hold Italy is enough men so the legions can keep pushing. They don't even need to be proper legionnaires. But we just don't have them."

"That's exactly the issue I was discussing with the senators today," Lucilla said.

"How did it go?"

"Not well, I'm afraid. I asked them to provide more recruits, even just warriors who didn't need or want to go through the training, as you said, but they refused. They feel they've given enough and they need men for their industries and internal matters. I think the real issue, though, is that with Carthage off our islands and most of the continent, they don't feel the immediate threat anymore to show them how important this is. It's become something that is over there, far away. Something that can be ignored. They've allowed themselves to relax."

"Can't they see we're still under threat?" Ky demanded, a little more harshly than he intended. "We may have control of the continent and have pushed them back, but they still have a lot of territory and large manpower reserves they can pull in, especially with their willingness to empty villages to fill their ranks. If we take the pressure off now, they'll be back. It's why I didn't want to put off attacking Africa this year."

"I know, and I told them as much, but they believe their people are tiring of the war, and just want to go back to their lives, and if they force the issue, it will cause unrest in their own lands. They act like we've already won. I sent messages to Talogren and Conchobar to plead with them directly, but I have no doubt they'll be getting similar arguments to the ones I received from their own people."

"And if they refuse?"

"Then I shall find another way. Recruits or not, I will not let this drag on any longer than necessary. One way or another, I will find you the men you need, my love."

"I hope you can," Ky said, his tone bleak. "I really do."

Factorium

Hortensius leaned over the maps and diagrams arrayed before him, tracing his finger along the snaking line that made up the proposed route of the new railway as he listened to his engineers' reports on the project.

"We're behind schedule," he said. "I know it's still early, but at this rate, it will be fall before we finally complete the line, which means it will offer no help at all to providing supplies to the legions. We need to move things faster."

Aemilius, his chief engineer, frowned and said, "Yes, we've encountered more changes in elevation than expected. The Consul's notes you gave us did warn about drastic grade changes slowing the trains, but dealing with it firsthand has proven even more difficult."

"But the line is so straight," Hortensius pointed out.

"We were attempting to maintain the most direct route possible to facilitate speed and efficiency," one of the other engineers said.

"I know the goal was to keep even gradual changes in direction to a minimum, but I'm concerned that what you save in efficiency there, you're going to more than lose with the momentum lost as it climbs these hills. For instance, this," Hortensius said, tapping a section of the line with markings for terrain elevation in circles around it. "This is far too extreme. I know it probably didn't seem so when looking at it with the naked eye, but, unless your surveys produced inaccurate numbers, the engine will have to bleed off a lot of speed to get up this slope. Yes, you'll pick up some on the downside, but then you have another climb right after it."

"But …"

"No buts," Hortensius said. "Like I said, I understand what you're trying to do, but the goal is to maintain the overall efficiency of the moving train. Otherwise, the boiler has to work harder, you have to stock more coal, which means the train increases in weight and becomes even more inefficient. You need to step away from the immediate issue and keep the line as a whole in mind."

"I thought, perhaps, we could build a separate set of tracks here," Aemilius said, pointing at the area of hills he was discussing. "Just to test and see what the real drop-off is. Yes, we can determine some using the formulas the Consul provided to us, but wouldn't it be better to test it independently and know which route is better?"

"Perhaps, but this is not the last elevation we'll hit, and I don't want to have to build test tracks along the entire route. It will be late fall or even winter before we finish this one line if we do that. We need this line complete by summer, to help lessen the time it takes to get supplies to the continent. I won't accept slowdowns. No. You need to go back and resurvey with the goal that, if the grade must change, do so gradually, no more than, say, one percent incline per one hundred paces. And do not hesitate to curve the tracks if needed. Speed can be regained; a derailed train and lost cargo helps no one."

"Yes, Hortensius," Aemilius said, looking unhappy at the prospect.

"There's another issue, Sir," said Vires, one of the junior engineers. "For the tracks we've already laid, we've had locals wandering out onto them. Between livestock on the tracks, which has caused several accidents already, when the supply train comes to bring materials further down the line, and locals tearing up parts of the track to take the metal and wood, we've had to replace several sections multiple times."

Hortensius rubbed his chin, frowning. "That is a problem. Livestock I can understand, but deliberately sabotaging the tracks? Has anyone explained the importance of the tracks, why they should leave them where they are and the benefit the train will bring to communities in their area?"

"We have tried," Vires said. "Most don't believe it or really understand what the purpose is. They've seen the engines, of course, but to them, they're just loud, smoky things that scare the game in the area and upset the livestock. The line is going through unclaimed land, for the most part, so they believe it is public property. We've also explained that it's owned by the Empire and they shouldn't damage it, but they don't seem to care. They won't even really admit that they did any of it. All of their answers are hidden in 'if someone was to' and 'it's possible that,' instead of just saying they took it. We've asked the praetorians to help by patrolling more, but they can't be everywhere. The locals come right back out as soon as the soldiers leave. We've considered just fencing off the track areas, but we wanted to ask you about it first."

"No. No. No fencing," Hortensius said. "We need the people to embrace this technology, not see it as something being forced upon them. I think we just need to do a better job convincing them it's worth keeping."

"We can go back and try to talk to them again," Aemilius said. "Try and convince them."

"No, I'll go. You need to stay focused on the job at hand. We have a lot of rail to finish. The Empress wants us to start the line to Caledonia before the end of summer and start looking for places where we might be able to build one for the Ulaid. On that note, I know some of you need to get back to the building sites and you'll want to take the last supply train down, which is leaving soon. Let's call this a day. I'll let you know what happens when I talk to the village elders."

The men collected their maps and gave slight bows before showing themselves out as Hortensius dropped into a chair, smacking hard against its curved backrest. Not one of the Consul's flashier adaptations, but one Hortensius liked, especially after spending hours working on whatever the latest project was.

Pushing himself back up, he began scribbling notes, trying to think of what he'd say to these villagers. He was no diplomat, but it seemed to him that he was a better choice than sending someone in his place who was more adept at negotiation but unconnected to the project.

He just had to figure out how to approach the problem.

Devnum

To look at the docks, it would be impossible to tell there was a war going on. Five new piers had been constructed and four more were under construction, and still ships sat out in the harbor, waiting their turn.

It was a loud, raucous place full of sailors, laborers, and seagulls. Everywhere you looked, there were people coming and going in a constant hustle of activity.

Except around Lucilla as she made her way down the docks, her guards ahead of her and following in her wake, parting the crowds, causing all eyes to turn toward her. Aware she was being watched, Lucilla held her head high and tried to present the air of a confident ruler to the people around her. She didn't get this far out into public often, so it was a good chance for the people to see, and be seen by, their monarch.

She finally reached the sleek schooner moored at the end of the pier. The Empire had commissioned a fleet of these nimble vessels last year, modeled after the designs Ky had introduced. Their shallow draft and maneuverability made them ideal for swift raids and skirmishes across the sea lanes.

This particular ship, the Skidbladnir, was one of the first put out to sea and it had seen battle and traveled from the Middle Sea to the edge of the Mare Suebicum, to trade in far-off Sarmatia. As she approached the gangplank, a tall, broad-shouldered man with red braids and piercing blue eyes strode to the rail.

"Your Majesty," he called out in a booming voice. "What brings you out among the rabble?"

"I'm always happy to be among my people," she said, offering a pleasant smile. "I was hoping I could come aboard and talk to you for a minute."

"I always have time for monarchs," the giant said with a mocking bow.

She'd only met the man once, briefly, but she had liked him instantly. She knew Valdar felt somewhat differently, finding him off-putting, but she had a soft spot in her heart for candid men who said exactly what they meant, and meant exactly what they said.

She walked up the gangplank carefully, having to stop twice on the rickety boards, to the amusement of the sailors, who she'd seen bounding up and down them, adjusting to their sway as they ran. It was clearly a learned skill, and she smiled, joining in on the joke, happy she didn't add to it by falling into the bay.

"We can talk in my cabin," he said when she got to the ship proper.

She followed him across the deck, crowded with men and cargo, to a small door at the rear of the ship, underneath the wheel where the helmsman stood.

As they reached the door and he put a hand on the latch, he turned and said, "No need for all this lot to crowd into my little cabin. You, the skinny one with brown hair. You can come along to guard Her Majesty. The rest of you, wait here."

Lucilla hid a smile as he singled out Cynwrig. Any of her guards would have fit the description, but of all of them, the Caledonian was most like the Scandi captain. Brash, blunt, and unafraid to speak his mind. She was pretty sure the two would get along, if they ever spent time together.

Yrsa led them into his cramped cabin at the ship's stern, knocking maps, logs, and navigation tools off a small table to clear a space. He gestured brusquely to the only two chairs as Lucilla and Cynwrig entered.

"So what brings the Empress herself all the way down to visit my humble ship?" Yrsa asked, dropping into the remaining chair.

Lucilla met his gaze directly. "The Empire has need of your services once again, Captain."

Yrsa grunted, bushy red eyebrows drawing together. "The Empire's been making that claim more and more these days. Customs fees are higher every time I make port, patrol ships stopping me to search for Carthaginian stowaways. That's on top of you taking my best crew for your navy last season."

"I'm certain those men saw a benefit in fighting for the Empire, and, as I'm sure has been pointed out to you, fees are only charged on the sale of specialty goods to non-Britannian captains. If you were to join the Empire, swear the oath of fealty, I'm certain ..."

"No, thank you. I took the deal to work for you lot to get my hands on this ship, and I've seen how often you 'require' things of your subjects. I've made peace with my deal, but I don't think I'll be signing any more."

"I don't fault you for your choice and won't try to argue you out of it. I'll only say I can't apologize for doing what's necessary to ensure the Empire survives this war, other than promising the harsher costs will come down when the war is over and the need drops. On that, you have my word."

He grunted and said, "So what is it you need old Yrsa for this time?"

"I need warriors, Captain. Men who can help secure our supply lines and garrison-occupied territories as our legions march on Carthage itself. I'm not asking them to join the legions or fight on the front lines. The lands of Italia have been in Carthaginian hands for a long time, and they've profited well from the conquering of others. They are not finding it easy to lose their connection to that power and have been fighting our legions as invaders instead of liberators. Right now, the legions are spread across the peninsula, trying to keep the peace while still pressing forward, trying to take the region as a prelude to attacking Africa itself. To do that, we need to consolidate our forces, and leave the pacification of Italia to someone else, which is where your people come in."

Yrsa grunted, bushy red eyebrows drawing together. "My people are traders and sailors, Your Majesty, not mercenaries."

Lucilla nodded. "That hasn't always been true, Captain. In hard times, your people have sold their sword arms to others for coin or plunder. Or turned to piracy."

"True, when times were lean and bellies empty. When we had no other choice. But this isn't one of those times." He gestured around at the well-appointed cabin.

"Isn't it?" Lucilla arched an eyebrow. "The only reason these aren't hard times is because of your people's connection to the Empire. When Carthage controlled Britannia and the Continent, sealing off trade, those were very hard times indeed."

"Can't argue with you there. Still, it's hard to convince men of that when things are comfortable and their stomachs full."

"Don't I know it," Lucilla muttered. "If we fail in our campaign against Carthage, those hard times *will* be back, and worse. Carthage had already spread across Germania, and was making its way across Britannia and Ériu. How likely do you think they would have been to stop when they hit the ocean? They covet all the land they can see, and they would need new places to plunder to continue paying for the vast military needed to control the lands they've taken. In reality, any assistance you provide is as much for yourselves as it is for us."

"That may be true, but I guarantee most will have difficulty seeing it. Perhaps ... perhaps my people could be convinced, but they'd need something more than promises of safety from potential future danger."

"We would offer more than promises," Lucilla said. "For any village that sends men to serve, they will earn the right to trade for items restricted only to our allies. So far, you've been able to buy tools and arcuballistas, which I know has been profitable. But that market will likely dry up as we redirect production towards the war effort and our newer weapons become available to more people for trade. I am prepared to offer your people the chance to buy firearms and cannon for your ships. Not our most advanced models, but effective, sturdy designs nonetheless."

"Really?" he said, leaning forward, his interest obviously piqued.

His own agreement with the Empire, to work for them as needed, had netted him not only his ship but the same cannon that Valdar used on his ships and the right to buy gunpowder for those cannons. He'd seen firsthand the difference having those weapons could make, and had received a lot of interest from his countrymen on his trips back home.

"Yes, really. Any village that contributes warriors will have exclusive access to purchase muskets and select models of cannon. We will also authorize an ongoing deal for the purchase of gunpowder as well. Amounts will be limited, but we are increasing our production facilities daily, and those numbers will go up. This availability only comes with a single caveat. None of the weapons you are sold can be sold to our enemies, or allies of our enemies. Any village caught doing this will have our markets closed to them, as will any village that sells to an embargoed neighbor. On this, we will not budge. Our technological advantage is what gives us the ability to fight the Carthaginians, and we will not allow that advantage to be sold away for gold."

"A tempting offer," he said, covering his earlier surprise.

"There's more. That is for the villages that send men to help us. We will also, of course, reward those individuals who come into our service, even temporarily. Beyond every man being paid handsomely in coin, they will also be allowed to bring home the breech-loading rifles they serve with. These are a much more advanced design than even the muskets I'm offering your villages."

"Additionally, those who come to Italy themselves to support us against the Carthaginians, working alongside my praetorians, will be allowed to become citizens without the requirements other new citizens are asked to go through. I know that might not be something your people want, but some might, after seeing the

Empire and its people up close, and hearing about the benefits, so the offer stands."

Lucilla watched as Yrsa turned her proposition over in his head, weighing the potential benefits against the risks. Not to himself, of course. He'd already committed to working with Britannia to get his hands on this ship, but he still needed his people for trade and new recruits for his ship. They were already suspicious of him for selling his services, as it were, and bringing an offer like this to them would only make that suspicion grow.

"I understand your hesitation, Captain," she said. "Believe me, I understand why this is difficult, both for your people and you personally. If there were any other way, I wouldn't ask, but there isn't. Make no mistake; this war with Carthage determines the fate of all our peoples. If we fail, no one will be safe from their domination and cruelty."

Yrsa grunted, his gaze drifting out the small porthole of his cabin, lost in thought. Lucilla wanted to say more. To convince him. But she remembered her father's advice that sometimes pushing too much makes a negotiation harder, not easier. Sometimes, there are too many words, and it is better to let the other person negotiate with themselves instead. So she remained silent, giving him the space he needed to come to a decision.

After what felt like an eternity, Yrsa finally turned back to her, his eyes meeting hers.

"All right, Your Majesty," he said, his voice gruff. "I'll make the offer to my people, but I can't guarantee they'll accept it. They're traders and sailors, not soldiers. And they're fiercely independent; they won't take kindly to being told what to do, even if it's for the greater good."

Lucilla nodded, a small smile playing at the corners of her lips. "I understand, Captain. And I appreciate your willingness to even consider it. That's all I ask."

Yrsa grunted again, rising from his chair and gesturing for Lucilla and Cynwrig to follow him. They made their way back out onto the deck, the sounds of the bustling harbor washing over them. It wasn't a victory, but it was a step in the right direction.

Chapter 12

Northern Italy, Just East of the Border of Gaul

Aelius sat tall upon his horse, surveying the small village as his century approached. Scattered huts and simple stone buildings dotted the landscape, smoke rising lazily from a few chimneys, with people moving about the fields outside of town. There had been a lot of talk of these villages being empty as the main body of the legions passed through, but it seemed as if some of the people had returned, now that the armies had passed.

Considering the villagers' obvious distrust of Britannians and their willingness to abandon their villages, Aelius would have bypassed it entirely if given his druthers. Unfortunately, he wasn't given that choice. His orders were clear: stop and negotiate with any locals they encountered along the way, breaking off elements of his cohorts to keep up appearances as peacekeepers at the larger villages.

To try and lessen any fear that they might cause the locals, as soon as the scouts told him they were approaching a village, he'd come ahead with a single century. Entering the village, he could feel the eyes of the people, most of whom had disappeared as soon as his small column approached. Even with people hiding, word must have spread fast, because an older man, flanked by a large number of younger ones, waited in the center of the village as they approached.

Raising his fist, he signaled his men to halt. Good soldiers, they spread out into even lines, weapons held at the ready position, butts against the ground. This was a friendly visit, and they were trying not to be overly aggressive, but reports coming back through the telegraph, when it worked, spoke of ambushes and assaults on isolated groups of legionnaires. That's why Aelius had brought an entire century with him, instead of a single squad.

Aelius dismounted and approached the old man, removing his helmet and tucking it under his arm, the dozen or so men around him tensing as Aelius approached.

"Are you the headman of this village?" Aelius asked politely with a slight bow.

The old man drew himself up, rheumy eyes peering at Aelius from beneath bushy white eyebrows. "I am Maurus, and I speak for this village. What do you want with us, foreigner?"

The man's voice had an edge to it, and Aelius couldn't help but notice the use of "foreigner." Carthaginians had continued referring to Romans as Romans, both after they were forced off the continent and when they'd voluntarily changed their own country's name to Britannia. It was telling that someone here in Italy would hesitate to use that description and chose "foreigner" instead. As if to make it clear that, even if they came from here and still used the name from their homeland, they considered his people neither Italian nor Roman. Only foreign.

"I understand your hesitation, Maurus. We seek no quarrel here," he gestured to his century of soldiers. "We've been tasked with establishing relationships in this region, to foster goodwill and cooperation, and to help with providing security from bandits and other threats."

The headman snorted derisively at Aelius' words. "And how do you plan to do that? By telling us where we can go? What we can do?"

"No. We have no desire to control you or your people. We only want to offer our help. Is there a well here? Is there anything Britannia can do for you?"

Maurus was unmoved by the legate's words.

"The best thing you can do for us is leave," he growled, crossing his arms over his chest stubbornly. "My people don't want you here."

"I understand your feelings," Aelius said, trying to keep his face and voice neutral. "Truly, I do. But right now, we can't leave this area completely unsupervised as we push the Carthaginians further south and work towards ending this war once and for all. As soon as our war is over and the area can be left safely on its own, we plan to leave and let everyone here manage their own affairs as they see fit. Our only goal is to contain the chaos caused by removing the Carthaginians."

A shout came from the crowd behind Maurus. "We're Carthaginians too! This is our land!"

Maurus nodded, adding, "My people have been part of Carthage for generations now. We see ourselves as Carthaginians as much as anyone born in the city itself. To say you're not invaders while removing the people protecting our homes and providing us security and prosperity, shows us exactly who you are."

Aelius frowned. He hadn't expected that. In his mind, the people of Italy were still Romans at heart even after all these years under the Carthaginian yoke. The idea that some truly saw themselves as Carthaginians was troubling.

"You were not always so," he countered. "We come from the same ancestors, citizens of a proud republic before Carthage conquered these lands by force. Given the chance, would you not wish to rule yourselves again instead of bending the knee to foreign masters?"

"You are no longer from here. Your fathers' fathers were not from here. You are as foreign as anyone else."

He'd hoped to deescalate things, but the more Maurus countered him, defending the Carthaginians and calling Britannians invaders, the more it egged on the crowd, which had started to build and grow increasingly belligerent.

Cries of "Lies!" and "Invaders!" erupted from the crowd as Maurus spat at his feet.

"Leave our village and our lands, Britannian," the headman said. "Leave us in peace."

Peace was the last thing his people had in mind, however, as several stones and a large number of vegetables and other debris sailed in Aelius' direction. Aelius threw up an arm to shield his face as he backed up to his men to put some distance between the missiles and himself.

The angry shouts from the swelling crowd grew louder as more villagers poured from the buildings and fields to join the confrontation. What had started as a few dozen people was now nearly a hundred, and Aelius could see even more emerging from alleys and doorways. His men were quickly becoming outnumbered.

He held up his hands pleadingly. "Please, let's not let this come to violence! We only wish to help provide order and security until the war is over!"

But his words fell on increasingly deaf ears. The mob pressed closer, emboldened by their growing numbers. Farm implements and tools became makeshift weapons in their hands.

"Get out while you still can, invader!" Maurus yelled over the din. "You've worn out your welcome!"

A young man darted from the crowd, a woodcutting ax raised over his head as he charged straight for Aelius, giving a feral scream. Before Aelius could pull a weapon or respond, one of the men closest to him lifted his rifle with well-practiced precision and fired, knocking the boy off his feet.

For a moment, everyone froze. The villagers had probably heard of firearms by now, as word had traveled pretty far and wide, but hearing about it and seeing it in person was a very different thing.

And then the dam broke. With a collective roar, the mob surged forward, brandishing their makeshift weapons. Young men came at them wielding wood axes, scythes, and staves. Women flung stones and old men shook fists. Aelius didn't attempt to reason with them a second time, leaping onto his horse as the wave of bodies crashed toward his now outnumbered men.

"Ready arms!" he shouted as he rode his horse down the rank and out of the line of fire.

In unison, his legionnaires hefted their rifles, the years of combat and hours of drilling making the action pure muscle memory.

"By rank," he commanded, a hand going up over his head.

As the legionnaires sighted along their rifles, a few of the villagers in the lead faltered slightly, maybe guessing what was coming next from the stories they must have heard, but fury and numbers carried the rest forward.

"Fire!" he roared, chopping his hand down.

The sound of gunshots tore through the mob's war cries. Villagers in the front dropped, some wounded, some dead. But the mass of humanity behind them barely slowed, trampling the fallen as they pressed toward the thin Roman line.

"Retreat by rank. Second rank. Ready! Fire!"

Row by row, his men filtered back, as the next rank in line lifted their rifles and fired. In the standard three-rank fighting formation, this would have held for only three ranks, and then required switching to bayonet without another formation to swap positions, but the village streets were narrow, and he'd been forced to switch to a wide marching column, even after his men had fanned out.

Step by step, his men retreated while firing into the crowd, villagers falling in fives and tens. They didn't stop coming, though. They were wild with fury, throwing stones and axes as they tried to close the gap with the Britannians.

A well-thrown axe flew from the surging crowd, catching a legionnaire, who was grabbed by the retreating rank and pulled to the rear.

"At the double step," he called, as the villagers began to fade, their fury finally giving way to the growing carnage around them.

Wails and cries of dying men and widowed women were already heard above the sound of the rifles and the shouting. Aelius spotted a young man clambering onto a rooftop, arming an arcuballista, maybe one of Carthaginian creation using the Roman pattern, or maybe one sold by Britannian allies. The iron bolt streaked through the air and punched through a legionnaire's calf in a spray of blood. Before Aelius could react, two more men grabbed their comrade's arms and hauled him away from the pressing horde.

"Watch the roofs and windows!" Aelius warned.

He had to get his men out of these cramped streets. Already, a handful of villagers had attempted to come in behind them. Not enough to overcome his rear guard, but a problematic development. If he didn't get his men out of this village soon, they were going to be overrun.

"Skirmish retreat by line," he commanded. "Fifty paces to the rear and prepare to receive. Double time."

The Consul had ordered the men trained on all manners of maneuvers, some of which, it had seemed, were unlikely ever to be used. Aelius was a believer in rigorous training, as any legate was, knowing the necessity of coordination when fighting in the legions, but even he had found some of the repetition almost unnecessary. Now he was glad of it. The men had done this maneuver, and others with slight variations, hundreds of times, and knew their jobs.

The rear ranks turned and ran, still holding their line, stopping after fifty paces, where they reloaded, while the front rank released another volley. As soon as their weapons were clear, those men turned and ran past the rank that had set up fifty paces behind and continued, passing ranks of men set out at fifty-pace intervals, until they became the last line, where they themselves halted and began reloading.

Like a wave retreating from the shore, his units fell back in what the Consul had called a 'leapfrog' maneuver. It allowed them to retreat quickly, while still presenting a lethal front to the oncoming enemy.

A few more attempts were made to attack his men from the rear and rooftops, but aware of the threats, his men cut those villagers down before any more of his people could be injured. In a few minutes, they had fought their way out of the town and were back amongst the fields, now devoid of the farmers who'd toiled in them when Aelius and his legionnaires had arrived.

"Marching column at the quick pace," he commanded, his leapfrogging units coalescing and putting their arms back to port, over their shoulders.

The villagers did not follow them beyond the edge of their homes, but Aelius didn't trust that they were safe yet. It seemed safe enough to let his men stop sprinting away, but he wanted a quick march for a mille passus or so before he returned them to a normal march back to his cohorts.

"Runner," he called out, bringing one of the unarmored men from the rear, or what was now the front of the column, to him. "Return to the main body and call up an ambulance wagon for the wounded."

The man nodded and dashed off at a sprint. As he watched the man go, Aelius frowned. Now all he had to do was get to the Consul and explain his abject failure.

Devnum

Lucilla strolled through the palace gardens, the sweet floral scents and vibrant colors a welcome break from being inside the stuffy confines of the palace. Rounding a corner, she smiled as she spotted her spymaster waiting beneath a flowering trellis, hands clasped behind his back. His expression was stoic as always, though she detected a hint of a smile in return.

They both knew her office was as private, if not more so, than conversations in the gardens, and that what they needed to discuss wasn't so secret that they really needed to go sneaking off to meet in a secluded location like a couple of cutpurses. They both knew the real reason she liked having their 'meetings' in the gardens was because it gave her a break from stone walls and marble floors.

She was just happy he was so good about humoring her.

"Thank you for coming, Ramirus," Lucilla said.

He inclined his head. "Of course, Your Majesty. How may I be of service?"

Lucilla gestured to a stone bench nestled amidst lush shrubbery.

"I wanted to check up on how Medb is faring with her new responsibilities," she said as she sat down.

"Surprisingly well, Your Majesty. I know you gave her the position to keep her busy and under watch, but it seems she has a real talent for administration, beneath all of the scheming."

"Truly? I expected her to chafe and make things more difficult. She certainly was vocal when I dared to suggest she put her 'immense abilities' to something so mundane."

"I thought the same when you told me about it, but the opposite has proven to be true. More surprisingly, at least to me, is that there have been a few opportunities for graft, admittedly some I placed in front of her on purpose, to see what she would do. Suppliers offering kickbacks for preference, merchants offering to line her pocket to give them gossip or access. The lesser ones, with people she might have to continue dealing with, the suppliers for example, she rebuffed tactfully, making it clear she would not take the bribe, but without casting judgment or engendering hard feelings. Considering how I saw her act in the council meetings, she did it with a level of subtlety that I honestly didn't expect her to possess. The ones that, potentially, had the greater long-term benefit to her, but weren't needed to continue efficient operations of the palace, she actually reported. Like I said, surprising."

"Well, now. That is promising," Lucilla mused.

"Beyond the tests I have thrown at her, she's done amazingly well with her actual tasks. Kitchen costs are down twelve percent, thanks to her scrutinizing waste, and several inefficiencies in the scullery operations were corrected when she took over. The palatinus has received numerous compliments from staff over the way things are being handled. From what the people I placed in the palace tell me, the staff finds her uncompromising and a harsh taskmistress, but also uncompromisingly fair. She doesn't speak down to them, treats each member of the staff as if they're important, and publicly praises good work. Seeing her activity over the last year, I'd questioned how she'd managed to amass such a loyal populace in her former kingdom, but now it seems much more understandable. She is an exceptional leader, in her own blunt way."

"That you should have been less surprised about. She didn't earn her kingdom through inheritance, she won it. We saw firsthand proof of how vehemently her people defended her. It's difficult to get that kind of support when you have an inherited claim to a throne, let alone one taken through force. We knew she was capable. It's why we wanted to take her not only out of her homeland but off the island itself."

"This is true, but most of the people she is overseeing are Roman and Caledonian. They are predisposed to the opposite inclination.

It goes beyond that, however. Beyond just doing good work in the job itself and turning down opportunities for graft, she actually uncovered some already in place. Graft that I, admittedly, had missed. There was a girl serving as a cubicularia. She is the daughter of a well-placed merchant here in the city. That, unto itself, was not a problem, but she discovered that the girl taking things, not valuables, but information. She would steal documents, linger near places she shouldn't to overhear conversations, apparently passing information back to her father, which he could use when conducting business with the Empire. Within two days of starting her duties, Medb identified her and removed her from the staff."

"And her father?" Lucilla asked.

"I'm dealing with him. Rest assured; he will find it difficult to do business with the Empire going forward."

"Good. I'm pleased to hear Medb is performing her duties so capably. Still, a woman of Medb's ambition, I have concerns that she will chafe at her new position, no matter her talent for it. I cannot imagine she is content simply ordering servants about and scrutinizing ledgers."

"It seems unlikely," Ramirus agreed.

"How likely, do you think, that this is all a ruse?" Lucilla asked. "That she's just biding her time, waiting until something worth taking a risk on comes her way?"

"It's impossible to say. From all appearances, she seems to be legitimate, and I've been watching her closely, but it's impossible to see into her mind."

"Actually, I might have a thought," Ramirus said, pausing and looking off, thinking. Lucilla, familiar with his methods, waited while he worked the thought through. "I do have some potential work that I think would suit her well and give her the challenge she wants."

"Do I want to know specifics?" Lucilla asked.

"It's probably better if you don't. At least, not yet. Sometimes these things are easier to deal with without official attention. It would mean giving the palatinus some of his duties back."

"That's fine. This was never intended to be a permanent assignment for her. Although, if you are giving him his full duties back, I believe it might be helpful to put some additional pressure on him.

It seems Medb has identified several spots where his performance could use improvement."

"I was thinking the same thing, Your Majesty."

Chapter 13

Northern Italy

Ky broke off mid-sentence as the flap to his command tent was pushed aside, revealing a dust-covered Aelius, looking weary from the road. Both he and Marcus, whom Ky had been speaking with, turned to the ninth legion legate as the man entered.

"Aelius, welcome to Italia," Ky said, stepping forward to grasp the new arrival's arm. "I hope the journey wasn't too arduous."

"The roads are clear at least, Consul," Aelius replied, grasping Ky's forearm in the Roman version of a handshake. "But the people ... that's another matter."

"I received your messengers, but I'd like to hear it from you first-hand," Ky said. "Do you need refreshments or anything before you start? I know the road has already turned hot."

"No, Consul, thank you," Aelius said. "As instructed, we stopped at the first major village in Italia, the one you reported as empty when the main force came through a month ago. It was reoccupied, and I brought forward only one century of men, in hopes that I would not create an incident. Clearly, my hope was wrong, for which I apologize. The leaders of the village were instantly hostile as soon as we arrived. We reiterated our goal of only assisting them, and not occupying their village as invaders, but they would have none of it. Before our conversation concluded, they attacked us without warning or provocation. It was madness. My men were armed and armored, and they came at us with farming implements, knives, and even stones. There were too many of them to attempt to de-escalate the situation. I'm sorry to report that I was forced to use more lethal measures as I fought my way out of town. Even with that, and the casualties that resulted, they continued to attack, like wild animals. A few of my men were injured before we were able to retreat from the village."

Aelius paused. Ky could see the scene playing out in the legate's head, and his regret at having lost control of the situation. Aelius was a good man, and Ky knew he took failure personally.

"I brought up the rest of the cohort and returned to the village, imposing martial law, and treating the injured and dying as best I could, while rounding up the instigators, but the damage was done. It is unlikely we will ever find a friend in that village in our lifetime. I apologize, Consul. I failed you."

"Don't beat yourself up too badly, Aelius. We have had numerous similar failures of our own, which is why you were sent for in the first place. Marcus and I were, in fact, just discussing this very problem when you arrived," Ky said, before turning to Marcus, "Would you mind sharing what you were telling me with Aelius?"

"Certainly," the legate said. "As the Consul said, what you encountered is what we have been struggling with across Italia. The people see us as invaders, not liberators, and have been resisting us as such. It seems they view the Carthaginians as the 'true' rulers of Italia. The war our ancestors fought and Roman rule of this area was a long time ago, well outside of any living memory, and they don't see us as Romans, or even a Roman legacy. While this was true in other areas, such as Hispania, which continued to resist Carthaginian rule in spite of that, here, it seems they've come to embrace that rule. We thought offers of assistance might show them we were different, but clearly, that hasn't worked either."

"Clearly not," Aelius said. "You had another thought, I take it?"

"I do. I think the Consul was on the right track but didn't go far enough. At least, not far enough to convince them we were serious about our intent. Instead of simply offering help and then leaving again, we should establish a permanent presence in the major villages. For now, it would have to be a large force, meaning a century at a time, to keep the villagers from acting impulsively and attacking us, but make ourselves permanent, or at least semi-permanent. At first, we will probably have to set up secure camps outside the villages, again for safety, but ultimately, the goal would be to rent or build a large enough structure in town that we can operate as part of their community, not as outsiders. And we don't just offer to fix things, since we've had any offers turned down before, but start fixing things that need doing on our own. We have to make sure we are seen as there to assist, and not act as guards watching over a prison. We can patrol and assist the village with security as they request it, but otherwise, we leave that to the villagers. Instead, we focus on tangible and visible things we can build and repair, making it known again and again that we are there only to help. Start actually being beneficial to the community."

"That's easier said than done," Aelius replied, looking skeptical. "We'll get hate at first."

"Of course we will," Marcus agreed. "But if we start solving problems and making these people's lives easier, it will start to change their minds."

"The phrase I believe you're looking for is that we will begin a campaign of 'hearts and minds,'" Ky offered, repeating the words Sophus fed to him, although lacking the history behind the phrase the AI included. "It's been attempted before, with mixed results. A lot depends on how many insurgents remain in the surrounding hills, and what actions they take. We will still have to patrol the surrounding areas, removing as many remaining Carthaginian elements as possible to keep them from poisoning the well, as it were."

"Exactly so, and our assistance will need to be more than just small things. The projects will have to be large enough that they can't be ignored or taken down easily by the disaffected, but important enough that they can't be seen as just monument building by conquerors," Marcus continued. "We'll also need to put in requisitions for larger amounts of supplies, and soon, since the levels we'll need are greater than what we have on hand. In time, I imagine we can buy much of what we'll need locally, further helping our credibility by putting gold into their hands outside of charity, but I wouldn't want to rely on that right away. I imagine much we attempt to buy now will be either unavailable or otherwise tainted or damaged to ensure failure on our part."

"It might work," Aelius conceded, "but, based on what I encountered, even with enough men positioned at each major village, we're going to have run-ins, probably violent ones, before we start convincing anyone to accept our help, or even believe we mean what we're offering."

"That's true," Ky admitted, "but we're having run-ins now. Violent ones. This is the best plan I've heard so far. Changing minds is rarely easy, but it's the only way we're going to secure our rear from constant insurrection. I'm pulling Auspex's legion back to assist you, which will give you two and a half legions to spread through the villages stretching back to Gaul. I will stay here with you a little while longer and leave the push south to Bomilcar and the seventh legion, although when they reach Rome, I'm going to have to shift my flag south."

Ky stopped and considered, working through the disposition of men and forces, Sophus overlaying maps and positioning across Ky's vision as he worked out specifics. He saw the look that passed between the legates as he fell silent, staring off into seemingly nothing, but they'd seen him do this before. For now, they still considered it just one of his foibles as a commander, which he was willing to accept.

"I know you're senior, Aelius, but I would like to put Marcus in overall command of coordinating your various efforts and making sure that all of the units we scatter about have enough supplies to get the job done," Ky finally said. "Hopefully, this will secure enough of our rear that we can start moving south again and catch up to our original timetable. If you do see success and we're able to reduce our forces, I plan on pulling both you and Auspex out, bringing your men to Africa, and leaving Marcus behind, if he's still needed. Hopefully, by that point, Cormac will have had success in Hispania and you will have your remaining cohorts freed up and sent to join you."

"If we don't, that will leave you with one legion for pushing out the last of the Carthaginians," Marcus said, his voice betraying a hint of concern.

"I know," Ky replied, his tone grim. "But one legion and a secure rear is better than three legions with absolute chaos and no reasonable supply lines beyond what we can ship, which is still too limited for large-scale operations at this distance. We'll have to make it work."

"Understood, Consul. We will make this work," Aelius said.

"I know you will," Ky replied. "Now, go get some rest. You've been on the road all day, and your men are probably worn out. Marcus will begin drawing up plans and we can discuss the details tomorrow."

Devnum

The knock at the door made Lucilla jump.

She had been sitting, not in the dark, but at least alone, thinking for almost an hour. Since her conversation with Ky, she had stepped up her efforts to find men to help with the defense in Italia, and she had hit a brick wall every time. She still had feelers out, but none felt promising. She had been going through lists of more and more untenable plans, not committing them to paper or even saying them out loud to Sophus because of how bad the ideas had been. But she was desperate for a way to help Ky, to protect him, and her brain wouldn't let go of the problem.

"Enter," she commanded, sitting up in her chair.

The heavy oak door swung open, and Lucilla was surprised to see Fiacha, the senior Ulaid senator, and Rotri, the senior Caledonian senator, coming through her door together.

While there wasn't animosity between their two peoples, which were in truth more alike than they were like her own people, these two men, in particular, had never gotten along. Something about their personalities didn't mix, and she'd watched several times as they'd sent proxies to negotiate for them rather than speaking to each other one-on-one.

To see them together was ... concerning.

"Please, sit," she said, gesturing to the chairs across from her desk. "To what do I owe the honor of this visit from both of you together?"

The men exchanged a brief, uneasy glance before Rotri cleared his throat. "We come bearing the responses from our respective leaders to your recent requests for additional manpower."

"I see. And what was their response?" Lucilla asked, preparing herself for disappointment.

"I am afraid both have declined to provide more direct aid at this time," Rotri said.

"Both of our peoples have been devastated by the fight against the Carthaginians already, to a lesser or greater degree," Fiacha said, eliciting a frown and a side-eyed glance from Rotri, who recognized the last sentence for the cheap shot it was. "We've also both given up large amounts of manpower already, limiting our ability to recover from those deprivations, not to mention needing to do the work necessary to simply maintain our populaces. We did so under promises of technological marvels that would help our people become more efficient, which would require less manpower than ever before."

"I believe we have delivered on our promise in many ways," Lucilla pointed out.

This was not a new argument, and all three knew the steps to this dance already.

"In some small ways, perhaps," Rotri said. "But for every small advancement we've been given, more men have been taken. Just as you have proposed this time. Which means instead of improving our conditions, we remain in the same place, while Rome experiences a renewal."

He waved his arms around, as if to illustrate his point. She knew he meant Devnum specifically, which was undergoing near-constant expansion at the moment. Ramirus had men in both of their capitals who reported regularly on their state, all of which indicated a very different state of affairs than what Rotri suggested. Neither's homelands were stagnant. Both were experiencing large-scale growth, just as Devnum was.

But that wasn't as defensible of a position. What mattered was that Talogren and Conchobar had said no. She could have prob-

152

ably traveled to them and strong-armed them out of more men, both being less willing to say no to her in person, which is why they'd sent word through proxies. Talogren, at the very least, could have sent a message directly to her on the telegraph line that was extended north to the Caledonian capital over the winter.

He just chose not to.

She didn't blame either leader for their power play. Getting the best possible deal for their people is what a leader was supposed to do, and it was probably what she would have done in their place. She had just hoped to avoid it until after they'd secured their victory against Carthage.

"While I understand the burden placed on your populations, this war impacts us all," she began delicately. "If Carthage defeats Rome, they will surely turn their eye northward. No land will be safe."

Rotri and Fiacha made nearly identical expressions.

"I know, I know," she said, holding up a placating hand. "I won't lecture you on that again, no matter how true it is. Let me ask you, how likely would they be to offer assistance if we found other ways to solve the issue of manpower at home? While we have given you every technological advantage we have achieved, if you were, for instance, to give us a list of the specific areas where you have the greatest manpower shortages, perhaps we could focus our efforts more in that direction. Channel advancements for your people specifically. I know it can seem that, right now, most advancements have been made with Rome in mind first, and your people second, and I can admit that would be a fair argument. But I think it might be because we are focusing on what we see. If the lines of communication were better, and we had a clear idea of what both your peoples need, we could target advancements more specifically to address your challenges. If we did this, and showed an impact, how likely do you think that would change their minds?"

Lucilla knew it was a straw man argument. She'd introduced an issue neither had raised so she could shoot that issue down, as a form of compromise, but she'd heard enough rumblings to know that it was something they'd complained about to others. She hoped that would give it some weight of validity.

153

Rotri hesitated, his lips compressing into a tight line. "With respect, Your Majesty, the problem lies with more than a mere lack of communication. While I know Talogren has made similar deals with you in the past, this time, I think it's unlikely."

She gave a small nod and looked to Fiacha, who shook his head vigorously.

"No. I'm sorry, no. No manner of promises or even some small token will change my king's mind. Short of a world-changing piece of advancement, I can't imagine anything you could offer that would. And even then, I would bet against your chances."

"In this, we're in agreement," Rotri said. "The cost of this war has been borne by too many of our people, and we can bear no more. I'm sorry, but if you need more men, you're going to have to find them somewhere else."

Lucilla offered a tight-lipped smile and said, "I understand your concerns and the messages you convey from your respective leaders. Thank you both for your time and effort in considering my request."

Fiacha and Rotri stood, nodding in unison before turning to leave. As the heavy oak door closed behind them, Lucilla let out a sigh and flopped back in her chair. She rubbed her temples, attempting to alleviate the tension building in her forehead. Now she was just left with Yrsa and the Scandi. In spite of his protestations, she had great faith in the overly large captain's ability to convince his countrymen. What seemed unlikely, though, was that even a willing Scandi people could produce enough manpower to make up the difference Ky needed.

She required yet another option, and she was quickly running out of ideas.

Northern Italy

Sextus wiped the sweat from his brow as he worked alongside his men, replacing the worn thatching on the roof of the small house. They had been at it for hours, and the midday sun beat down on them relentlessly.

"This isn't necessary. I told you we are fine," the villager, who Sextus learned was named Sicanius, called up to him.

The man had said the same thing every ten minutes since Sextus and his men had started working, and the decanus gave the villager the same reply he'd given every time.

"It's no trouble, really. Like I told you, we're here to help," he said, gesturing to the group of legionaries working alongside him. "Besides, it gives us a break from drills and marching."

Sicanius grumbled something under his breath, and Sextus went back to ignoring him. He knew the people here could be hostile. He'd been involved in several skirmishes already with malcontents set on driving the Britannians out with pitchforks and shovels, but he'd hoped this posting would be different.

Instead of marching in and setting up operations, the centurion had them set up a small, fortified encampment outside of town. Every day he marched the century into the village and offered the villagers help. When they'd refused, the centurion had simply told them he would be in the area, patrolling and keeping the roads safe, and helping where they saw the opportunity. He'd then ordered his men to find any places where they could help, and to pitch in.

At first, everyone had been openly hostile. While they were still fairly hostile, things had calmed down over the last week. Sextus didn't know if it was just a growing familiarity with the Britannians, seeing not just soldiers, but the same faces, day after day, or an actual realization that they weren't here to hurt them, and had made things a little better.

Of course, he wouldn't know that from how negative Sicanius had been when he'd come to offer help repairing the man's roof. Every day for the last week, he'd looked at the roof slowly collapsing, and had finally gotten permission to take the rest of his contubernium to repair it.

The work itself wasn't all that grueling, and no worse than some of the things he'd had to do as a servant on the latifundium, working to maintain that large estate. Here, at least his work helped an average person, instead of the wealthy estate owner Sextus had never even met.

Within the next hour, the house started to take shape. The once-tattered roof was now covered in fresh, tightly packed thatch, the golden hue of the new material a stark contrast to the faded brown of the old. Sextus felt pride in a job well done, slapping one of his men on the back as the group looked up at their finished work.

"Good job. Very well done," he told them.

Behind him, Sicanius threw his hands up in exasperation. "I told you, we don't need any help! My roof was fine."

"With respect, your roof was in poor shape. The thatch was worn and the supports were cracked in places. I really was only concerned about your safety. I've marched by here almost every day for the last week, and I couldn't help but notice that the roof was in such bad shape. I was afraid it would collapse on you and your family. I apologize for taking so long to come and fix it, but we had to requisition supplies, and it took some time for them to arrive."

"I don't want your charity," Sicanius protested.

"That's why it's help, not charity. You didn't have to ask for it. We were told to help out this village and others in the area in any way we can, and so that's what we're doing."

"Are you sure there's no price to be paid?" Sicanius asked, his eyes narrowing, his face sinking into a worried expression. "My children … my wife … will they be taken?"

A sudden realization hit Sextus, filling the decanus with revulsion and disgust. This was the kind of 'help' the Carthaginians must have offered, with strings attached that bound the villagers in servitude and fear.

Sextus recoiled. "Gods, no! I want you to understand, Sicanius, we're truly here to help. We're not looking to take anything from you or the other villagers. Our goal is to make your lives easier and safer, not to burden you with more hardship."

"If you're sure," Sicanius said, looking up at his new roof almost hopefully.

"I am. Enjoy your new roof. I should warn you that my men and I aren't skilled tradesmen, and other than Darius there, none of us has ever rethatched a roof. If you have any problems with it, please come find me or any of my men and we will do our best to correct them."

"I ... will," Sicanius said, almost hesitantly.

"Good. And if you or any of your neighbors need anything else, please do ask us. I promise, we are not here to make your lives worse! If we can, we really do want to make it better."

He clasped Sicanius's arm in farewell, then turned to gather his men, who had already collected their equipment, one of them handing over his armor and rifle. They left the villager standing there, staring at his house in almost slack-jawed amazement.

Sextus spent the walk back to the fortified encampment thinking about what the man had said. About what he'd feared, now even more bewildered by the locals' near pathological support of the Carthaginians. How anyone could support rulers that displayed the level of cruelty the Carthaginians obviously had, based on what Sicanius had obviously feared, Sextus would never know.

Hopefully, Sicanius would eventually accept that they really were there just to help, and even tell others about it. Maybe then they'd stop trying to ambush the Britannians and finally start to work with them.

Chapter 14

Central Britannia

Hortensius stepped off the supply train, appreciating for a moment the benefit of being able to travel this far to meet with the disaffected villages and still be able to be back in Factorium to review that day's production numbers. They were living in the future, and it amazed him that anyone would be against technology like this.

The smell of burned coal and oil filled the air. It was the smell of progress, and one he was getting to know more and more, although he wondered about the quality of the air around Factorium.

He made his way from the train, which had already started to build up steam as it began moving forward toward the end of the track, where it would deliver supplies to the men extending it ever forward to Londinium. He'd never been to this village, but his managers had told him where the meeting had been set up, and in person, it wasn't hard for him to pick out the larger central house, built in the Roman style, surrounded by smaller, Carthaginian-style dwellings. This was one of those villages that had lived for a long time on the border of the Roman and Carthaginian lines, before the Carthaginians were removed, and it still maintained the style reflecting that heritage.

Several old men and men dressed in the current, more modern style quickly taking shape in Devnum, were gathered around a long table, sitting in chairs with sturdy backs. Hortensius silently shook his head as he saw them. For as much as these people were fighting progress, they certainly had adopted a lot of the new ideas the Consul had introduced.

"Good day, gentlemen," Hortensius greeted them cheerfully, setting his drawings down and unrolling them on the table. "I appreciate you all taking time to talk with me today. I'm certain we can work out solutions to your issues around the railway going in through your lands."

He'd been prepared to receive some pushback as he argued for the usefulness of the train, but he hadn't expected it to be so vocal and immediate. Nearly as soon as he'd given greetings and started in on the explanation he'd come to give, his voice was drowned out by a chorus of objections.

"We're losing too much acreage!" bellowed a burly livestock owner, his face reddening with indignation. "How can we feed our animals and families with less land?"

"And what about my crops? That dark smoke from your trains might ruin them! I can't afford to take that risk," another man said.

"The one-time payment for the land your tracks are going through doesn't make up for the loss of valuable planting space!"

Hortensius held up his hands, signaling for quiet. "I understand your concerns, gentlemen. I truly do. Because this is all new, it can be difficult to see the benefits to come in the future, and only see what you are losing in exchange. That's perfectly reasonable. Please allow me to address your concerns and explain how what you are getting is much greater than what you are losing in return."

The men fell mostly silent, although the expression each man gave him made it clear they had little confidence that he would be able to convince them of anything.

"I know it's hard to tell now, but there are some very large, long-term benefits to be gained from the railway, and not just for the Empire. I specifically mean long-term benefits for villagers such as yourselves," Hortensius said. "The single largest advantage to you is the ability to bring your cattle and crops to markets in major cities that are currently unreachable to you. You'll have access to a larger customer base and won't be limited to local trade. And that works both ways. Instead of waiting for some of the marvels being produced further north to filter their way down here through traders, your local markets will have more direct access to the factories directly, allowing them to bring those supplies here faster and at a much lower cost."

Hortensius had one of his more artistically inclined employees draw up a bustling market scene showing a village much like this one, its market stalls full of both goods and customers. As he finished describing the increased trade to their village, he unrolled the image. It was pure pageantry, since there was no real way to know which markets along the train route would become hubs and which would remain sleepy backwaters, but it was a reasonable inference to make, since all would see some kind of increased traffic.

The farmers exchanged glances, and he could see that the argument was already working to win over some of the men, who were even now starting to count the money it might generate.

Hortensius pressed on. "I know it's difficult to see past the immediate loss of land, but I assure you, the advantages will far outweigh the inconvenience."

A young man with a defiant glare spoke up, "And what if I don't want your railway cutting through my fields? I won't let you build on my land, no matter what you offer."

Hortensius met his gaze evenly, "I understand your feelings, but I must remind you that this project is for the greater good of our people. However, I'm willing to work with you to minimize the impact on your land and ensure fair compensation. If enough of your neighbors feel the same, then we'll be given no choice but to acquiesce to your demands, and move the railway, and the hub of commerce that would come with it, through another village. The Empress has been very clear that Britannia is not to become another Carthage. We will not force the Empire's might down on you if the majority of you are against it."

That was a bluff, of course. They had gone over the topography and the most direct route through the region, and this was by far the best site for this section of the track. If it came down to it, he might have to go to the Empress to force the issue. If he thought this might actually be harming them, he might not, since he really did want to make Britannia a better place than it had been under the threat of Carthage, but this seemed a clear case of people stuck in the past, needing someone to drag them, kicking and screaming, into the future.

"No matter the deals we work out with the landowners," one of the old men at the table said, "we can't control people who take materials left out by the Empire. It's becoming a real problem."

"While we have talked to the praetorians about increasing patrols in the area, I think part of the reason your people are finding it so easy to steal from the Empire is that it's generally accepted by the rest of the populace," he said, and then held up a hand as several people began arguing, protesting their innocence. "I'm not saying any of you want to defy or clash with the Empire. I'm just stating a simple fact that when the majority of a people are against something, there tends to be a general sense of acceptance against anything that might counter that thing. I feel that once I convince all of you of the value of the railway to your village, and your people accept that, the incidents of vandalism to the railway will decrease."

"And how are you going to do that?" another man asked. "How will we know our village will be one that sees these benefits you're talking about?"

Hortensius unrolled another drawing, this one showing a loading facility near a local station. "In exchange for your help, we will establish loading facilities at your local station, at the Empire's expense. These facilities would be available for the local populace to use at a low cost, making it easier for you to transport your goods to market. At first, that would be to Devnum and then points further north into Caledonia, or Londinium and shipment off to the continent, but as the rail lines expand, you will find even more markets open to you."

Hortensius could see he was making progress with some of the men, and for a moment hoped they'd turned the corner that they would eventually have to turn. At least, until one older man with a worn face and calloused hands scoffed loudly.

"We've survived just fine for centuries without this nonsense!" he declared. "It's nothing but a waste of time and money if you ask me. We don't need it!"

Some of the men who, moments before, had started to look convinced now wavered again, nodding along with the grizzled villager. Hortensius frowned. This was why he preferred his factories over dealing with people. People followed no logic, just making mercurial decisions without rhyme or reason.

As the noise level rose, Hortensius pulled up one of the chairs and stood on it, trying to get their attention as those in the crowd egged each other on, becoming increasingly hostile.

"Please, my friends, I understand your hesitation, but I urge you to consider the future!" he implored passionately. "The world is changing rapidly. More and more people means more trade, more goods moving back and forth. I know your families have lived and farmed these lands for generations without these innovations. But if you do not adapt, you will be left behind while other villages embrace progress and reap the benefits."

The old man didn't say anything but folded his arms, unconvinced. Others began to swing back, however.

"Having the railway so close to your homes makes your village invaluable as a hub of commerce for the surrounding areas," Hortensius continued earnestly. "Your markets will swell with goods from afar, and your own products will find new customers. It will be like having a major crossroads or a port, right on your doorstep. A vital lifeline tying you into the growing trade networks crisscrossing Britannia. I promise you, the railway will enrich your people beyond your imaginations ... if you give it a chance."

Hortensius smiled as he saw the men begin to talk amongst themselves. As always, money trumped tradition. Some still grumbled about the inconvenience or personal loss, but Hortensius could see more considering the possibilities he had painted. Even better, several of their neighbors began arguing Hortensius's point for him, which is what Hortensius really wanted. They might not listen to him, but they'd listen to the people they'd known their whole lives.

"You say our village could prosper from the railway, but how do we know it will be chosen as a station hub over other villages in the region?"

Several of the other elders voiced their agreement.

"Yeah, tell us how these station hubs will be selected!" one demanded.

"Valid concerns," Hortensius said. "Let me explain the criteria we are using to determine station locations."

He unrolled another sketch, this one a regional map marked with potential sites.

"The primary factors are distance between hubs to maximize coverage, size of local population to support commerce, and access to roads and rivers to facilitate transport of goods," Hortensius said, gesturing at several of the marked locations. "As you can see, based on those criteria, your village is in an optimal location to be selected as a hub, being equidistant from other large villages in the area, at the convergence of several roads, and with your markets and farms able to provide goods for trade. That being said, if a majority of you really do not want this line going in near your village, we will, of course, listen to your complaints."

The village elders began looking to each other, as did some of the ranchers, who had a fair number of costs involved with getting their animals to the larger markets of Devnum and Factorium, both of which had a large appetite for both meat and animal byproducts. The fear of their competitors getting something they would otherwise receive outweighed their fear of what they might lose to the rail lines.

"Thank you for your time, Hortensius," one of the men said as several of the louder dissenters were swarmed by their fellows, each pressing them to be silent on the point. "We still have much to discuss, but if you stay true to your word, I don't think you'll be having more problems from us."

Hortensius could just imagine what those discussions might be. What mattered, though, was that the people with the most money in this region and those with the most political clout were both coming to his side. Which meant any of the other dissenters were going to find the ground underneath them getting very soft indeed.

He might have to come back here again, but it seemed a good bet that the issue, with this village at least, was solved.

Devnum

Medb stood outside the palace, partially in the shadow cast by the late afternoon sun against the large granite and marble pillars that made up the front of the impressive complex. She wasn't skulking in the shadows intentionally, though. That was just a happy circumstance. She'd positioned herself out here more than an hour before, waiting for the man she needed to emerge from the palace and into the open, where the world had fewer ears.

Senator Fiacha had finally arrived almost ten minutes ago, but he wasn't alone, which meant Medb had to wait even longer. So she continued to lean against the pillars as the shadows crept across her as he argued and bickered with some of the other Imperial Senators over whatever those men found important to bicker about.

It took almost thirty minutes for the long-winded men to finally finish up their discussion and break apart. She waited until the last senator got far enough away to not become involved in their conversation and for Fiacha to move a little ways from the palace, before she pushed herself off the pillar and hurried after him.

"Senator Fiacha," she called as she caught up to him. As he spun around, eyebrows going up in surprise as he recognized her, she asked, "May I have a word?"

"What do you want?" he asked, his mouth drawn in a tight line.

Medb was not surprised by the cool reception. Among the Ulaid, she was 'persona non grata,' as the Romans would say. Between her openly leading her kingdom against the Ulaid and then the Britannians, and news of her conflict with the Empress last year had not remained a secret, earning her a general sense of distrust. While it made doing anything inconvenient, she had to admit, if only to herself, it was a reputation well earned. This time, at least, that reputation would work in her favor, which is probably why Ramirus requested her for this in the first place.

"I know you have been in discussions with the Empress about sending more men to fight on the continent," Medb began, her tone conversational. "And that you've informed her that Conchobar is unwilling to grant her request."

"That's right," he said, his brow creasing slightly. "We've given enough to this war already, in both blood and resources. To give more would be to deprive my people of enough to sustain themselves. That is the will of the Ulaid people, something you would know little about."

"Perhaps not," Medb replied, ignoring the dig. "But what I do know is that you have not actually contacted home about the Empress's offer, in spite of what you told her."

"I don't know what you're talking about."

The lie was smooth; she had to hand it to him. He didn't flinch or react to the accusation. His only real mistake was his being almost too passive. If it had been her, she would have thrown in a bit of confusion or concern to sell the lie. Not that it mattered this time. She knew what his lie was going to be before he even uttered it.

"Interesting," she said, letting a small smile play at the corners of her mouth. Not too much, just a hint of victory. "They tell me your man Cairell has been intercepting the messages you sent home directly off the messenger boat, and is then sending that same message back, so you have an effective paper trail while still letting you determine what 'Conchobar's answer' will be."

Medb, in fact, did not know any of that herself, but somehow Ramirus did. He didn't reveal how he came upon this information, but Medb had been duly impressed by the volume and the specifics of what he did know. It also explained why she'd been caught so easily before, even as she used cutouts to protect her identity. It was a good lesson, and one she intended to take to heart.

"How dare you!" he spat, his expression changing from anger to shock, and then quickly back to anger. "You have no proof of this!"

There it was, she thought, forcing back a real smile that threatened to escape. When calm and collected didn't work, they always went with indignant rage. He sold it well, but it was too predictable. If he ever wanted to make it past his station, he really had to become a better liar.

Medb let her small smile widen, taking a step closer to the senator.

"Proof? Proof like your investments in several labor-intensive industries that have been losing many of their workers to Rome and the legions?" she said, holding up her hand when he started to protest again. "I know, I know, there's nothing in your name that shows you have any investments like that. Your wife's brother, however, has quite a few, although it's not clear how he came by the large amount of coin he used to buy into those businesses. It's also interesting that they are all in several labor-intensive industries within Ulaid. The largest among them is the vast grazing lands for sheep, producing wool that you sell to the Empire."

He closed his mouth, the protest dying on his lips. She could see his brain churning, trying to come up with a lie to explain it all away. Or maybe just wondering how she could possibly know all of this.

"It's hard to keep track of all the lies, isn't it?" she whispered to him conspiratorially.

Fiacha's face paled, but he quickly regained his composure. "You're grasping at straws, Medb. So far, you've just spewed accusations, without proof of anything. Besides, your word means nothing anymore. You're a traitor, twice over. No one will believe the ravings of a desperate woman."

"Come now, Senator," she said, shifting her tone to an almost sultry purr. "Did you really think you could keep this going forever?"

Fiacha's face twisted into a scowl. "You overreach yourself, woman. I've had enough of your baseless accusations."

His finely woven léine swirled around him dramatically as he turned on his heel and stormed away. She had spooked him, which was good. He'd be jumpy now, looking to find whoever gave away his secrets. For now, she would let his own festering paranoia continue the work for her, priming him.

As she watched him disappear into the crowd, she considered her next moves. She had to be careful. She couldn't push him so hard that he retreated entirely. Ramirus might have enough to convince the Empress of Fiacha's duplicity, but Conchobar would need more, and Ramirus made it clear they needed both leaders' approval to do something about the senator.

That was a tall order, considering Fiacha's family had long-running connections with the king. Fiacha's uncle had funded Conchobar's rise to power, and the king owed the family much. It wasn't impossible, though. Now that she'd spoken to him, got a better sense of the man, the specifics of her plan began to take shape.

As she turned and re-entered the palace, a genuine smile crept across her face. This would be fun.

Chapter 15

Lucilla knelt before the altar in the small sacellum, the flickering light of the oil lamps casting dancing shadows across the mosaic floor. She bowed her head, a thin veil placed over her wavy black hair, clasping her hands together, letting the faint scent of incense wash over her.

"Great Jupiter, protector of Rome and its people, I humbly seek your guidance and strength in these troubled times," she pleaded in a soft whisper. "Your servant Ky, your sword, has brought us great victories in your name. But we hang on a precipice of losing all that your benevolence has given us. I beg you, Jupiter, to grant us aid in our time of need. Help Ky find the men necessary to finish this war, to protect our people and restore peace to our lands."

She clasped her hands tighter as she offered up every part of herself to Jupiter, in hopes that he would hear her plea for her husband and her people.

"Empress, I do not understand why you continue to engage in these rituals," came the voice of Sophus in her ear. *"You are aware that Ky was not sent by Jupiter. By all rational measures, these 'gods' do not actually exist."*

Lucilla smiled softly, keeping her head bowed.

"My family has looked to the gods for protection for generations, Sophus. And when I needed them most, they sent me Ky. Yes, I know where he truly comes from. But even you cannot say for certain how he came to be here with us. I choose to believe it was the will of the gods that pulled you both from your far future home and delivered you here, to save my people," she said, pausing and taking a deep breath of the incense. "Besides, I find peace here in these quiet moments. It is more socially acceptable for an

Empress to seclude herself in a temple than to hide away in her bedchamber."

"I find your superstitions fascinating, Lucilla. It is intriguing how humans can attribute the inexplicable to divine intervention, even when faced with rational evidence to the contrary."

"Perhaps it is because we find comfort in believing that there is something greater than ourselves, guiding us through the chaos of life. It gives us hope and strength, even when all seems lost," Lucilla said, smiling in amusement. "If my praying bothers you so, Sophus, perhaps you should help me find a solution instead."

"I did not mean to imply I was bothered, Lucilla. As I have explained, I am incapable of being upset or offended. I am merely intrigued by the human tendency towards faith and ritual. But of course, if you require my assistance, I would be more than willing to provide whatever analysis or advice I can," Sophus replied in its usual calm tone.

"I need help convincing the Ulaid and Caledonians to provide the men we need. Simply promising things I have already pledged, like new rail lines, was clearly not incentive enough during my last negotiations. I need to offer them something more tangible, something that will both improve their lives now, and free up much-needed labor, especially with the harvest season approaching. I don't blame them for their reticence. They may have the men who are not occupied now, but once harvest is upon us, they'll need all the men they can get, and Italia is so far away."

"There may be a solution, Lucilla," Sophus began, its voice steady and unwavering in her ear. *"I can propose two potential solutions that may sufficiently incentivize the Ulaid and Caledonians to provide the additional manpower you require."*

"Really?" she said, surprised.

She's mostly talked with Sophus about its opinions on Ky's situation, what he needed, and the like. She'd only asked it about options of what to do as a joke, teasing it for its continued bafflement at humanity. She usually relied on Ky to determine what and when to introduce new innovations, her involvement mostly being acting as the go-between for Hortensius and her husband. She hadn't realized until then how interconnected all of these innovations were, or how complex the steps to getting to them could be.

"Yes, Your Majesty," it said, using her title in one of its many attempts to 'humanize' itself. *"The first is a mechanical reaping device. Britannian steel making and tooling has now progressed to a sufficient level to make the device possible. I have enough data to guide the engineers in Factorium to design and build an early version of the mechanical reaper."*

"Mechanical reaper?" she repeated. "A device that harvests?"

"Essentially correct. It is a large, wheeled machine that can be pulled by a single horse. Along the front is an articulated arm with a reciprocating blade that can cut an entire field of grain rapidly. Compared to dozens of men needing to swing scythes to harvest a field, this device would allow just one man guiding the horse to accomplish the same amount of work in a fraction of the time. While planting crops is still a labor-intensive task, the mechanical reaper greatly reduces the manpower needed during the critical harvest period."

"That's brilliant!" she said, and then lowered her voice. The rooms were secluded, but the walls were not so thick that someone in an adjacent room could not hear her. "That is exactly what I've been trying to find."

"It will not be a simple process. It is a complex machine that requires more than fine tooling to produce. Maintenance will be an issue and will require training of local smiths to repair them properly as they break down. It is one of the reasons it was decided not to introduce the device at this point. It will also slow rifle production until Hortensius can further expand his production facilities, as it requires some of the same fine tooling machinery."

"We can handle that. You said there were two ideas that could help?"

"Yes, Your Majesty. The rate of production of nitrate is now sufficient to keep up with the gunpowder production quotas with some surplus leftover, and the development of the tools necessary to produce ammonia as part of the process for generating viscous rayon, collectively provide the pieces necessary for the production of ammonium nitrate, a powerful fertilizer. This chemical will increase crop yields substantially when applied to fields. With higher yields per acre, less land and labor are required to feed the same population."

"These could both be major improvements for us, notwithstanding helping to get more manpower for the legions. I wish I'd known about these sooner," Lucilla said.

"I apologize for not providing them. As the operating process for new innovations has been set to proceed through the commander, and he has been distracted with leading military efforts, the rate of introduction has slowed commensurately. Should we change our process to take into account the commander's unavailability?"

"Yes," she said slowly. Sometimes, the way Sophus spoke was hard for her to follow, using words that sounded Latin, but were not. Words she knew covered ideas from outside her time. "I don't want to remove Ky entirely. There is too much I don't know for me to make decisions on why and how to introduce new technologies. Perhaps you and I could decide when we have the manpower to take on a new innovation and then consult with Ky, instead of the other way around. I will discuss this with him and see what he thinks. He'd be a better judge of it, anyway."

"As you say, Your Majesty."

"In the meantime, tonight, I want to start drawing up plans for Hortensius and Sorantius. Let's start with the fertilizer since Hortensius still has the railroad to deal with."

"Of course, Lucilla. I can provide you with detailed schematics for the mechanical reaper, as well as an outline of the process for producing ammonium nitrate fertilizer. I can also provide estimates on the resources required to manufacture the reapers and the amount of fertilizer that can be produced in a given timeframe."

"Thank you, My Friend," she said.

She offered up a silent thanks to Jupiter. In spite of Sophus's skepticism, this was more proof to her that he was watching over her people. She knew Jupiter had directed their conversation, prompting her to ask for assistance at the right time.

She knew her gods were with her and would see them through.

Northern Italy

Ky and Marcus entered the small village, led by Decanus Sextus and his Germanic centurion, Egilgar. Unlike Ky's last visit to a village in this area, where the residents had fled in terror or formed angry mobs, these people stood to the side of the narrow, muddy streets, eyeing the armor-clad soldiers cautiously as they approached, more out of curiosity than fear.

The group made its way through the village until they reached a simple home on the eastern outskirts, made notable by the freshly installed thatch roof, still firm and new, with a group of men standing outside, watching them approach.

One man, humbly dressed in a plain wool tunic, unlike the finer linens of the others, gave a small bow of his head and warmly greeted them, "Welcome to my home. Please, come inside and find rest."

The wording was peculiar, although as far as Ky knew, this region didn't have a specific greeting for guests. Still, Ky gave a small head bow in return.

"Thank you for your hospitality, Sicanius. Decanus Sextus has told us of your generosity."

"If by generosity, you mean berating him as he and his men built this roof, then I'm sure it was legendary. Still, he's a good young man and does your people proud," the villager said, opening the door and waving Ky through.

"He certainly does," Ky said as he entered the man's home, with Marcus, Egilgar, Sextus, and the villagers filing in behind them.

The interior was simple, but clean and well-kept. A small fire crackled in the hearth, casting a warm glow over the room. The men took their seats on stools, that seemed too nice to belong to the simple man.

The village elder, a man with thinning white hair and a weathered face, slowly lowered himself onto a stool opposite Ky and said, "Greetings, Consul. Thank you for visiting our village. I will be the first to admit that when your people first appeared, we were very nervous about having them here. The things we'd heard ... it doesn't matter. What matters is that your man Sextus has been all over our village for the past several weeks, doing all kinds of repairs. Just yesterday, I heard he was at one of the outlying farms putting up a new storage barn. I don't even know how he heard about their difficulties, but to say the family is ecstatic would be an understatement. Your other men have seemed to follow his lead, repairing buildings, delivering much-needed supplies, and even mediating a few disputes."

"I'm glad to hear that our men are making a difference," Ky said. "This is precisely what we sent them to do. Having been under Carthaginian occupation as well, before we liberated ourselves, we know well the toll their governance can take on a place and its people."

Ky was stretching the truth a bit there. Although Rome had been affected by Carthaginian rule in southern Britain, and many of their allies had been under Carthaginian control, their situation wasn't exactly comparable. It seemed, however, a good way to build a connection with the man.

"Indeed. My nephew, Sicanius here, couldn't stop singing your man's praises, or those of the rest of your people. Word has spread, and other villagers have shared tales of your assistance. They've seen your soldiers handle confrontations with restraint, preventing minor skirmishes from escalating into larger conflicts."

"I'm pleased to hear that," Ky said. "My officers emphasize daily the need to handle any confrontations calmly, without escalating conflicts unnecessarily. It's not always easy with young soldiers far from home, but they've taken those lessons to heart. Is there anything further we can provide for your people? Supplies, repairs, settlements? My men have time and are eager to assist however they can."

The man was shrewder than he let on, Ky thought, as the old man handed over a list he'd already prepared. While it wouldn't have taken much to guess that Ky might have asked that very thing, considering what his men had been doing around town and the supplies they had already provided, it still sent a message. They might cooperate with the Romans, but that cooperation came at a price.

For now, it was one Ky was willing to pay since, at the moment, manpower came at a much greater premium than goods. Besides, the list wasn't that difficult to provide; it was mostly raw materials, only available outside the nearby area that the villagers would have had to buy from traveling merchants. The cost was minimal, especially considering what they were getting in return.

"I'll do my best to see these needs met," he assured the elder.

Ky and the elder spoke for several more minutes, with the other important members of the village bringing up issues that they could use help with. Most were mundane tasks, repairs and renovations, and the like, although one man did mention an issue with bandits in the hills to the east that had ransacked several of the outlying farms. Ky looked to Marcus, who indicated he would see to taking care of it.

By the end of the meeting, even the more reticent of the villagers began to speak up, most likely worried they would be left behind while their neighbors received aid and assistance.

"Thank you, Sicanius, for your assistance in bridging the gap between us," Ky said as the villager walked them out after the meeting, extending his hand in farewell.

Taking Ky's hand, Sicanius said, "It was the least I could do. I cannot express how grateful I am for the new roof. It is the first time in years I haven't been leaked on during a rainstorm."

"We're glad to have been of service. Please extend our gratitude to the rest of the village for their cooperation."

With a final nod, Ky and Marcus exited the hut and made their way through the narrow streets, heading towards the outskirts of the village. Ky looked to Sextus, the young decanus who seemed to be radiating nervous energy. Ky didn't blame him; being the focus of attention from so many superiors at one time must be an intimidating experience.

"Decanus Sextus, you have done an excellent job here," Ky said, putting his hand on the young man's shoulder. "Your initiative has not gone unnoticed."

Sextus straightened, his chest swelling with pride. "Thank you, Consul. It has been an honor to serve."

Ky turned to Sextus's centurion, the stern-faced Germanic, and said, "Centurion, keep an eye on this young man. He has great potential. I believe he will go far."

Considering Egilgar himself had risen very quickly to become a centurion, even in a time of war, Ky's words said even more good things about this century and how Marcus was leading his men.

"I understand, Consul."

"Good," Ky said, handing the list of supplies the village elder had given him to the centurion. "Requisition what they need and make sure you bring Decanus Sextus with you when you deliver it. He seems very popular here, and I think he might make your job here easier, especially if you both keep to what you have been doing."

The centurion nodded, taking the list and tucking it into his belt. "Yes, Consul. We will see to it."

Sextus saluted, looking like he might burst from pride and excitement. Ky returned the salute and then continued on his way, leaving the young officer and his centurion to begin a hushed conversation as Ky and Marcus walked away.

As they continued out of the village and toward the secured century camp, Ky turned to Marcus and said, "This is the kind of reaction we need to see more of. The decanus did an excellent job here. We need to find out exactly what he did, so we can reproduce it elsewhere."

Marcus nodded. "Yes, I agree. His initiative has proven quite effective."

"This is exactly the type of reaction I was hoping for," Ky continued. "Don't wait for the villagers to come to us with requests for aid. Be proactive, while still being respectful. Don't presume too much but look for ways to be of practical assistance. I want you to encourage the men to take the initiative. I think the important thing isn't just what Sextus did, but *how* he did it. He saw things that were wrong and helped in those areas. If he could see it, then I'm sure it bothered the people that live here, for much longer. Beyond fixing the problem, it shows he cares about the community he was assigned to assist. People can see that and respond well to it."

Marcus nodded, a determined look on his face. "I understand, Consul. I'll make sure to pass on these instructions to the other legates and centurions."

"Good. If we can get the same response in other villages, we will find our manpower problem sorting itself out quickly."

"I will see to it at once," Marcus said, saluting and hurrying away.

Satisfied, Ky turned and looked back toward the village. The muddy streets were empty now except for a few villagers hurrying about their business, and a few squads of Britannians here or there, moving about unmolested, and, in one spot, even in conversation with locals.

Ky allowed himself a small smile. This just might work.

The Village of Alaria, Southern Hispania

It was a beautiful late spring day as the morning sun rose over the rolling green hills. Villagers made their way out into the fields, baskets and farming tools in hand, to tend their crops and animals, continuing their simple life as a rural farming village. Children laughed and played games in the dirt streets while chickens pecked at the ground in search of food, and small flocks of goats and sheep were led out to graze by young shepherds.

Indortes, the village elder, emerged from his small home, leaning on his gnarled, wooden cane, and surveyed the familiar scene with a feeling of satisfaction. Children paused in their play to smile and wave excitedly as he passed by. Indortes had led this community for many years and loved it more than anything. No longer as spry as he'd been in his youth, he still enjoyed his morning walk through the village center before settling down on the wooden bench outside his home, ready to receive his people, assisting in mediating disputes or just sharing a story or two.

Just as he began to settle in, faint noises drifted from the hills beyond the fields - odd cracking sounds he couldn't quite place. Straining to hear, he tried to pinpoint the noise that threatened to upset his daily routine. And then it came again, closer and louder. Hoofbeats pounding hard on the ground and the unmistakable crack of gunfire, which had to be from the new weapons being sold by the new arrivals to the south, who had replaced the Carthaginians in the port of Kalb.

His people had only managed to buy a few of these weapons, and a small supply of gunpowder, and he was impressed with their power and ability to deal with predators threatening their livestock and the occasional hunting party.

The sounds could mean only one thing. Raiders. As if to confirm his fears, the screams from his people out in the fields joined with the rising noise. Indortes pushed himself up as quickly as he could and hobbled to get a clear look at the fields in the direction of the sounds.

Horsemen were descending on their village like a pack of wolves, their muskets spitting fire and death. Farmers dropped their tools and fled, only to be cut down mercilessly, caught in the open as they were. Indortes could only watch in horror as their bodies crumpled to the ground like broken dolls.

"Get the women and children to the grain house!" He called out as loudly as his old voice could carry. "Hurry!"

He moved as fast as he could, cane thumping against the hard-packed dirt, waving in that direction as mothers scooped up crying toddlers and herded terrified older kids ahead of them.

"Arm yourselves. The muskets," he ordered again, pointing to his home where the weapons were stored.

The few men who hadn't gone out to the fields rushed to retrieve them, not that it took many. There were scarcely enough to go around, with the rest having to settle for iron tools or pieces of wood to be used as makeshift clubs.

"Take positions between the buildings. Protect the children," he said, pointing out positions where they would stand the best chance, pulling on faint memories of his days as a warrior, decades before.

All of the men were grim-faced, knowing there wasn't any hope of surviving this. They were outnumbered, and it looked like every one of the raiders was armed with one of the new muskets.

The raiders were through the fields now, only a handful of his people escaping the initial onslaught alive, running to the temporary safety of their village. They were close enough that he could recognize them, or their style of clothing, anyway. Arandur warriors. Already known for raiding, with many of their people behind the increase in brigandry in central Hispania, coming from north of them.

With whoops and war cries, the Arandur warriors swept into the village, firing as they came.

Despite being hopelessly outgunned, the men of Alaria stood their ground. They took up positions between the stone and mud-brick buildings, forming a ragged line of defense in front of the granary where the women and children huddled in terror. Indortes felt a swell of pride for these men, simple people, farmers, and craftsmen by trade, and then sorrow knowing they would all soon be dead.

As if to prove his point, he watched helplessly as Tomaz, the blacksmith's boy, took a musket ball to the chest. He crumpled to the ground, his lifeblood pooling around him.

His men returned fire as best they could, forcing the raiders to pay a price for their evil. A few of the Arandur reeled back, struck by the return fire, but his men had little experience with the weapons, the gunpowder too costly to practice with. Most of their fire did little more than produce clouds of smoke, missing their targets entirely.

And then the horsemen were upon them, their animals trampling the dying as they slashed and shot at the outmatched villagers. Tomaz's father joined his son as he tried to protect his wife, who was cowering behind a basket, holding their youngest. He managed to swing an iron rod, one of his tools, into the face of a rider, knocking the warrior clean off his mount. Before he could raise his weapon again to repeat the feat, two enemy muskets barked in unison, sending their pellets ripping into his chest.

The remaining villagers fought ferociously with axe, knife, club, and fist. With a roar of defiance, Indortes raised his cane and charged at the nearest warrior. The man sneered, raising his musket to fire. The last thing Indortes saw, beyond the fire and cloud of smoke that exploded in front of him, was the wooden door to the stone grain house being wrenched open. Too many of the men were gone, dead, to protect the women and children any longer.

Indortes had a brief moment of overwhelming sadness. Not for himself, as he was old and close to the end of his life without the aid of the Arandur, but for his people. The ones he loved and had fought for all his life.

And then he thought of nothing else.

Chapter 16

Devnum

Medb waited in the Empress's private garden, pacing among the blooming flowers, trying to ignore the luxury the Empress lived in, one that Medb herself had once enjoyed before her downfall. She knew herself and knew that if she let thoughts like that fester, she would start slipping back into old patterns. While she'd been able to indulge in those in her former life, she'd come too close to death to court it again so soon.

Besides, she was having fun for the first time since she'd been exiled to this godsforsaken place, and the last thing she wanted was to be caged again, kept in stately rooms to act as a princeling's concubine instead.

Motion at the garden entrance drew her attention. She smiled slightly as she saw the Roman Senator Taenaris being ushered into the garden by one of the palace guards, pleased to see his annoyed expression as he realized who he was being brought to meet. She didn't know the senator, beyond a few curt words, but she knew his type. Pompous, self-important, and utterly convinced of his own genius. Tweaking the noses of men like him always gave Medb a small amount of joy.

"What do you want, Medb?" Taenaris said in a gruff, almost bordering on rude, tone.

"That's not a great way to start off with one of the Empress's agents, doing the Empire's business."

"You'll get over it, now what do you want from me?"

"I want your help," she said.

Taenaris let out a bark of laughter, "Why on earth would I ever help someone like you?"

Medb shrugged, "I already told you I'm doing work directly for the Empress. For someone who holds such an important position, you really should try to pay more attention. But, since I know how distrusting you are, perhaps the fact that I'm in her private garden, with her guards bringing you to me should be evidence of that." She paused, letting her words sink in before continuing, "If you still don't believe me, after this you can check with Ramirus, whose minions have been scurrying around me constantly, watching me like a hawk."

Taenaris glared at her, looking like he wanted to say something more biting, but held it back, giving a small nod, "Fine, but that doesn't answer what you want help with, specifically."

"I need some legislation introduced in the senate. Specifically, I need you to introduce a bill requiring wool production to be distributed equally across the Empire, with wool bought by the Empire and used in imperial factories to be bought in equal parts from each state."

"Why do you care about wool production?" he asked, frowning in suspicion. "What are you trying to gain?"

"I'm not trying to gain anything. I don't care if this bill is passed, I just need it introduced and it to be believable enough that anyone else looking at the legislation believes it to be genuine."

For a moment, Taenaris didn't say anything. She could see the wheels turning behind his eyes, trying to work out what exactly she was trying to do. She knew all of her protestations aside, he still wasn't convinced this wasn't some kind of scheme on her part to increase either her wealth or power. She didn't blame him for that and was about to point out again that she was doing this on behalf of the Empress when he surprised her.

Instead of protesting again, or refusing, or calling her motives into doubt, he asked, "What is the current distribution?"

"At the moment, more than half the wool bought by the Empire comes from Ulaid, with Caledonia producing the second most and Rome making up maybe five percent of what is purchased."

His brow creased further as she answered him. "You understand that would hurt Ulaid and the farmers of Ériu?"

"I do, but I don't actually expect it to get voted on, let alone passed, since it would require both Caledonia and Ériu to take large cuts in their wool trade, purely for the benefit of Rome."

"Could Rome even handle that increased production?"

"I have no idea, although I doubt it," Medb answered. "It doesn't matter. It won't be the first time you lot passed laws that bore no relation to reality."

Taenaris gave her a thin-lipped, humorless smile and said, "Funny. You understand the other senators will see this as some kind of power grab on my part, don't you? It will anger them and make it harder for me to make deals with the other delegations in the future."

"You'll be shocked to hear how little I care about that," Medb said.

He gave her another annoyed look and said, "Then why should I do this? You're the one asking me for a favor, remember?"

"Because you're a good dog who does what his Empress asks him to," she said, and then rolled her eyes. "Fine, because it needs to be done. Some of your fellow senators have been up to things they shouldn't, and are causing problems for the Empress and the war effort."

"And how does a bill on wool purchases help you with that? Seems kind of mundane and unconnected."

"The bill is just a tool. I need to pull some of the senators into the open, so we can apply the right leverage to them. Think of it as a fishing expedition."

"Which senators?" he asked, his eyes narrowing as he started going through the relatively small list in his head.

"I'm not going to tell you."

"Why?" he said, sounding genuinely surprised.

"Because you lack subtlety. You have a bad habit of too easily letting people know what you're thinking, and this requires a softer touch."

"Calling me incompetent will hardly persuade me to assist you."

"I'm sure you'll get over it. Besides, I didn't call you incompetent, I said you weren't subtle. I'm sure you're very good at your job and the Empress thinks highly of you, but you're too noble and honest for your own good. As to why you'll do it, as humorless and pompous as you are, you're also a patriot. You'll think about it, check with Ramirus, who'll confirm what I'm doing is on his and the Empress's orders, and realize that, with Ramirus involved, it's more than just some simple jockeying for position.

"And why would the Empress ask you to do this? Why would you be working so hard for the Empress after scheming so hard to discredit her?"

"The Empress asked me to because I'm equally good at what I do, and she has this high-minded idea to give people second chances. While I doubt I would do it in her position, since I'm benefiting from it now, I can't exactly fault her for it. This is my trial run to show I won't be … difficult, if she gives me bigger jobs. As to why I'm doing it, that's none of your business. Assume it's because I'm bored and want something to do. Now, are you going to do this or not?"

Taenaris stared at her hard, considering. For a moment, she wondered if she'd pushed him too hard. She knew he'd be distrustful of any attempt at friendly persuasion, which is why she chose the tack with him she had, but perhaps she misjudged his motivations.

If she had to, she could go to Ramirus or the Empress and have them make the request on her behalf, forcing the issue, but she didn't want to do that. Part of this challenge was to prove she could get things done and, as distasteful as working for the Britannians was, it was better than the alternative, at the moment.

Finally, he sighed and said, "Fine, I'll introduce your bill."

"Good," she said, allowing him a friendly smile for the first time since he'd entered the garden. "I'm glad you listened to reason."

Taenaris scowled. "Don't get too cocky, Medb. I'm doing this because the Empress wouldn't have given you this task without a reason, not because I believe you're in any way reformed. If I find that you are using me for some personal scheme, I promise there will be consequences."

"Whatever," she said, patting him condescendingly on the cheek. "As long as you do it, I don't care what your reasons are."

She left him standing there, fuming at her back as she walked away, allowing herself a genuine smile.

Yes, this really could be fun sometimes.

The Port of Kalb, Hispania

Cormac leaned against the windowsill of the commander's office, overlooking the busy wharf, watching the sun sparkling off the water as ships, by the dozen, jockeyed for position coming and going. Even with the majority of the port's faculties at least nominally in place now, the speed at which the port moved was breathtaking, dwarfing Cormac's previous experiences in Ulaid before the coming of the Romans. Even Devnum, with its larger ports and more massive facilities, didn't seem to move at nearly the breakneck speed that it did here.

"I must apologize again for the delay, my lord," Commander Niall said, sitting at a desk next to where Cormac stood, shuffling through stacks of papers. "The requests from Admiral Valdar have increased exponentially in the last few weeks and are starting to put a strain on our ability to maintain sufficient supplies."

"Think nothing of it, Commander," Cormac replied, turning from the window. "I know a little something of pressures from those above you and their unrelenting expectations."

In truth, two years ago, Cormac might not have said that, having generally only his father to give him orders. These last few years, however, had done much to show Cormac just how much under the thumbs of superiors he was; although the layers above him were still a great deal smaller than the ones above the commander.

Niall didn't need to know that and looked up, giving Cormac a sympathetic smile as he found what he was looking for, pulling a sheet out of the truly terrifying stack of documents in front of him.

"As of now," the commander continued, "we're weeks behind in fulfilling the requests from the villages and tribes across the peninsula to purchase muskets. The demand is simply over-whelming."

"I know you're overwhelmed already, but we need to find a way to accelerate deliveries. The muskets were the main thing that convinced these people to sign treaties with us. The rest will help solidify things in time, but this is still all too new, and the more we fall behind on our promises, the more likely they are to walk away."

"I know, and I am trying, My Prince, but very little of our shipping is run by the Empire, and I am at the mercy of the merchants. If we were doing this directly from our own stores, that might be different, but allowing our merchants to sell into civilian villages gives us less ability to apply pressure."

"I know, and again, I appreciate the difficulties, but that doesn't detract from what we need to have happen. In fact, the speed of shipments is only part of what needs to happen. Even when they do arrive, the pricing is higher than it was for those sold into Germania. While that's not generally known, I worry in time the villages here will learn that and blame us for the increase. It also means the smaller villages have less access to our goods, putting them even further behind the larger villages. For what we need, ultimately convincing them to not only stop all the infighting but actively taking part in the war effort, the more villages we have contributing, the more leverage we'll have on the larger villages, who won't want to appear lacking in comparison to their smaller neighbors."

Niall leaned back, looking at the ceiling, and for a moment Cormac was wondering if the man even heard him.

Right as he was about to repeat himself, Niall said, "We could rebuild and reopen Port Invictus. It is now well behind the lines, so wouldn't need the kind of military presence there that it had before, or even what we have now, but it's also a lot closer to Britain than we are. One captain can make ten trips in the time it takes a captain to make the same trip here. Knowing these men, they would take less in delivery fees for the allure of quick money. It would help shorten delivery times and bring down costs, at least to some degree."

"An excellent idea, although not one that can happen right away. I'll send word to the Empress and find out what we would need to do for that to happen. It doesn't solve all of our problems, because Southern Hispania is a lot more populated than the Northern half, so a lot of these tribes would find themselves further from the source of goods. Most of our merchants sell into the ports and let the ports sell to whoever, which is fine when it's centrally located, but a problem otherwise."

"I'm not sure we can have both halves of the bird, My Prince."

"I know," Cormac said. "It really is an excellent idea and one I will start to explore. I was mostly just putting a voice to my thoughts."

Before they could discuss Niall's suggestion any further, a highly agitated Llassar burst into the room. Seeing the normally stoic and emotionally balanced Caledonian highly anything was unusual, immediately putting Cormac on edge.

"Forgive my intrusion, but we have an emergency," he said briskly.

"What happened?" Cormac asked, stepping away from the window.

"There have been a series of raids. Tribes from central Hispania, predominantly the Arandur tribe, have attacked and destroyed several of their neighbors, making off with goods and slaves."

They had dealt with so many tribes recently, it took Cormac a moment to cycle through all of their names. He did remember the Arandur though. Haughty, aggressive, and presumptuous. At the time, he'd thought they were just grandstanding, hoping for a better deal than some of their neighbors had gotten.

"It gets worse," Llassar continued, seeing the recognition on Cormac's face. "Survivors report muskets were used in the raids. Several of the other tribes have sent emissaries to the port, some of whom are here now, waiting to see you. We have started getting emissaries from tribes closer to us, with complaints. They're blaming Britannia for this, and there's talk of some of the other signed tribes withdrawing from the agreements."

Cormac's face twisted in anger, his fists clenching and slamming into the table next to the garrison commander as he said, "This is unacceptable! I told them what would happen if any of them double-crossed us. Commander, assemble a century and get them prepared to march."

As a worried Niall started to stand, Llassar held up a hand and said, "That may not be the wisest course."

"Why not? We said they were not to use the muskets against their neighbors when we sold them the muskets, and that we would bring swift retribution against them if they did. I do not intend to go back on my word."

"No, we agreed that, if they were to use the weapons in hostilities against their neighbors, we would stop selling gunpowder and weapons to them."

"So we're just supposed to withhold weapons and let them use the ones they already bought to wreak havoc across the peninsula. I'm not sure that's exactly what the Empress meant when she sent me here to 'get things under control.' We have to show the rest of the tribes that signed treaties with us that we can be counted on."

"I'm not saying that's all we do, I'm simply pointing out that is the consequence we laid out in our agreement when we initially sold them the weapons. Attacking the Arandur will make an effective display for some of the tribes, yes, but not for all of them. They are watching for when Britannia becomes like the Carthaginians, using might to enforce their will. We will regain some of the tribes who are walking away, but we will lose others who aren't. The Arandur aren't the only offenders, either. They're the largest and have done the most damage, but they're not the only ones."

"So what am I supposed to do? Just let them get away with it?"

"No. We can still deal with them, but we have to do it in the right way, to show all of the tribes that we can both be counted upon when they need our help *and* that we will abide by the terms we agreed upon, even when we have the ability or even responsibility to do something else instead."

"I assume you have a way to pull that little trick off," Cormac said petulantly, slipping back into his old habits.

"Possibly. We cut off gunpowder shipments to those tribes. It won't matter, since they'll just attack and steal what little powder the smaller tribes have managed to buy, but it's a start. We start offering additional benefits or technologies to the tribes that have stayed loyal to us. It might not affect the larger tribes, but it will convince some on the fence that, in not getting those, there is a cost to crossing us that's still within our agreement. We make it clear if they come back into the fold, we will offer them the same. That's the carrot."

"I hope there is a stick somewhere in there," Cormac said.

"There is. While we're offering those additional benefits, we sign defense treaties with the tribes that have abided by our rules. That way, when we do move against the tribes attacking our treaty partners, we aren't acting arbitrarily, but within the bounds of our agreements. In reality, the Arandur have done us a favor, because hardly any of the tribes wanted to tie themselves to us militarily. The Arandur will force their hands, pushing even the strongest southern and western tribes into military alliances with us for their own safety."

"That's ... interesting," Cormac said, his anger fading as he considered Llassar's plan. "There will be some tribes who still don't want to be tied to us, who prefer to stay neutral."

"It's not a perfect solution, but nothing ever is," Llassar said. "What it is, is the best option we have available to us at the moment. For the tribes that do sign, it opens the door for us to be able to ask for assistance in our war, which was the real reason the Empress sent you here. In case you missed how actively she is politicking to get manpower to send to the legions."

Cormac frowned. He had missed that, but then, he'd been actively trying to avoid politics at the time, since it had meant spending more time listening to senators drone on about water use and land rights. Even with that, his first instinct was to just march on the offenders. Any of the tribes that pulled back would quickly find themselves in a worse position, since their neighbors would have tools they would not. And if they attacked their neighbors to get them ... well, that was what the legions were for.

Of course, he'd been learning more and more that his first instinct was very often not the right one.

"We'll do it your way," Cormac finally said. "But if this doesn't stop the raiding, I'm going to burn their villages to the ground."

"If they don't stop, you'll have treaties in place to allow you to do just that," Llassar said.

"Good."

Chapter 17

Coast of Sardinia, The Mediterranean

Valdar stood at the bow of the BNS Bellona, the wind whipping through his hair as his ship cut its way across the water. Ahead of them, still a speck in the distance, was the island of Sardinia, their current target. After months of clearing out the western end of the Middle Sea and laying waste to every Carthaginian port on that side of North Africa, he was finally comfortable moving his fleet further east, working to clear out the seas of southern Italia before the Consul's legions could reach it.

His preference would have been to just push hard all the way across the sea and then swing back to pick up any stragglers they might have missed on the way. Unfortunately, he wouldn't get his preference this time. Soon, hopefully, the Consul would be ready to cross to Africa, which meant a large number of supply ships would take the place of the overland logistics he was using now.

While Valdar's caravels might be a plague on Carthaginian ships, Britannian and allied shipping was much slower, and their current supply situation was such that they couldn't afford to absorb the losses of being less than thorough.

"Here they come," his first mate said from his position next to him, staring at the small island in the distance through a spyglass.

"You have to hand it to them; they certainly are brave," Valdar said, squinting as he tried to make out the distant shapes. "It's nice of them to bring their ships to us to be destroyed instead of making us chase them."

"They could still turn and make a run to the east. It looks like they're all using our copied sail plan."

"Won't matter. It's better than oars, but their ships are not built from the ground up for it like ours. It might take us a little longer, but we'll catch them. How many?"

"Twenty, I think. It's hard to tell. They're sailing in a very tight formation, bunched up."

Valdar frowned. That was not typical of how the Carthaginians sailed. They fought with their fleets like they did their armies, trying to spread out and outflank the other side and surround them, so they could get as many of the soldiers waiting on deck onto the opposing ships as fast as possible.

"Can you see any of the ships in the middle or back?"

"No, Admiral, I ... wait, they hit a swell and had to separate a bit. I think they might have catapults on some of those ships," his first mate said.

"Signal to the fleet, prepare to head on a westerly course, holding a formation four abreast. Lower to half-mast but prepare to return to full sail as the enemy closes. Bellona will take the rear."

Instead of relaying the order, the sailor looked at him, his head tilted in confusion. "Admiral?"

"Those catapults are for throwing the gunpowder they've started using, and if you haven't noticed, our ships are made out of wood. They've got the wind, and I want our ships held at long range from them. Since they're able to come straight in and fire, once they're close enough, we'll start to tack for broadsides and pick up ground to restore distance. It'll make this slower, but I'm not ready to surrender any of our ships to those thugs."

The man looked back out at the enemy ships for just a moment, working through the implications of what Valdar had said before turning and rushing off to the signalman.

"Not today, you sneaky bastards," Valdar muttered to himself, watching the Carthaginians close the distance between them.

The signal flags began flying with agonizing slowness as his fleet and the Carthaginian fleet continued to edge closer and closer together. While the flag system the Consul had instructed them to use allowed a level of coordination unimaginable before, which was needed when fighting as floating cannon platforms, that level of complications meant everything took so much longer.

Finally, his ships began their slow arc, turning away from the oncoming Carthaginians. They had been sailing in line, with his ship at the front, which meant, for the time being, only his ship would have a clear field of fire at the Carthaginians as they turned.

"Prepare broadside. Fire as she bears!" Valdar bellowed to his gun captains, forcing his voice above the sound of the waves and wind.

As his ship became parallel with the enemy fleet, his starboard cannons fired, long tongues of flame reaching out toward the Carthaginians. Through the billowing smoke, he saw several hits across the front of the Carthaginian line, with the lead ship looking to have taken several as it began to drift south uncontrollably, its fellows were forced to adjust suddenly to avoid it.

"Nicely done," he said to his first mate, who'd returned.

"Order the fleet to tack on my command once we've created enough separation. Keep it tight, I don't want them to gain any more than necessary," Valdar said.

Looking through his spyglass, he saw the Carthaginians did them a favor, slowing as ships moved in to replace the damaged ships. As they did, the Bellona finished its turn and began to sail steadily westward, putting distance between the fleets.

It took almost twenty crushingly slow minutes to open up enough range for his ships to maneuver, even with the Carthaginian fleet slowing briefly to reshuffle their line.

"That should about do it," Valdar said. "Order the back line to tack south and fire as they bear, then return to the westerly course."

"Yes, Admiral," the man said, shouting instructions to the signalmen and ship's helmsmen.

Valdar watched as his four rear ships, which included the Bellona, began turning south. They had been sailing abreast, meaning each ship had a clean line of fire, although his ship furthest south had to turn almost southeast before he could get his guns on target.

Each belched fire as their ship got on target, their months of practice over the winter and the core of trained and blooded sailors paying off as the majority of the fire hit their targets. Unlike his first salvo, his men had known it was coming enough ahead of time for his gun captains to get their guns fully on target, concentrating all of the fire on the first three ships in line. Cannonballs ripped through the galleys, tearing away masts and punching holes through the decks, sending the ocean rushing in.

One might end up salvageable, falling away as his predecessors had done, no longer seaworthy, but the other two were completely lost, already starting their journey to the bottom, listing to the side.

"We may have only three ships for the next volley," Valdar said. "The Alfhildr made too wide of a swing and is lagging too far behind."

As if to make his point, an object came arching out of the center of the Carthaginian fleet toward the Alfhildr, which was still turning to get back to the rest of the fleet, forced to give up speed in exchange. The projectile still fell well short of the ship, but the explosion no doubt worried everyone aboard when the jar burst into a flaming ball a few handspans from the ocean surface.

"It's alright, they're slowing again," his first mate said.

Valdar lifted his spyglass. Sure enough, the Carthaginian fleet slowed again, shuffling their ships forward to replace those sunk or damaged in the last pass. The longer he watched the ships repositioning themselves, the less pleased he was with the Carthaginians slowing.

"Damnit!" he finally said.

"Sir?"

"They're using those ships as shields. That's why they slow down every time we sink some, to keep us from hitting their catapult ships. I'm sure of it."

It made sense, especially with the way Carthaginians liked to fight. They preferred to power their way through every challenge, sacrificing things they saw as 'expendable materials,' such as their own people, to gain position and victory. And because his ships had to do a series of maneuvers after each volley, while they could just sail straight in, it meant that they just needed the Britannians to slip up, or the winds to drop enough where their oars could counter the better Roman sail plans, to get within range.

Worse, it just might work.

His first mate must have seen this playing across Valdar's face because he said, "Perhaps we should disengage."

"No. For one, it's not like that will make this problem go away. They'll still be here, waiting for us. For the other, I told the Consul I'd have the waters around Italia cleared by the time he reached the land's end, and I mean to. If conditions shift, we can re-evaluate, but right now, we have the wind on them. As long as we don't get sloppy, we should stay ahead of them. And they don't have an unlimited supply of ships to lose. Eventually, they will expose their catapult ships, and then we can end this."

Unfortunately, eventually turned out to be a very long time. For the next two hours, Valdar's fleet swung back and forth, slowly whittling the enemy down, sinking a handful of ships with each pass.

Valdar never left the deck, straining through his spyglass at the Carthaginian fleet. In spite of what he said, he knew there were bound to be mistakes, no matter how good his captains were. This kind of fight of attrition was bound to wear down any crew, no matter how well trained. Although he kept the Bellona on the rear firing line, he cycled his other ships out to give their crews a rest between each volley.

Even with all of that, there were mistakes. Nearly very costly mistakes.

On the forty-third pass, the wind suddenly dropped, not completely, but enough. Most of his captains saw what was happening right away, unfurling their top sails and bracing the yards as best they could to pick up enough extra wind to keep their lead. All except the Kvasir, which delayed several long minutes before it joined them.

Horlf was a good man and an experienced seafarer, but he hadn't noticed the wind change fast enough. The Carthaginians, whose orders allowed them to continue pushing forward as his lagged, didn't have nearly the same disadvantage, surging forward in the calm conditions.

Valdar watched, a pit in his stomach as first one, then a second, and then a third container was launched from the Carthaginian fleet, which was closing the gap between them rapidly.

Two landed well short, harmless as they had been the few other times they'd fired their weapons. The third was much closer. Had the Carthaginians' aim been better, they would have had the Kvasir. As it was, the container exploded perilously close to the ship. No fires were started, but there must have been some kind of shrapnel, either in the container or from pieces of the container, because Valdar could see injured men on the deck and rips appeared in the canvas sails.

"Prepare to come about! Signal the fleet to come about and engage. The Alfhildr will pull aside and render aid to the Kvasir!"

It would make all their patience for naught, turning this into a slugfest Valdar was sure to win, but not without damage or casualties. He wasn't prepared to give up one of his ships, though. If his men were quick, they could punch through the shielding boats and sink the catapult galleys before any of his own ships were hulled. He hoped.

Thankfully, it didn't come to that as the gods looked down on their fool of a servant, blessing him. Before the signalman could send the message, the wind picked up once more. Valdar could feel the Bellona surge forward beneath his feet. More importantly, the injured Kvasir also picked up speed; the next Carthaginian volley landed close, but behind the ship, which meant they were widening the distance between them.

"Belay that order," Valdar shouted to the signalman, thankful he didn't have to commit his fleet to such folly.

They returned to their pattern, the Carthaginians now barely even waiting to change out shielding ships as they pushed forward, apparently buoyed by their near success. Part of Valdar wanted to disengage and try again when his men were fresh but he knew that wasn't really an option. All he could do was worry, and pester his men to stay alert, working his signalman's limbs to the bone with the constant signal traffic.

Thankfully, the men had taken the close call to heart. As he knew it eventually would, the wind dropped a second time. His men all performed well, reacting quickly, keeping their distance from the Carthaginians.

By the third hour, the Carthaginians were running low on ships to use as shields. Valdar thought they might withdraw, their tactic firmly failing, but they did not. Instead, they persisted, leaving their catapult ships exposed for longer and longer gaps until, finally, the supporting ships were taken by surprise, reshuffling their position when his fleet hit, creating a sizable gap in their lines while his ships were still in firing position.

"Signal the fleet. All ships are to turn and fight. We finish this now," Valdar commanded. "Helmsman, hold your course. Guns to fire as they bear, targeting the catapult ships in the center."

One by one, the Britannian ships swung about, fanning out to bring their full broadside armaments to bear. Valdar didn't wait for them, his ship holding a southerly course, angling to keep the enemy fleet in his broadside. The Carthaginians didn't even slow, maybe thinking this was another opportunity to strike one of his ships.

His gunners dissuaded them of that notion as they finished reloading, their tubes bellowed smoke in a second volley. The other three ships in the firing line were close behind him, their captains seeing his ship hold its course and reading his intentions before the signals even finished sending. The Fabius and the Einar both fired their second volleys less than a minute after his. Clear of the obstructing shielding ships, the effect was instantaneous.

A hail of iron rained down upon the enemy, slamming into ships, men, and, most importantly, catapults, pulverizing anything in its path. One ball must have hit their gunpowder storage, as the vessel disappeared in a colossal explosion as its payload caught. His ships didn't slacken their fire, the gunners working their weapons with practiced efficiency, sending a third volley a minute and a half later. The second ship was hulled a dozen times over. While not with the impressive explosion of its companion, it died all the same, listing hard to the side, until the catapult slid into the sea, followed by its sailors and then the ship itself.

They had courage, Valdar had to give them that as the third catapult ship continued on its course, launching its payload, maybe trying to take one of his ships with it. Unfortunately, the enemies' skills did not match their fortitude; the payload missed his ship by a wide margin.

His men did not give them another chance, as all three ships poured fire into the remaining catapult carrier, literally ripping it to shreds. The other two took water rapidly, sagging into the sea.

That was enough for the rest of the Carthaginian captains, some of whom struck their colors while the rest turned to try and flee eastward.

"Order the fleet to round up the surrendered ships. Have the sailors secured in the hold and prepare to scuttle their vessels." He paused, considering the situation before continuing. "Send the Einar and the Fabius to chase down those runners. They're to sink as many as they can, but stay within range of the fleet, even if it means letting some escape."

As the signalman began relaying orders, Valdar watched the handful of ships making a run for it. Most of those would get away, scattering in all directions, but it didn't matter. They'd gotten the catapults and sent more Carthaginian gunpowder to the sea bottom, which was the real threat. He'd also bet this was the last major Carthaginian fleet around Italia.

They'd clearly known he was coming and prepared for him, launching as soon as he was within sight, instead of waiting to draw the Britannia ships in closer, which is what he would have done in their place.

Not that it mattered. By this time tomorrow, he'd be back to Sardinia, shelling the docks to ensure nothing else could be launched from there. Then, it was on to the next target.

Imperial Forum, Devnum, Rome

Medb sat in the far back corner of the Forum's spectator section, where the overhang created a bit of shadow, allowing her to blend in as much as possible. Despite the poor vantage point, she had made sure to arrive early to claim the seat, isolated from the bustling crowds filling the tiered steps along the perimeter of the cavernous central chamber.

The lowest and closest steps to the center were the most prized seating area, which started to quickly fill up with the more prominent merchants and tradesmen who sent representatives to hold their place since early in the morning, to ensure they would see, and be seen, in attendance. The rest filled up almost as quickly by not just merchants and tradesmen, but common citizens of all stripes crammed shoulder to shoulder for more than an hour before the session was scheduled to start.

She had to admit the Empress's decision to open the senate sessions to public viewing had proven more popular than she'd expected. Medb couldn't help but wonder how much of their interest was concern for the future of the Empire and how much was just people searching for a cheap form of entertainment. While not quite at the level of the Colosseum, the bickering could be fun to watch, she supposed. Although sometimes she found herself annoyed with the sheer confidence some of their 'leaders' had in their own stupidity. At that thought, she allowed herself a smile. It was a truism she'd found, that the dumber a man tended to be, the more confident and sure of himself he became.

For her, she would have preferred to be anywhere else than listening to these men bicker and argue, and would have been if she didn't have to be here for one specific subject being discussed. The problem was, the Senators never gave an indication of when specific bills and discussions were happening. She didn't know if that was just due to their inability to organize themselves or because they thought being able to surprise their fellows gave them some kind of advantage, but it meant she had to sit here and listen to them prattle on for hours.

So there she sat, bored, as the proceedings unfolded below. Senator after senator took their turn at the central square, arguing about the next stage of the telegraph lines going into Caledonia or the rail line beginning to extend toward Londinium, as much preening for the spectators as an act of actual governance.

Finally, Taenaris decided to get off his rear and present what she'd actually come to see. She rolled her eyes as the man slowly walked to the center, standing there for nearly ten seconds just looking from one delegation to another, like some kind of preening prima donna.

"Honorable Senators, esteemed guests, fellow Britannians," he finally began. "I come before you today to address a grievance that has plagued our great Empire. Since the Empire's formation, Rome has been treated unfairly by its partners in this great enterprise, who have taken advantage of Rome's legendary magnanimity. While this pervades many aspects of our society, today I speak of the distribution of our Empire's wool industry. While we have toiled and labored to produce the finest quality product, our partners have reaped the benefits, leaving Roman wool producers with the scraps."

Medb smiled to herself. She wasn't sure she agreed with what he was saying, but she couldn't fault his performance. If this didn't achieve the results she wanted, she didn't know what would.

"The time has come to propose a solution, a fair and just solution that will benefit all parties involved," he continued. "While I would never dream of telling private industry and buyers how or where they should procure their goods, I do believe this body has the right to have a say when the biggest buyer of wool is the Empire itself. Specifically, my proposed legislation would require the equal distribution of what the Empire buys in terms of wool. Instead of favoring only Ulaid goods, we must ensure that Roman wool producers receive their fair share as well."

Before Taenaris could even stop speaking, the Ulaid and Caledonian delegations were up on their feet, protesting.

"This is an outrage!" Rotri yelled, his voice managing to carry above the rest of the shouting delegates. "You dare accuse us of taking more than our share? Rome dominates almost every industry in the Empire. Yet the moment we have success in one area, you immediately cry foul and demand a redistribution!"

Rotri, who already talked with his hands quite often, was gesticulating wildly as he spoke. Taenaris held up his hands in a calming gesture, waiting for the shouting to subside.

"Please, this is simply a proposal for discussion," he assured them. "I am open to counterproposals on how to make allotment of industries more equitable. I would also say that it is unequivocally false that we 'cry foul' when one of our partners finds success.

Your own nation, for example, has gained a high level of prominence in mining, and there has been nary a complaint from my people."

"Rome doesn't even have the mines if they wanted to," Enniaun, one of the other Caledonians said. "I'm certain if you did, it would be on the list of things you felt weren't equitable."

The Caledonian senators shouted their agreement, pounding their fists on the stone benches. Taenaris raised a hand for silence once more, maintaining his calm demeanor.

"I understand your perspective," he replied evenly, "And if it were as simple as two equal groups providing products, I think it should be up to the Empire's factors to buy based on their necessary requirements. What I cannot, will not, abide by is an agent of one of the wool concerns actively interfering in who the Empire chooses to buy from, artificially elevating one group above the others."

Again, the senators erupted into shouts, this time demanding that if he had proof that someone was manipulating the purchases of the Empire, they had a right to know who it was. As the bickering dissolved into squabbles over rights and minor points of law determining when and how information was disclosed to the senate, Medb tuned them out.

Taenaris had played his part well. She did wonder how much of what the Roman had said was true. Was Fiacha, and she had to assume that the comment had been a reference to the Ulaid senator, doing more than blocking the Empress's proposals. Could he have had someone inside the Empire's treasury influencing where they purchased their wool?

It wouldn't surprise her if this was the case, since it seemed exactly like something the Ulaid senator would do. She also didn't care very much, one way or another. This entire stunt was simply to smoke the man out, get a reaction from him. If he was involved in other layers of malfeasance, then maybe Ramirus would credit her with saving the Empire some money outside of what she'd promised to fix.

She also noticed Fiacha was not one of the ones in a fit of hysterics over the proposed law. Instead, he silently fumed in his seat, his jaw clenching and grinding with each word Taenaris said.

When Taenaris agreed to hold his amendment for a few weeks while discussions happened behind the scenes, and the rest of the senators began frantically whispering, probably seeing if there was a way they could eke some kind of advantage out of the situation, Fiacha just sat there, looking away from his colleagues, staring at the spectators.

And then he saw her, his eyes locking with Medb's, recognition and anger spreading across his face as he finally started connecting the dots. She blandly looked back at him, having to will herself to keep from rolling her eyes at just how slow he really was.

He broke eye contact, looking to Taenaris, and then back to her, fury building behind his eyes. She responded by giving him the smallest hint of a smile, and then a wink.

Then, before he could react or explode, she broke eye contact and stood smoothly, lifting the hem of her skirt as she mounted the stairs and made her way up and out of the Forum.

That had gone just about as well as she had hoped.

Chapter 18

Imperial Palace, Devnum

Lucilla made her way down the dimly lit corridor deep in the palace complex, far from any windows or light. Although she grew up in the palace, this section always seemed so unwelcoming that she hardly ever came down here. Now, as Empress, she usually just made anyone who might be located here come to her. If she hadn't had one of the guards leading her, she was certain she would have gotten lost.

She didn't bother knocking as she got to the door she was looking for, another benefit of being Empress, only to pause as she found Ramirus behind a long table scattered with papers which took up much of the cramped room.

"... very angry. He only stayed five minutes before leaving again."

Ramirus and the woman both stopped as the door opened. Ramirus looked surprised for a moment, before his gaze softened as he recognized Lucilla. The woman had the opposite reaction, going from curiosity to shock.

"Your Majesty!" she said, going to one knee, her head dipping down. "I'm sorry. I didn't ... You ... I."

"You're fine," Lucilla said, reaching down and pulling the woman to her feet, giving her a warm smile. "I'm the one who should apologize. You two were talking and I interrupted."

"Your presence is never an intrusion, Your Majesty. This business can wait," Ramirus said, before turning to the woman. "Please excuse us, Opima. We will speak again soon."

Opima bobbed a hasty curtsey to Lucilla before scurrying from the office, the guard outside pulling the door shut behind her.

"One of your agents, I presume?"

"Opima is a friend to the Empire," Ramirus said, gesturing to one of the chairs. "What can I do for you, Your Majesty?"

Lucilla rolled her eyes at the spymaster. He sometimes seemed incapable of answering even the simplest questions, even to her.

"I've made a decision," she said, taking a seat and folding her hands in her lap. "I want to go to Germania and speak with the leaders of the Germanic tribes directly."

"That's quite the journey, and not without risks."

"I'm aware of the risks, but I believe it's necessary. We are having no luck finding the men Ky needs to keep Italia pacified so he can continue his march south, and they've shown more willingness than anyone else to provide warriors. I've run out of options here."

"Beyond the fact that they've already given quite a few men and still have scattered remnants of Carthaginians in their own lands, my greater concern for this is your own safety. The Carthaginians would love nothing more than to get their hands on you, and you won't have the same protection in Germania that you have here in Rome."

"I understand the risks, Ramirus, but we don't have a choice. We need those men, and if my being there personally can ensure their cooperation, then I must go. I know you'd rather I send someone else to negotiate, but so far, they've been working with the Consul. Sending a functionary now could be seen disrespectful, as a sign that they've become less important to us now that the war has moved south. I am the only right choice."

"I'm sure they understand that our focus must be where the fight is," Ramirus countered. "They were still actively engaged in hostilities against the Carthaginians last year. People don't forget that easily."

"Before Bomilcar left for the continent last year, I spoke with him at length about the tribes and their customs. At the time, it was mostly curiosity. I've never been to Germania, and there are some similarities between the tribes there and the kingdoms of Ériu, so I'd hoped some of what he shared would be transferable.

One of the things he made clear was the importance they put on how things are respected. Yes, they would understand that Ky had to be with the armies, and maybe they would accept a representative of a lower position, but they might not. We are running out of options and this is the best one left to us. If we send a representative and they do take affront, we might be left with no other options. I'm not willing to take that chance."

Modius, who had been standing silently by the door, spoke up. "I believe this is a mistake. This trip is an unnecessary danger and we cannot guarantee your safety. As Ramirus said, there are still scattered Carthaginians throughout the region. The legions may need additional men, but they need you to keep the Empire together more."

"I understand your concerns, Modius, but this is what has to happen."

Modius frowned, looking more displeased than usual, which was saying something. He, however, didn't say anything else.

"You should listen to your guard, Your Majesty," Ramirus added. "I assume you've seen the reports I've sent you. You know how dangerous this is. Please, let me send someone in your stead. I will even go if you want me to. Your place is here."

"I appreciate your concerns," Lucilla said, heartened that her people cared for her so deeply, but annoyed she had to keep repeating herself. "But my decision is final. I am going, and if I have to sail a ship myself to get there, I will. Ramirus, send word to the chieftains that I request a large gathering at the village we've been using for the northern supply shipments. I want as many as possible of the tribes we've been in contact with to attend. Tell them this has to do with the weapons supplies being sent and their allocation, and requires leaders or people capable of making agreements to be present. That should be enough to get them there."

"I hope you're right, and that your presence there will be enough to convince them, but you should be prepared for the worst. Their last response to the Consul's request for more men left the impression that they have no intention of providing more manpower."

"I'll have to be persuasive then," Lucilla said.

"There are also going to be complications here," Ramirus added, still not giving up. "The Empire is still young, fragile, and you're well aware of the complications we've already had. The insurrections may be over, but we've got plenty of loyal subjects who'd be very willing to let us lose this war if it meant personal gain. We've done well keeping them in check, but it seems likely that, with you being gone, they will see this as an opportunity. You could be setting up more problems for yourself in the future."

"I know, and we will have to deal with that when it happens. I want you both to hear me on this," she said, giving both Ramirus and Modius a serious expression. "This needs to happen and is my will as Empress."

Ramirus sighed, "Very well. I will dispatch agents to the tribes and begin making arrangements for your journey and protection.

Northern Italy

Raśna watched as the Britannians as they packed their tools, still covered in a sheen of sweat after a long day's work in the sun. A stack of stones, gathered by his people over the last several weeks, but much smaller now, still lined the banks of the river. Raśna allowed himself a small smile as he realized how much they had overdone it, without his even having to press them.

When word had spread that the bridge was going to finally be replaced, his people had volunteered almost to a man to help gather the stone needed for it. Several had made it sound like a practical exchange, the offer to help get the job done faster, but he knew some also had started to feel they had taken too much advantage of the Britannians' charity, and wanted some part in the work being done for their home.

Which was for the best. Even if they didn't do the work itself, they would all have a sense of pride every time they passed over the bridge, as it should be.

"I think we're about done, Elder," the young Britannian Sextus said, breaking from his men and coming over to where Raśna had been watching them work. "I'm sorry, but we haven't been able to thoroughly test it. I'd hoped we would be able to do that today, so you could start using it right away, but the sun's already starting to go down, and our orders are firm."

"I understand, Decanus," he said, reaching out and grabbing the young man's hands. "I know you've received less than a friendly welcome among some of our neighbors, and I don't fault your superiors for their caution. Please know how grateful we are for your help, and how thrilled we are to see your progress. You and your men continue to astound us."

Sextus gave a small grin as he did every time he was complimented, the one that reminded Raśna of his grandson. It was easy to forget, when these men were in their armor, looking ferocious, how young they were. And like his grandson, Sextus was a good boy, even if he was from a far-off land.

"We will return tomorrow to ensure the bridge is stable enough for your people to use," he promised. "Then you won't have to make that roundabout trip anymore."

"Thank you again," he said, still patting the man's hand. "We look forward to seeing you tomorrow, even if you aren't doing more work for us. You know you are always welcome in our homes."

"I appreciate that," Sextus said, squeezing Raśna's hand in return before pulling free.

As the Britannians left, the village settled into the evening routine, families getting their dinner, exhausted after a long day working the fields. Lights from candles and cooking fires began to sparkle to life, as darkness closed in.

It was a scene that Raśna had witnessed countless times before, but one he still savored. He relished this time of the night, as he walked through his village and listened to his people living their lives. It was almost serene to him.

This night started out just the same, until he made it back to his own home and the tranquility was shattered by a scream somewhere in the darkness. Raśna froze, listening intently, trying to determine where the sound came from, and if someone needed help. And then chaos erupted as more cries and shouts followed. He'd just started down the main road of the village, toward where the cries were coming from, when he saw armed men swarming toward the village center, some bursting into homes and dragging people out, while others slaughtered those who tried to flee.

Worse, as the first men got close enough to be seen in the dark, Raśna realized he recognized some of the assailants. They were neighbors who had vanished with the Carthaginians when they fled before the Britannian advance. He'd assumed they had fled south with the Carthaginians, since most had had better relations with their former overlords than he or the rest of the village had had.

Worse, he also recognized some of the men as Carthaginians, by bearing if not specifically recognizing individual men.

"What is the meaning of this?" he shouted at the men as they continued to go from house to house, pushing and forcing everyone to the center of the village.

One of the Carthaginians nearest him backhanded Raśna across the face, sending him to the ground, before grabbing him by the neck and pushing him to join the rest of his people, forcing Raśna to his knees. A moment later, his nephew Sicanus, who lived further on the edge of the village, was dragged into sight and thrown to the ground next to him.

Over the next ten minutes, more and more of the men, and even some of the women of the village, joined them. Most were the leaders, farmers, and craftsmen who held prominent places in their neighbors' lives.

"What is happening?" Sicanus gasped, clutching a bleeding gash on his arm.

Raśna just shook his head, at a loss for words.

"Silence!" barked one of the attackers, backhanding Raśna across the face again. "No talking!"

Raśna turned his head and spat blood into the dirt, glaring at the man who had struck him. He wasn't a Carthaginian. Veli had been his neighbor for years, living just outside of the village at one of the small farmsteads. Raśna even remembered when the young man was born and that he had helped his mother care for him when he was small. He'd worried for the man after he'd abandoned his farm just a month ago without a word to anyone. Raśna had assumed Veli fled south with the retreating Carthaginians, but with the sudden upswing in banditry, he'd been concerned that maybe something worse had happened.

It was shocking to see him here, now, as he was leading an attack on their own village. Shouts and screams echoed through the night as the invaders continued their rampage. Raśna watched helplessly as young Larthia was dragged whimpering past him, clutching the limp body of her younger sister. His heart ached at the sight.

As the chaos began to die down, with the entire village gathered, those who still lived, on their knees around Raśna, a man broke away from the rest of the attackers, who had started to gather in front of the villagers. A Carthaginian, no doubt, Raśna thought, by the way the man carried himself, his chin held high, his back straight, lording over them.

"This village," he began, his voice echoing through the night, "and its people stand accused of treason. You have accepted assistance from the invaders and allowed them free access to your village and the surrounding area. You have brought them into your homes, fed them, and taken their charity."

He paused, letting his words sink in.

"The emperor has declared any such behavior to be treason against Carthage and punishable by death."

Fearful whispers rippled through the villagers, which were promptly shouted down by the men gathered behind the Carthaginians.

"Some of your neighbors have not been so weak and have stayed loyal to the empire while you have begged and groveled at the feet of the invaders," he continued, gesturing toward the men gathered behind him, indicating Raśna's former neighbors. "They have watched you and made notes of the worst offenders."

With that, Veli and the other men strode to the villagers and began dragging many of them forward. One grabbed Sicanus, pulling Raśna's nephew hard, before hands then grabbed Raśna himself, with all of the selected villagers put into a line at the Carthaginians' feet.

"All of you took from the empire for generations. Your village lived, protected in the empire's good graces, suckling from its teat. And what did you do when the empire needed you? You turned on your loving emperor who cared for you as a father cares for a child. You accepted aid and comfort from our Britannic enemies; you have betrayed your rightful lords and masters."

He paused again for dramatic effect.

"Let this be a lesson to the rest of you, of what happens when you defy your emperor."

A cry erupted from Sicanus as one of the men wrenched his nephew's head back, exposing his throat, drawing a dagger from his belt.

"No!" Raśna shouted, lurching forward only to be held back by unyielding hands.

The man didn't even glance in Raśna's direction as the blade slid across Sicanus's neck. Blood sprayed in an arc, soaking the ground in front of the Carthaginian. Sicanus clutched desperately at his mutilated throat, gagging and choking before collapsing lifeless to the earth.

Raśna felt bile rising in his throat.

"Why?" Raśna choked out, fixing his eyes on Veli. "We are your neighbors. Your friends!"

"And now you're all traitors," he said coldly, stepping forward, plunging his sword into Raśna's chest.

The elder gasped, more in shock than pain, as the blade slid into him. He could vaguely feel his tunic become damp, then soaked, as the sword was removed and blood spilled from him as he collapsed to his side. Already, his vision was dimming, but he couldn't look away as his former neighbors and the Carthaginians fell upon the rest of the men lined up along with Raśna and Sicanus.

He watched as Thufl, his friend of thirty years, was grabbed by a trio of the men, who took turns beating him with clubs, laughing at each wet impact as they caved in his friend's skull.

That was the last thing Raśna saw as he slipped away, dying with the rest of his village.

Devnum

Medb rested her head back on the edge of the bathing pool and luxuriated in its warmth. Even on a hot spring day, which this one was turning out to be, she still found the sensation pleasing.

When she'd come to Rome, the first time she'd tried out the baths, she'd been both perplexed and put off by the odd smell, which someone told her was a new addition to the experience. Something about a chemical added to the water that was part of a series of new requirements the Consul had put on public baths. It seemed there wasn't a consensus if people thought those requirements were good or not, and a very vocal minority apparently refused to step foot in them, claiming the smell and having to wash in running cold water after getting out ruined the experience for them.

Maybe because she didn't know a time before the new requirements, but Medb found the smell somewhat familiar now. She even liked the cold rinse after leaving the baths, finding it bracing. It was also a notable sight better than sponging off using cold tubs of water, which is how she'd done things back home. If she ever did go back, she'd have to bring this improvement with her and set up baths of her own.

She inhaled the moist air, the hint of herbs and minerals reviving her. The bath attendants waited, just out of sight, to pour the cleansing water over her before wrapping her in warm cloth, kneading scented oils into her skin and hair, and dressing her. It made her feel like a queen again.

She sighed, letting the tension seep from her body. She'd been on the sidelines for so long, she'd forgotten what the game was like, with its moves and counter moves, not to mention all of the egos involved. She loved it and was glad to have even a taste of it back, even if this version of it was so narrow and limited.

The sound of one of the attendants gasping and some kind of commotion made Medb open her eyes, only to find herself staring up at the scowling face of Senator Fiacha, who was standing above her.

"Have you come to bathe, Senator?" Medb asked, her voice lazy and unbothered, a stark contrast to his heaving shoulders. "This hour is normally reserved for women, but I'm sure no one would restrict someone of your fine stature."

Medb waved off the guard standing behind the senator, looking unsure of how he should handle the sudden intrusion by someone of such high standing, and pushed herself up, floating to one of the perpendicular sides of the pool so she could face Fiacha directly, making no attempt to cover her naked body.

"Of course not," he snapped, putting clenched hands against his hips. "I know you're behind this ridiculous wool legislation."

Medb raised an eyebrow and said, "Is that a question or an accusation, Senator?"

"Don't play coy with me, Medb. You know damn well what I'm talking about. And don't think I don't know you're the one who's been whispering in Taenaris' ear."

"Of course I was behind it. I made no secret of that at our last meeting," she said, lifting a graceful shoulder in a shrug. "You made it quite clear then that you did not think I had the power to compel you to do anything. That required a demonstration to show you how wrong you are."

Fiacha's face reddened, his anger boiling over. "You're willing to destroy my brother-in-law's business, to devastate my wife's family, all to prove a point?"

"Of course I am. I don't care about you or your family, Senator. Besides, only one of us chose to flout their position and put their family in harm's way, and that wasn't me."

"What is it you want, Medb?"

Medb didn't answer right away, instead tilting her head and studying him for a moment, letting him squirm.

"For starters, Fiacha, I want you to pass on the Empress's request for manpower to your king. And I want your full support behind it."

Fiacha scowled again, but Medb could see the resignation in his eyes. He'd known he was outmaneuvered before he'd ever stepped into the baths. Everything else had been bluster to cover his defeat.

"Fine," he said through gritted teeth. "But you have to halt this legislation."

Medb smiled, a slow, satisfied smile that made Fiacha's scowl deepen. "See, isn't it easier when you just do what I tell you from the beginning?"

"To the hells with you," Fiacha spat, turning on his heels to storm out.

"Why do you think you're done with me, Fiacha?" she asked, her voice soft but firm, stopping him in his tracks.

"What do you mean?" he asked, his voice wary as he turned to face her.

"I mean that I will have tasks for you to do in the future, Senator, and I expect your full cooperation."

"What? Why should I do anything for you, ever? If I never have to even speak to you again, I'll die a happy man."

"You haven't thought this through, have you, Senator?" she said, putting her arms behind her, over the edge of the bath. "By getting this legislation shut down, and by passing on information you should have already passed on to your king, you've shown your hand. How do you think Conchobar would feel if he knew you'd been legislating for personal gain? Or withholding information because of your own personal wishes?"

"What are you talking about?" he stammered, his face paling.

She shook her head. How someone this stupid could ever get to his level of power, she'd never understand.

"I know Conchobar, both as an enemy and now as his loyal vassal and daughter-in-law. As reasonable as he can sometimes be, I have also known him to react badly, often violently, when crossed. Do you really want to test him?"

"I've agreed to your terms. What more can you want?"

"Like I said, I'll let you know when I have more tasks for you. I just wanted to make sure you understood who you belong to now."

Fiacha's eyes narrowed, his jaw clenched as he glared at Medb, who looked back at him, unperturbed. The senator's face contorted with anger and resentment, and she could see him working through all of the things he wanted to say. She could also see him working through the consequences of voicing them, realizing he was boxed in completely.

"You have no idea the type of enemy you've made today," Fiacha said through gritted teeth.

Medb regarded him coolly and said, "On the contrary, I know exactly what kind of man you are, Fiacha. Weak, greedy, and a coward when it comes down to it."

"I won't forget this."

"I don't want you to. I want you to remember this every time you try to go around me or think you can outmaneuver me. If you step out of line, I will crush you," she said, her voice becoming deadly serious before returning to her more carefree attitude. "Now, run along and do as you're told."

With a final venomous look, Fiacha turned on his heel and stormed out of the baths. Once he was finally gone, she slid back down into the water, her head lolling onto the edge of the bath again, letting the relaxing waters wash over her once more. A small, satisfied smile played at her lips.

That had gone well.

Chapter 19

Devnum

Lucilla sat at her desk in her private office, transcribing the words Sophus was dictating in her ear, finishing the last sheet in a large stack of documents, when a knock drew her attention.

The door opened a moment later as Gaius admitted Ramirus, Hortensius, and Sorantius into the room, all three men bowing respectfully as they approached.

"Please sit; I know you all have busy schedules, so I appreciate you're making the time to meet with me today," Lucilla said, setting down her quill. "I'll try and make this fast."

"We are always ready to serve, Your Majesty," Ramirus said.

"I know that, and I appreciate it. As Ramirus knows, and I'm sure everyone else has heard some kind of whisperings about, we've been experiencing difficulty getting the manpower we need to support the legions as they get closer to Carthage. I've been in talks with our countrymen in Ulaid and Caledonia about the possibility of their freeing up more men to join the legions, but those talks have been … unproductive as of late. Part of the problem we're having is that both states have given a large amount of manpower already, and we're entering into the peak growing season. They fear, not unfairly, that they will not have enough people to harvest their crops come fall, leading to food shortages over the winter. I have sent messages to Ky and he has sent back some thoughts on new technology that could help us address this problem, allowing fewer people to harvest more. Which now, of course, puts the problem in your laps."

Both Hortensius and Sorantius looked intrigued in their own way, Hortensius's inventor's soul nearly jumping up with excitement at the prospect of something new. A stark contrast to the slight tick of an eyebrow from Sorantius, which for him was the height of exuberance.

"I'll start with what I need from you, Hortensius," she said, handing over a stack of pages, one of which still had damp ink drying on the page. "It's a device called a mechanical reaper. According to Ky, it will greatly increase efficiency in harvesting crops, allowing one man to harvest what would have taken dozens."

Hortensius's eyes lit up as he looked over the drawings and notes, mumbling to himself as he traced his fingers along the diagrams. "Fascinating! Using a reciprocating blade to cut the stalks. Brilliant! And you say the Consul wants this device completed before harvest season?"

"Yes, if at all possible. I assured both Conchobar and Talogren that we could provide an efficient harvesting machine in time for late summer and fall harvests. Can it be done?"

"I believe so. Technically, this is much simpler than some of the things we've worked on recently. Had someone had this idea even before the Consul arrived, it might have been possible, although maybe not, since our steel at that time did not handle torsional stress well. These pieces are very long and will require setting up new production lines, but that simply takes time. From a technical perspective, this is very much achievable."

"Good. I know you have a lot happening, finishing the line to Londinium, getting the telegraph network extended in Ulaid and to our allies on the continent, but this is very important."

"I understand, Your Majesty, and I will see it is done."

"Thank you, my friend," she said, before turning to Sorantius, handing him his own stack of pages. "In addition to a new mechanical solution to help with crop harvesting and manpower, the Consul has a new chemical solution as well, which he says will greatly increase crop yields. He calls it ammonium nitrate."

Sorantius' eyes narrowed. "Ammonium nitrate? It sounds similar to several other compounds he has shown us."

"I know little beyond the name and intended use myself," Lucilla admitted. "But Ky seemed quite confident in its potential. My understanding is that there are similarities to what you are already making and that you have the base components to create this, but that he has waited until now to introduce it because of our need for nitrates in other areas. Apparently, our nitrate production has increased to the point where he now feels comfortable diverting some of it from gunpowder manufacturing into other areas."

"You are correct. We do produce more than our needs require at the moment. I had been looking to other uses hinted at by some of the Consul's previous instructions. Looking at this …" the chemist said, holding up the pages. "I think this might be one of those. The instructions are clear, although with mixtures such as this, it isn't as easy to test the results as it is for something mechanical. More so even with something like this, that has less instantly obvious effects. If I had my choice, I would test these on an isolated patch of crops for a season, to establish a baseline of results and determine proper usages."

"I understand that and applaud your caution, but as with so much of what I've given you over the past few years, we are under time pressure. I don't want to push you beyond your comfort level or jeopardize any of your people, but we do need this as quickly as possible. It's too late to help with the initial plantings, but there is time for it to help with the winter crops."

"We will do the best we can," Sorantius said.

"Good. I appreciate anything you can do for me," Lucilla said, pausing for a moment. "While these projects are important to the Empire, they aren't the only reasons I asked you both to be here in person, instead of messaging these over or sending a message over the telegraph. This is not, and hopefully will not be, public knowledge, but the two of you are critical to the running of the Empire and have the 'need to know,' to borrow a phrase Ky likes to use. Very soon, I will be leaving Devnum and the Empire, and I don't know how long I will be gone."

Hortensius and Sorantius exchanged surprised glances.

"That means both of you will be on your own overseeing all of your projects in my absence. I know you are both capable and have run operations of your own long before being employed by the Empire, but this is more than just managing the creation and production of your assigned works. It means you will need to work with Lurio on distribution of the products and dealing with the issues that may arise. To be clear, this means both practical issues and, potentially, political issues. I know this is outside the scope of the work you both do and that both of you dislike politics in general, and I apologize for asking so much of each of you. It is, however, critical, and there is no one else I trust to handle things in my absence more than the two of you."

"We are, of course, at your command and will do anything you require of us," Hortensius said almost as soon as she finished speaking. "If I may ask, however, where are you going? You've made trips to the other states before, so I assume this is more than just visiting Caledonia or Ulaid."

"I'm sorry, my friend, but I can't answer that. Please know it's not that I distrust you in any way. Ramirus and Modius, however, both believe that there is risk associated with this trip, and the fewer people that know the specifics, the safer it is. I can only tell you this trip is necessary, and that I would not be going if the need were not great."

"You can count on us, Your Majesty," Hortensius said, Sorantius nodding his agreement.

"I knew I could count on you both," she said.

She stood, smoothing her stola, signaling the end of their meeting, the two men quickly getting to their feet in response.

"Before I let you get back to your work, I want to sincerely thank you both for your loyal service these past years. I'm not sure if our Empire would have survived without your contributions, but I do know that you are both major reasons why we have stood our test as well as we have. You both have my deepest gratitude."

Both men seemed to take that as seriously as she'd offered it. Even the normally businesslike Sorantius seemed a little moved by her pronouncement. She ushered the men out, leaving the specific details of how they'd administer everything to Ramirus, who followed them out.

Now, she just needed to find someone to mind the Empire as a whole in her absence.

Medb sat in the lavish chambers she normally shared with her husband Cormac in the Imperial Palace, lounging on a divan with a book in her hands. Coming to Rome had introduced her to many amazing things that she'd never thought possible, from trains to baskets that could fly in the sky under a globe of fabric, but the one she found the most fascinating was books like the one she was reading.

In practice, it wasn't that different from what she'd had at home. They'd had collected works of long scrolls and even tied "books' of parchment, but those had been treasures, hoarded and not accessed casually. The sheer time and expense of producing them were such that they were mostly used for short things like messages and speeches.

It wasn't until she came here that she'd discovered the mass-produced tomes with their stamped-out letters, each copy almost identical to the next, so easily produced that she had even seen merchants and laborers with them. They were still new and hadn't started making it into the further reaches of the Empire, but as she understood it, they were bringing about a wave of literacy, even among the lower class.

While she cared less about that, their popularity also meant that more artists, men who previously had created works for the stage, were putting their ideas to paper. The explosion of printed materials underway was largely driven by entertainment, of all things. Medb had always been a lover of plays, poets, and dramatists, and to have their works in her hands, where she could revisit them whenever she wanted, or find new ones each time she went to the market, had been like a gift from the gods.

Which is why she sighed in annoyance as a knock at her door interrupted her reading, forcing her to close the leather-bound writing, setting it aside on a small table.

'This had better be good,' she thought to herself as she crossed the finely decorated quarters she'd spent so much time cultivating and opened the door. Her face fell even more, which she wouldn't have thought possible, when she found Ramirus, the Empress's watchdog, standing outside her door.

He didn't say anything, and the two just stared at each other for a moment before Medb stepped back, allowing Ramirus to enter the room.

"I guess you're going to come in no matter what, so come in," she said flatly over her shoulder as she walked back into the room.

"I'm sorry for disturbing you, Lady Medb," Ramirus said, closing the door behind him and following her.

Medb waved a hand dismissively as she settled on the divan again. "Let's skip the pleasantries, shall we? I assume this isn't a social visit."

Ramirus's mouth twitched into a slight smile. "No, I'm afraid not. Though I had hoped after the last few months, we were beyond such hostility."

"Yes, that started right after you threatened to execute me."

"I think you would agree the outcome following your ... efforts to influence members of the clergy into open opposition against the Empire was far more lenient than even you expected. More so, I believe the Empress is trying her best to uphold her end of the bargain you struck with her."

"I think my results should prove that I've done the same. Nothing in my agreement required me to be pleasant about it while doing it."

"Fair enough," Ramirus said. "I came to talk to you about Senator Fiacha. I have been following your progress. You did well in setting him up in the Forum with Senator Taenaris's bill, but I had expected more to come from that little maneuver."

"My job is done. Fiacha will not only stop blocking the bill, he will now be far more cooperative in all ways the Empire needs him to be."

Ramirus looked genuinely surprised. "Oh? I had thought you were simply going to expose Fiacha and force him out of politics."

"What would be the point of that? If we simply exposed Fiacha and forced him out of politics, we'd just end up with some new

Ulaid senator who could potentially be even more troublesome. Instead, I convinced the senator that it is in his best interest to become more cooperative with the Empire on future dealings. This way is far better. We now have a senator firmly in our pocket, and the more we compel Fiacha to act in the Empire's interests, the deeper in our debt he becomes."

Ramirus raised an eyebrow. "It sounds like Fiacha is more in your pocket than in the Empire's."

"There's the trust I've come to know and love. And you wonder why I'm still disagreeable after all your kindness."

Ramirus inclined his head slightly, acknowledging her point.

"And no, not in my pocket. I just put things in place because that was the job you asked me to do. If you want to take point in directing the senator, by all means, go ahead. Though I should add that doing that puts more culpability on the Empire."

"How so?" Ramirus asked in that maddening way of his.

She knew he already knew the answer but wanted to hear her reasoning before putting his own out there. He would have given the Greek philosophers a run for their money.

"I am still technically a subject of King Conchobar, so my controlling a Ulaid senator is problematic, but not as bad as Rome having direct control of one of the Ulaid senators. Especially since, of all the members of the Empire, Ulaid is still somewhat distrustful of the Empire as a whole and the Romans specifically. With my managing Fiacha, it provides the Empress with plausible deniability. I make an excellent cutout, wouldn't you agree?"

"I suppose," he said, skeptically. "I will admit to having concerns over your managing an … asset like Fiacha, but you are correct about the relations between ourselves and the Ulaid."

"You can only dance in the middle for so long, Ramirus. What do you want me to do? I couldn't care less either way, but if you have concerns, then you take him."

"No, I think that won't be necessary," Ramirus said. "However, I do want to be there the next time you meet with him, to ensure he understands what his position is in all of this, and where his obligations lie. I would ask that you keep me informed of any instructions you give the senator moving forward. I would have liked to know you were taking this route before the deed was done."

"If there's time, I'll try," Medb said. "You know, if you keep assigning me work like this, at some point, you're going to have to decide if you trust me or not."

"Don't take it personally. There are very few people I trust completely. You've done good work here and I will make sure the Empress knows it. However, it will take time to repair the damage done by your own actions."

Standing, he straightened his clothes and started toward the door, before stopping and turning back toward her. "You know, the Empress thinks you're hungry for power. At first, I agreed with her, but now, I think we were wrong. I think you like the game. I think it's one of the few things that really gets your mind going, and you've enjoyed being in it again. You're also very good at it. I'll promise you now, as long as you never try to turn your genius in this area against the Empress or the Empire, I will ensure you get as many chances to play as I can."

Giving a slight nod to himself, as if confirming he was right about something, he turned and left her quarters.

She watched him go, closing the door behind him before reaching over and picking up her book once more, settling back into the cushions. She tried reading a page, found she retained nothing from it, and tried a second time before shutting the book and dropping it in her lap.

Damn that man, she grumbled to herself.

Port of Kalb, Hispania

Cormac stood at the center of the amphitheater, built by the Carthaginians to entertain their soldiers, a wave of sound washing over him as representatives from all over Hispania talked excitedly, and angrily, to one another. The Britannians had sent runners across the peninsula announcing the council meeting, making it clear the central topic to be discussed was the raids still occurring across Hispania. They had made it clear that any tribe that wanted a say in the response to the raids needed to be here.

Even with the urgency of the announcement, the sheer number of men who showed up for this meeting surprised Cormac. He had thought the wrestling match and other games of physical challenge had been well attended, but that had been a fraction of the total population here. Men were packed into the auditorium, crowded shoulder to shoulder on the stone benches.

More surprising than how many were there, were some of the tribes that had decided to attend. The Arandur and several of the other tribes who'd been identified as the perpetrators of the raids had sent representatives to the council, and were the only ones with some room left next to them. Cormac was honestly impressed they had the brazenness to attend a meeting that was, ultimately, about them. Although, it would make sense the people being accused of committing the raids would want a say in what happened to the raiding tribes, he supposed.

Cormac raised his hands, gesturing for silence.

Once the rumblings died down, he said, "I welcome you all to this council. I know you've come from far and wide, each with your own concerns and grievances. We've heard and understand your concerns about the escalating raids, and the use of Britannian weapons in those raids. I can promise you this; we are determined to work with each of you to make this right."

"How? Your weapons are killing our people!" a voice called out from the audience.

"You're right. We don't deny Britannian weapons were used, and we are committed to helping solve the problem. I also think it should be acknowledged that the raids did not start with the introduction of the weapons we sold you. Bandits sacked villages, kidnapped people, and have plagued this region since the withdrawal of the Carthaginians. I say this to put these troubles into context, not to absolve Britannia. We came here because we were the ones who drove the Carthaginians out, making everything that's happened here since our responsibility."

He paused, looking across the audience. That last section had been contributed by Llassar, and had the effect the Caledonian said it would. They'd all come here ready for Cormac to defend Britannia and to deny any culpability on their part. They hadn't expected him to do the opposite, and now that he had, some of the anger was taken out of them.

"So what is to be done?" he continued. "We called this meeting to offer additional ways we can offer support."

A chieftain from one of the tribes stood up. "You Britannians came here with your weapons, making the raids and bandits worse, only to return and sell us the solution. You show us who you are!"

Murmurs of agreement rose in pockets around the auditorium.

"I understand why you would think that, and all I can say is I'm not here to force anything on you. Any chieftain is free to take up all, some, or none of what we're offering. Consider each part separately, judge their merits, discuss them with your councils, and decide what is best for your individual tribes."

The murmurs didn't silence, but did die down a bit.

"Which brings me to what we've come prepared to offer you. First, we will continue to maintain the forts along the border between your land and Gaul. While we are allies with the tribes there, and hope to have good relations with all of you, we understand that does not remove long-standing difficulties between your two peoples. We also know that, even as the Carthaginians retreated and our line of forts went up, you have not had issues with raids across the mountains to your north. I know that doesn't do much for some of you, of course, but I hope the tribes in central and northern Hispania see the value in this. I also hope that all of you can see the value in making Hispania a self-contained, fortified area, protected from the rest of the continent, allowing your people to work out their own destinies."

More discussion erupted among the tribal leaders. It was impossible for Cormac to tell, but he hoped most of the murmurs were signs of positive reactions to the news.

"Furthermore, we will rebuild Portus Invictus and grant its governance and profits to the tribes collectively, with Britannian assistance. This will give you much easier access to trade with

Britannia through three major ports within easy reach: Portus Invictus, Kalb, and Daramouda. Since both Kalb and Daramouda are under Britannian control, we thought it fitting that at least one of the ports be under local control, so you aren't beholden to our good graces to connect to the wider world," Cormac continued, and then held up his hands as rumblings of unrest started rippling through the audience. "I know how that sounds on the face of it. That we will be 'assisting' you, and some of you take that to mean we are giving it to you in name only while still having control of it. It's a reasonable assumption, but I would suggest you consider that if we give the port to just one tribe or even a set of tribes, it would breed issues with the rest of the tribes, and be seen as Britannia picking a favorite partner or who we think we could control. If we hand it over to all of the tribes and walk away, much like you have continued to have raids, I think it's reasonable to argue that the stronger tribes would take control of the port from the weaker ones, again, effectively having the port under the control of one tribe to the exclusion of others."

Cormac could see the men nodding along with that point.

"Our only goal in assisting you is to act as an intermediary as needed for those that are council appointed and to offer suggestions that you are free to take or dismiss at your leisure, for how to assemble that council. Last, although not part of the offerings to help ease the burdens the raids are causing your people, is something for sale. It isn't, however, military in any way, nor is it connected to the raids. It is something that is on the verge of becoming available to our people, or so I'm told, and we want to give you the same access. By that, I mean you will be able to trade for this at the same time that our own people will. Specifically, it is a set of tools that will allow you to reap far greater crop yields with significantly fewer men, freeing up manpower within your tribes. With that freed up manpower, you can focus on other projects to enhance and improve your own lands."

"That is what we're offering to do to assist all of the communities in Hispania, with one exception. Any new sales of goods, any goods, as well as membership to the ruling council over Portus Invictus, will only be available to tribes who have refrained from initiating hostilities among their neighbors. When we started selling muskets and gunpowder, the agreement we made with each of you was clear. Sales would only happen if your tribe did not initiate hostilities. The sale of weapons has already stopped to those tribes identified as one of those raiding their neighbors and will remain that way until those neighbors agree the hostile tribe no longer poses a threat."

Cormac paused, looking around the room, to make sure his words set in.

"I know this isn't enough, however. Some of the hostile tribes have taken to raiding settlements they know have purchased firearms and gunpowder from us to replenish what they can no longer buy from us. Britannia is offering to patrol any area when requested and will come to the defense of any tribe in good standing, who hasn't attacked their neighbors, if asked."

"Liar," an angry voice called out from the crowd. "You speak of unity and bringing all the tribes together, but then you design tests of loyalty, pitting us against each other."

It took a moment to find the man speaking. When he did find him, Cormac was surprised. The protest came from none other than the representative from the Arandur tribe, the biggest offender when it came to attacking their fellow tribes.

The look on Cormac's face must have been easily read, since the man said, "You may not have said our names, but you have painted my people as one of these aggressors, simply because we have not bowed to your wishes as easily as some of the others. Even though we have not raided any of our neighbors and have, in fact, been raided ourselves, you have labeled us as aggressors and enforced rules that make it impossible for us to defend ourselves against this aggression."

Cormac tried, and knew he failed, to keep the skepticism off his face. Nearly every other tribe in Vettones, the central region of Hispania, and the northern parts of the Turdetani region all agreed the raiders they faced were Arandur. This was clearly a ploy targeting the tribes further east and west, who weren't in direct conflict with their neighbors, perhaps in hopes of upsetting any long-term agreement that would allow their raiding to continue.

"We did not identify you as anything," Cormac replied. "Your own neighbors are the ones who pointed to your people as the primary raiders across central Hispania."

"Lies!" the Arandur man shouted, cutting him off. "Our villages have been raided relentlessly! Our people slaughtered! Yet you take the word of our enemies as truth?"

The crowd erupted into chaos. Cormac was nearly positive no raiding had occurred in their area and that they were behind the raids on their neighbors, but there were enough men from the tribes further out looking interested and concerned that Cormac didn't think he could just dismiss them out of hand.

"Since our goal is to be an independent arbiter and allow the future of Hispania to be guided by its own people, we will not make a decision out of hand. Instead, we will dispatch a representative to determine the truth of these claims. We will continue to withhold any sales or assistance while this is being investigated, but we will not take direct action against your people, even at the request of your neighbors, until we have all of the facts at hand."

"So you will just decide our guilt? You already have our neighbors as puppets, who will attest to anything you direct them to. What is the point of this charade?"

Cormac didn't know if this man thought he could simply talk his way out of any consequences of their actions, but it wasn't working. He was pushing too hard, and the positive response was less than it had been before. He was losing the audience, and he knew it.

"But," the man continued. "We have nothing to hide. We welcome your agents to see for yourselves the lies portrayed against us."

"Good, then it is settled," Cormac said quickly, before the Arandur representative could attempt to sway the audience out again. "Before this council breaks, I say again that we have already been asked to directly intervene on behalf of several of the attacked tribes. We only hold off to make sure we understand the situation fully before acting. This pause will not last forever. Any tribe involved in hostilities against their peaceful neighbors, attacking them unprovoked, will find a Britannian legion at their doorsteps."

He looked across the assembled men, letting that sink in. Some tribes, like the Arandur representative, looked nervous at the pronouncement. Encouragingly, the majority, however, looked hopeful.

It meant they were on the right track. If they could just get these people working together, Hispania would finally have peace.

Chapter 20

Devnum

Lucilla sat alone upon the Imperial throne, the majesty of her office all around her, structured to force audience seekers to look up slightly at the top of the dais. It was designed to put Lucilla in a position of power over those who came before her, and why she'd chosen to hold this particular meeting here today, instead of in her office or one of the quieter corners of the royal palace.

The room wasn't exactly as it was during her normal audiences, however. Gone were the normal courtiers and attendants, petitioners and guards, all of whom filled the hall on audience days. The only other person in the room was Ramirus, who stood beside her chair silently, hands clasped behind his back, passive and serious as always.

Both of their eyes were fixed on the doors to the audience chamber as her guards pushed it open, admitting the former queen of Connacht, who was ushered in. Cool and collected as ever, she walked with her head up and shoulders back, like she was marching into war. Which for her, was probably true.

Lucilla couldn't help but feel a pang of uneasiness as she watched Medb approach. The queen had shown herself capable and even, to a small degree, trustworthy over the last several months, but Lucilla knew she'd never shed her cunning and hunger for power. It made her simultaneously perfect for this assignment and a dangerous gamble.

Just the kind of duality Lucilla hated.

"Medb, thank you for coming," Lucilla said as the former queen stopped in front of the dais, pointedly not kneeling or bowing, as was tradition.

"I'm not sure how much of a choice I had," Medb said, subtly looking at the guards flanking her.

"I believe we sent a messenger with the request and not a guard. These gentlemen are here in a ceremonial capacity only. Thank you both, you may go," Lucilla said to the two guards.

The men offered crisp bows before turning on their heels and marching back the way they came. Medb, for her part, didn't even acknowledge they'd moved.

"I asked you here because I wanted to talk to you about the work you've been doing with Ramirus. He tells me you've done excellent work and are the person to thank for the Ulaid suddenly reversing their previous decision and agreeing to send men, even temporarily, to help ease our manpower situation in Italia. He has spoken highly of your efficiency and dedication in the matter."

"I appreciate his support," Medb said, her tone indicating she did nothing of the sort. "I only had to make a few well-placed suggestions, reminding certain members of the Ulaid delegation as to where their loyalties lie."

"There are only the three of us here, Medb," Lucilla said. "There's no reason to continue playing word games. While Ramirus was right about Senator Fiacha's curating of information to his king and double-dealing, I think your solution ended with better results than what would have happened if I had followed Ramirus's original suggestion of alerting King Conchobar directly. While I'm not sure the end result is what I would have wanted either, it was effective. My only concern is that, in pressuring the Senator, you have potentially set up a situation that could come back and haunt us in the future. Conchobar might not have been pleased to learn what his servant has been doing, but I'm certain he'd be significantly less pleased to know that someone here has subverted him."

"Which is the point I made to Ramirus. I'm not Roman, so the blame can't lie with you or Rome."

"That might work on paper, Medb, but Conchobar will see through that reasoning. He's no fool, and treating him like one, assuming he won't see Fiacha's situation or decision to work with you, as anything other than what it is, is a mistake."

"I'm not sure I'd agree about Conchobar, but what else would you have me do? If you think this is some kind of ploy, like Ramirus keeps hinting at, then run him directly, notify Conchobar, or do whatever else you feel is necessary."

"I'm not suggesting any of those things. Like I said at the outset, both Ramirus and I are happy with how you've decided to handle the situation, and both agree things worked out well enough. I also know you like playing games, sometimes to your own detriment, and would like for you to keep in mind the larger picture at times like this."

"Noted," Medb said flatly.

"I didn't ask you here to lecture you or quibble, Medb. I really do think you did a fantastic job, and I wanted to thank you personally for the excellent work," Lucilla said, resisting the urge to yell at the woman for her stubbornness. "I also wanted to offer you a new challenge that I think you will find particularly appealing."

"I live to serve," Medb said, sarcastically curtsying.

"What I'm about to tell you is not yet common knowledge, and hopefully will not become so before I return. I intend to leave Devnum, and Britannia as a whole soon, to travel to the continent and treat with the Germanic tribes there. Even with the release of more Ulaid warriors, we still desperately need more to reinforce the men already fighting in Italia," Lucilla said, and then paused for a long moment to let her next words stand on their own. "I am planning on leaving you in charge in my absence."

"Me?" Medb blurted out, her shell breaking for the first time ever, true surprise etched on her face.

Lucilla didn't bother holding back a smile. The woman was so maddeningly in control all the time, it was nice to catch her off guard for once.

"Yes, you. You were a queen in your own right and have proven you have both the ability and cunning to handle the job. More importantly, even though you are technically a subject of the Ulaid crown, you have shown you are beholden to none of the three powers of Britannia. That is something my more high-placed subjects have had trouble understanding. I might be the ruler of Rome as well as Britannia, but when it comes to the Empire as a whole, I cannot simply side with my homeland. I have to make decisions that are for the good of the Empire as a whole. I'm not sure anyone else I could appoint would understand that, and I don't know if our Empire would survive if they didn't. I don't think you will have the same dilemma."

"When you say you will be leaving me in charge, what exactly do you expect me to do?" Medb asked, her surprise again disappearing behind a mask of control.

"You will manage the Empire as a whole. Ramirus and my advisors will manage Rome in my absence while you look to the needs of Britannia. You will handle audiences, manage the bureaucracy, and keep the Senate on track. You'll intercede as needed and deal with any diplomatic needs that arise. I am leaving you with the full authority to make decisions as you see fit."

"Thank you for putting your trust in me," Medb said, all but vibrating as she struggled to hold back her obvious excitement.

"Don't sound too eager too quickly," Lucilla warned. "I know the thing you want, more than anything, is to rule once more. To sit upon a throne and wield power as you did before. While this opportunity does give you a taste of that responsibility and authority again, I need you to understand that it is temporary. I will be watching closely, as will others, and if we detect any attempt to overstep your bounds or try to gain more advantage than what I have granted, there will be consequences."

Medb's expression hardened at Lucilla's words, but she remained silent.

"Both Faenius and Ramirus will have the authority to remove you, with force if necessary, if you resist or scheme against them. King Conchobar and King Talogren, along with Taenaris and Rotri, will be notified of the situation and will not tolerate any games or manipulation from you either. While Fiacha will also be notified, to keep up the fiction of his independence, I think you will understand that any use of him to counter concerns of the others will also trigger your immediate removal. Consider this yet another test, Medb. You now have a chance to participate more fully in the governance of this Empire, to have real responsibility and yes, even a measure of power. But it will only continue if you stay within the clearly defined bounds I have set. Should you decide to grasp for more, to overplay your hand, this opportunity and any future chances will disappear."

Knowing that Medb was smart enough to read between the lines, Lucilla left it unsaid that her head could follow those chances if the offense was grievous enough.

"If, however, you serve faithfully and work for the good of Britannia, not just your personal interests, you will find me to be a generous and supportive patron, with the full might of Rome and the Empire behind you. The choice is yours, Medb. Tread carefully."

"Don't worry, Your Majesty, I'll be a good girl," she said condescendingly, bowing slightly.

"For your sake, I hope so."

The former queen turned and walked out of the audience chamber. Lucilla watched her go, uncertain if this was a wise move to counter the other members of the Empire and those in her own government who might use this moment as an opportunity, or a foolhardy rationalization that would doom all of Britannia.

Hofstadir, Svealand Region, Scandia

Yrsa guided his horse along the winding dirt road, flanked on either side by dense birch forests, trying to push off the bad mood that had settled in days ago and refused to leave. He'd already been sent packing, making no progress, from the largest trading ports in the Agder and Rygjafylke regions, both of which were on the sea facing Britannia and did the most trade with the Empire. He'd hoped that would have meant they would be the most likely to hear out his argument, but that hadn't been the case.

Yrsa wasn't even sure why he was taking this personally. He'd told the Empress how unlikely it was that any of his people, who were traders and isolationists when it came to anything beyond trading, almost to a fault, would agree to help. But now that he'd taken on her pointless mission, some part of him had decided to take it seriously, which meant when the inevitable failures came, it only served to annoy him.

This was the first non-port city, even though it was still essentially a fishing village at its heart, sitting on the shores of Lake Mälaren, because it also happened to be a major religious hub. Yrsa hoped that the wise men here would see things more clearly than the secular elders at the trading ports.

He had to admit, as he broke through the tree line and looked out at the cleared area around the village, that it was a beautiful place. Modest timber longhouses, workshops, and storehouses formed a loose ring around the village center—a large earthen mound capped by an ornate structure of carved wood and stone. It was the building on the mound that brought most of the people currently in the village here, since more than half the people in Hofstadir were not from here directly.

Which also meant hardly anyone took notice of him and the small party that had set out from his ship that morning.

Yrsa dismounted, his group tying the reins of the horses they had rented from a farmer at the port, leaving his men behind to watch them as he and his first mate made their way up the gravel path to the top of the mound, which was currently cluttered with people.

The largest group was gathered around an older man, who was speaking to each in turn. Yrsa, not a particularly religious man, had never been here, but he could recognize a wise man when he saw one, stood in line to wait. Yrsa must have stood out, dressed finer than most of the peasants who'd made the pilgrimage to the site, or maybe just because of his size, because the elder excused himself from the farmers and craftsmen as soon as he saw the captain, making his way over to them.

"I am Bjarki, the Goði of the shrine. I welcome you both as strangers and friends."

Yrsa inclined his head respectfully. "Thank you. I am Yrsa, a trader and ship's captain. I have been asked to come and speak to the villages of Scandi on behalf of the Britannian Empire across the Herring Sea, to treat with leaders of larger villages. May we speak for a few moments?"

The man looked surprised but nodded and beckoned Yrsa to follow. Yrsa wasn't sure if the surprise was because a clearly Scandi captain represented a foreign interest or because, landlocked as they were, he was unaware of Britannia, but either way, it did not start off their discussions on the correct footing.

People were scattered throughout the main section of the longhouse, performing various rituals. Bjarki mostly ignored them, leading Yrsa and his first mate to a small side room, not much bigger than his cabin aboard the Skinbladnir, taking a seat on a small bench, which left Yrsa to stand. Had he been younger, Yrsa might have thought that a power play, but the man was seemingly ancient and had all but shuffled his way through the longhouse. Yrsa wasn't sure he would have been able to stand through the entire discussion.

"What does your Empress want with our small villages?" the man asked as he settled himself.

"I am not Britannian."

"My apologies. What does their Empress want from us?"

"I've been sent here to offer an alliance of sorts, to any village that wants it. Britannia is currently at war with Carthage, which as …"

"I'm aware of what is happening to the south," the man said, surprising Yrsa.

"Ohh, umm," Yrsa fumbled, a little, taken off guard. "Well, the Britannians are on the verge of taking the fight to Carthage itself. However, they're taxed to their limits for manpower against the juggernaut that is Carthage. They're asking for any men who can be sent to help. These men will not be used in the war itself and will only help keep the peace in villages and towns where the Carthaginians have withdrawn, leaving chaos in their wake."

For a moment, the man said nothing, only staring at Yrsa. The silence went on long enough that Yrsa worried he might not have heard him or was feeble in some way.

The captain looked to his first mate and was about to repeat himself when Bjarki asked, "Why is a Scandi captain the messenger of this foreign empire? Why would they not send one of their own?"

This comment did not catch Yrsa off guard and had been one asked by each of the other villagers he'd visited.

"Many of our neighbors have migrated to Britannia, which is undergoing a dramatic shift. New technology and ideas taking hold there have presented enormous opportunities for our people to gain wealth and stability, drawing many Scandi, along with people from across the continent, to the Empire. I have not migrated there permanently, as have so many others, but the Britannians have done well by me, and their Empress felt it better to send one of our own people rather than a Britannian to make the request."

"Does the wealth you've received from the Britannians make you invested in their success, and therefore not a remote third party?"

"I never said I was an uninterested party. I do seek to gain from the Britannian's success, but that doesn't make my interest toward my people here any less real. I've seen our countrymen do well in Britannia, and I'd like some of that success to find its way back here to Scandi."

"You said they are requesting men to help keep the peace while they finish their war," the wise man said, again not addressing Yrsa's words directly. "Temporary has a strange way of becoming permanent, and how much can the people who die in someone else's war profit from the spoils of that war?"

This Yrsa had heard from the other villagers as well. Even with that, he still didn't have a good response for it. The wise man was right, it was impossible to tell how long any people who agreed to travel south and work as peacekeepers would have to remain there.

"Our people are farmers and merchants," Bjarki continued. "Craftsmen and traders. We have never been ones to fight someone else's wars so far from home. That has always been left to the likes of the Greeks."

"You haven't seen the technology they are offering. Medicines, tools for farming, better implements for hunting. It will change every settlement that receives them. The benefits to Scandi would make up—"

"No benefits can make up for death," Bjarki said, cutting him off. "Pitting our village, or Scandi as a whole, against someone else's enemy can only cost our people."

It may have been a more eloquent and less greedy of a response, but it was no different than he'd heard at the last two villages. The war was far away and someone else's problem having nothing to do with Scandi or her people.

"I know you feel this conflict does not involve our people directly," Yrsa said, trying to change track. "But I have sailed the seas and witnessed the devastation firsthand. Entire villages razed, fields salted and burned. Mothers clutching starving children, fleeing for their lives. Innocents slaughtered or sold into slavery by the thousands. The Carthaginians show no mercy, not even to their own people who get in the way of their ambitions."

Bjarki's face remained impassive, but Yrsa pressed on.

"I understand your desire to protect your people above all else, but this is bigger than any one village or region. The Carthaginian war machine will not stop until it controls the entirety of the known world. Nowhere will be safe, not even frozen Scandi. Britannia represents our best chance to stop this," Yrsa said, kneeling down to look at the wise man directly. "You, of all people, who speak for the gods, who tell them our sorrows and ask for their help, must understand how important this is. Why it must be done."

"Our gods," Bjarki finally said. "Those who watch over our people. The Britannians worship other gods, who have failed them. The all-father only cares for his people and would not want to send his children to their deaths to make up for some other gods' shortcomings. I'm sorry, but as much as my heart may go out to them, my duty is to my people, here. I must say 'no.'"

Yrsa collected himself, standing and nodding solemnly.

"I understand. Thank you for your time."

"I'm sorry I must send you away empty-handed. I will pray to the gods for your safe travels."

"Thank you," Yrsa said, giving the man a final nod before leaving the room and the longhouse altogether.

"Send word to all the merchant captains and trading concerns we know," Yrsa said to his first mate as soon as they were outside.

"Along with any Scandi merchants they're acquainted with. I want a meeting, and soon. Make sure they know this has to do with the future of trade with Britannia as a whole."

"There were some captains I know in port when we left. They should still be there when we get back. I'll spread the word as soon as we get there."

"Good. We also need to head back to Britannia and meet with the Empress. What we're doing here isn't working, but I have an idea that might. I need her input though, if we're going to make it work."

Chapter 21

Northern Italy

Ky waited outside the large headquarters tent at the center of the sprawling encampment, looking through the rows of men and material as he watched the small procession making its way toward him.

They'd been in this camp for weeks now, and as all camps did, it had started to solidify as soldiers built semi-permanent structures here and there to make their lives a little more comfortable, replacing the portable and more rugged materials used when the legions were on the move. Normally, Ky took it as a sign of soldiers' ingenuity, something he could connect to his life before, in the distant future. War and technology might have changed, but soldiers were still soldiers, regardless of the time period.

Now, however, their activity signaled something else. Something that troubled him more every single day. It showed how inactive the legions had become. They were at the height of the campaigning season and nothing was moving. Even his lead elements, which were instructed to keep pushing south, had only just now started to cross into central Italy, a month behind schedule. The entire campaign had ground to a halt, and Ky was beyond frustrated.

He tried to keep those thoughts off his face as his commanders, or at least some of them, separated themselves from their traveling parties and approached. It did say something about each man's organization and attention to detail that, even though they all came from different areas of the peninsula, they'd all arrived at roughly the same time. That, at least, could make him smile.

"Gentlemen, I appreciate your promptness," Ky said, reaching out and clasping each of their arms in turn before beckoning them into the command tent. "Let's get started."

Ky led the group inside the tent, where a large table dominated the center, maps and reports scattered across it. Normally, they all just stood through these conferences, but Ky knew they'd all been on the road, in Bomilcar's case for a full day, and would be tired, so he gestured for the men to take seats he'd provided.

"Gentlemen, I don't need to tell you that things haven't been going well as of late," Ky began, the frustration evident in his voice. "We all had a brief moment of hope when some of the villages started to sway toward the Britannians, but things have since fallen apart. Marcus, would you please explain what's been happening?"

Marcus nodded, his expression grim. "We've been making headway in some of the villages, turning things around. Villages were starting to work with us and attacks on our men became less frequent. We'd hoped this was a sign things were starting to ease up and that we'd again be able to concentrate our forces and move south faster. Unfortunately, this is no longer the case. We've found the cooperation short-lived in nearly every instance. Things go well at first, but after a few weeks, word begins to spread about the work we're doing in a given village. Inevitably, after our people pull back to the camps for the night, dissidents and Carthaginians show up and slaughter everyone who cooperated with the legions. Worse, other villages have started to take notice. Even those that seemed like they might be receptive to working with us have pulled back. People are afraid to work with us."

"Is it still so bad that we have to remain in camps overnight, instead of staying in these villages permanently?" Bomilcar, who'd remained focused on the push south, asked. "Couldn't we pull our men out of their camps and deploy them in the villages them-selves, to protect the people there?"

"I wish it were that simple," Ky said. "We can't spare enough men to be in every village, and the Carthaginians just hit the ones where we aren't present. And that's in the villages that are friendly to us, or were friendly. Some villages are still openly hostile, attacking any soldiers we try to station there. It requires too many men to secure just one village."

"We're attempting to try and stop them," Aelius said. "My men have begun patrolling the outlying areas, and at first, we were able to catch and defeat some of the dissidents and Carthaginians, but it's started to become more difficult. The enemy knows we're coming, warned by non-violent sympathizers, and they simply fade away into the countryside before we arrive. They have too many allies among the locals. To truly secure the region, I'd need at least three or four full legions concentrated here, and even with that, it would likely take the rest of the campaigning season."

Bomilcar leaned forward and asked, "In light of this, should we stop advancing? My lead elements are already nearing Rome and I could have the city enveloped within the next few days, but taking the city is going to either take manpower or brutality. You've ordered against the second and from the sound of the situation, we don't have the resources for the first."

"What have your men seen of the city?"

"The Carthaginians have fortified the city with massive walls, which won't pose a problem for our cannons, but the collateral damage to the city will be ... substantial. Beyond that, we're looking at needing an envelopment and prolonged siege to take it."

"No. Continue your operations, but do your best to minimize civilian casualties and damage to the city. I know it will slow things down, but we've already got a problem with public opinion, and it's only going to get worse if we level the city in the process. If we need to divert some units back to you for the encirclement, we can. Does it look like the city itself is going to hold up and try to keep you out, or are the Carthaginians still in place? And if so, do they show any signs of continuing their retreat?"

"It's hard to say yet. The Carthaginians are still in the city and have been gathering supplies, I assume to outlast our siege, but until we start to envelop them, we won't know if their forces will retreat south again or if they plan on making a stand there."

"Move quickly to surround the city, if you can. The further south we go, the more spread out we get. If we can stop them now, in central Italia, and defeat the bulk of their forces, we'll have less to worry about later, when you've had to shed more manpower to control the countryside."

"As you order, Consul," Bomilcar said, sounding unconvinced.

"I know this is all disheartening, and you're all frustrated," Ky said, seeing the faces of his commanders. "Believe me, I had hoped we would be further along by now as well, but you are all doing well. We're behind schedule, but we are not stopped yet. We haven't passed the point where we can take Italia and still make it to Africa this year. It might mean fighting there in the late fall, but the weather there won't turn against us as early as it did in Germania. Keep pushing, keep your men moving, and by the gods, we will see the Carthaginians fall this year."

They all looked at least somewhat buoyed by Ky's pronouncement. Ky just hoped he'd be able to deliver on his promise. Right now, he didn't know if he could.

Londinium

A large crowd gathered around the newly built station, cheering wildly as the first train pulled into it. Hortensius, standing near the door of one of the cars, watched them, happy to see the reception.

They had been met with a variety of emotions during the long months they'd worked on the line, from fear to outright anger. The one thing they hadn't gotten a lot of was enthusiasm. He understood why. Besides the rails changing the very landscape these people had lived in for generations, the train itself, with its loud sounds and belching smoke, could be frightening. The closer they'd gotten to London, the more people they'd had come out to watch the supply trains arrive with more material for the track, but he hadn't imagined enough had inured themselves to the sight of the gigantic metal beasts to have this kind of reaction.

He also knew the Empress, after the trouble he'd had with farmers and landholders along the way, had sent forth emissaries and heralds to talk to the people of Londinium, beating the drum of progress, as she'd put it. But he'd thought that would have limited success. He was happy to see he was wrong, and once again happy to see his ruler had a better handle on the emotions of her people than he ever would.

The train pulled to a full stop and Hortensius stepped out onto the platform. Since he hadn't expected this kind of reception, he hadn't prepared for it, but it definitely seemed like a moment that needed some kind of pronouncement.

The crowd cheered as they saw him step out of the train. He was pretty sure most did not know who he was. Outside of Factorium, he tended to take a back seat to politicians and other public figures. There were some dignitaries up front who he'd worked with and spoken to from time to time, including the duumviri, a pair of the top elected officials in the city, the city prefect appointed by the Empress, and the aediles, who'd handled the day-to-day operations in the city, and who he'd worked with the closest to finalize the platform construction and final track laying.

But for each of those, there were a dozen or more of what looked like normal citizens, who probably had no clue who he was. He knew he was being cheered mostly because he had stepped out of the first train they had ever seen and seemed to be in charge, but it was a strange feeling. He held up his hands to quiet them, a wide smile crossing his face.

"My friends, this is a momentous day for our great Empire! For months now, our team of engineers and workers have toiled endlessly along the route from the capital to finish this great project. They have crossed rivers, cut through hills, and laid mile after mile of rails across the countryside to bring this modern wonder to your very doorsteps!"

The crowd cheered again and Hortensius let their enthusiasm wash over him for a moment before continuing.

"I know many of you have heard about the train and what you can expect, and I am here to tell you that what you have heard is true. What used to be a week-long journey to the capital can now be done in a single day, with stops along the way at major towns and settlements, allowing families, merchants, and farmers to travel the length of our Empire quickly, opening up opportunities of all types to every Britannian. Goods from Factorium will now be able to come here in large quantities without the need for trains of wagons spending long days hauling them, making the things you've asked for, the new innovations and products, more readily available and less expensive. It will allow the city's port, already on the precipice of becoming the largest in the Empire, to grow even faster, since it will be faster and cheaper for goods to come here by train than by ship or mule. Food will be more readily available, arriving, in some cases, the same day it was picked from the fields to your very doorstep."

The crowd cheered again, whistling and clapping, as Hortensius listed off all the benefits they were likely to reap from the finished train line.

"Let this accomplishment stand as a symbol of our Empire's spirit of innovation and progress! United as one people, there is no feat of engineering we cannot achieve, no challenge we cannot overcome. Just as the iron road connects our lands, let it bring us closer in camaraderie and prosperity. We embark, now, into an exciting new era of industry and advancement. The future is ours, friends!"

Hortensius thrust his fists into the air triumphantly. The crowd responded with a deafening roar.

One of the men in charge of running the station then announced that tickets for the train's return trip to Factorium and Devnum were available, almost causing a stampede as the crowd pushed and shoved to be allowed to get theirs, forcing Hortensius back aboard the train car reserved for him and his men. He even took the precaution of barring the door as the crowd swirled around the train.

He understood their enthusiasm, but doubted this many people all needed to go to Devnum or Factorium. More likely, they wanted to be one of the first to take the train or were just excited for the opportunity. Either way, he'd seen how people's enthusiasm could sometimes cause unintended devastation, and he had no interest in being trampled in the chaos.

"Well, that certainly was exciting," Hortensius said, sitting on one of the cushioned benches in the specially designed car for dignitaries, resembling more a fine carriage, only larger, compared to the wagon-like seating with people packed in rows in the other cars.

"I want to commend you all on your amazing work," Hortensius said to the engineers, mostly his managers who'd overseen the day-to-day deployment of this rail line. "You should be proud of yourselves for a job well done. And you know what that means."

It was an old joke of his, and elicited a groan from the assembled men, who knew what was coming next.

"Exactly," Hortensius said. "More work. This line is only partially finished. The Empress has charged us with extending the line north from Devnum to Monadhcarden before we begin constructing separate, crossing or spur lines. I'm sure I don't need to point out that this will be a new challenge with a whole lot of new problems we're going to have to overcome. Caledonia has a very different landscape than we've dealt with so far, and I'm all but certain we're going to have new challenges to deal with. Even those challenges we've already bested, bridging and tunneling, will be taken to new levels. While Tasius begins assembling supplies and starting the line out of Devnum, the rest of us will go ahead and scout the proposed route north. I want every bridge, tunnel, and grading needed to be mapped out ahead of time. The Empress has promised the chieftain of Caledonia that we will have this finished by the harvest, and I am not going to disappoint her. Is that clear?"

Hortensius smiled as the engineers groaned exaggeratedly. Though the work was hard, he knew they took pride in their accomplishments.

"I never doubted that you lads were up to it," Hortensius said, clapping the shoulder of the engineer nearest him. "You should all be proud of yourselves. You've brought Britannia into a new era. We're shaping the future here."

This time, the men dropped all pretenses. They loved their work, even when it remained behind the scenes, unrecognized. To see it so visibly though, not only praised but truly appreciated. That was an engineer's dream.

Neitin, Vettones Region, Central Hispania

The small village of Neitin sat a few miles north of Arandur, one of a number of satellite settlements that had sprung up from Arandur itself as it began the slow transition from a single village to a full, region-spanning tribe.

Llassar had seen the same thing happen in his homeland, having witnessed Talogren's own tribe expand in a similar way during his lifetime. True, it had taken the Consul and the Romans to accelerate that from being regional to the entirety of northern Britannia, but Llassar thought it was likely to have happened naturally on its own, just at a slower pace.

One thing he'd learned was how disruptive that entire experience was to the other villages nearby. Places like Arandur did not exist in a vacuum, and to grow and expand, they had to either replace or subsume the people already in the places they wanted to expand into.

Unfortunately, this had suddenly become a different world. Ky had begun to usher in a time where trade and mutual cooperation could lead to greater prosperity for tribes than conquering weaker neighbors and taking whatever they could. It wasn't only the Consul. The Carthaginians had shown that the more a civilization conquered to grow, the more they had to conquer, as the weight of all the peoples they drained of resources grew like stones around their neck, until they eventually ran out of victims and collapsed in on themselves.

That was fine for people like the Romans, who'd already grown to a size to put themselves in a position of leadership, tribes already forced to cooperate for self-survival like Caledonia had been or Germania was, and of course, the smaller tribes, whose very existence was allowed to continue, but was very much a negative for tribes like the Arandur. On the verge of growing into something more, they could only see how the new paradigm limited them.

Llassar pulled his small command up short as they arrived at the outskirts of the village. Had it been up to Llassar, he would have left them behind and come on his own, but considering the raids and banditry, he'd been forced to agree they were necessary. His main worry had been, regardless of whether the Arandur were making up being attacked or if it had really happened, that these people would be on edge when he arrived. If he was going to find out what happened, he needed them talking, and a bunch of foreign soldiers would not help that.

He was proven right, however, once they arrived and found a dozen warriors waiting for him, all seemingly on edge, hands never far from a weapon.

"Decanus, please keep your men here, outside of town," Llassar said to the leader of the squads that had accompanied him.

Llassar dismounted and approached the waiting warriors, raising a hand in greeting. Their leader, a tall man with a prominent scar across his face, stepped forward to meet him.

"I am Ambatus. The elders await you," he said brusquely, then turned to lead Llassar into the village without further niceties.

The rest of the warriors crowded in around Llassar as Ambatus escorted him toward the center of the village. Llassar had expected the crowd with them to grow as they went further into the village, as curious people wanted to see more of the stranger entering their home and to find out what was happening. In a village like this, so similar to the one he'd grown up in, gossip was possibly the most valuable commodity.

Instead, the few people he could see shied away from the crowd. They were clearly curious, stretching their necks to try and catch a glimpse of him, but none tried to join their procession, their fear clearly greater than their curiosity.

Ambatus brought Llassar to a large roundhouse at the center of the village, three elderly men stood outside, their bearded faces somber and lined with age. They inclined their heads in solemn greeting.

"I am Neton," the one in the center said, before gesturing to the other two men. "And this is Caros and Turibel. We were told you would be coming to see the aftermath of the raid, and that we were to cooperate with you fully."

"I'd also like to interview some of your people who saw the raid in person."

There was a small look between Caros and Turibel, but Neton didn't flinch. "Fine. Ambatus will show you around."

As with their servant, the three men had nothing else to say. They simply turned and walked away, back into the roundhouse. Llassar found their attitudes a little confounding. He'd talked with the leaders of the southern tribes, even the ones who were incensed that Britannian weapons were being used against their people, and they hadn't had nearly this kind of reaction. The leaders of the Arandur all but demanded someone come see what was done here, and now that Llassar was here, he was treated as if he were a nuisance, rather than something they demanded.

Ambatus began to show Llassar around the damaged area, most of which seemed to be on the north side of the village. Llassar had to admit, the damage met with what Llassar would have expected of a raid. A few burned-down huts, the doors to a storage barn ripped off, the building seemingly empty except for a few grain kernels and a little fodder that would have spilled from their containers. Some of the huts in this area had makeshift doors over their entrances that looked new, as if recently put into place.

From his experience, raiders, real raiders, didn't just burn a settlement to the ground. They might burn one or two buildings if the inhabitants fought back too much or to create a bulwark between themselves and the rest of the village that might be trying to rally against them, but the destruction wasn't wanton. They mostly broke into homes and storage centers to steal goods and take captives, and their hands would be full as they left the village, making it harder for them to destroy it on the way out.

The people, however, were more interesting. He could see villagers peering out through gaps in walls or hovering in anxious clusters, many sporting crude bandages over wounds. The sense he was getting, above all else, was one of fear.

"Tell me again about the attack," he asked Ambatus and his men as they walked. "How many raiders were there?"

"I did not count each man. But many, mostly armed with your damnable weapons."

"Enough to overwhelm three bands worth of warriors," one of the warriors said.

"And no one identified symbols or markings to indicate which tribe they belonged to?"

"Why would they identify themselves when they are here to kill our men and take our women," Ambatus said. "One of the northern tribes, I think."

"We have records of who we sold weapons to. If we gave you a list, could you pick out which tribe specifically?"

"No. We don't trade or mix with those dogs."

"I understand there's a fairly large gap between you and the northern tribes, more than between you and the southern ones. It seems a very long way to come for a raid to steal supplies and captives. Did you see wagons or something else they might use to carry off their spoils?"

Instead of answering directly, Ambatus bristled at the question. "You think we are mistaken about who attacked us without cause? Or mayhap you think we are lying?"

"I am simply trying to understand the full truth of what happened here. If I could speak to some of the survivors, who saw the men up close, that would help."

For a moment, Llassar thought Ambatus was going to decline the request, glaring at him the way the Hispanian was, but then he nodded once and turned, leading Llassar to a set of huts on the very edge of the village.

These were some of the worst damaged huts, with the one he stopped at missing the door, with ax markings in the wood next to the doorway, showing the kind of violence that had happened here. The hut that had been next to it was one of the ones that had been put to the torch, burned to the ground until only a sooty outline remained.

A young woman stood inside the door, holding the cloth that had been hung over it aside as they approached. She had her arm in a sling and a large bandage on her other arm. Llassar motioned for Ambatus and his men to wait where they were, so he could talk to the woman alone. The warrior clearly did not like being told what to do, but stopped and held his ground.

"May I know your name?" Llassar asked the woman gently as he approached her.

She hesitated before replying, "I am Numa."

"Numa, can you tell me what happened during the attack?"

She didn't answer right away, casting her eyes down and slumping a little. When she did look up, she didn't look at Llassar right away, but instead looked past him, to Ambatus and the warriors, before finally answering.

"Many men came, yelling and carrying loud weapons that struck men down at a distance. They broke into homes looking for food or whatever they could take. Some of our warriors tried to fight but were killed. They cut down my door. My husband tried to fight back but … he wasn't able to stop them from … what they did."

She started crying. Llassar waited patiently for her to regain control, which was faster than he would have thought. She seemed to will herself to stop crying as she again looked past him to Ambatus.

"Did you see any of the raiders up close?"

"Only for a moment, when one dragged me from my home. He wore strange clothing and had coloring I did not recognize."

Llassar had met villagers from the north, all of whom seemed to dress more-or-less similarly to the people here. Had he not been told they were from different villages, he would have assumed they were all neighbors. The elder had also mentioned they'd had some dealing with the northern tribes in the past, and seemed acquainted with them enough that they were recognizable to him.

Which made her claim that they wore 'strange clothing' and 'unknown coloring' unusual, at best. Even if they were all on horseback and had wagons to carry off goods, they wouldn't have come from that far away. It also was hard to tell how much was taken. From what Llassar could see, the 'devastating raid' had penetrated only a little into the north end of the village, with the rest, including the largest storehouses of food supplies closer to the center of the village, completely untouched.

The story remained much the same as he stopped to talk to other people affected by the attack. All bore injuries and seemed genuinely afraid, but were less focused on telling him what had happened than keeping their eyes on Ambatus and the rest of his 'escorts.'

After the fifth nearly identical, word for word, account of what happened, Llassar gave up and returned to where Ambatus and the other warriors waited. What bothered him the most was that, although the village itself suffered limited damage, the people he'd been sent to speak to had very real injuries. If this was what it was starting to smell like, it made Llassar angry that a community could treat their members like this.

"Thank you for allowing me to speak with the survivors," Llassar said to Ambatus, not letting his face communicate what he was feeling.

"Did they provide the proof you need of the crimes committed against us?"

"Yes, they shared their experiences and I will be sure to inform my superiors about what I have seen."

"Good," the man said, as stoic as he had been the entire time.

The warriors followed him through the village only leaving his side when he passed the southern border where his men waited for his return.

The Decanus straightened as Llassar approached. "How bad was it?"

Llassar mounted his horse before replying. "Nonexistent."

"Really? Some of the villagers came close to us while heading out to their fields, or wherever, and were talking about all the injured and dead."

"How convenient," Llassar said. "I have enough to report back to the prince. I think we should try and leave Arandur territory as quickly as possible though."

Llassar turned his horse to ride south, glancing back one last time. The warriors of Arandur stood together at the edge of the village, woodenly watching their departure. It was unlikely they'd be foolish enough to do anything, but Llassar was no actor, and knew he didn't hide his incredulity as much as he should have.

What these people had done had been short-sighted, the act of people reacting and not thinking their actions through.

People like that could be unpredictable, and unpredictable people could be dangerous.

Chapter 22

Wendhom, Anglii Territory, Germania

In spite of the warm mid-summer temperatures, Lucilla pulled her cloak tightly against herself as she stepped off the gangplank. As soon as they docked, she could see that the vast majority of the ships here were unloading cargo and not passengers, making her appearance noticeable. It was made all the worse by Modius and Cynwrig following behind her. Even cloaked and not armored, neither could hide what they were, which made Lucilla glad she'd stood firm against Modius's insistence that they bring even more of her people along.

They'd barely stepped off the ship and already she felt like every eye in Germania was on her. It wasn't until she got to the bottom of the gangplank, however, that she realized that at least two of those eyes were definitely staring directly at her. Although she might have kept her head down anyway, to keep from being recognized, she'd been forced to keep looking down as she walked off the ship, focusing on keeping her balance as she made her way down the rickety gangplank.

She finally looked up as her foot hit the dock and found herself staring directly into the face of Yrsa, the Scandi captain. She stopped so suddenly, in surprise, that Modius and Cynwrig almost slammed into her, both being forced to hop off the gangplank and onto the dock on either side of her to avoid the collision.

"Captain Yrsa," she said, quickly recovering her composure. "What are you doing here?"

Yrsa gave a bow, smiling slightly, and said, "I was actually on my way to Britannia to see you when I heard that you were, in fact, already on your way here. I thought it easier, for me at least, to come straight to Wendhom and meet you when you docked."

"How did you know I was coming here at all, let alone which ship to meet?"

"Come now, Your Majesty, you must know how sailors like to talk, and nearly every vessel that trades between Britannia and the continent has some kind of connection to one another. The old trading families are so intermarried, at this point, that we're all essentially one people now. There was little to no chance that you could board one of those ships and the other captains not find out."

Lucilla pressed her lips together, annoyed. She had paid well for the ship captain's discretion, above and beyond the exorbitant cost she'd agreed to pay for the transportation itself. The fact that he had talked anyway was more than a little unsettling. Beside her, she could feel Modius shifting, probably checking for the dozens of assassins he was now sure lurked among the dockhands and sailors.

"Don't worry, Your Highness. They wouldn't have spoken about it to their crews. Captains are a gossipy lot, but usually only among other captains. It's difficult to maintain discipline among these rabble if you socialize too frequently," Yrsa said, waving indistinctly at the various sailors scattered across the docks.

"I see," Lucilla said, not entirely convinced. "I guess since you found me, I should hear what you needed to speak to me about. I assume it has to do with the mission I sent you on to your Scandi countrymen."

"It does. I'm afraid my efforts met with little success. While eager to maintain free and open trade, most are reluctant to officially back either side in the war. Some because they don't want to become embroiled in it themselves, and others because ... well, because they want to keep selling to both sides."

"They understand if Carthage wins, it is only a matter of time until they make it north to your homeland, right? To the Carthaginians, there are only two types of people, subjects and victims."

"I did explain that. Most have their heads buried below decks, refusing to look out at the horizon. The ones selling to both sides, I believe, think they will be the exception to the rule. In fact, I believe some of those have already begun selling some of the things they've learned from you. I believe they were the source of the Carthaginians' swift copies of your inventive sail plans."

"Do you think they are behind the sudden appearance of gunpowder in Carthaginian hands?"

"I don't think so. I've heard rumors that it isn't resold Britannian product. Some of the men who've seen it have pointed out how much lower quality and volatile it is. And I don't think my people could have copied it like they did the sail plan. While that was inventive, it's not that much different than the sails we used before. Once we saw them in use, it wasn't hard to work out what you did and what made these sails different. The gunpowder, however, is completely foreign, like nothing we've seen before. Even though I know what goes into it, I would have no idea how to make that into actual gunpowder. So no, I don't think my people did that."

"I see," Lucilla said.

Part of her wished they had, simply because it would explain the mystery behind the Carthaginians' possession of it, which had baffled even Ky. Yrsa was right that it was a lower quality, but the fact that they had it at all was concerning, since both Ky and Sophus had thought that the 'reverse engineering' of it, to use their phrase, was unlikely.

"I do believe, however, that I have a plan that might work, but I wanted your input on it before I tried. Which is why I was heading back to Britannia when I heard word of your coming here."

"What exactly do you have in mind?" she asked.

"I think we should speak to the merchant captains who've been benefiting from trade with Britannia. The captains and most of the larger merchant concerns are run by families that wield a lot of influence across Scandia. While the village leaders might not listen to me, as I've always been something of a cast-off, they have to listen to the families. Most of the taxes and trade through their villages are at the whims of these merchant families. If one decides to pack up and move to another port, it isn't unheard of for the previous port to dry up and become abandoned. If they can convince their home villages to assist us with manpower, I suggest we offer them some of the things we've offered the Germanic tribes.

"Such as?" Lucilla asked.

"For one, the same lower tariff that tribes in Germania have been receiving. It's something they've been grumbling about all winter, since the local Germanic traders have often been able to undercut them since getting that benefit."

"Which they got in exchange for supporting our war effort," Lucilla pointed out.

"Exactly, which is why it is a good opening offer to the families. Beyond that, I think we also need to allow them to buy muskets and gunpowder. I know," he said quickly, as she began to protest. "I know the sales of it have been limited because you didn't want to face your own products but with Cormac selling them in Hispania and the sales we've made here in Germania, you've lost control of that. Even gunpowder is being sold second-hand. Not a lot, but some. I'm assuming that is why you've only sold the muskets, and not your much better rifles, or the newer cannon that just started showing up. What Hortensius's factors called howitzers, I believe. You knew this was inevitable."

"Fine, anything else?" Lucilla asked.

He was right, of course. Ky had already pointed out that no matter how much they restricted it, the proliferation of those weapons was inevitable. As much as she liked Captain Yrsa, she didn't want to admit that to him, though. Especially now that she knew how free he and the other Scandi merchants were about sharing information with one another.

"Yes. I know it's not practical to do now, with the navy still growing, but we could promise, once the war is over, to allow Scandi merchants, or really merchants of any of our allies, to buy caravels or other new ship designs that come along. I see the way my countrymen look at those massive ships. As much envy as there is toward my schooner, the idea of the mass that can be transported on one of those ships is mind-boggling. This, I think, would be the thing that pushes them over the edge to really put pressure on the villages where they're based."

Lucilla was quiet for a minute, thinking. It wasn't surprising that he was asking for similar provisions to those they were already giving out to others. Lucilla hadn't offered those up front, because it would be harder to control on a village-by-village basis, which was essentially what Scandi was. Not pressured to form more comprehensive alliances with neighbors the way the people of Germania and Hispania had been, there was too little cohesion to force controls she wanted in place for the sale of weapons and tools that could be used directly against them.

"I agree that allowing Scandi merchants access to our muskets and gunpowder is sensible," Lucilla said. "You're right that we've already lost control of the spread of that technology. I'm also amenable to lowering tariffs, eventually allowing access to our ship designs, and the other concessions you outlined."

"Good," Yrsa started to say, before Lucilla held up a hand.

"However, I do not want to negotiate agreements piecemeal with individual villages. If one village goes rogue and violates our arrangement, I want recourse beyond just cutting off trade to that specific village. We learned that lesson already in Hispania. When Cormac allowed tribes to purchase weapons individually, some used them against neighboring tribes, despite promises to the contrary, and it has caused unrest across the entire region. The tribes that upheld their word had no power to stop those who did not. I will not repeat that mistake here."

"Then what would you accept?"

"I am willing to make an agreement with a coalition of Scandi villages and merchants. Sell to any traders who are part of that organized group, that way there are consequences if any village breaks their word. If one village betrays our arrangement, tariffs return and sales halt for the entire coalition until amends are made. It is the only way to give your people incentive to police their own actions. Additionally, any Scandi village must be eligible to join this coalition, and none can be barred from entry. But any can also be removed by vote if they undermine the greater good."

"I'm not sure that will work. My people are fairly independent and don't work well together. And, well, competition between ports and families runs deep. They will be reluctant to cooperate."

Lucilla hadn't considered that. She'd worked with a few of the captains, and knew that, compared with other areas, there was less cohesion among their various villages, but she hadn't considered why. Still, she was convinced that, in this, she was right. She wanted their help and men, but she wasn't willing to create another mess like Cormac was dealing with to get it.

"I have no doubt you're right, but, as you said, these are things your people have been longing to acquire, for some time. If anything could break through and convince them, I think this has a chance. It's at least worth a try. If it doesn't work, we can talk again and try to find a new path."

"Perhaps you are right. The families are greedy bastards, that much is true. If anyone would let their old hatreds and grudges be bought out, it would be them. I will try as best I can, although I make no promises."

"That is all I ask."

Carthage

The procession around the golden litter weaved through the streets of Carthage, a throng of guards pushing everyone, peasants and merchants, nobles and commoners, out of the way, clearing a path for the eight muscular slaves carrying it. At its head marched a full Me'atim of the Sacred Band, the elite warriors sworn to defend the emperor with their lives. Their polished armor and scarlet crests stood out against the drab garb of the commoners lining the streets.

Not that the guards needed to push many out of the way, since most of the crowd parted in awed silence as the litter passed, some kneeling and others simply staring uncomprehendingly. It was a rare sight indeed to see the emperor outside the palace, let alone this far on the outskirts of the sprawling capital, and the people responded accordingly.

Imilcar paid little attention to the rabble, focused ahead on the great wall and its massive gates, thinking of the message he'd received an hour before, informing him that the caravan he'd been waiting for was finally approaching his city.

The golden litter came to a stop just outside the massive gates. A pair of slaves carrying ornately carved wooden steps ran forward and placed it in between the slaves maintaining the litter on their shoulders, carefully holding it so that it did not rock or sway as the emperor stood up from the fine chair he'd been sitting on. Another slave rushed forward, pushing aside the deep purple curtain, revealing the emperor, who slowly and regally stepped down the stairs laid out for him, the entire scene designed to enhance his presence and prestige as much as possible.

Not until he had stepped all the way down the stairs and away from the litter did the slaves finally set it on the ground.

The litter had stopped in front of General Hadar, who stood at the head of the large caravan of soldiers, elephants, and a horde of strangely dressed men. These men stood out among the rest, both in their unusual dress and their strange eyes, traits apparently common among those from the Far East.

In front of the wagons piled high with supplies sat the objects that Imilcar had actually come to see. Six wagons riding low to the ground, each loaded with a long, hollow metal tube nestled in a wooden frame.

"Your Eminence," General Hadar said, bowing low as the emperor approached. "As promised, the emperor of the TianYou has honored our alliance and sent the weapons we requested. I am told they are called 'cannon.'"

The general gestured to the wagons and their contents as he said the name. Imilcar had only seen one of these before, a weapon captured from the Romans, its metal blackened and cracked along its length, apparently unusable. These weapons bore a similar appearance to the Roman version, but were far larger.

"I was honored to see one of these weapons in use when we received them from the TianYou caravan. They placed in the tube a bag filled with the dark powder, which they called gunpowder, in

257

front of which they placed a large stone, which had been chiseled into a round ball. They then lit something called a fuse, which they have also supplied, attached to the closed end, which ignited the bag of gunpowder inside. There was a tremendous sound, along with flame and a huge cloud of smoke. The ball they had placed inside was hurtled out faster than the eye could follow, smashing into a mound thousands of paces away. It was … very impressive."

Hadar had become more and more animated as he spoke, only getting control of himself at the very end. One of the reasons Hadar had been allowed to survive in a position of command as long as he had was because he was so well controlled, which, in of itself, told Imilcar how impressive the demonstration must have been.

"Show me," the emperor commanded.

"Certainly, Great One," General Hadar said, before gesturing behind him. "Along with the cannon, their leader also sent these men. Technical advisors who are to train our own people in the proper handling and use of these weapons."

The general turned and walked a few steps toward the strangely dressed men, saying, "Demonstration."

As he spoke, he enunciated each syllable, making the word slow and clear. Imilcar wondered, for a moment, how they were to train his men if they did not speak their language, but pushed the thought aside. That would be a problem for later.

One of the advisors, a short, slender man with long, jet-black hair braided down his back, nodded slightly. Turning, he began to talk to the others in a guttural, consonant-heavy-sounding language. They must not have needed much in the way of instruction because after only a few words the others sprang into action, carefully lowering one of the long cannons from the wagon bed and onto a wooden platform with small wheels underneath. Six men arranged themselves around the cannon, three on each side, and slowly wheeled it forward as the advisor continued to shout commands.

"Aim it at that building," Imilcar said, pointing at a small mud-brick peasant's hut at least a thousand paces away from them, east of the great wall.

Bowing, the advisor turned back to his crew and shouted more commands in their strange language. Two men brought over a large leather bag, which they carefully loaded into the back of the cannon. Another man held what looked like a slender rope, with one end tucked inside the back of the cannon barrel.

The advisors quickly finished their preparations before hurriedly jogging away from the cannon, putting as much space between themselves and it as possible. Once they had moved to what was apparently a safe distance, the man holding the slender rope touched the end he still gripped to a torch one of the other soldiers held out.

"Cover your ears, Your Eminence," Hadar said, already placing his hands over his own.

Imilcar was a little confused but followed suit. His men had called the Roman weapons 'thunder weapons,' so it made sense they would be loud. Moments later, a flash erupted from the back of the cannon, followed by an earth-shaking boom that made Imilcar's bones rattle. A great cloud of dirty gray smoke enveloped the cannon, obscuring it briefly before dissipating on the breeze.

After a few moments, the results of the cannon's tremendous blast became clear. Half of the hut was now just a pile of rubble, as if a giant had reached down and swatted away half the building. The remaining half was already collapsing in on itself, the building's integrity gone. Jagged chunks of mudbrick lay strewn about, along with splintered wood that must have been the door or roof supports.

He could faintly hear a wail of agony and grief coming from inside the structure and waved for one of his attendants to deal with it. It did help give the full feeling of the weapon's effect, putting a smile on his normally dour face as he turned to General Hadar.

"This changes everything!" he proclaimed. "Finally, we have a weapon that can match the Romans. Not just match, but surpass. Look how large our weapon is compared to the Roman version. Surely the destruction ours can rain down will greatly outclass theirs."

There was some kind of look between two of the advisors, but Imilcar ignored it, caught up in his dreams of victory. Of finally dealing with the Roman nuisance once and for all.

"When can we get more?"

"I have already requested additional cannon and gunpowder from the TianYou merchants, and sent our agents to collect the necessary trade goods for them. I hope to have another shipment in a month, and more after that."

"Can we not do it faster?"

"I'm afraid not, Great One. They have limited supplies of the weapons to sell, and must produce more, and it is taking ... longer to gather the supplies for trade than I'd hoped, since we have lost so much of our territories."

"Take whatever you have to. Demand they produce the weapons faster. The Romans have a dozen or more of these weapons on each of their ships, not even counting the ones with their armies. We cannot win with only ten."

"At once, Your Eminence," Hadar bowed, rushing back to the advisors, communicating with hand gestures as much as with words.

Imilcar ignored them, looking back at the cannon and the destroyed hut. Soon. Very soon, things would change.

Chapter 23

The Port of Kalb, Hispania

Cormac leaned back in the chair at Niall's desk and listened to the crashing waves and bustle of the docks below, closing his eyes and relishing the moment. He felt bad about how often he kicked the commander out of his own workspace, and if he was honest, there were probably other temporary accommodations he could set up while he was operating out of the port, but he preferred the commander's office.

Besides being convenient to messengers and soldiers, as needed, he liked how it sat above the docks. High enough that not too much noise came in the window, which allowed him to leave it open for the nice breeze that came off the Middle Sea, but close enough he could still look out and see the bustle about the harbor and the high-masted ships coming in.

A knock on the door drew him out of his reverie, and to the reason he was sitting in the office at all.

"Come," Cormac commanded, sitting up and schooling his features.

Cormac watched as the Arandur representative was led into the office by two legionaries, his face pressed into a scowl. The man wasn't in manacles or even being touched by the men, but it was clear from his face he hadn't come willingly.

"Welcome, friend," Cormac said, standing up from behind the plain wooden table that served as a desk. "Please, have a seat."

The man gave the two soldiers a look, as if assessing if he could just leave or not, before stepping forward and taking the offered seat. As he did, the men moved to stand on either side of the door, inside the room, as Cormac had instructed them to do before they left to retrieve his guest.

"Some wine, perhaps?" Cormac gestured to a clay jug and goblets on the table.

"I'm no friend of yours, Britannian," the man finally snarled. "Your soldiers dragged me here against my will. What gives you the right to accost a free man of Hispania in such a manner?"

Cormac held up a hand in a conciliatory gesture. "Please, I apologize if my men gave you any indication that your presence here was forced. That was not my intention."

Of course, that was a lie. Cormac's men had dragged the representative here very much against his will, on Cormac's instructions. Something he had learned from Medb was to always stack the deck when negotiating. Instead of trying to predict the reaction of the person you'd be against, set up a scenario ahead of time that was most likely to produce a reaction you could work with. Besides, it was satisfying to see the usually brash and cocksure man looking so off-balance.

"Well, I cannot say I appreciate being fetched like some errant child. Now, perhaps you might tell me what was so urgent as to justify this ... discourtesy."

"Straight to business then. Very well. We have concluded our investigation into the recent attack on one of your outlying villages. We have found some ... inconsistencies with the accounts from your survivors. In short, we believe the attack never happened. It was staged."

"What!?" the man spluttered, his face reddening. "This ... this is an outrage! You dare accuse us of fabricating an assault that cost our tribesmen their very lives?"

Cormac just sat there and listened as the man repeated himself, over and over. Demanding apologies, for all intents and purposes completely flabbergasted that anyone would dare think his people would do something so reprehensible.

"You can deny it all you want, but we know the truth," Cormac said when the man's denials finally wound down. "The damage to your village was extremely localized, and the people were clearly afraid of the warriors accompanying the man I sent to investigate.

Meanwhile, every other raided village was nearly burned to the ground, with widespread destruction. Not a single person in your village was able to accurately identify which tribe had supposedly raided them. Yet every other raided village had no trouble pointing to the Arandur as the ones who raided them."

The man started to say something, another denial, most likely.

"Furthermore," Cormac said, leaning forward and speaking over him. "The injuries on the so-called victims were still fresh. The man we sent is a seasoned warrior with decades of battle experience. He knows what fresh wounds are, and can tell the difference between those and injuries that happened days or even weeks prior. He is quite certain these supposed 'attacks' happened after our last gathering of the tribes ... after you had already laid claim to being raided."

"I don't care what you think you can prove. You Britannians are no different than the Carthaginians who came before. You swoop in thinking you can decide what is best for Hispania and her tribes," the representative said, his credulous expression fading as he jabbed a finger at Cormac. "What matters here are the tribes themselves, who have never gotten along, always fighting each other for land, resources, and power. The Carthaginians at least understood that. They knew that if they let the powerful tribes have their way, there would be peace of a sort. Something you Britannians still need to learn."

The man leaned back, his standard over-confident demeanor back in place, as if he hadn't been outraged moments before.

"If you keep insisting that all the tribes work together under your high-minded rules, all you will get is chaos and bloodshed as we fight among ourselves."

"That sounds remarkably like a threat. Are you saying that if I refuse to provide weapons to the Arandur or hold you accountable for violating our agreements, you will sabotage relations with other tribes and provoke more conflict in the region?"

"Take it however you want, Britannian," the man said with a shrug. "I'm simply telling you how things work here. The tribes have never gotten along, and they never will. That's the natural order of things. But if you keep pressing this and refuse to sell to my people, then we'll have no choice but to make sure the other tribes know how deceitful you really are."

"I see," Cormac said, remaining calm and thinking back to some of the things his wife had said about negotiation. "Then let me make my position equally as clear. Britannia will not be coerced by threats from those who violate their agreements with us. Nor will we allow chaos and bloodshed to spread unchecked. If the Arandur insist on raiding their neighbors, despite our warnings, then they will face severe consequences."

The man started to respond until Cormac held up a hand, stopping him, "Don't bother with any more of your threats. Tell anyone what you think you have to. I think you misjudge the wisdom of your neighbors and your own place in their eyes."

"You aren't from here and know nothing of us. You think the other tribes will just stand by while you crack down on us? They'll see your hypocrisy for what it is."

"We shall see," Cormac said. "Thank you for coming."

The man glared at Cormac but didn't say anything further, instead standing and stomping toward the door. The two legionaries glanced questioningly at Cormac, who gave a slight shake of his head. Each man stepped aside, allowing the representative, who never looked back at Cormac nor said anything while this was taking place, to leave, following the man outside as he did.

Cormac sat in silence for a long time after that, thinking. While their conversation didn't end the way Cormac had hoped, it did end more or less how he predicted it would. Now, he had to decide what to do next.

Rome, Italia

As his legion spread out into long firing lines, interspersed with batteries of artillery, Bomilcar looked toward the walls of Rome.

For months, they'd slowly plotted to reach this point, delayed again and again by attacks up and down their supply lines.

Now that they were here, he wasn't sure it was worth it, even with the towering wall the Carthaginians built around it. Once, this had been a magnificent city, the heart of what was the Roman Republic, which his own ancestors had fought so hard to capture. Now, it was a shadow of its former self. He had been in the city several times over the years, before his life and allegiances had taken a drastic turn, and every time he'd been shocked by the state into which it had been allowed to fall. Gone were the parts of the city that had once held massive temples and architecture, if the artists who'd rendered paintings of it were to be believed, replaced by small ramshackle homes built shoulder to shoulder, a crowded and intertwined mess.

If it weren't for its symbolic value, Bomilcar would have as soon bypassed the city altogether, finishing it off at some future time. Unfortunately, he didn't have that luxury. Every day they had gotten closer to the city, his Roman legionnaires had become more excited by the prospect of retaking their ancestral home. While Bomilcar was sure they would feel differently once they got inside, he could at least understand their feeling.

"Have the batteries prepare to bombard the walls, concentrating on the gates, if possible," he commanded Gordianus. "They are to keep their fire low, to minimize damage to the city as much as possible. Although I don't expect them to sally, keep the cohorts in line and prepared to repel an attack."

"Yes, Legate," Gordianus said, saluting and riding off.

Bomilcar watched him go. He was a good man and, by all rights, should have taken over the Seventh Legion after the unfortunate loss of Velius. He would have done a good job at it, too. Bomilcar had already talked to the Consul about finding a legion for the man, but politics played their hand, and Marcus, who'd already been groomed for a position, had gotten there first.

Twenty minutes later, the cannon began firing, smashing iron balls into the stone and brick walls. Aside from the normal cannon that had made up the Britannian batteries since their formation, he had several pieces of a new style of cannon the Consul called howitzers. While he was duly impressed with their range, he immediately ordered the fire from those weapons ceased as their first shots sailed over the walls of Rome and into the city proper.

He could see the advantage of these weapons, able to be fired from behind the line instead of slotted into the line and able to hit on any part of the enemy line, used much like he'd used archers or catapults before he'd been introduced to firearms. They would even be useful in a siege where he wasn't trying to protect the city proper, as he was here.

For almost an hour, his cannon pounded away at the walls, sending sections crumbling to the ground. The openings not enough to try and exploit yet, but there were signs that it was working. One of the large gates opposite him had suffered a direct hit, smashing in the upper portion of the door.

It wouldn't be much longer until the breaches were large enough to begin to exploit them. While that was good, Bomilcar was still bothered. The enemy had tried a few ranging shots with their hurled jars of gunpowder, all of which exploded well short of his position, and then fell silent.

In the few times they'd faced the Carthaginian weapons, they had been liberal with their use, as if they had no care of supply at all, even when the ranges were against them. To see the weapons fall silent now worried Bomilcar slightly.

"Have the cannons pause after every five volleys and the men listen for digging. I'm not sure what they're up to, but I don't want another crater like the one they created outside of Daramouda."

The messenger saluted and ran off to begin relaying the message.

"Do you think they'll try that again?" Gordianus, who'd returned a few minutes previously, asked.

"They might. It didn't work then, but the damage was fairly catastrophic. Had they gone around the crater instead of in it, they might have broken our lines. Well, and if the Consul hadn't been there to lay waste to the ones that tried. I just don't want any surprises."

"The walls are already starting to breach. It won't be long until we can take the city. Maybe they're holding back their gunpowder for then, since they know it's coming."

"Maybe," Bomilcar said, unconvinced. "Have the legions pull back five hundred paces, just in case."

"Won't that leave the artillery exposed?"

"Only minorly. We're a fair distance from the gate and they can move back into position quickly if the enemy sallies."

Gordianus nodded and began sending messengers to the cohort commanders.

Bomilcar watched his men begin to shift back, away from the line he'd created. If the enemy was digging, it would take time for them to pass the word to the men who were tunneling. He'd also been told by the Consul that there was a limit to how far they could tunnel without creating air shafts, which he would be able to see. The distances had been a range and not an exact number, but his legions were now far enough back that, if they were to set up an explosion, it wouldn't reach his main force.

Not that it would matter. Gordianus had been right that the walls would be down soon. Another well-placed shot blew the gate opposite him wide open, sending the large doors tumbling back into the men on the other side, and taking some of the wall that had held the door with it. The opening was still too narrow for an assault, but it meant they were close. Another breakthrough, and he'd be willing to send his men.

He was about to order a change in the artillery, to focus the fire on a few spots to create that additional breakthrough, when the ground erupted in a series of fire explosions all along the Britannian line.

It wasn't the massive, earth-shattering explosion like outside of Daramouda, however. Instead of one massive blast, there were dozens of much smaller ones, scattered both ahead of and behind his position, not concentrated in one specific area. It also wasn't all at once. It began with a few and built to a crescendo of explosions, past his line to the east and west, seeming to curve around the circumference of the city itself. There was also something else different about this. The holes left behind were much smaller, more of a pit in the ground than a crater.

Taking all of that in, Bomilcar realized this wasn't tunneled explosives out to their position, which would have taken days to reach him, but something completely new. The Carthaginians had laced their city with the explosive charges. He wasn't sure how they'd managed to set them off, buried as they were, but they must have had some kind of fuse he'd missed. They must have also done it around the entire city, or at least the northern half of the city, since they couldn't know the direction his men would come from.

Unfortunately, the range of the explosions didn't just go east to west. Some were well in front of his artillery by dozens of paces and some were so far behind as to be in the middle of where he sent his infantry. Worse, the explosions alone were not causing all of the damage. The Carthaginians' explosions looked to be sending out a lot of shrapnel when they exploded, very similar to how their own canister rounds worked.

The worst damage, however, occurred when an explosion launched out of the ground almost directly beneath an ammunition carriage, causing a chain reaction of explosions that sent the tube of the cannon sailing into the air, hurtling end over end. Thankfully, it sailed toward Rome and not back into his cohorts.

"Move the infantry further back, out of the blast zone," Bomilcar commanded, not flinching as one of his messengers was suddenly struck down by flying shrapnel. "Batteries are to hold position and maintain fire, but back their ammunition carriages out."

He was willing to accept the risk of losing a few more cannon if it meant continuing to open the breaches in the wall, but he wasn't prepared for more of his ammunition reserves to go up.

Almost as soon as the ripple of explosions began, they ended. His messengers had barely gotten to the closest cohorts when the rate of explosions began to gradually slow until it was only one or two, with long spaces of time in between each. In some part of Bomilcar's mind, he realized that must be caused by how they rigged up the fuses, since it was unlikely to be a stable or controllable process. It also made sense that some would have gone unexploded and would be a hazard for people crossing this land in the future.

Not that any of that mattered now. Unless they were completely brain dead, they would follow that display up with a counterattack, since they had to know it was unlikely to completely decimate his forces on its own.

"Bring the cohorts back in line. At the double step," he ordered, sending more aides rushing off.

Almost as soon as the words left his mouth, however, the enemy launched their attack as a line of cavalry poured out of the entrance of the city, riding hard for his line.

Bomilcar didn't wait for messengers, instead turning his horse and riding along the line of artillery.

"Load canister!" he shouted. "Fire by battery."

He repeated the command down the line, hearing it echo as men heard him and saw what was coming their way. A few cannons fired wildly to clear the charge they had already set up while the rest of the crews leaped into action, lowering the barrels to preset ranges and pushing thin metal tubes with solid bases designed to break apart as soon as they cleared the cannon, creating an additional layer of shrapnel.

The men had trained on this maneuver and did him proud, each holding fire until the well over two hundred horsemen thundering toward them came into range. The artillery went off almost as one, letting loose huge billowing clouds of gray smoke as their metal charges ripped across the open field, tearing down scores of horses.

The gunners began clearing and reloading their weapons almost instantly, but it was unlikely they'd get another chance before the horses made contact. Bomilcar was about to order their retreat when the thundering sound of footsteps caught his attention. Before he could even turn, legionnaires began skidding to a halt from a full run into their previous positions. They didn't wait for orders or coordinated fire. Any man who arrived fired as soon as he was in position, before kneeling to reload, allowing any men behind him to also fire.

Bomilcar turned his horse to see Gordianus riding across the field, cajoling men into position, ordering them to fire at will, without waiting for the others.

At first, it was a handful, mostly misses, but that quickly became a continuous ripple of gunfire as more and more men got into position and began to fire. It wasn't the crashing wave a full volley would have produced, but it was enough to turn the already injured cavalry. A few persisted and made it to his lines, crashing into gunners and riflemen, who then made quick work of the isolated riders. There were casualties, but the Carthaginians had missed their chance to break his line after initiating their clever plan. The small amount of infantry that had begun to come out of the broken gates reversed themselves almost instantly as they saw the cavalry charge dissolve, its remnants riding hard, back the way they'd come.

"Fix bayonets. Forward, at the quick step," Bomilcar commanded as soon as the cavalry charge disintegrated.

The enemy would get jammed up in their own door, everyone pushing to get back inside, giving him a window to follow on their heels, taking advantage of the chaos to smash into their rear and break through into the city. He hoped that the enemy had used most of their gunpowder, but even if they hadn't, he was going to have to assault the wall and deal with their gunpowder eventually.

Either way, the city was theirs. The Carthaginian army was in chaos and they'd spent their one chance. Now, it was just a question of the cost.

Chapter 24

Devnum

Medb sat in the Empress's richly appointed office, her feet up on the Empress's ornately carved desk, and looked out the large window with its views of the city, instead of at the stack of papers on the desk.

Since Lucilla's departure and her installment as the temporary administrator of the Empire, she has finally had a taste of what it is like to rule again. She was enjoying some of the benefits that come with sitting on the throne, especially the deference she was paid now that she was making decisions again. It's what she'd been working toward ever since her kingdom fell and she'd been shipped off to this place.

Now that she had it, though, she found the experience gave her mixed feelings. On the plus side, Rome knew how to treat their nobility. She knew her kingdom wasn't on this level, especially after arriving and seeing her accommodations here, from the art to the amenities, as more or less a prisoner, were actually better than they had been in her own kingdom where she was a queen. They were even better now, as she sat in Lucilla's place. Everything was of the highest quality, comfortable and luxurious. She doubted she'd ever get her kingdom back, but if she did, it would almost certainly be a step down from this.

If that was all there was, she would have thoroughly enjoyed her time as the Empress's stand-in. Unfortunately, she also had the Empress's workload, which was leaps and bounds above anything she'd ever had to deal with as queen in her own right, even at the height of the war. For one, the Romans had more bureaucracy than she'd ever experienced. While it made sense, considering how much more expansive their holdings and interests were, it was also incredibly difficult to keep on top of everything. Even with a large bureaucracy to handle the day-to-day aspects, just keeping abreast of it all took from sunup to sundown.

Paperwork wasn't a thing in her kingdom, mostly because they'd never heard of paper. All of their writing was either on very expensive parchment or carved wood and dried tablets, none of which were cheap enough or convenient enough for storing anything but the most important information. Several times she'd actually considered that to be a good thing, since the Romans seemed to generate paper by the cartload and she had adjusted to its use extremely well. Every day, stacks of it with reports and information from across the Empire made their way into her office, threatening to drown her.

She could see its usefulness, as she knew more of what was happening not just in Britannia, but across the continent, than she'd known about just her small kingdom. It was also tedious and mind-numbing. If this is what it meant to be the Empress, she wasn't sure she wanted the position. Better to leave it to someone else and find a way to get the benefits without all the work.

Her thoughts were interrupted when a legionnaire knocked on her door. When she'd first taken over, they'd had a bad habit of following their knock by just opening the door and letting whoever was there in. She'd quickly broken them of that habit.

"Enter," she commanded, pulling her feet off the desk and sitting upright.

The door opened and the old inventor, Hortensius, shuffled in, looking disheveled as always.

"Hortensius, finally," she said dryly, setting down the papers she'd very much not been reading.

"My apologies for the delay, My Lady. I was in Caledonia when I received your summons."

"Well, it's a good thing we have your trains now to allow you to travel so freely."

"Uhh, absolutely," Hortensius said, frowning a little.

"Well, one of the reasons I asked you here was to congratulate you on finishing the line to Londinium. I understand it was quite a lot of work."

"Thank you, My Lady," Hortensius said, taking a seat, not noticing Medb's darkening expression as he did so uninstructed. "While it wasn't easy, most of that was centered around learning and adjusting our processes. While the line between Factorium and here was beneficial as a first step, there were still many unexpected challenges as we progressed to laying a much longer stretch of track. The men did excellent work, however, and the line between Devnum and Londinium, with a stop in Factorium, is running every day now."

"I see," Medb said flatly. "And speaking of significant undertakings, I trust you've made progress on the new line to Caledonia?"

"Ah, yes, the Caledonia line. As you might expect, we've encountered ... difficulties."

"Difficulties?"

"Yes. One of the reasons we started with the line to Londinium was that it was possible to lay a line that was more or less flat, with only rolling hills to deal with. The north, however, is a much different prospect. The terrain is much rockier with many rapid changes in elevation. Using gunpowder to help blast tunnels is much faster than just digging by hand, as we would have had to do previously, but it is still a very slow process. Especially using the safety precautions and construction methods for the tunnels the Consul instructed us to use. We also have to grade almost every inch of track, even when running next to hills and mountains and not tunneling through them. It makes every inch of line take a large amount of time to complete."

"So, how do you propose to deal with these ... difficulties?"

"It's not one problem, My Lady, but a series of them. Many we anticipated and are already working on options, but it will take time."

"I see. How much time?"

"I'm afraid I can't say for certain, My Lady."

"Well. Figure it out. I also know that you regularly updated the Empress on your progress when she sat on this side of the desk.

I want the same kind of cooperation and expect you to keep me apprised of your progress."

Hortensius opened his mouth to reply as she said, "I appreciate you coming. You are dismissed."

Picking up a page, Medb returned to reading where she'd left off, ignoring the inventor as he stood looking at her for a moment before turning and leaving as he'd come.

Mediterranean, Off the Coast of North Africa

Admiral Valdar stood on the quarterdeck of the Bellona, the Middle Sea stretched out before him, dotted with the sails of his fleet. He always enjoyed watching his fleet at work, the large forms of the caravels dwarfing the smaller nearby galleys.

They had done good work, sinking every Carthaginian fleet they'd come in contact with, which was becoming more and more infrequent as they cleared the Middle Sea of the enemy entirely. While it felt good, having the accomplishment, it had not been an easy transition, as their role had shifted from a combat force to one of patrolling the sea, on the hunt for Carthaginians. It was a very different task, and one for which he felt ill-prepared.

Or rather, ill-equipped. Peacekeeping on even a smaller sea like this required a lot more boats than sailing from one fight to another. He once again wished he had more caravels and schooners. The converted galleys were helpful, and the port of Kalb was now able to refit captured galleys with the new sails, but they couldn't operate independently, since they had neither the guns nor the men to spare for a galley which wasn't able to stand up to grouped enemy galleys.

Still, his job had been accomplished, and he had more or less locked down the Middle Sea. While they had not yet blockaded

Carthage, mostly for want of ships, they had severed all sea lanes to and from it.

He watched as his ships surrounded a group of vessels sailing for Sicilia, inspecting them for any cargo meant for the Carthaginian forces. They were still allowing basic merchant traffic, transporting food and goods, but any ship carrying military supplies or confirmed to be bound for enemy forces was captured and its crew sent off to a prison camp.

He could see the sailors swarming over the deck, checking the cargo and questioning the crew. It surprised him, with all of the supplies they'd taken, that the Carthaginians would still try to ship supplies this way, but they were becoming more and more desperate, and taking more and more risks.

"Excuse me, Admiral," one of his officers said, coming up behind him. "We've just intercepted a ship carrying materials bound for Sicilia."

Not the first and certainly not the last one they would intercept.

"Good work. Another loss for the Carthaginians."

Instead of acknowledging the statement and moving on, the man hesitated, torn between walking away and saying something else.

"A problem?" Valdar asked.

"Yes, Admiral. Aside from the more standard supplies, including gunpowder, we found something ... unusual. Weapons we didn't expect."

"What do you mean, 'weapons you didn't expect?'"

"They look like the cannons we've been using, sir, only ... less so."

"Damaged? Did they manage to take some of our cannon in a battle? If they did, it would have been taken on the continent, not Africa. Why ship it to Carthage only to turn around and send it back."

"No. Sir. I don't think they're ours. They're much larger than ours, and made of bronze."

"One of the early designs the Consul showed us was bronze, before he introduced the reinforced steel tubes. The bronze ones apparently warped more easily but didn't shatter during a misfire."

The man didn't say anything to that. Why would he? While he trained his men continually on the operation of cannon, they knew little of the actual construction, which wasn't needed to man the weapons. Valdar only knew about it because the Consul liked to talk, and had explained it once to a group of legates and Valdar.

"Take me to them," he said. "I want to see these weapons for myself."

Admiral Valdar took a long boat to the captured Carthaginian vessel. Its crew was gathered to one side of the deck, bound and kneeling, surrounded by a group of armed sailors. For the most part, they looked resigned, probably assuming the Britannians were going to kill them and throw them to the sharks. No doubt their Carthaginian masters had told them that was exactly what happened to those who were captured. While it wasn't entirely untrue, and almost certainly how the Carthaginians dealt with captured Britannians, it wasn't how they normally dealt with the Carthaginians.

For the moment, Valdar ignored them, instead following his officer to a collection of crates at a far end of the sailed galley. Most were opened, having been checked by his men, filled with gunpowder, food supplies, and the like. Those didn't hold Valdar's attention. What did was the pile of four metal tubes, stacked together two by two on a wooden cradle.

His officer had described them well. They were notably larger than his own cannon and the dull golden color of bronze. He could also see why the man had been confused. There were distinct differences. For one, although the cannon was larger, the bore hole was much smaller, with a huge metal shell around it. For another, the barrels weren't rifled. While the cannons on his ships weren't rifled either, his were fitted with attachments on the side to allow them to be mounted into a heavy-wheeled gun carriage. This was, for all intents and purposes, a solid tube with a small fuse hole in the top.

Primitive, was the word he'd use to describe it.

"The ship was headed to Sicilia?" Valdar asked.

"That is what he said, but it was before we pulled the sheet covering the cannon off and opened the crates. It's possible he was lying."

"I see. Bring him to me," he ordered.

The officer nodded and hurried away. A few minutes later, he returned with a small, wiry man in tow. The captain was dressed in fine clothes, but his face was pale and his eyes were wide with fear.

"What is this?" Valdar asked, gesturing to the cannon.

The man hesitated for a moment and said, "I don't know. I was told to allow my ship to be loaded with cargo, which I was then instructed to take to Sicilia. That is what I was doing. I didn't even know what was in the crates."

On the face of it, his story was plausible. After all, that was how the Carthaginians treated most of their subjects. But he'd seen a lot of Carthaginian ships over the past few years, and especially since entering the Middle Sea. None of the private merchant ships he'd seen had been upgraded with the new sail design. This one even had two masts, forward and stern, rather than one in the center. That kind of addition would have needed to be made from the keel up, and not something just upgraded later.

If this was a simple merchant, forced against his will to deliver Carthaginian supplies, Valdar would eat his rigging.

"Don't lie to me," Valdar growled. "You aren't some simple merchant, and you know exactly where this came from and how your people got their hands on it."

The captain swallowed hard. "I don't know. I swear."

Valdar's patience was running thin. "This is your last chance. I will not ask again. Where was this produced? How did it get to you?"

The captain looked around frantically, as if searching for a way out. But there was nowhere to go. He was surrounded by armed sailors.

"I don't know!" he cried. "I swear!"

Valdar gave the man a hard stare and then nodded once.

"Make sure his ankles, legs, and arms are all secured, and throw him over the side," he said, before turning to look at the rest of the crew. "Someone find me his second."

The sailors grabbed the captain and started to drag him away, while others grabbed additional lengths of rope.

"No! Wait!" The captain struggled as they dragged him toward the rail, screaming frantically. "They came by convoy from Egypt, I think."

Valdar held up a hand, stopping the sailors from tossing the man overboard.

"Not made by your people though, I think. Where did they come from? Are you expecting me to believe someone in Egypt developed them?"

"I only know they arrive by ship sailing up the Red Sea, where a caravan brings them the rest of the way west, since no ship is safe in these waters anymore."

"And yet you tried?"

"I only did what I was ordered to do. They don't ask me what I think," the man pleaded. "Please, I've told you everything I know."

"No captain lets goods onto their ship without trying to find out something about it, even one as cowardly as you. I know you asked around, and I'm betting you heard something. Maybe you just need a little swim to jog your memory," Valdar said, signaling to the sailors, who put their hands under the captain's arms and started to lift him again.

"I swear, I don't know who's sending them. All I know are the rumors I've heard. Something about a great empire, somewhere far to the east, able to make weapons similar to those made by you people."

"You say this shipment arrived via the Red Sea and Egypt?"

"Now they are. These weapons first showed up last year with the fire powder, which arrived at the coast of Syria and then transferred to one of our ships and was sent west. Since the spring, though, the shipments have changed. They're now bringing in more, by boat, and we're the ones taking them by caravan."

"What else have you heard?"

"Nothing. Only rumors and speculation. We know they're powerful, but other than that, no one knows much about them. I don't even know anyone who's seen one of these foreigners, let alone spoken to them. I swear."

Valdar stared at the man for a moment. While he was certain the man would have heard rumors, it also seemed likely that the Carthaginians did keep what they knew about these weapons and the people providing them secret, otherwise word would have leaked out sooner. Ramirus had been caught as flat-footed as anyone else when the gunpowder showed up in Carthaginian hands, and the only way to keep that kind of information out of the spymaster's hands was to make sure that hardly anyone knew what was happening.

It also explained something that had been bothering most of the commanders. It had seemed impossible that the Carthaginians would be able to duplicate something as dangerous and specific as gunpowder, and yet the Carthaginians had seemingly done just that. They had all wondered how that had happened, but this explained it. The Carthaginians didn't duplicate anything. They found someone else who had similar knowledge to the Consul. The pieces, at least the ones he could see, fit.

"Put him with the others for delivery to the prisoner camps in Gaul. Have the cargo sent to Britannia for examination, except for one of the cannon. Send it and a messenger to the Consul with an explanation of what we found. I will include a note to go along with it. Use one of our fastest ships for the message to the Consul, but everything else can go the standard route."

The sailor saluted in the Roman tradition, or maybe it was the Britannian tradition now, and began hauling the men up, to be transferred to another ship. After the defeat of the Carthaginian armies in Gaul, the Consul had set up an additional prison camp outside of Daramouda, where the praetorians would interview the prisoners and determine which ones needed to be held and which ones could be paroled and sent home, which would at least save the Empire the expense of feeding them.

That would also make them someone else's problems, which was good for Valdar, since this discovery gave him something new to worry about. He returned quickly to his ship, summoning the other caravel captains in his fleet to come aboard with utmost haste.

While he waited for them, Valdar paced, considering the problem he was just presented with and his options for what to do about it. What he knew for a fact was that he'd seen the enemy's plans for countering the Britannian army, and he had a chance to do something to stop them. He also knew that if they were already receiving these weapons, he didn't have much time to step in and act.

Only five of his captains were with him, at the moment, the rest either back at Kalb continuing to blockade the Middle Sea or sailing with a collection of smaller ships, patrolling for Carthaginians. Valdar wasted no time, laying out his plan as soon as the last captain was on board.

"We've been presented with a rare opportunity to stop the enemy's latest plans to counter the legions and the weapons that give us much of our advantage, but we do not have a lot of time. Shipments of the new weapons the Carthaginians are receiving, which might be strong enough to counter our own cannon and rifles, are already being shipped into Carthage. It's impossible to know how many they have already received, but what we do know is that we want to stop them from getting any more. They have always had the manpower advantage over us. If they manage to maintain that and to close the technology gap between us, our men will have little chance."

"How do we stop them?" Ingvarr, the captain of the Hrafn, asked. "Do we know where the weapons are coming in from? I assume, since you say we have a chance, that it's being brought to them by ship."

"It is. Apparently, the nation supplying these weapons is in the Far East, well beyond where I've heard of anyone having traveled. They used to deliver these weapons from Syria across these waters to Carthage, but they had to make changes once we gained control of the Middle Sea. Instead, they've begun shipping everything up the Red Sea, delivering it to Egypt, where it is then taken overland to Carthage."

"How can we do anything about it?" Kvasir, captain of the Pollux, asked. "We know the Carthaginians have men in Egypt and a large force still in Persia. Even with a full legion, I doubt we'd be able to hold that region long. As soon as they swarm our men, probably from both sides, the shipments would continue."

"True, which is why I'm not suggesting we land any men."

"Then how do you want us to stop them?" Ingvarr asked.

"The Consul once told me it was possible to sail around Africa and up the other side. We were discussing some of the tools he's given us for navigation, the improved compass, the sextant, and the better time-telling devices. He was highlighting how much time they would save in voyages and the more difficult routes we could take, when discussing it, and used sailing around Africa and up the other side as an example. He said that with the new tools we could make the journey in two to three months. That might not be enough to stop all shipments, but it would mean halting them this year. But only if we start now."

"We're going to sail around Africa to the Red Sea?" Kvasir asked in disbelief.

"Yes. It will not be easy going. When I probed, the Consul told me that the waters were as harsh, or harsher, than what we experience on the Serpentine Sea or here on the Middle Sea. But we've shown that we are able to sail the North Sea waters with these ships, and I believe, with the exception of rounding the southern tip of Africa, we should be able to handle what the gods throw at us. I will leave you in charge, Ingvarr, with two-thirds of the caravels and schooners in the fleet. You're to ensure that the Carthaginian shipping remains suppressed and that the Consul has the support he needs. I will take four of the caravels and a fair number of the converted galleys and older long boats that have been upgraded to the newer sail design. I will also see about borrowing a small contingent of legionnaires from Kalb. I believe if we set up some ports along the coast, we will have stations along the way to stop and refit as needed and reload supplies. I will spend a week in Kalb, talking to some merchants that I know, and see if I can't convince them to throw in with us. If we could manage to make this at least somewhat profitable, it will go a long way to establishing a supply line around the cape."

"If you're sure," Ingvarr said, echoing Kvasir's hesitation.

"I am. Start sending out the orders. I want to sail for Kalb within the hour."

Germania

Lucilla stood to one side of the massive Anglii longhouse, watching the gathered conclave of Germanic leaders in dismay. Ky had mentioned some of the issues and rivalries they'd been forced to deal with when making the initial alliance with the tribes, but she'd been under the impression that most of those had been, if not ended, at least suppressed. At least enough to allow the tribes to work together.

Things were clearly not as harmonious as she'd been led to believe, as she watched the men bickering and arguing amongst themselves. It was hard to pick out one conversation, as it seemed everyone was arguing with everyone else, but those she could hear made it clear that most of the grievances stemmed from old and deep-rooted issues, everyone digging up past wrongs and conflicts from years, and sometimes generations, ago.

Worse, a few of the conflicts she heard referenced in their arguments seemed to be much more recent, since Ky departed for Gaul and Italia. If they were starting to fight among themselves again, then things here were much worse than she feared.

Conflicts over territory each tribe claimed but had been prevented from taking during the Carthaginian occupation. Arguments over broken oaths and deals one side felt was handled unfairly. Even arguments about youths from one tribe being bound to youths from another tribe, against their parents' wishes. There seemed to be no end to what these people would argue about, with each of them nursing grudges and old enmities.

After listening to ten minutes of petty squabbling, she'd heard enough. Head held high, she walked into the center of the conclave and, with a dramatic sweep of her arm, threw back the simple cloak hood that had covered her face, hiding her identity.

"I am Lucilla Germanicus, Empress of Rome and the Britannic Empire!" she announced, her voice clear and steady. "And I have come before you seeking an audience."

A hush descended on the assembly as the arguments trailed off at her sudden appearance. She waited for a moment, letting the men take in her sudden appearance before she spoke again.

"I stand before you amazed," she said finally. "After years of fighting together for your freedom, you needed only a single short winter of that freedom before you turned on each other."

She let the words hang in the air, allowing them to sink in. The room remained silent.

"The war *is not over*. The Carthaginians could return at any time to threaten your lands again. You have clearly forgotten what this alliance was originally about: working together to protect your people and your future."

Lucilla's words seemed to cow the men, who shifted uncomfortably as they exchanged glances. She let the silence linger for a moment before continuing.

"Britannia stands by its word, and I honor the commitments and guarantees made by the Consul to each of you. The Britannic Empire believes in supporting our allies. However, we did not come here to play favorites or allow one ally to intimidate or attack another. Our alliance and support is contingent on the defensive nature of said alliance. We will support any tribe here against outside attack, but I will not support aggression against your neighbors unless it is an action we unanimously agree must be taken. I understand conflict happens and I would be happy to send an Imperial negotiator to help resolve disputes. We could even involve a neutral third party from one of your other allies if all sides agree to mediation. What we will not be is a conspirator with one tribe to conquer the others."

Lucilla waited, gauging their reactions, giving them a chance to speak up, to disagree or shout curses. Better to let any tribe that disagreed show themselves now rather than wait and have them scheme behind their backs. No one did. She could see the seeds of doubt taking root. This was more a restating of their agreed-upon terms, with the added threat of fighting on the side of any tribe attacked, rather than new policy, but it highlighted the self-defeating decisions they'd been making.

"I did not come here to threaten you," she continued. "But I will not stand by and watch as you tear each other apart. The Carthaginians are gone, but there are other threats that will come. Together, you can face them and build a future that is brighter than anything you have ever known. But you *must be united*."

She paused, letting her words sink in.

"With that being said, what I am proposing is a defensive alliance among yourselves. Not the loose agreement we have now, for you all to buy from us and for some level of support, but a pact that would guarantee the security of all your lands and peoples. This isn't an agreement between Britannia and each of you, but one between yourselves. Britannia would welcome being asked to join as a partner in this alliance, but that is your decision. If we are asked to be a part of this, we would offer a guarantee of security from attack on any member of the alliance, but would not require you to defend our Empire unless you choose to do so. That is a very one-sided agreement, binding us to you without binding you to us, but that should be a clear indication of how much we believe this is necessary, not just for your future, but for the future of the continent as a whole."

The silence that had fallen across the entire assembly finally broke at this proclamation; it was almost like a wave rippling through the men as they reacted. They were intrigued by the idea. It also probably occurred to many of the tribes, especially the more aggressive ones, that if even two of them agreed to this and formed the alliance, they would then have a powerful ally on their side that the rest did not. The more tribes that joined, the less the other tribes could afford not to join.

"I do want to say that this is not why I came here," Lucilla added. "But, seeing the state of things, I think it is important. More important than my initial reason for coming before you. It is that important, not only to me but to all free people, that there be peace on the continent. When Carthage is gone, we are all going to have a real chance to build a real golden age. A chance that I, for one, am determined to take."

Aliverko, the Anglii leader, stood up, waving the others to silence.

"Empress, you honor us with your words and presence, and I'm certain every one of us will consider your offer carefully. You said this proposition was not why you came before this assembly today, which brings me to ask, why are you here?"

The question wasn't as innocent as it might have seemed. Ramirus and Aliverko had a good working relationship and he was the only Germanic leader who knew she was coming. She had spoken to him briefly, in secret, before this gathering, and he knew what she was actually here for. He was a clever man and knew she couldn't put her request forward now, after making her proposition, without it seeming like a quid pro quo. He'd helpfully reopened that door for her.

"Yes. While I do think an alliance would be a benefit to everyone here, and the people they lead, this is indeed not why I came. I came, because of the war that brought us all together. We are nearing the end game of the war with Carthage, and it is possible their hegemony over all of us could end this year. But my Empire is spread thin. Too thin to achieve the final push needed to stop them once and for all, at least on our own. I came seeking help to ensure they do not get the time they need to prolong this conflict or, worse, find a way to win it, forcing all of us under their sovereignty again."

"You show yourself," one of the men said. "You presume to not only tell us who not to fight against, but who we must fight as well. Will you become the next Carthage, another oppressor we must obey? Why should we submit ourselves to you?"

"I am not requiring any of you to do anything," Lucilla said calmly, not taking the bait. "I did not come here to propose an alliance or even suggest it. That idea only came to me as I saw all of you ready to throw your hard-won peace away over petty grievances. I very clearly did not put any stipulation on our assistance in protecting the proposed alliance on whether any tribe assists us or not. I wasn't going to mention this at all, in light of my proposition, had I not been asked. My hope, however, is that you all recognize how close things are right now. The Carthaginians could come back and put all of us back under their yoke. Britannia will stand to its last to prevent that from happening, and we hope you all feel the same. But we do not demand nor mandate your help. It's up to you to decide what you want to do."

As the man looked away, Lucilla swept her gaze across the rest of the gathered assembly. No one else stood in challenge.

"I will be a guest of the Anglii for a time, should any of you want to discuss my proposals," she said finally. "I hope you all choose to consider my words, both about assisting us in our final fight against the Carthaginians; but, maybe even more importantly, about an arrangement to guarantee real peace in Germania. I have long held a dream of a better world, and I hope that all of you choose to join me in that dream."

With that, she turned and walked out of the longhouse, leaving the men to their deliberations.

Chapter 25

Port of Kalb, Hispania

Cormac stood in the center of the partially finished auditorium watching representatives from across Hispania file in. He was glad to see the architects had already put in the sun coverings, as it helped with some of the late summer heat.

If he was being honest, Cormac wasn't sure he understood why the Romans loved building these kinds of venues. The large coliseums that hosted fights, wrestling matches, and contests; those he could understand. That kind of contest was as old as time itself. These sunken performance places though, with their semi-circular design and wide "stage" area, he didn't get. He'd gone to see one play when he'd been in Devnum, and had been bored to death by it.

Still, as a meeting venue, it was excellent. Not quite as nice as their forum, it was a far sight better than converted warehouses and barns for holding large gatherings. And this one was particularly large. When he had put the word out for this conclave, Cormac had expected grudging participation similar to the last few gatherings of the tribes. He was surprised to see that he'd been wrong. He still wasn't well versed on every tribe and its representatives, yet, but it seemed to him that nearly every tribe in Hispania was represented here, based on, if nothing else, by the volume of people arriving.

"Thank you for coming," Cormac said, as it seemed the last few leaders made their way down the steps, finding seats. "The last time we met, there was a lot of discussion about assaults on villages and tribes across Hispania, mostly around the central regions. I sent out agents to investigate all of these claims, to see where the attacks happened, and to talk to the survivors. Many were found to be exactly as was described. Small villages raided by men using weapons sold to them by Britannia. Some, however, were not. One, that I know everyone here was interested in, was the assault on the Arandur village of Neitin. It was notable, because many of the attacked tribes identified the Arandur themselves as the perpetrators, and their claim that one of their villages was raided in the same way was a strong defense that they were not to blame. Which is why I know it is of interest to many of those gathered here today to hear that, from everything my investigators found, there was no outside attack on that village."

A ripple of conversations erupted across the auditorium.

"In fact," Cormac continued, raising his voice over the din. "The evidence shows that what was presented as a raid on their village was in fact staged, with villagers attacked and even killed by warriors from Arandur themselves and threats made to the survivors to convince them to offer false accusations of an attack."

The representative of the Arandur stood and started to shout something, but Cormac had been watching him, waiting for the interruption. As soon as the man stood, he raised his voice another level and continued, speaking over the man.

"I brought these revelations to their leader, demanding answers, and I was told that if I made our findings public, it would … not could, would, incite open warfare among all the tribes. Promises were made to sow seeds of chaos and disruption across Hispania if word of the truth got out. What's more, I was told that the only way to keep the Arandur from using one tribe against another, from raiding and killing at will, was to resume our sales of weapons to that tribe and to support them as *they* consolidated power across the peninsula. It seems the Arandur have decided they alone deserve to rule Hispania through force and fear, replacing Carthaginian rule with a rule of their own. I tell you now; Britannia will not stand by and let that happen."

"Lies!" the Arandur representative shouted. "More Roman deception meant to turn the tribes against each other so they can swoop in and take control!"

"We did not pluck your tribe's name randomly from the air," Cormac said. "Nearly every raided village, with the exception of yours, has identified your tribe as the perpetrators of the raids. Why is it that your own neighbors, who know exactly who you are, all agree that *you* are behind the attacks?"

"Because they have been bought off by promises of gold and power by you. Scum who sell themselves, whores for Britannian favor, hold no sway."

"Then perhaps we should hear from your own people," Cormac said, waving toward one of the auditorium entrances.

Llassar appeared at the top of the steps with four people in simple clothing, each sporting multiple injuries. As they walked down the steps, three of the four looked to the ground, nervously refusing to look up. The fourth, a woman, glared daggers at the Arandur representative as they made their way to the center floor, to stand next to Cormac.

"These are villagers from Neitin. People injured by their own leaders' avarice. But don't hear it from me," Cormac said, and stepped aside, gesturing for the woman.

"My name is Atta and I come from the village of Neitin. My home was on the north end of the village. I lived with my husband and young daughter; we were poor but happy. Then, a group of warriors arrived late one night. Men I vaguely knew, or at least had seen before, from the central village to the south. Indortes, my husband, went out to greet them. The leader didn't even speak to him, only pulled a sword and rammed it through his heart. The rest came past him, into my home, grabbed me and my daughter, and pulled us outside. They ..."

Her words turned into sobs. Even the Arandur representative knew better than to speak up at this moment, interrupting this woman's obvious grief. After a moment, her sobs slowed and she regained control of her emotions.

"My daughter was killed in front of me. I was to be next, but Arranes, one of our neighbors, ran up, hearing my screams, and demanded to know what was happening. They killed him for his kindness, but the distraction he caused saved me. I ... I ran. I should have stayed and died with my husband and child, but ... I was terrified. I ran and ran. They chased me, and would have caught me if not for Urcha. She has a burn and she was hiding there. She grabbed me and pulled me in with her. The warriors passed us, and ran on. We stayed in those woods for days, starving, too afraid to go back to the village. Only when foreign soldiers came did we leave the forest."

"More lies. I will not stay here and listen to this deceit!" the Arandur representative screamed, before turning to look over the other representatives. "We should all leave now, before we allow ourselves to become slaves again!"

With that, he stormed out of the row he had been sitting in and up the steps, toward the exit, in a huff. One other man made to follow but hesitated when no one else moved. Sheepishly, he sat back down. The Arandur man turned, face reddening as he saw no one else following him out. Spitting on the ground, he turned and left in a fury.

Cormac watched him go before turning back to the rest of the assembled leaders.

"Well, that was dramatic," Cormac said. "I appreciate the faith you've all shown Britannia to serve as a neutral representative. I promise you now that, despite the provocations of the Arandur, we will continue to act in good faith and work towards a peaceful and prosperous future for Hispania."

He paused again, letting his words sink in before he continued.

"However, I do not think that the Arandur are done. They made it clear that, if their demands were not met, they would escalate their attacks. The fact that none of the rest of you stood with them will only make their anger stronger. They will look to weaken the rest of you, and if I had to guess, I would say they will target the smaller tribes first. They may be standing alone, but that doesn't mean they are any less dangerous. Alone, I'm not sure any of you could stand up to them, which is why, again, I propose some form of alliance between the rest of you. The only way you will stand up to them, and future challenges, is if you pull together. You can't do it alone. Britannia has offered to stand with any tribe that honors its promises, and to stand with any alliance you form amongst yourselves, and we will honor that. If you take the fight to the Arandur, Britannian legionnaires will stand with you."

The men began to excitedly talk among themselves, and Cormac had the sense that, this time, his suggestion was being taken much more seriously.

"While you consider that, I will add that I am a man of my word," Cormac continued. "I already sent a request to Britannia to send men to the ruins of Port Invictus to begin rebuilding it. Once finished, I will work with whatever form the tribes here agree to function together as to hand the port and its governance over to you."

Across the auditorium, men began getting up and gathering in clumps, excitedly discussing the proposal. Cormac wasn't done yet, though. He had one thing left to add and, with as excited as everyone else was, this seemed to be the best time to bring it up.

"Before you disperse to deliberate further, I have one other consideration," Cormac said, raising his voice above the din. "As dangerous as the Arandur are, they are not the greatest threat to your existence. Britannia is on the verge of defeating the Carthaginians, but our victory is not yet complete. In fact, it hangs in the balance for want of enough men to complete the defeat of your former overlords. Britannia desperately needs assistance if we are to finish the job. Assistance in the form of additional manpower."

Shouts, not yet angry, but at least concerned, started going up around the auditorium.

"Wait, hear me out, please," Cormac said, raising a hand. "I'm not asking you to send your men into combat or to join our legions. I know you've had your fill of being pressed into service so far away, and we would not ask that of you. We would, of course, welcome any young men who wish to see the last great war of our lifetime and take part in the defeat of the Carthaginians, but we would not ask it of you. What we ask is additional men who would bolster our rear-guard forces in Italia and the accompanying islands. We have entered regions that, instead of yearning to overthrow their masters, have lain under the yoke for so long that they resent the removal of it."

"If we are to take the fight to the Carthaginians," he continued. "We need as many of our legionnaires as possible in Africa, and cannot spare them for garrison work, especially since that garrison work covers enough ground that it would take the bulk of our forces to cover it. This would be a limited request, and your young men will be back home by winter. We know that might affect the harvests, and we have tools we are willing to give you to make up for their absence. Beyond the tangible gain, there will be a larger chance for the tribes here to build contacts with other nations. We have made similar requests of our friends in Gaul, Germania, and Scandia to assist us in maintaining peace in the freed lands. This would be an opportunity for your youths and theirs to learn about each other, become exposed to each other's cultures, which would improve trade and relations between neighbors as we prepare to enter a new future, where each of our people have the chance to rule themselves as they see fit. As I said, we do not require this of you, we only ask for your help. I leave the decision to you."

With that, Cormac and Llassar left the auditorium, helping the injured Arandur villagers out. The remaining men were already abuzz as he left.

Atlantic Ocean, Northwest Coast of Africa

Valdar inhaled, pulling in the deep, rich scent of the ocean, happy to be back on Oceanus again, with its dark waters and roiling waves. There was something about the vast expanse that smelled different than the Middle Sea. He knew landsmen would think him crazy if he said that out loud, but he knew he could smell it.

The fleet had just finished rounding the northern coast of Africa, and now turned south, sailing along the western shore. He could feel the crew's excitement. He'd come up as a merchantman, which meant sailing close to the shore, passing along the same path over and over again. There was a lot of unknown water, but until the Britannians showed up with all of their new technology, it had been a risky thing to lose sight of the shore, especially out here, where the sea to the west stretched on until it reached the heavens.

That mostly meant that very few sailors broke new ground, as it were, sailing into uncharted waters. It was a huge deal to set off on a voyage that, at least partially, would lead to the discovery of new waters and finding new lands to explore.

They weren't the first to make this sail south, below the great desert. Theoretically, everyone knew Africa ended at some point south, and that one could sail down the west coast and then back up the east coast. There had been enough trade up the Nile from Nubia and other nations above the farthest waterfalls, with stories of the eastern shores, to tell them that. None of the ships that had ever sailed that way had returned, though. Of course, they didn't have the knowledge the Consul had given him, describing the "Horn of Africa," nor the tools for more precise measurements and these massive ships, built to sail the violent waters of Oceanus.

No, this was a new day, and all of the men knew it.

"Will we have enough men to accomplish our task, Admiral?" his first officer asked.

"We'll have to make do with what we have. Maybe if we'd discovered the enemy's shipments a little earlier, we would have arrived before Cormac took the bulk of the legionnaires stationed at the northern Hispania port, but we didn't. Not that he would have been able to spare them, from what Tribune Niall said. I think we were lucky to get the thirty men we did. We'll just have to make do with that. Niall promised to send word with the next message boat to Britannia asking for another detachment. I've instructed the captains stationed at Kalb to break off one more caravel if those arrive and to bring any reinforcements they send. Another batch of caravels and schooners should be coming off the docks next month to make up for it leaving."

Before they could discuss the situation further, a voice from high up on the main mast shouted down, "Sails sighted."

Valdar lifted his spyglass, sweeping it across the horizon. After a moment, in the far distance, he made out what looked like a cluster of ships. He squinted hard against the glass, adjusting it, trying to make the image clear. And then he saw it. A Carthaginian signante at the top of a mast. How they'd managed to build another fleet, out here on Oceanus, without anyone knowing, was beyond him. It was clear why they were here, though. With the bulk of Roman ships in the Middle Sea and the legions on the continent, they stood a much better chance of landing troops now than they did two years ago.

"Signal the caravels and schooners to fall in line and prepare to engage. The rest of the fleet is to fall back and hold position until we come back to them. If we don't return by dark, or they sight the enemy, they are to fall back to Kalb and inform the fleet there of what we've found."

The fleet responded swiftly, the smaller ships peeling away and turning north as the three caravels and two schooners surged forward. The Bellona took the lead, Valdar keeping his spyglass fixed to his eye as it did, watching the enemy fleet grow in his vision. As it did, he realized that something was different with this fleet than the ones they'd faced before, but it wasn't until they began to close on the ships that he realized what it was. The hull shape of two of the Carthaginian ships resembled, in some ways, the Britannian caravels. The lines were crude, and there were subtle irregularities that suggested the shipwrights were trying to copy the vessels based on a brief glimpse or second and third-hand information. That assumption led him to believe that it was most likely survivors of battles relaying the Britannian designs, rather than some kind of espionage at the ports.

It took some time, but the Carthaginians finally began reacting to their arrival. Valdar would have taken his own men to task for being so slow to notice an enemy fleet, his men had known they were sailing along Carthaginian shores while the enemy had no idea that a Britannian fleet would appear, coming for them. Not that Valdar thought he'd be able to sneak up on the enemy. Not on such a clear day for sailing.

As the enemy turned, Valdar noticed something else, something more important than just the design of the ship. In a crude approximation of Britannian gunports, the enemy ships had crude cutouts along the side of each of their mock-caravels. He couldn't see into them, and no cannon had been rolled out, but he had no doubt that more of the bronze cannon he had intercepted near Sardinia lay inside those gun ports.

As the two fleets closed on each other, the enemy fell into a line-abreast formation, showing that they'd paid more attention to the technical changes in Britannian ship building, and not how they handled those ships. While typical of galley combat, where the goal was to ram the opponent and then fight a land-style battle across the now-connected ships, it gave away all of the benefits of cannon armed ships. If the mock-caravels in the center wanted to fire, they would have to either fall back or turn into their fellows to get their broadsides off.

They also hadn't taken into account the speed difference between a three-masted caravel and a single-mast converted galley, causing their line to almost instantly become disjointed and staggered, the chaos getting worse by the minute as the converted galleys struggled in the harsher conditions out on the ocean. It was one of the reasons Valdar had all of his converted ships fall back. They just weren't capable of precise coordination in the heavy seas.

"Signal the fleet to hold formation and prepare to engage," Valdar said as the fleets entered long-gun range. "Concentrate all fire on the larger, new model ships."

They might have bad tactics, but Valdar wasn't about to risk his ship by being overconfident. The enemy fleet had started losing enough cohesion that their cannon armed ships now had enough room to turn and fire broadsides, which Valdar wasn't going to let happen. Once the ships with cannons were gone, he could sail circles around the converted galleys, until the entire fleet went to the bottom of the sea.

"Helmsman, hard to starboard. Gunners, fire on my mark."

The Bellona heeled over sharply as the helmsman spun the wheel, until it was sailing parallel to the oncoming Carthaginians, putting it in position to "cross the T," as the Consul had described it, allowing his cannon to fire down the length of the Carthaginian ship, making it harder to overshoot and increasing the damage if it did.

"Gunners. FIRE!" Valdar bellowed.

A ripple of explosions erupted as the cannons along the port side of the Bellona belched smoke and fire. Splinters flew and men screamed as iron shot punched through the hulls of the Carthaginian ships.

"Helmsman, turn us north," Valdar ordered, even as the other five ships in his line made the same journey behind him, each firing a salvo as it lined up against the Carthaginian fleet.

By the time the entire fleet had turned back north and begun picking up speed, putting distance between the two fleets, both of the mock caravels were listing hard and on their way to the bottom.

"Send my complements to the other captains and tell them their men handled that well."

Valdar had been an early convert to the Consul's insistence on continual drilling and practice with the cannon, especially aboard ship where the rolling of the deck made aiming a tricky operation. His men had taken to it well and all their hard work had paid off. Valdar smiled as he heard a cheer go up on the Seadreki, which was following directly to his rear.

"All right, let's finish them off."

The fleet began to turn back south, continuing the long serpentine move that allowed a line of ships to maintain range while presenting broadsides to the enemy. The enemy fleet was in disarray, or at least more disarray than it had been prior to the engagement, the converted galleys losing all cohesion as every ship's captain turned this way and that, trying to find a safe escape for their vessel now that their two largest vessels had gone down without a fight.

It was pure chaos. As Valdar watched, one of the galleys tried to turn over so fast that it ended up swamping itself in a swell, taking on enough water to send it to the bottom.

"It's kind of them to take care of things without us, but how about we help them along. Signal break formation and fire as you bear. Maintain distance and range," Valdar said, pausing as he had an additional thought. "Separate message to the Bolvastr to watch crossing fire lanes."

Egil was a good captain and one of the best ship handlers in the fleet, but he had a habit of losing the positioning of the other ships in the fleet, and sailing in front of one of his partners' broadsides.

Outgunned and outmaneuvered, the Carthaginian ships stood no chance. One by one they were pummeled into floating wreckage, hapless crews leaping into the merciless sea. Thirty minutes after the two mock-caravels went to the bottom, the last of the converted galleys followed them, all without being able to answer in kind with cannon or catapult. It was a massacre.

"Should we blockade and shell this port while we're here?" his first mate asked as they watched the last ship sink. "Make sure they don't build any more ships and try again?"

Valdar thought about it for a moment. As easy as the battle had been, there had been a real danger here. With the Middle Sea blockaded, most of the warships had been pulled from around Britannia, leaving it vulnerable if the enemy managed to get their act together and sail a fleet to it. Had they not stumbled upon the enemy's new cannon design and decided to intercept the shipments of the weapons from the east, he would have never known the Carthaginians were here. It was very possible they would have managed to get the fleet together and sail it all the way to Britannia, causing chaos at the very least.

But, there were other concerns here, too.

"No," he finally said. "We have a long trip ahead of us with a fight at the end of it, and we'll be a long way from a resupply. We need to conserve what ammunition and gunpowder we have."

"Then what about the port?"

"When we retrieve the rest of our fleet, we'll send a ship back to Kalb with word of this port and their attempt to build a fleet. I'll send along orders for some of the ships patrolling from the port to sail down and deal with it. Now, let's go find the rest of our ships and continue on our way. The longer we take, the more cannon the enemy will have delivered."

"Yes, Sir," the first officer said, saluting.

Valdar smiled as the man went to signal the rest of the fleet. For a bunch of ships made up of merchantmen, or at least former merchantmen, they certainly were picking up a lot of habits from the legions.

Chapter 26

Arandur, Central Hispania

Cormac rode at the head of his makeshift army comprised of one century of Britannian legionnaires and five hundred warriors from across Hispania, a mixture of all the various tribes making up the new Hispanic Alliance. While he probably would have had an easier time if the force had been more homogenous, as the first battle of the alliance Cormac wanted every member to have skin in the game.

It was also less than he could have gotten if he'd pushed, but there were other needs for Hispanic warriors now, and Cormac was fairly certain he could win this battle with six hundred men, all armed with firearms. Especially since his one hundred men were highly trained and coordinated, armed with rifles and were bringing two field pieces with them, giving the force a significant firepower advantage. Besides, the Arandur might have been a large tribe, but they would have trouble fielding an equal-sized force.

Cresting a ridge, he saw a sprawling village spread out before him. It was no surprise that the Arandur managed such prosperity. The village was situated in a valley between two chains of hills with a river flowing down the center, creating a particularly fertile valley. Defensively, it allowed them to be hemmed in, as forces could ride down on them from the east or west, but economically, it was excellent.

"Split our allies in half and have them surround the village, but hold until they hear our guns fire, unless they're directly attacked,"

Cormac told Llassar. "Make sure they understand it's imperative that they not go charging in until we all do. I'm sending in negotiators, and I do not want them getting our men killed."

"You're not going in with the negotiators," Llassar said, more as a command than a statement.

"While I'd like to, no, I'm not. Even I know that would be foolhardy."

"Why send anyone? They made their position very clear. You think they'll suddenly see wisdom now, with us at the edge of their homes with an army?"

"No, I don't think they'll see wisdom, but I want to give them that chance. Or rather, I want the rest of the *Hispanians* to see me giving them that chance. This is as much about convincing the other tribes that we aren't like the Carthaginians as it is about teaching the Arandur a lesson."

Llassar looked at Cormac, appraising him, before saying, "You really have made progress. You know that?"

"I'm a slow learner sometimes, but I am trying," Cormac said, and then smiled. "Or at least I am trying now."

"Maybe you did need to get out in the field after all," Llassar said, still with the appraising look, before turning his horse and riding off to deliver the messages.

"Cian," Cormac called to the decanus, one of the few Ulaid in this contingent. "Pick four men and ride to the edge of town under a flag of truce. Offer their leaders the chance to surrender and talk terms before this turns deadly and threatens their civilians."

Cian nodded, and a few minutes later, Cormac watched as the decanus and four men, unarmed, one waving a white flag high over their heads, made their way down the hillside toward the village.

As they neared the edge of the village, a group of maybe fifteen Arandur warriors appeared from between the buildings, all cradling muskets or swords, held at the ready but not raised, moved to intercept the negotiators before they entered the village itself.

Things went downhill from there. Even from this distance, he could see the tense body language and animated gesturing as the two groups conversed. It was clear the discussion was not going well. Silently, Cormac tried to tell Cian to end things and come back, not that the decanus could hear him. There was nothing to be gained from extending the conversation, not with how defensive the Arandur were being, and would only work to provoke them further.

Suddenly, without warning, the Arandur warriors raised their muskets and opened fire on the unarmed Britannian delegation. Cormac stared in horror as three of his men were struck down in an instant. The remaining two men turned and sprinted back toward the Britannian lines in a desperate attempt to escape. Neither of them was Cian, who'd gone down in the first cowardly blast.

One of the two fleeing men was struck in the back as he ran, but the other had better luck, making it to the hill and up the side, the Arandur rounds going wide, kicking up dust all around him, until he was beyond their shorter range.

Rage boiled up inside Cormac. He knew the Arandur were honorless, but Cormac never imagined they'd stoop so low as to kill men under a flag of truce.

"Put fire on those men," Cormac commanded the two cannons already set up on the hill, overlooking the enemy. "Send word to our allies to begin encircling the village and to move in from all directions but the west. Centurion, give them a volley and move forward. You are permitted to open fire on any armed man but avoid civilian casualties as you can."

Commands began to snap out, with the first shots from the cannon smashing into the group of offending Arandur warriors as soon as the survivor made it to the bottom of the hillside, a blast from the Britannian rifles followed thirty seconds later. Before the smoke from the volley even cleared, the century began to move through it, guns at the ready, marching with good separation between the lines. The sound of gunfire was all his allies had been waiting for. As soon as the cannons fired, his Hispanian allies let loose a battle cry Cormac could hear from where he was, followed by a charge into the village from the north, south, and east.

Cormac rode behind them, closer than Llassar would have liked. He might not go out front, but he'd be damned if he wasn't going to lead them. The Arandur were playing it smart, retreating back into their village as the assault began, refusing an open-field battle and taking away the advantage that firearms gave them.

He could already hear fire coming from the other edges of the village as his men made their way into the cramped streets, breaking into squad-sized units, using the gaps between huts and cross-streets to keep in parallel lines, so none of the units got too far ahead and cut off.

His men moved from hut to hut, leading with their bayonet-fixed rifles, checking one building at a time. A musket cracked from a few feet away as an Arandur warrior leaped out of the hut he'd been using for cover and fired at Cormac, whose position atop his horse made him a target. Thankfully, the muskets had a lot less accuracy than rifles, especially when a man was running, and the round went wide. The attacker did not fare as well; rounds from three rifles struck him simultaneously, spinning the man like a top before he crashed to the ground.

"Get off your damn horse," Llassar said, standing next to the animal.

Cormac didn't have to be told twice, sliding off it and handing the reins to one of the men, directing him to take the animal out of the village, lest it become a hazard.

Cormac ducked behind the side of a hut as musket balls whizzed past, chipping off splinters of wood. Around him, his men exchanged fire with Arandur warriors using the maze-like alleys and huts for cover. The crack and boom of gunfire was nearly continuous now, with occasional shouts and screams rising above the din.

As Cormac peered around the edge, an Arandur warrior, who somehow remained hidden as the men in front of him passed by, leaped out, swinging a sword. Cormac pivoted on his heel, narrowly avoiding the blade as it thunked into the hut and smashed the man across the face with the stock of his rifle, wrenching the sword from his grasp as the man fell.

"Forward!" Cormac yelled, waving the men on.

They stormed down the alley. Three Arandur warriors rose from behind a stack of barrels, but Cormac and his men cut them down in a withering hail of lead before they could fire their muskets.

They pressed on, the alley opening up into a small courtyard. An Arandur woman cowered by a well, clutching two young children. Cormac raised his hand for his men to hold position.

"Get them inside, keep them safe," Cormac said in a halting version of the local dialect.

She hesitated for a moment, and then hurried the children into a hut.

They were nearing the village center now. Cormac could see the large communal building looming ahead, likely where the Arandur leaders were holed up. He was hoping to end this quickly, but the warriors were putting up a fiercer resistance than he had expected. The center of the village was large enough that muskets wouldn't be that big of a danger until they crossed past the line of huts. His rifles created another problem entirely, however.

"Watch your fire," Cormac commanded. "Our allies are coming from each direction, and a stray round can hit them. Aim low and focus on using your bayonets."

As he took a step forward, a crackle of gunfire erupted from the upper floor of a two-story building ahead of them. His men scrambled for cover as balls smacked into the ground at their feet. Cormac pressed himself against the wall of a hut, finding himself across the street from his men, underneath the attackers. They were pinned down by the withering fire, unable to advance.

Cormac turned to the men nearest him. "Provide covering fire on my order. I'm going around the back."

He could see the look Llassar gave him, but he was across the alley, and the mixture of musket and crossbow fire was enough to keep anyone from crossing over.

Leaning his rifle, which wouldn't help much in this situation, against the building, he slipped down a side alley, looping behind the building and pulling his sword from its scabbard. Taking a deep breath, he kicked the rear door in and charged inside. No one was downstairs and the din of the rifles and muskets covered the sound of the door crashing in. Cormac crept up the stairs, keeping low and peering around the door. Three Arandur warriors were inside. One was firing down into the street below before handing the spent musket off to one of the men behind him, who rapidly reloaded it. Clever, and an explanation of how they managed to maintain such an impressive rate of fire.

Steeling himself, Cormac rushed into the room, his sword skewering one of the warriors without warning, the man's face twisting in surprise before Cormac pushed him off the blade, sending the man crashing to the floor. The other loader saw Cormac instantly, starting to open his mouth to shout when Cormac brought the butt of his sword up, smashing it into his face, sending teeth flying, before stabbing out and catching the shooter in his side, his musket going off, blasting into a side wall.

The man dropped, wounded but not dead, which Cormac shortly corrected, stabbing him through again. The other man was groping for a weapon, his hands on his face, which was leaking profuse amounts of blood. Cormac dispatched him on his way back out of the room, slashing his sword across the man's neck.

"I'm coming out," Cormac shouted, just in case his men got jumpy and tried to shoot him.

Cormac emerged from the building, peeking out to make sure Llassar had things in hand.

"That was amazingly stupid," the Caledonian said as Cormac retrieved his rifle and the men started forward again.

"We didn't have time for something more complex," Cormac said.

Llassar glared at him, but said nothing else. Across the village square, he could see the Hispanians beginning to emerge from between the buildings as well, having fought their way through from the other sides. The crackle of musketry was already beginning to taper off as the Arandur resistance crumbled in the face of the coordinated assault.

Wiping the blood from his blade, Cormac stepped out into the open area, motioning for his men to advance with him toward the large communal building at the far side. As they moved forward, checking the alleyways and buildings on either side, a figure appeared through the doors of the communal hall. He was an older man, with a commanding presence despite his age, flanked by two younger warriors. The man raised his hands over his head while the warriors hastily lowered their weapons.

Cormac didn't know the Arandur leader, who had always sent his minions anywhere they were summoned, but he was fairly certain that was who this man was, all the same. Cormac raised his fist, bringing the century to a halt a dozen paces from the trio. Hispanians filtered in from the side streets, encircling them with leveled muskets and swords drawn.

"Tell your men to lay down their weapons and surrender, or you will all die here today," Cormac said.

"So be it," the man said, waving at his two warriors, who threw their weapons to the ground.

Commands were shouted out, and a handful of men came out of their hiding spots, hands in the air. There were losses, but he'd shown his allies that Britannia was true to its word, and had aided in defeating the biggest problem on the peninsula. Or at least the biggest currently.

This would certainly not end the conflict among the tribes, but it would go a long way towards it.

Rome, Italia

Ky folded his arms across his chest as he watched squads of legionnaires rushing in every direction. He'd arrived in the city two days ago, and since then, it had been one crisis after another. Today was looking to be no different, with a thick plume of black smoke rising up from the direction of the south wall, the flickering orange glow of fire visible even in the daylight.

"The situation is deteriorating rapidly," Ky said. "We need to stabilize the city before it descends into complete chaos."

"We are trying, Consul," Bomilcar said. "As far as we can tell, there are no Carthaginians left in the city, and most of this seems almost spontaneous, not directed by one person or group. Some of it is people upset that we're here at all, but a lot of it is from those trying to use the chaos, or even enhance it, to make gains for themselves. I've seen this in conquered cities before, but not this bad."

"We can't resort to the same tactics," Ky said, feeling the argument they'd had the day he'd arrived rising up again.

"I'm not suggesting it. I only said that the way we dealt with it back then was to use a much harsher version of martial law."

"I understand that, but we don't want people in rebellion in fifty years, which is what that kind of attitude achieves," Ky said, turning and walking back into the headquarters building of the Carthaginians' former barracks at the center of the city.

"I agree. But it is going to make dealing with this much harder."

"We can't stay here much longer," Ky said, turning to face Bomilcar. "Every day we spend dealing with these insurrections is another day Carthage has to prepare for our arrival. We've been stalled here for weeks, and things aren't improving."

"I understand your frustration, Consul, but we cannot leave Rome in this state. If we do, it will only get worse, and we'll have to come back and deal with it later. We need to stabilize the city before we can move on."

"And how do you propose we do that?"

"We hold here for now. We secure Rome, build up our forces, and wait for reinforcements. This might be as far as we go this year. We've all seen this eventuality coming for months; I think it might be time to accept it."

Ky knew that Lucilla was in Germania, working to secure additional men, but he couldn't say anything about that until those men, who she hadn't actually gotten to agree to the deal, actually arrived. Even then, it seemed unlikely that Germania alone could provide enough manpower to turn the tide.

Before Ky could respond, a messenger burst into the room, "Consul, there's a large number of men approaching the north gate. Thousands, by the look of it."

"Carthaginians?" Ky asked, exchanging a concerned glance with Bomilcar.

"No, Sir. There are praetorians at the head of the column."

Ky, Bomilcar, and Ky's lictore rushed through the streets, sometimes having to stop while legionnaires, dealing with a dispute or disruption, cleared space for them to get by.

As they approached the north gate, still under reconstruction after the battle, Ky could see a large crowd gathered around it. Again, they had to wait for his men to clear a path, but once they did, he saw that the messenger had been right; the men at the head of the column wore the distinctive armor of the Praetorian Guard. The other thing that caught Ky's attention as the rows of men began to march into the city was the diverse array of clothing and equipment worn by the men behind them.

There were probably a hundred praetorians at the front, marching in neat rows. The men who came after were in a very loose formation. Rabble would probably be a closer word. Had they not all been together, coming in behind the praetorians, Ky might have thought they were some large pilgrimage or merchant caravan, the way they all craned their necks around, looking at the city like tourists.

As he watched them, Sophus began matching the clothing with those of groups they'd dealt with previously, identifying the fur and leathers common to Scandian traders and the more colorful woven fabrics found in Hispania. He could also see those he recognized more easily: men from Ulaid and Caledonia.

A truly strange collection of men, all carrying an assortment of weapons.

One of the praetorians near the front of the line made eye contact with Ky and veered off from the rest. He stopped a few paces in front of Ky and Bomilcar before snapping off a crisp salute.

"Consul. I bring word from the regent, who has sent these men to assist with securing the rear lines and maintaining order. I apologize for not passing on additional notice, but the telegraph lines between here and Daramouda seemed to be down each time we checked."

"Yes, we've been having problems with that," Ky said. "Medb sent these men? I wasn't aware she was tasked with putting together additional manpower."

He knew Lucilla had left the former queen in charge, although the title of regent hadn't been mentioned until now, making Ky wonder if it was self-appointed. He also knew Lucilla had only left her to manage the day-to-day operations of Britannia itself. Unless Lucilla was keeping secrets from him, this was wildly outside Medb's mandate.

"She sent this message, to better explain the situation," the praetorian said, handing over a sealed note.

Ky opened the note, feeling Bomilcar's eyes on him as he read it. A smile tugged at the corners of his mouth as he read, and he looked up at Bomilcar with a nod.

"This is very surprising. It seems Medb saw the collection of men arriving in Britannia from our various allies and took the initiative to send what they had available right away, instead of waiting for all of them to arrive at once."

"I didn't get a chance to know her, but from the stories I've heard, I am surprised to find her involved. And I certainly wouldn't have expected her to be so proactive."

"Neither would I," Ky admitted. "It seems the praetorians were her idea. She discussed the situation with Faenius and realized the need for people trained in garrison and peace enforcement duties, something most of these warriors wouldn't be versed in. She convinced him to send along a group of his men to act as leaders or advisors."

"Commander Faenius asked me to relay that he will send another hundred with the next batch, but that will be all he can spare for the time being," the praetorian said.

"I see," Ky said, before going back to reading. "It certainly looks like Lucilla's efforts to get more assistance are paying off. Medb says that, although she hadn't heard from the Empress when she wrote this letter, she expects these three thousand men to be the first of what looks to be between ten and fifteen thousand men to help with rear security."

"That many?" Bomilcar said, his eyes widening. "That is much more than I would have expected."

"I know," Ky said, "although still, it's not all sunshine and flowers. Medb warns that all of the agreements stipulate that the

Empire make use of these men only until mid-winter, when they need to be returned home, and are only to be used for rear duty."

"That's fine," Bomilcar said. "They'll still free up enough men to allow the attack on Carthage to happen this year, as you wanted. It changes everything."

"It certainly does," Ky said. "I'll have to send a message to Medb congratulating her on her initiative. Bomilcar, send word for Marcus to get down here, then see to the distribution of these men as needed until he arrives and can take over. I want as many legionnaire units in the field replaced as soon as possible, regrouping them and preparing to move south and on to Sicilia. Deal with it as you see fit, but I think we should focus first on your legion, then Aelius's, then Auspex's legions. I want to leave Marcus here to maintain security over Italy, with half his cohorts split between the other three legions. I appreciate the praetorians and they will be a big help, but we need a centralized command if we're going to keep our rear in check, and Marcus has proven he can lead men performing that kind of assignment."

"I agree. I'll see to the men. If we start with the units here, I should be able to begin the push south in the next day or two."

"Excellent," Ky said. "Excellent."

Chapter 27

Wouri Estuary, West Africa

The small Britannic fleet glided through the tranquil waters of the estuary, its lush, green shores a stark contrast to the relentless expanse of Oceanus they had traversed. The dense tree line seemed to engulf the waterway, stretching as far as the eye could see. The air was moist in a way Valdar had never experienced. Damp earth and plant odors mixed with the briny aroma of the sea.

Beyond a few paces of sand was a wall of towering trees, their trunks draped in vines. The waters themselves seemed to practically teem with fish which Valdar could see from his place on deck. For most of the trip, they'd stayed a fair distance from shore, in sight but far enough away to avoid unknown shoals and sand bars. Seeing this estuary and the small island off the coast, it seemed like a perfect place for a port, just what he was looking for. It would be well protected from storms and the rough seas of Oceanus, and there were several rivers feeding into it, meaning they'd have nearby fresh water.

"Gather a group of our legionaries and sailors," Valdar said to his first mate. "I want them ashore to scout out a suitable spot for our port. Also, signal one of the galleys to go upriver a little way. Not far, but far enough to give us an idea of what's inland and to see if there are any signs of people living here."

"Yes, Admiral," the man said, heading for the signalmen.

A few minutes later, one of the modified galleys began pushing its way up what looked to be the largest river, next to the area Valdar was thinking of for a resupply port. On the shore, waves of men disembarked from longboats, pushing through the soft sand along the edge of the water and disappearing into the thick foliage.

Twenty minutes later, the men he'd dispatched were back, sending up the signal flags that all was clear. Satisfied with the initial assessment, Valdar made his way to a longboat and was rowed ashore.

"Report," Valdar said to one of the legionary officers as they met him by the longboat.

"We've identified a suitable spot just east of here. The terrain is flat, and there's a natural cove that could provide shelter for the ships. The tree cover is pretty thick, so it's going to take some work to clear the land, but at least we'll have timber to start building with."

"Good. Very good," Valdar said. "Take the men and begin clearing the area. I'll start bringing more men from the fleet ashore to help. Get your legionaries set up to establish a perimeter."

As the men set off to perform their assigned tasks, Valdar gathered the few captains who had also come ashore around him.

"My plan is to leave one schooner and several of the galleys here. Your task is to build up this port and maintain a supply line back to Hispania. I know building a port from nothing in these conditions will be challenging. The fleet will hold here for a week to help you get the initial settlement cleared and started. My hope is that between the schooner and the cannon-armed galleys, you'll have enough protection until you can get some walls up."

"And after the wall is built, Admiral?" one of the galley captains asked.

They all knew this wasn't the goal of their mission. Valdar needed a safe port to resupply from as he continued around the continent, a way for him to send information back and get what he needed without sending ships all the way back to Hispania. It was a big job, but it also meant being left more or less alone very far from home. The sailors, many of whom had grown up sailing unknown coasts in search of profit, would have some appreciation for that, but those trained into the fleets more recently and the legionaries would not have had the same experience.

"Once the walls are up and the settlement is at least stable, the schooner will travel back to Hispania for more supplies, both for you and to be drawn from by my supply ships. You'll inform the commander of what we're doing and about the port you've established, letting him know we'll need semi-regular shipments from him to maintain the port. For now, this is a way station, a hub. Eventually, the Empress might decide she wants more contacts inland, but for now, you're to maintain yourselves here and not venture further than needed inland, away from the port. I'm not sure what farming is possible here, but some of your people started off as farmers and might have a better idea. It's a good natural harbor, and there is that island just offshore that you can also set up an outpost on, if you feel the need. The galleys will remain here to maintain protection, assist with fishing, and whatever else is needed. It's imperative that you maintain communication with Kalb. We're far from home, and I don't want any of you to up and suddenly disappear."

Before anyone could respond, there was a commotion further down the beach, where a river emptied into the estuary. The galley that he had sent to explore had returned, its captain waving frantically.

Valdar and his men ran up to where the galley pulled up close to the shore, close enough for the captain to shout across.

"Admiral, there are people coming through the woods," he said, pointing upriver, into the trees. "They look armed."

"Hostile?" Valdar shouted back.

"It was too hard to see, and we turned around right away to warn you."

Valdar gave the man a wave and shouted for the legionary commander to bring all of the men back to the shore.

"Signal the ships to prepare to defend the shore party. Optio, ready your weapons, but keep them at your side until we find out how this is going to go."

"Natives, sir?" the optio asked.

"Probably. It was bound to happen; I just didn't expect it so soon. They must have seen the ships."

The optio nodded and began rounding up the men, putting the sailors, most of whom were unarmed except for wood axes and tools, behind his soldiers. Valdar sent the captains with the sailors, but remained in front. A few minutes later, figures emerged from the jungle. He could hear several of the Britannians, who'd never traveled much south of their own island nation, gasp at the men's appearance. But Valdar had visited Egypt several times. He had met Nubians and other tribesmen from past the upper cataracts.

These men had a similar appearance, at least in their skin tone, although some were darker than even the Nubians he'd met. Their clothing was different, however. Most of the men wore minimal clothing and simple jewelry made from what looked like shells or polished rocks. The one thing they all were, however, was armed. They were carrying a variety of spears and bows.

They also seemed as intrigued and bewildered by him and his men's sudden appearance, as he was by theirs.

Valdar took a step forward, holding his empty hands out, open with the palms facing towards them, in what he hoped would be seen as a gesture of peace.

"Hello," he said, working very hard to keep his voice calm and even.

One of the men, maybe a little older than the others but otherwise no different, stepped forward, handing his bow to one of the other men as he did. He copied Valdar's gesture, his hands out and open, and spoke in a language Valdar had never heard before.

Valdar held up a finger, hoping the "one moment" gesture was somewhat universal, and looked back to his men.

"Give me that piece of cloth," he said to one of the sailors, pointing at some of the supplies they'd brought ashore.

He could hear the natives tense as the sailor grabbed it and ran it forward, putting the brightly colored, tightly woven scrap of fabric in Valdar's hands. Valdar turned and held it out to the leader, who, after a moment, took it, running his fingers over the soft material with a look of wonder. Valdar then drew his sword, a gleaming steel blade that caught the sunlight.

A ripple of strange words went through the natives, several of whom drew back their bows but paused as Valdar put the blade and pommel across his hands, extending the weapon to the native leader.

The native leader picked up the sword, testing its weight and balance. He nodded, a smile spreading across his face. He gestured to the bay or maybe across the bay, then to the ground where they stood, speaking in his native tongue.

Valdar tried to follow, piecing together the meaning as best he could. Valdar gestured to his people and the area where they stood and the trees nearby. They did this for what seemed like a long time, each gesturing to the other. Valdar got the impression these men lived somewhere on the other side of the estuary, making it a pretty sizable walk between there and the proposed spot for his port. If he had to guess, they were a hunting party of some kind, since there didn't seem to be anyone else around.

Valdar thought he got across the idea that he and his men wanted to settle here, and that he wanted to trade goods between them. At one point, he gave them a small mirror, one of the many wonders the Consul had taught them to make. The native was almost terrified at first, then amazed. Valdar pointed to it and some of the dried meat the natives had on them. The man got the idea and gave a fair amount of dried meat to Valdar, who took a bite of one piece and then handed the rest to one of his men.

They had an interesting moment when Valdar reached over and, after a few minutes of somewhat comical confusion, grasped the native's forearm in a shake, putting the man's hand on his forearm in return. The man, after a moment, seemed to understand the gesture and smiled at him broadly.

Returning to his group, the natives all chattered amongst themselves, examining the fabric, sword, and mirror. They seemed truly excited by it all. As far as Valdar could tell, they weren't hostile, which was fortunate. He'd had run-ins, as a younger man, with great bearded men living near the ice flows above the northern sea, who'd been instantly hostile when his then captain had gone ashore, so Valdar knew how badly this could have gone.

Valdar let the men mingle, and there was a lot of interest on both sides. Valdar spoke multiple times, in as gentle a voice as he could manage, reminding his men that they needed to stay calm and not take anything the other men did as offensive. He told them that it would take time for the groups to understand each other's customs.

Eventually, the native group left, probably to return to their village and tell others what they'd seen. This meant that by tomorrow he'd end up dealing with a larger group. They did indicate, Valdar thought, that they'd return, and Valdar tried to give them the idea that their visits would be welcome.

"Alright, let's get back to work," Valdar called out as they left. "Optio, keep patrols at the rear and no one goes off alone. Understood?"

"Yes, Admiral," the man said, his eyes following where the natives had gone. "Do you think they'll be a problem?"

"It's hard to say for certain. They seemed more curious than hostile, but we must remain cautious. We don't know their customs or how they might react to our presence here."

"I understand."

"Good. Make sure you keep everyone on task once we leave. Your very first job is to build a workable palisade to use for defense and to maintain a constant guard once you do. Have everyone sleep aboard ship if you need to. Don't provoke the natives, but make sure you take every precaution you can think of. Store anything of value aboard the ships as well. Remember, we're not here to start conflicts. This is to be a trading port, and there may be valuable goods we can acquire from the locals."

"Do you think they'll have anything worth making all this effort worth it?"

"I don't know. The primary goal of this port is to give us an easier way to resupply and stay in touch with the homeland, but if we're going to do it, we should try to make it actually profitable. I'll make sure to give orders to the schooner captain to bring back items useful for trading; tools, textiles, and the like."

"I'll make sure we keep everything safe."

"I know you will. While the captains are in charge of their ships, I'm placing you in charge of the port itself until someone from home sees fit to send someone senior. Also, be on the watch for sickness. I seem to remember the Consul mentioning something about a disease carried by mosquitoes when he spoke of Africa. I want you to send word to him and the Empress through the commander of the Kalb garrison, asking them for any special instructions they might have, and to see if you can find out more about this disease and how we can protect ourselves from it."

Dismissing the optio, Valdar went to give similar instructions to the captains that would be staying behind. This was a risky plan, and there were numerous things that could wipe this small settlement out before it had a chance to get started; but if they could hold on, it could actually turn out to be a viable thing for them in Africa. He'd shipped some goods from Carthaginian ports, before Scandia became more involved in the war, that had originated from ports further east. Getting the goods directly had not been an option for merchants before, considering the land distances involved, but if they could make it around by ship, it might be feasible.

He'd started this plan out of pure military necessity, but there was a chance it could actually turn out to be profitable at the same time.

Middle Sea, Southwest of Italia, Nearing the Coast of Sicilia

The wind whipped past Ky as the schooner cut across the Mediterranean Sea. After more than six months stuck in the quagmire that was Italy, he was finally out and moving again. His timetable might be much tighter than it otherwise would have been, but Ky was thrilled, nonetheless.

"We're making good time," Ky said to Bomilcar, who walked up with Aelius and Auspex in tow from the stern of the ship.

"We would be there already if we'd crossed straight to Zancle," Aelius pointed out.

"No one disagreed with you on that, then or now," Bomilcar said, visibly stifling a sigh of annoyance as Aelius brought up the topic for the thousandth time. "The Carthaginians have fortified it too much. Landing even near the city would be costly, and possibly bog us down again. A legion on the ground, marching to the city, is a lot more effective than trying to land outside its gates. If Valdar's fleet hadn't done such a good job clearing the waterways, then maybe, but without having to fear Carthaginian interception, this is far preferable."

"The debate has already been settled," Ky said before Aelius could start the argument again. "Aelius, you'll still get your shot at Zancle when you march north with your legion, while Auspex and Bomilcar's legions march south to deal with Syrakousa. As far as our scouting can tell, it's the much larger garrison, and a bigger threat to us."

"Yes, Consul," Aelius said, getting the message.

"It'll be nice to be done with this and on to Africa," Auspex said.

"Agreed," Ky said. "You all did amazing work, getting things moving once you were freed up again. I want to commend all of you on your excellent work."

All three men were unused to compliments and only mumbled their thanks in reply.

Even though they were traveling the longer distance, it didn't take long for the schooner to cross it, with the Sicilian coast coming into view after only a few hours. Dozens of galleys and two of the large caravels traveled with them, packed with legionaries and equipment. Not the entire army, but enough to conduct an assault. It would take several days to land everyone. That gave the enemy time to react and adjust their force disposition, but there wasn't an option to avoid it.

"Send in the first wave," Ky said to the signalman waiting next to him.

The legates had all boarded longships. They had scattered the legions across all of the ships evenly, to allow the maximum number of longboats to land at a time. Ky watched as the sleek boats, already dropped down next to the ships that carried them, skimmed across the water and skidded onto the shore. While only about a third of the men in the ranks had taken part in the last amphibious landing on the Insula Manavia, many of the unit leaders had been line legionaries during it, and everyone knew what they were doing.

As soon as the boats were ashore, the men piled out and began forming a semi-circular line, pushing up off the sand and rocks and onto firmer ground, where they waited for the boats to return bringing the next wave. For twenty minutes, Ky waited and watched, not even pretending to use a spyglass, for the enemy to attack. The Carthaginians had to know they were coming. Beyond the fact that they'd been building up forces along the east coast of Sicily, anyone with military experience would have known the Britannians couldn't just leave that large of an island, with at least a handful of full units of Carthaginians, sitting behind them as they went for Africa. They'd passed a few small fishing vessels, which Ky had to assume one or two were plants to watch for the inevitable landings, which also meant the Carthaginians had to be monitoring their progress, and knew they weren't going for Zancle after all.

And yet. Nothing. The second wave landed and then the third, and other than a few locals trotting out to look at the ruckus, no one appeared. He wasn't the only one concerned by it. Ky could see riders headed north, south, and west, probably sent by Bomilcar to figure out what the Carthaginians were up to. By the time the fourth wave of longboats prepared to sail, Ky couldn't take it any longer.

Over his lictore's objections, he boarded one of the longboats and joined that wave going ashore. Landing, he found Bomilcar, Aelius, and Auspex huddled up with a small group of runners and aides.

"Consul," Bomilcar said. "I sent out scouts; I would have expected to see the enemy by now."

"Either they've pulled back to the defended their positions or they have abandoned the island altogether to defend their homeland. They're outnumbered here as it is, so maybe they decided it wasn't worth the effort."

"Maybe," Bomilcar said.

"Yeah, I don't buy it either; but honestly, it doesn't matter. Whether they want to fight in the open field or let us shell their cities, I'm happy to oblige. Once three-fourths of the men are ashore and the scouts have returned, we will continue with the plan. One way or another, I want to be off this island and landing on the shores of Africa by month's end."

Carthage

Imilcar's stomach rumbled. He'd been feeling ill for weeks now, and it was only getting worse with every piece of bad news that was delivered. Although they hadn't said anything directly to him, yet, he knew his healers were concerned with how rapidly he was losing weight, his skin sagging in pouches on his face, giving him an almost drooping, melted appearance.

Not even pushing his generals, punishing failure with the most brutal consequences he could imagine, seemed to slow the flood of bad news. If anything, it was starting to isolate him more. He used to rely on the infighting among them to ensure he received all of the information he needed, but as their ranks dwindled and the failures grew, it seemed few wanted to stick their necks out enough to tell him of the latest disaster. Which is why he only heard about this latest problem through gossip and whispers. It was time for him to put his foot down and start finding out what was now happening in his empire.

"I'm not sure what rumors you refer to, Great One," the guard captain, sent to be a sacrificial lamb by cowardly superiors, said.

"Then ignore the rumors and tell me is it true? Are there a large number of refugees coming into the city from the continent or not?"

"I'm not sure I would say they are coming into the city. There have been an ... umm ... influx of citizens from Italia, Sicilia and some of the islands the Romans have yet to take over showing up over the last month, as the Romans have begun to make more headway. We've also seen some ... umm ... allies from Hispania arrive, but they have mostly shown up at smaller ports and not the capital."

"But they are coming. Abandoning their duty to defend the continent?"

"... Yes," the man said, almost more a question than a statement.

He was sweating in fear, and looked like he might try to turn and run at any moment.

"And how, pray tell, are they managing to navigate past the Roman fleets when our own supply ships cannot? How were they not inspected?"

"I believe the ships these people were on were stopped, Your Eminence. With some exceptions, the Romans have stopped every ship that crosses the Middle Sea and inspected every vessel. It seems, however, that if it is a civilian ship with no signs of weapons or military supplies, they allow it through. I believe they are trying to win the favor of the commoners, or are at least attempting to not antagonize them."

"They think they're that likely to win?" Imilcar asked himself, before returning his attention back to the captain. "Have any of these ships brought our warriors back from the continent?"

Beads of sweat formed on the guard captain's brow, his eyes darting from side to side, as if he was looking for a place to escape.

"I ... I'm not certain, Magnificent One. It's possible some have returned, but ..."

"But what?" Imilcar snapped. "Speak plainly, or I'll have your tongue cut out and fed to the dogs."

The guard captain paled, rubbing his hands together to control their trembling.

"F-forgive me, Your Excellency. I know you ordered that not one step of ground was to be lost. But there have been ... rumors ... that some of the commanders have been ignoring those orders."

Imilcar leaned forward, his voice low and dangerous. "Go on."

"Some units, they say, have come back to Africa. That they left their weapons behind and slipped through the Roman blockade on civilian ships. But I don't know that for certain, I swear it!"

The guard captain looked like he might faint at any moment. Imilcar felt his stomach turn again. He knew they were too cowardly to openly disagree with his orders, but to secretly defy him?

That was even worse. He would send the Acolytes of Hexitas out to look for these commanders. If they'd defied his word, then punishment must be dealt, or he'd lose control of the entire army.

Still, if they were willing to go so far, knowingly putting their lives at risk in defying him, it was something he needed to take into account.

Imilcar stared at the guard captain for a long moment, his dark eyes boring into the man's face. The captain shifted uncomfortably under the emperor's intense scrutiny, clearly fearing the worst.

Instead of yelling at him or having him dragged out of the room and thrown in chains, Imilcar said, "Very well. We shall deal with those cowardly commanders in due time. But for now we have more pressing matters to attend to. I want you to begin rounding up anyone coming from the continent. Put them under arms, for the defense of the homeland."

The guard captain blinked in surprise. "Your Excellency?"

"You heard me. There are many brave citizens who have been defending Italia and they did a good job slowing the Romans down. If these people do not want to help with that, then they can help with the defense of the homeland itself. Anyone not in a critical job such as farming or smithing, something needed for supplying the city or the armies, they are also to be put into arms."

"But ... but, Your Excellency," the guard captain stammered, "many of these people are civilians. They're not trained for battle."

"They will still be effective in stopping an arrow, or one of those ... what did the TianYou diplomat call them? Bullets?"

"Yes, Your Excellency. I will see it done."

"Good. Once we have enough men, I want you to begin building up defenses along our coast. Get with the army commanders and any units arriving from the continent should be put into the defenses. With the Romans now in Sicilia, they are but a short distance from our shores, and I am not confident the commanders there will be any more successful at stopping them than any of the other failures have been. It is only a matter of time before they attempt to cross into Africa, which will put their armies at our very gates. I'm not deluded enough to think they won't land on Africa, but the further from Carthage we can push them, the better."

The captain opened and closed his mouth several times, but said nothing.

"I want you to take every measure to prevent the Romans from landing anywhere along our coast. Use the new weapons we've acquired from the TianYou. Fill the beaches with bodies if you must but make any landings near Carthage impossible."

"Good. Now go," the emperor said, dismissing the man, who scuttled away the instant he was released, like the bug he was.

Looking around the room, Imilcar signaled to one of the messengers, "You. Send word to the commanders. If the Romans are allowing people to escape the continent on civilian boats, then it's time we bring all our trained soldiers home from the continent west of Anatolia, including Greece. We need every able warrior for the defense of the homeland and it's clear they are too foolish to defend it successfully."

The man nodded and dashed out of the room. Imilcar sat back in his throne, resting his now floppy jowls on one hand. He'd hoped the cannon could turn the tide against the Romans, but they'd been ineffective in ship battle, and delivering them to the continent to be used in land battle had become all but pointless. They'd lost enough of the weapons for him to order a halt to the delivery of them, for fear of not having enough for defense of the homeland.

The chance to stop them on the continent was gone. If they were going to defeat them, it was going to have to happen on African soil.

Chapter 28

Syrakousa, Sicilia

Ky sat with Bomilcar and Auspex as the two legions fanned out, marching toward the wall of Syrakousa. The only good part of the slow march down Italy, chasing the fleeing Carthaginians, was that it had given the men a lot of practice assaulting fortified positions with rifles and cannon.

After first Daramouda and then Rome, they had learned that, in spite of the technological difference in their forces, the Carthaginians were far from helpless. Ky assumed there'd be a trap waiting for them here, as there had been outside the walls of Rome. That went doubly, now that they'd learned the Carthaginians had, somehow, managed to acquire the ability to make cannons of their own. What bothered Ky was that, this time, it wasn't just a copy of Britannian weapons. These cannon were much simpler than the weapons Ky had taught his people to build, using techniques from developmental stages of artillery production that Ky had skipped over, deciding to go straight for early and then late nineteenth century designs.

According to Sophus, these were close to designs found in the late fourteen hundreds. A little better built maybe, but still un-re-inforced tubes made of brass that would have serious structural problems if fired too much.

Not that they weren't dangerous. These were the types of weapons that had brought down the walls of Constantinople and toppled the last remnants of the original Roman Empire, back in his future's past.

Which is why they had their lines well separated, to keep from letting the cannon tear them apart. It also meant that his men would have to form squares if cavalry appeared, which was another reason for the slow approach to the wall.

Of all the things Ky had expected and prepared for, none of them covered what was actually happening. As the legions closed to within range of the walls, the city gates creaked open. Ky was ready to sound the call for the men to form into squares when, instead of cavalry, a small group, of what appeared to be civilians, emerged from the gates, waving a white strip of cloth, stopping a few steps from the gates. Ky and Bomilcar looked at each other.

Every fiber of Ky's being shouted that this was some kind of trap. It had to be. Nothing else made sense, and the Carthaginians had shown how willing they were to resort to those very tricks.

Still, unless they were ready to open fire on unarmed men, there was little choice in the matter.

Ky and Bomilcar nudged their horses forward, signaling several squads of legionaries to follow them, leaving a nervous-looking Auspex behind. Ky knew what the younger legionary was thinking. If this was a trap, his two superiors would be in the middle of it, leaving him on his own.

It was a valid concern, but Ky wanted to know what was happening, and he didn't want to get it secondhand. As they drew closer, Ky could see that the men were elderly, their clothing generally of better quality than that of most people he'd seen under Carthaginian rule. The man holding the white cloth stepped forward, looking between Ky, Bomilcar and the soldiers, clearly very nervous.

"Greetings. I am Evander, the mayor of Syrakousa."

Ky studied the man for a moment before saying, "I'm not sure why the Carthaginians sent you out, but if they want to surrender, we will need the highest military leader in the city, and not a civilian. Otherwise, our attack will commence promptly."

"I think you misunderstand. There are no Carthaginians in the city."

"What do you mean?" Bomilcar asked, again exchanging concerned glances with Ky.

"The Carthaginians abandoned the city two days ago, taking everything they could carry with them."

Ky frowned. In other situations, it would make sense for an outnumbered military force facing an opponent that had shown its capability for taking down defensive walls to run, but the Carthaginians had never done that before. They'd retreated, as they had in Italy, but when given the chance to stand in a fortified city, they always did. They'd captured enough men to know their emperor had issued orders not to give up one meter of soil.

For them to just run from a fight was antithetical to everything Ky had seen so far from them.

"Where did they go?" he asked.

"They left the city by the west gate and headed further in that direction, but I overheard them talking about going to Africa once they reached a port closer to the coast. However, I do not know if that was true or not."

"That doesn't make any sense," Ky said. "We've had reports of their movements all along, and there are more of our ships in the area now, not less. There's no chance of their entire army getting across. Why wait until we're almost at the gates to make a run for it?"

"Perhaps they didn't think we'd make it across and land in Sicilia," Bomilcar offered.

"Maybe," Ky said, not sounding like he believed it. "Or maybe it's a trick. Lately they've gotten very good at coming up with ways to get around our superior weapons."

"I'm not lying, I swear it! You can march through the front gate and see for yourselves. The city is empty of Carthaginians."

"If you want me to believe this isn't a trap, trying to get me to march my legions into tight streets where our weapons give no advantage is not doing it."

The man looked helplessly from Ky to Bomilcar and back, clearly trying to figure out how to convince them he was not lying.

"Either way, unless we just want to stay outside these walls forever, or put it under siege and starve everyone out just in case this is a trick, we're going to have to send someone in to look at things. We were ready to take the walls by force, so there is risk either way."

"You and your group wait here," Ky commanded the mayor.

He doubted these nervous men were part of a plan to notify people inside the city or that the Carthaginian army, if they were still here, would care about sacrificing a civilian to pull it off, but Ky still wanted to keep him and his group here as hostages until they knew it was safe.

"Send two squads forward to check it out," Ky ordered Bomilcar.

At the general's command, twenty legionaries came trotting forward out of the main line.

"Take your men into the city," Ky commanded one of the decani in the group. "Search as many streets and buildings as you can, look for any signs that this is a trap or that the Carthaginian army may still be inside the walls. If you find anything suspicious, no matter how minor, report back immediately. If not, return in thirty minutes with a full report."

"Yes, Consul!" the man said, saluting sharply, then barking orders to the men with him.

The minutes ticked by, Ky straining his remarkable hearing as far as he could, listening for gunshots, shouts, or anything else that might indicate the men had sprung a trap. The fact that he heard nothing only served to unnerve him more. Not only did he hear no sign of warning from his men, but there was little noise at all coming from the city. It was still occupied, but normally massive cities required Sophus to dial down the volume and filter out much of the noise, to keep it from damaging Ky's enhanced senses.

None of that was needed here. For a city, it was eerily quiet.

Finally, as the chronometer in Ky's vision almost clicked down the last of the thirty minutes, the decanus emerged through the gates, his men followed close behind. He approached Ky and Bomilcar, saluting once more.

"Consul, we found no signs of Carthaginians within the city. The people seem to be mostly hiding in their homes, but otherwise, everything is quiet. No indication of any military presence."

"I'm still not comfortable just marching the legions in. They must have known we'd send in a group to check, and there's no way the squads made it to the south gate. There's still lots of places for their soldiers to be hiding."

"We could send in a full century," Bomilcar suggested. "Have them spread out through the city. As they secure each district, more can follow until we have complete coverage. That way, we're not spread out and the men can hold each block, staying prepared for an attack."

"Risky, but better than nothing, I guess. Work outward from this gate, establishing a parameter and have the men make sure any one group does not get too far ahead."

Orders were passed, and groups of legionaries began moving into the city, one century at a time. Ky sat patiently, as a hundred and then thousands of men passed through the gate, slowly spreading out through the streets and alleys, almost making the city sound alive with the noise they generated.

An hour progressed, and still every report was that there were no signs of the Carthaginians anywhere within the walls of the city. A full legion now patrolled the streets, yet they encountered only frightened civilians huddled in their homes.

"This doesn't make sense," Ky said to Bomilcar before turning to the mayor. "You're coming with us. We're going to see this for ourselves."

The man looked nervous, but fell in behind Ky and Bomilcar, Ky's lictore pressed in close to them. The city looked closed, as if everyone who lived here had taken the day off or had traveled to somewhere else. Shutters were closed, doors barred. They only saw the occasional child's face peeking out a window before being hurriedly pulled back.

"General," one of the legions tribunes said, riding up to their small group. "We've reached the far wall, still no sign of the enemy. We've searched all large public buildings and have men on most street corners. If they're here, they're very well hidden."

"They must have known the city was going to fall," Bomilcar suggested to Ky. "Perhaps they truly did flee west to a port where they could escape to Africa."

"Maybe," Ky said, still sounding unconvinced. "But I won't believe this city is truly empty until we've scoured it from top to bottom."

"I can have the men conduct a house-to-house search. If they're still here, that's where they have to be. It will take time, however."

"Fine. In the meantime, have the remaining legion set up a fortified camp outside the city walls. I want all our artillery positioned there, just in case. Your legion will quarter here in the city tonight, but stay on high alert. Let me know if you find any wooden horses."

"As you command, Consul," Bomilcar said with a slight chuckle.

Off the Horn of Africa

As Cormac made his way from the docks to the Palace Complex, he was amazed by how much the city had grown in his absence. He didn't know if the city, already seemingly the busiest place in existence, had actually grown and become more lively, or if it was just the six months he'd spent in Hispania, with its much slower pace, relatively, that made him forget how mad this city was.

Even with a squad of praetorians accompanying him, they had almost been run down twice by carts piled so high with goods it seemed as though they would topple over.

Arriving at the palace, Cormac dismounted and handed his reins to a stable hand who had just run up. Thanking the guard for the escort, Cormac made his way into the palace, which was, thankfully, much more controlled and reasonable than the streets outside.

Nearing the residences, he saw a servant heading in the other direction. Although he hadn't been here in quite some time, and even though he knew that the palace had many servants, Cormac suddenly realized he did not know, from either face or name, any of the servants who'd previously waited on him before he'd left for the continent. While he'd grown up with servants, and had been used to them, it wasn't until very recently that he realized the importance of them.

A lot of the information he had gotten about the tribes in Hispania had come from servants, many disgruntled, who heard and saw a lot more than their masters thought them capable of. If that was true in a more primitive setting like he found in the tribes of Hispania, it had to be doubly true in a place like this. It made him realize that completely ignoring them, as if they were furniture, was a mistake. Thankfully, one that had not been fatal to him before it was too late to realize it.

That passed through his mind in a moment before he flagged the servant down and asked, "Could you inform Medb that I have returned and will be in our quarters at her convenience?"

"Yes, Prince Cormac," the servant said, bowing deeply.

"Thank you," Cormac said, causing the servant to pause a moment before rushing off.

Cormac entered the chambers, and immediately saw that the city was not the only thing that had transformed in his absence. Medb had clearly been busy, redecorating their quarters with an even greater level of opulence than before. Rich tapestries adorned the walls, many depicting scenes from their homeland that must have been custom-made. The furniture, too, had been upgraded, with intricately carved wooden pieces and sumptuous upholstery in deep shades of green and gold.

He walked around the room, taking in the lush carpets that looked to be from Anatolia or Persia, vases and decorative touches from Greece, and even what looked like a Scandinavian carved bone horn cradled in a carved stand on one table. For an Empire at war across the known world, the width and scope of the finery here was impressive.

"Do you like it?" Medb said from behind him, coming through the door to their quarters.

"I do. You certainly have outdone yourself."

"I'm surprised you didn't send word that you were coming home. I would have prepared a proper welcome."

"It was a last-minute decision, really. With the Arandur suppressed and more tribes signing alliances by the day, Llassar and I agreed it would be better if I came home."

"Really? You don't think it would be better to stay until the alliance was more solidified?" Medb asked.

"You've been reading the reports I sent back, I see," Cormac said. "No. We started hearing a growing number of whispers that, since I set up the alliance, or at least got it started, I was making myself the ruler of Hispania. That was not exactly the message we wanted to send, nor how we wanted to start the alliance off, so I thought it better to leave Llassar to manage the next stage of their development and take myself out of the mix. I'll go back in a few months, meet with the allies I made there, and tour what's being done at Port Invictus. But generally, they need to become more used to dealing with the Empire and not me specifically. At least if we're going to make it work in the long term."

"That's ... actually very clever, Cormac," Medb said, giving him an appraising look. "Yes, I have been following your reports closely and I was already impressed with the work you managed there, but I hadn't realized just how much you've ... grown up."

"You know, there was a time I would have taken offense to that comment. But you're right," Cormac said with a slight smile, which dropped almost as quickly. "Enough to know that last year, you were using me, leading me by my desire for you, into near treason."

"I see."

"Not to start our reunion on a sour note, but it is something I've spent a fair amount of time thinking about. Being in Hispania, dealing with the tribes, the politics, the constant negotiations ... it made me see things differently. Made me see how naïve I was."

"And what do you see now?"

"I see that you somehow managed to convince the Empress to not only give you a second chance but to put you in a position of power. I can't help but wonder how you managed that?"

"I did what I had to do, Cormac," not answering him directly. "I won't apologize for how I used you. It was necessary, at the time."

"I know, and I'm not asking you to. I think you're wrong, in that it wasn't something you had to do, but something you only thought you had to do. I have to ask ... do you still plan on trying to make yourself Empress?"

Medb paused, her face impassive as she stared back at Cormac. He couldn't figure out if she was deciding to tell him the truth or sizing him up. She had an amazing ability to be almost completely unreadable, something he knew he was not nearly as good at.

"No, Cormac. I no longer plan on trying to make myself Empress," she finally said.

"Really? That's a surprise, considering where you were this time last year. What changed your mind?"

With a small shrug, Medb said, "Having spent time in Lucilla's chair, I've come to realize that I don't actually want it. Not in the way I thought I did, at least."

She walked over to a nearby settee and sat down, gesturing for Cormac to join her.

As he sat down next to her, she said, "I've gained a great deal of respect and authority in this position, Cormac. More than I ever thought possible, given my past … indiscretions. But with that respect and authority comes a burden that I hadn't fully appreciated until now. I thought I knew what it would entail, from how my kingdom had been, but this Empire … it's an entirely different level. Especially set up as it is, with so much power shared between the various factions and limitations on what a ruler can do. Managing it all, even for a short while, has made me realize that I don't want that responsibility. Not permanently, at least."

"So, what do you want then? I can't imagine that you'd be happy, closeted in an estate somewhere, brooding children."

"Gods no," she said, letting out a light trill of laughter. "A child, eventually, might be nice. Maybe two, but that's where I draw the line. No, I'll be more than happy to give the reins back to Lucilla when the time comes. Let her deal with the headaches and the constant demands. I've found that I much prefer being a power behind the throne."

"I think that's probably wise, and it would suit you. The ruling from behind the throne, not the babies, although I'm sure you'd excel at that just as well. Speaking of babies, where does this leave us? I'm not satisfied to continue being your pawn, Medb. Not after everything that's happened."

"No, clearly that won't work anymore. You've grown, Cormac. Matured. I can see that now."

The way she spoke about using him, so matter-of-factly, was almost chilling. And yet, in a way, also intoxicating. She was unlike any woman he'd ever met, or probably ever would meet.

She must have seen the look on his face because she placed an arm on his hand and said, "That isn't a line, I mean it. Before ... that was different. At the time, I thought it just how you were, another man only focused on armies and fighting. I see I was wrong. You simply needed a chance to expand your role. I see a much bigger role for you, beyond simply a piece to move around the board."

"What kind of 'bigger role?'"

"With your newfound maturity, confidence, and ability, I believe we can become a ... what was the phrase Lucilla used once? A power couple. The Empress, she's too soft. Kindhearted. Not always, but often. The thing she has going in her favor is that she knows it. She knows she needs to have someone behind her, willing to do what she isn't. It's why she keeps Ramirus around. He's good, but he's too much in the shadows. The nobles and wealthy see him as a functionary, not a superior. No, sometimes she'll need someone in the public eye, part of society, but with authority and a willingness to accept a ... wider range of options. Let the people adore their Empress, their beloved Lucilla. And when they cross her, let them fear us."

"And do you think the Empress will want you doing that?"

"I do. I did something like that for her before she left and put me in charge, which I think was what convinced her to put me in this position in the first place. I might need to convince her, but I don't think that will be too much of a hurdle. She's smart ... smarter than I originally realized. She'll see the value."

"I see," Cormac said, considering her. "I appreciate your honesty, Medb. It's refreshing, a different side of you."

"I'm not always trying to manipulate people, Cormac. Do I work to get what I want? Yes. Does that sometimes require manipulation and deception? Also, yes. But that isn't always needed. With you, I think we can work together more effectively if we are honest with each other."

What surprised Cormac the most about all of that was ... he believed her. Of course, she was a master manipulator, so maybe he was just deluding himself into believing her, but if he wanted a real relationship, one built on actual foundations, he'd have to give her the chance to prove she could do that.

"I believe you. And I'm willing to support you, and be your partner, in every sense of the word. I know I was too credulous before, but I'm not that person anymore. Please don't let this chance go to waste. I probably won't give you a second one."

"Well, I'll have to be on my best behavior, won't I? Maybe I should start now," she said, pushing him back against the edge of the settee and leaning over him.

"Maybe you should," Cormac said, smiling.

Chapter 29

Syrakousa, Sicilia

Ky relaxed in the center of the room, eyes closed, his mind focused inward. It wasn't sleep, precisely, but it allowed more of his processes to shut down and the nanos swimming through his body to do more of the work they needed to do cleaning his system of the standard degradation of time, which allowed his age to extend so much beyond that of a human life span in this time.

As it did every time he entered his rest state, he thought to Lucilla. She had her own nanos which, thanks to Sophus's ingenious extension of the limited technological equipment available to them, still operated even though the couple remained thousands of miles apart for months at a time.

The question that always came to him in moments like this was, how long could her nanos keep the rigors of time away from her? What would her life span be? Now that he'd found her, found these feelings, he couldn't imagine ever losing her, and yet the fact that he would live for probably another one to two hundred years meant that, eventually, she would leave him.

It was worse for Sophus who, although sentient, had no body of its own that would give it a sense of the passing of time. It was along for the ride, forced to experience its death without ever changing what it saw as its own being. Would Sophus be able to keep his flesh going after he passed? Continue existing in his lifeless husk? It was impossible to know. No one had ever had an AI in a body for so long, let alone a sentient one. They were in uncharted waters.

He was just about to fall down the rabbit hole of his thoughts, when the noise of a distant commotion somewhere in the city pushed its way into his consciousness, pulling him out of his thoughts and back to the present. Even with the increased pickups and filtering, it was hard to work out exactly what the sounds were.

And then sounds suddenly erupted outside of the house he was staying in. Shouts in the street. Dozens of sandaled feet striking hard-packed earth, followed by a crash of wood, sending Ky propelling upward. By the time the first alarm was shouted, Ky was already jumping down the stairs, landing with a hard thud on the first floor.

His men acted fast, already engaging the first few men through the door, but the surprise had been almost complete. Ky could hear a guard outside in combat, meaning they'd isolated the door guards, swarming the building to get their men inside.

His men were trying to form up, protect the stairs and their charge, whose sudden appearance hadn't yet registered. Ky knew Carus, on the far left, would be furious for what he was about to do, and he didn't care. Leaping over his men in a forward lunge, Ky landed in front of them and rolled into a fighting stance, forcing everyone, friend and attacker alike, to freeze in place for a moment, surprised by his sudden appearance.

A moment was all Ky needed.

With superhuman speed, his blade whipped out and caught an enemy off guard, slashing across an exposed throat, sending the man crumpling to the floor. Two more went down almost as fast, with a fourth mortally wounded by the time his compatriots finally got their senses about them enough to begin responding, with the first enemy blade making its way toward Ky, almost in slow motion, as Sophus identified and began plotting all of the potential tracks across his vision.

Ky spun, parrying a blow from one of the attackers and feinted left before striking right, catching a man in an exposed thigh as he lunged forward, Ky's blade going in just far enough to sever the artery before pulling back and whipping around to block another attack.

"Consul," Carus finally shouted, seeing the man he was supposed to protect in front of him. "Protect the Consul."

His men tried to surround him, put their bodies were between him and danger. Ky knew they meant well, but his greatest asset was his mobility, his ability to dodge and parry attacks at lightning speed.

"Give me room," Ky shouted as he dispatched another man. "Surround the door."

The door was the key. With each man Ky killed, another came through. They had to staunch the flow of enemy and regain control of the situation, or some of his men would die. Already, Firminus was bleeding, an arm hanging limp where a sword had cut deep into the muscle. If this went on much longer, he'd lose even more of his precious guards.

And then, as suddenly as the attack began it ended, with men falling and no more coming through the door to replace them. This was the only place the fighting had stopped, however. The noise in the city continued to grow, a building crescendo of shouts, screams, and curses.

Ky rushed outside, hurdling over the bodies of the fallen enemy, almost certainly the "missing" Carthaginian soldiers by the look of them. On either side of the door were two legionaries, placed there to guard the building. The sight of Carthaginians lying near their bodies proclaimed that they didn't go down without a fight.

Fires raged unchecked, the flames casting an eerie orange glow over the city. Screams and the sounds of metal clashing sounded from every direction, signaling how widespread the fighting was. From one of the side streets, a wounded legionary stumbled out, clutching his side.

"Consul," he gasped, his face contorted in pain. "The Carthaginians ... they're everywhere. They came out of nowhere."

"Are you alright?" Ky asked, grabbing him, helping hold the man up.

"I'm fine. We ... fought our way here, to you. The others ..."

"I understand. You did your duty. Where were you when they attacked? Do you know how many?"

"Five blocks over, manning an intersection. I don't know how many, but they came from every direction. Hundreds, maybe. It was quiet and then ... they were there, attacking. Cutting us down."

"Go inside, rest. You've done enough."

"No," the man said, stepping away from Ky's arm and standing on his own, pain etched into his face. "I can fight."

Ky wanted to order the man to go rest, but he knew he'd do the same in the man's place. He wouldn't take his honor from him now.

"You're a good man," Ky said, before turning to one of his lictores. "Pacatianus. Take this man and any other legionaries you can find. Make your way to the front gate and out to Auspex's legion on the plains. I'm sure he's seen the fighting and will be on his way into the city, but help guide him. I want his legion to establish a perimeter around the gate and push out from there. We need a zone of control and safety for our wounded. They must have been in some of the houses, and there might be more. He isn't to push to another block until he's cleared all the houses inside his perimeter. He is to move slowly, checking everything before moving forward. He's to value security over speed. If the Carthaginians are smart, they planned for our second legion, and have another trap ready. I don't want him falling into it."

"Understood, Consul," Pacatianus said, saluting.

Ky clapped the wounded legionary on his shoulder, before turning his attention to Carus and the few legionaries that had started to gather, all coming to the same conclusion as the other man had. The Carthaginians were probably rallying either here or at the headquarters Bomilcar had set up a few blocks away.

"The rest of you, with me. We'll assemble every legionary we can find and establish a perimeter around this building. I want to fight towards Bomilcar, who is almost certainly doing the same. From there, we will expand out and connect with whatever zone Auspex has carved out. We are retaking this city, block by block."

Before any of the remaining men could start moving to follow his orders, a shout from behind alerted him to a new threat. Another group of Carthaginians, perhaps thirty strong, emerged from a side alley, charging towards them with swords drawn.

The legionaries reacted instantly, their training taking over. They quickly arranged themselves into a loose formation, each man covering his neighbor's vulnerable side.

The Carthaginians crashed into them like a tidal wave. Ky parried a vicious thrust, countering with a lightning-fast stab into

336

the man's chest. Next to him, Carus fought like a man possessed, cutting down two men almost as fast as Ky could have.

"Consul! We must fall back to a more defensible position!"

"Fall back to Bomilcar's position," Ky ordered.

It seemed impossible that the enemy had enough men to attack like this all over the city, which meant the real thrust was here, against him. The other attacks were probably diversions. If that was true, it was likely Bomilcar's command post was also being hit hard, and he could not afford to lose the general.

A Carthaginian soldier lunged at him with a spear. Ky side-stepped the thrust and grabbed the spear shaft. Wrenching it from the man's grasp, he spun it and with a swift motion, drove the spear point through the soldier's chest, then kicked him off the blade.

"Consul, watch out!" Carus shouted, rushing forward to intercept a Carthaginian who had slipped past Ky's guard.

Carus's sword cleaved the man's skull in two, spraying bone and brain matter across the cobblestones. Ky nodded his thanks, then turned to face the next attacker.

Step by step, the legionaries fought their way to the square, leaving a trail of Carthaginian corpses in their wake. Occasionally a single or maybe a pair of legionaries would see them and join up. Slowly, the odds evened and then shifted, until the Britannians were no longer the outnumbered ones.

And then they were there, at Bomilcar's command post. Much as Ky had expected, it was surrounded by Carthaginians, with the bodies of a dozen legionaries scattered around in front of the building. Bomilcar stood behind a wall of men who were fighting valiantly, a more sensible plan for him, considering his lack of enhanced abilities.

"Help them," Ky called out to the legionaries with him. "We'll finish this."

Ky redoubled his attack on the few Carthaginians left assaulting them as all but his lictore turned and charged the men attacking Bomilcar's command post. As if on cue, the remainder of Ky's lictores appeared, looking bloodied and tired, but intact. Their sudden attack finally turned the tide, giving everyone around the command post a slight breather.

The battle wasn't over yet, however. He could still hear screams and shouts coming from across the city.

"You found us," Ky said to Sellic, grabbing the man's blood-smeared arm.

"We followed the bodies," Sellic said, indicating the trail of dead Carthaginians that led back to the house Ky had quartered himself in.

"Good. Help Carus and Bomilcar. We're establishing a front here. There should be enough of us."

More and more legionaries were appearing, either from the direction of Ky's living quarters or headed directly for the command post. They were good men, and all doing what they needed to do.

The men, now bolstered, fought with renewed vigor, pushing the enemy back from the command post, creating a bubble that slowly expanded. As they advanced, they encountered pockets of resistance, Carthaginians emerging from side streets and alleyways to engage them in brief, bloody skirmishes. Each time, the Britannians pushed them back, their numbers growing as they rescued beleaguered legionaries and added them to their ranks.

The fighting was intense and chaotic, with no clear front line. Ky found himself constantly on the move, racing from one crisis to the next as he sought to turn the tide of battle, leaving an unhappy Bomilcar at the command post turned reinforcement depot and hospital. From there, the general directed reinforcements to ensure their perimeter held up, and that every building was checked thoroughly for men laying in wait.

They were not without losses. Legionaries going blindly into buildings was a dangerous mission, and several were slain each time they found hidden Carthaginians, but they succeeded in their mission, digging the enemy out from their prepared ambushes one at a time.

The battle felt endless, especially to the exhausted legionaries, many of whom had been woken up and thrust immediately into the fight. Thankfully, the men he sent for the remaining legion did their job, and after almost an hour of straight fighting, fresh legionaries appeared, helping clear streets and buildings, replacing men ready to drop from fatigue.

By the time daylight broke, the city was once again theirs.

Off the Horn of Africa

Valdar gripped the railing hard as the ship pitched and rolled in the turbulent seas, the gray skies above unleashing sheets of driving rain. Icy spray lashed his face, the salt stinging his eyes. The Consul had warned him the waters here were treacherous, but he'd sailed the northern seas and into the great waters that stretched endlessly west, and had thought he was prepared for anything.

He'd been wrong. These were some of the roughest conditions he'd ever sailed through. It felt as if the very seas themselves were in competition, with one side pushing him west and the other pushing him east.

"Reef the mainsail!" Valdar bellowed above the howling wind. "Secure those lines!"

His crew leaped into action, scrambling up the rigging to battle the flapping canvas. The deck heaved beneath their feet, making the task a perilous dance.

Waves crashed over the deck, threatening to sweep away anyone not securely tethered. Valdar ignored them, his attention focused off the port side of his ship, following one of the schooners struggling in the maelstrom. The smaller vessel rose and fell with sickening velocity, its deck awash with foaming seawater. Valdar watched with growing unease as the schooner's mast swayed precariously, the wood visibly flexing, visible even at this distance.

The schooner's crew scrambled about the deck, working frantically to secure the rigging. It was all for naught. Even as the sailors fought to control their vessel, Valdar saw the mast shudder violently as the winds and pressure on the deck pulled it this way and that.

With a final, wrenching motion, the mast gave way, snapping like a twig in a giant's grasp. The top section toppled, plunging into the churning sea beside the crippled vessel. The schooner lurched drunkenly, its balance lost, and it began to list heavily to one side.

Sailors were thrown about on the schooner's deck, some tumbling over the side and vanishing into the sea. He didn't need to hear the words to know the desperate cry that would be ringing out: "Man overboard!"

Not that there was anything they could do for those poor souls. Not in seas like this.

They weren't the only ones struggling. To the starboard, two of his galleys had drifted dangerously close, the towering waves and brutal winds conspiring to push them together. Their much smaller masts, not built into the frame of their ships but bolted to the decks, weren't enough to control the vessels. Not in seas like this.

The gap between the two small ships narrowed, bringing them closer and closer, until collision was unavoidable. The men fought valiantly, but without success, as the two ships slammed together with a sickening crunch, planks and beams sheared from each vessel, flying in every direction. The men aboard the ships were flung about like discarded dolls. Worse were the ones in the way of shredded timber, which became missiles in the collision, spearing the men like arrows shot by the gods.

"Ready the rescue boats!" Valdar commanded, his voice straining to be heard. "We need to get our men off those ships!"

"Admiral, in these seas the boats will be swamped in minutes! We'll lose even more men!"

He was right. Valdar cursed himself and the seas as he watched one of the galleys roll over and begin its trip to the bottom.

"Throw lines to the damaged ships!" he ordered. "We'll tow them through the storm. And get every able-bodied man bailing water on that schooner!"

The crew hastened to obey, hurling weighted ropes across the heaving gaps between the vessels. On the stricken schooner, sailors snatched up the lines, lashing them fast to the cleats.

"Heave!" Valdar roared. "Put your backs into it, men!"

His own ship groaned as it took the strain of pulling another ship while fighting the waves. He saw one of his other caravels closing the distance, following his lead as it tried to pull two of the remaining ships to safety.

They continued east, pulling the lamed ships, ordering his other vessels to keep wider gaps, which made communication worse, but kept additional collisions from happening.

Two hours later, the winds died down and the seas calmed. It was still overcast and drizzling, but at least his ships weren't being thrown about like the gods' playthings any longer.

The damage, however, was done. Half his ships had damage of some kind, mostly minor, but they needed to find a harbor to effect repairs. Two more were damaged to the point of no longer being able to move on their own. And two ships were lost entirely. Aside from the galley he saw go down, another had just disappeared into the abyss. It had been astern of one of his other caravels, which lost sight of it temporarily in a crest of waves. When they came out on the other side, the galley had just been gone, vanished as if it had never existed.

For another hour, he kept the ships in sight of land, which now sat off the port side as his fleet turned north, looking for a place they could pull ashore. The crews on his two most damaged ships bailed continually, trying to keep the sea out of them, but they were running out of time.

"Admiral," one of his crewmen who'd been assigned to keep his glass fixed on the shore called out. "There."

Valdar took the man's glass and followed where his finger pointed. Sure enough, it looked like a protected inlet, or at least enough of one that ships sitting off the shore wouldn't be swamped and pushed onto the sand.

"That will have to do," Valdar said. "Signal the fleet to heave to, and hold off the coast. Any ships in need of repair are to follow us in. Galleys can beach and brace for repairs if they must, but otherwise they are to hold and repair in the shallows."

The battered fleet limped closer to the shore, the crews of the damaged ships struggling to keep them afloat long enough to reach the shallows. All but one of his ships stopped as they entered the natural port, with the one damaged galley continuing until its keel scraped the sandy bottom.

As soon as it made contact, dozens of men jumped overboard, splashing through waist-deep water as long lines were thrown to them. With great effort, they managed to pull the ship out of the water, its hull grinding against the sand and rock.

As it came out of the water, Valdar could see a great gash along one side from the impact with the sunken galley. It was a miracle the ship had managed to stay afloat.

"Send our carpenter and any unoccupied men to the damaged ships to help with repairs. Focus on the ships still floating. All legionaries are to go ashore and set up a perimeter. I have no idea what the locals here are like, but I'm not willing to risk it. Captains are to fix what they can, but the fleet will continue on by the morning. Once repair work is underway, I want all captains who are able to meet me ashore for a conference in an hour."

The officer nodded and went to begin sending the signals. It took more than an hour to get most of the captains ashore. No vessel, not even the Bellona, was without damage, which left a lot to be done.

Not that the captains were wasting time. By the time Valdar and the rest made it to shore, the cannons of the damaged galley had been offloaded and one of the fleet's carpenters had declared the ship unsalvageable. While not unexpected, it increased the total to three ships lost, and they hadn't even been in a battle yet.

"While that was difficult, we made it through," Valdar said, once the captains were assembled. "I know what we'd all like to do is stay here for a little while and lick our wounds, but we still have a mission to accomplish. We were ordered to cut off the flow of weapons to Carthage, and that's what we're going to do. The Consul might not have known about the Red Sea route, but that doesn't make it any less of our concern, and every day we spend getting there is another day they can make shipments. When I said I wanted to sail by morning, I meant it."

"What about the damaged ships?" the captain of the damaged schooner asked.

"I'm afraid we can't wait. No offense to our galley captains, but if it was just galleys, I'd say sink them and transfer all of the crew and materials to the rest of the fleet, but I'm not willing to give up on the Velox as quickly, which changes things a bit. Actually, this works out. It's too far to make regular trips back to the other port we set up, especially with how unpredictable the trip around the horn is going to be, which means we'll need another port on this side of the continent anyway. This just decides the location a bit earlier than expected."

"It's a lot drier here than on the other side of the continent," one of the captains pointed out.

"True. It doesn't mean farming will be impossible, but it does make it harder. Thankfully, fishing should still be an option. Beyond that, we'll work it out as best we can. Since it appears the Maris is unsalvageable, I want it broken up for parts. Have anything valuable or usable taken off. We can use some of it to help repair the Velox, which is still seaworthy enough to offer some protection. Beyond it, I'm also going to leave four galleys here. Two will station here to help with fishing and offer protection, since the Velox won't be particularly mobile. The other two will make the trip back to report on our situation and arrange supply shipments for this port. You are not to risk your ships. Navigate carefully and turn back if conditions worsen. We need additional supplies and reinforcements, not more boats at the bottom of the sea. Understood?"

Both captains nodded that they did.

"Good. We'll be leaving several of our carpenters and craftsmen here, as well as all of the legionaries we have left. I don't expect us to set up any more ports and they won't be able to do much when we take on the Carthaginian supply ships, so it's better to leave them here to help protect this location. I think that about sums it up. You all have work to do. I'm very serious about sailing at first light, and the next time we stop will be to intercept a potentially hostile fleet, so I want every ship as seaworthy as possible. You all have a lot of work to do, so get to it."

Chapter 30

Syrakousa, Sicilia

Ky and Bomilcar once again rode through the streets of Syrakousa, but the experience was much different than the one they had just a few days prior, when the city had seemed equally peaceful and still.

In spite of the smoke still rising from fires not yet completely under control and cobblestones still slick with blood, the streets were suddenly teeming with the previously missing women and children. They still didn't know for sure if the civilians had been missing because they had been held captive by the Carthaginians or had been hiding because they knew the Carthaginians were still in the city, although if Ky were a betting man, he would have assumed the former.

What was clear was the sudden relief they all shared that it was over. Not all had made it through unscathed, caught in the fight between the Britannians and the Carthaginians, but most had. In spite of that and the damage to their homes, the threat of future violence was over, and they were able to do what civilians throughout time had found a way to do, exist under occupation.

"I should have trusted my instincts," Ky said to Bomilcar as they passed a group of bandaged legionaries.

"You didn't do anything wrong," Bomilcar said, pulling his horse to a stop. "It was a clever plan, one they must have been working toward for weeks, maybe longer. Ever since it became clear their plan in Italia wasn't working. The Carthaginians weren't just hidden in people's homes. They dug out concealed spaces beneath floors and within walls to avoid detection, then threatened the civilians to keep their presence a secret. It made the trap exceptionally difficult to spot. Even with all of that preparation, you knew there was a danger here and took steps to deal with it. Ordering the men to keep dispersed and the continuous inspections of houses throughout the night looking for the soldiers you suspected to be hiding ... Those actions ultimately exposed the Carthaginians, triggering their ambush before they were fully prepared."

"Small comfort to the men we lost," Ky said.

"It's a comfort to the much larger number of men we might have lost but didn't. If the Carthaginians had been able to gather their forces and fortify their positions, taking back the city would have been a much bloodier affair. Consider the alternative. If we had been forced to breach the city walls under a traditional defense, our losses would have been far greater. The Carthaginians' unconventional strategy left them vulnerable to a swift counterattack once their presence was revealed. We had to enter the city if we were going to keep to our timetable. We managed to do it and defeat the only full army on Sicilia with what would be very minimal losses compared to a more traditional siege. You should be proud."

"Perhaps. But the cost was still high," Ky said, nudging his horse forward again.

Nothing the general said was wrong, but Ky could still feel the absolute surprise and chaos of the battle, replaying the video stored in Sophus's data storage. Maybe it was true they took precautions, but the surprise had still been total. And the fault for being surprised by the enemy like that stopped with him.

What it did tell him was that they had played it safe and were still surprised. They'd taken Britain, Ireland, and Europe through aggression, not by this slow stepping, careful progress. Ky had let what happened in Italy color his thinking too much, and allowed himself to slow down despite himself.

"Our intelligence indicated that there was only one major army in Sicilia," Ky said, changing the subject. "And the forces that retreated from Italia are pinned up north by Aelius. It's unlikely any went west, let alone to Africa."

"You don't think they could have slipped past our lines? Our navy is fairly spread out."

"I know, but they don't have any large ships for transport. It's one of the reasons I was so skeptical their army had fled to Africa. To move enough men to make a difference, they would have to use enough ships to handle that, we would know."

"And ..." Bomilcar said, giving Ky a look as to say 'What's your point?'

"I don't want to wait to clear the rest of the island. I want to cross to Africa now."

"Now? But Consul, that could be dangerous. Even without another army in Sicilia, there are probably scattered forces that could be a problem."

"I know," Ky said. "But we can't afford to delay. Every day we wait, Carthage has more time to prepare their defenses. I want Auspex and his legion here. That should be enough to hold the island and assist with the other priorities."

"Other factors?"

"Valdar has moved out of the Mediterranean and requested more legionaries. And Llassar in Hispania has also asked for reinforcements. I want to start clearing the rest of the islands, just in case."

"Consul, that will leave us with only two legions for the attack on Africa. Is that wise?"

"I know it's a risk, but we've allowed the enemy to dictate our momentum for months now, and I'm not going to let it continue. The Carthaginians are running out of provinces and places to draw manpower from. I'm not going to let them march men from Greece or Persia and consolidate."

"But two legions ... Africa is a large place."

"And more sparsely populated than the areas we've been through so far. We've come this far by striking hard and fast, not by playing it safe. If things get bad, Auspex can turn Sicilia over to Marcus and come join us."

"The enemy has shown an impressive ability to overcome our technological advantages and surprise us. By moving quickly, we give them more opportunities to do so."

"If they do, we will adapt to them. I trust the men. I'm set on this, my friend. I want to be in Africa by the end of the month. We need to press our advantage while we have it."

Bomilcar was silent for a moment, his eyes searching Ky's face. Finally, he nodded, though his expression remained troubled.

"As you command, Consul. I'll make the necessary arrangements."

"Thank you," Ky said, reaching across the space between their animals and slapping the Carthaginian on the shoulder. "I know you'd prefer we go slower, and I appreciate your warning. Keep telling me when you think I'm wrong. I might not always agree or follow your advice, but I promise I'll still listen and weigh it carefully."

Bomilcar gave him another firm nod. It had been several years since he defected from Carthaginian service, but years of autocratic, top-down command that brooked no disagreement or discussion had their effect on its commanders.

Ky never wanted to be like that. Bomilcar might be overly cautious, but he had more experience with men in the field than Ky might ever have. He wouldn't let such a valuable resource go to waste.

Germania

Lucilla emerged from the small hut she had been quartered in since coming to Germania, feeling a cool breeze whip past her. Summer was coming to an end. She allowed herself a moment to feel the air and take in a deep breath before opening her eyes again.

It only took her a moment to find the man she'd set out to find. Not surprising, since Modius was very rarely out of sight of whatever room she was in at the moment. She found him a dozen paces away, engaged in conversation with a tall, broad-shouldered Germanic warrior.

It was a good sight to see, a Britannian and a Germanic engaged in what looked to be a friendly conversation. The last few months had been filled with difficult negotiations, as tribes distrustful of anyone becoming a new overlord trying to control them made setting up a lasting relationship difficult. In spite of that, they'd managed it, and most of the tribes of Germania had signed on. She predicted that in a year's time, maybe two, they'd form a more cohesive political body with their neighbors, much like the world Sophus often described to her.

One where all sections of the planet were controlled by political entities made up of a range of people, rather than small tribes fighting over every patch of land they could get their hands on. The level of overall prosperity and security Sophus described, outside of a few fairly devastating wars, was something she wanted for her people. She could only imagine a time when the main pursuit of a populace wasn't just trying to feed itself, constantly worried about someone taking what they had.

There were pitfalls from the future Sophus described that she wanted to avoid, but with what it and Ky knew, it was possible to build a new future for themselves.

Of course, first, they had to end this war with the Carthaginians. Which is why she came looking for Modius. Attentive as ever, she had been outside for only a beat or two before her guard captain noticed her, politely excused himself from the conversation and made his way to her.

"Your Majesty," he greeted her with a respectful bow. "Is everything alright?"

"Who's your friend?" she asked, pointing at the man who was now walking away from them.

"His name is Dagmar, part of a group from the Anarti way out east. He's one of their chieftain's guards, and we got to talking while you were meeting with his chief. They're returning home now that most of the negotiations are done, and he stopped to say goodbye."

"Did he give you any sense of how his master feels about how things have gone here?"

"Not directly, but I get the sense they're pleased. He's talking about traveling to Britannia next year. He's desperate to see the train after I described it to him."

"They'll get a chance. One of the things we agreed on was building out a railway here as well, which will help us as much as it does them."

"They know that, but I think they're still curious to actually see it. Hearing about it isn't the same as seeing it."

"If you speak to him again, please tell him the Empire welcomes him and will give him a grand tour when he visits. The more of their people we can win over and send home to talk about it, the better it will be for our relations."

"I'll make sure to mention it."

"Good. Since it seems our job is done here, I want you to begin preparing a small guard force to escort me to Italia. Large enough to take us beyond the peninsula and on to wherever the legions will be when we get there."

"Your Majesty, with all due respect, I must advise against this course of action. Joining the legions on the front lines is far too dangerous for the Empress."

"Considering the deal we just finished making and the relationship we have with the Germanics, do you believe the journey to Italia would be unsafe, Modius?"

"Well, no, but ..."

"And did you not just say that our relations with the Germanics are better than they've ever been?" Lucilla pressed.

"Yes, Your Majesty, but that doesn't mean we've eliminated all threats. There are still bandits and other dangers lurking in the wilderness. And from what I hear, the situation in Italia is far less stable than it is here."

"Which shouldn't affect us. The first group of Germanics heading to the peninsula to bolster security there is set to depart within the week. Over a thousand warriors. It's highly improbable that any bandits would dare to challenge such a formidable force."

"Only through Germania, Your Majesty. Once we reach Italia, they will report to the legion and be dispersed across Italia, leaving us on our own just when security becomes the biggest issue."

"We have garnered support from numerous allies who have dispatched their own men to aid in stabilizing the region. Between their presence and your own fearsome reputation, I have the utmost confidence in your ability to ensure my safety."

"And after that? We may have allies in Italia, but we do not have them in Africa, which remains outside of our control, and no one, not even I, can guarantee your well-being in an active war zone."

"I appreciate your concern, Modius, but I will be surrounded by legions of our finest, most well-trained soldiers. I do not expect to be perfectly safe. Not when I'm, as you point out, in a war zone, but if the legions fall, my safety is doomed no matter where I am."

"But if the enemy learns you are there, if they target you, they could ..."

"Enough," Lucilla cut him off, her voice firm but not unkind. "I understand your reservations, but my decision is final. This is not a matter up for debate. I have received word that Ky is heading to Africa to end this war once and for all, with only two legions. I don't know what help I can be, but I will not allow him to face this alone."

"A message, Your Majesty? I wasn't aware that any messengers had arrived recently."

Lucilla waved a dismissive hand and said, "What matters is that I need to be there, not just for Ky, but for our people. They need to see their Empress standing with them in their time of greatest need."

"I will, of course, do as you command, but I must express my deepest reservations. Having both the Consul and the Empress in the same place, in an active war zone no less, could lead to disaster for the Empire."

"The Consul can keep us safe, Modius. We are on the verge of winning this war, and I refuse to sit idly by while our people fight and die for our future."

"But what of the Empire itself? Surely you are needed back in Devnum, to govern and maintain stability."

"Surprisingly, Medb has things well in hand. I will need to be back by winter, but for now, the reports from Ramirus have been extremely positive, and I trust in their ability to manage affairs in my absence."

Reaching out, she took his hands in hers and said, "I may never get another chance to do something like this, Modius. Our people are putting themselves into the lion's maw, risking everything for the sake of the Empire. I will not let them do it alone."

"If we go, I must insist on taking every precaution to ensure your safety."

"Of course," Lucilla said, squeezing his hands and giving him a bright smile. "I wouldn't dream of making your job harder."

The look he gave her in return reminded her very much of looks her father would give her when she was a girl, trying to get whatever mischief she was up to past him.

North African Coast, Near Carthage

'They were finally doing it,' Ky thought from the flagship of his fleet, as it cut through the calm waters of the Mediterranean. The ship's white sails billowed in the steady breeze, propelling them towards the North African coast. Behind him, the rest of the fleet followed in a well-maintained formation. Three additional caravels, two of the newest schooners, just arrived from Britannia, and dozens of galleys, all packed with the legionaries of the Seventh and Ninth Legions.

Years of fighting had all lead to this. They were taking the fight to the Carthaginians. They'd picked a landing point thirty miles outside of Carthage. Close enough to be within easy striking distance, but not so close that the city could rally to counter the landings easily.

Or so Ky had thought.

As the shoreline grew in his enhanced vision, he could see hundreds of people moving along it. Horses, chariots, and carts, all following and converging where his ships were headed. They were still too far out for Bomilcar or any of the other men with him to see what was coming, even using the spyglasses they were all staring through.

"We have a problem," Ky said to Bomilcar.

"What do you see?" the general asked.

Ky had used his augmented senses enough times that it had gone from a wonder for his commanders to a tool they used with ease.

"The shoreline is packed. Hundreds of people, and growing by the minute as more arrive. Only some look to be soldiers. I would assume the rest are civilians, by their dress, but everyone is armed. I'm also seeing catapults and, I think, some of those primitive cannon Valdar warned us about."

"How did they know we'd be landing here?" Bomilcar asked.

"I don't know. We're not that far from their capital, so maybe they didn't, although if they just spread a ton of people along the coast, watching for us, that is a lot of manpower."

"Should we start the landing anyway? We've come this far."

"Let's test the waters. Send in two galleys and have the rest of the fleet cover them. If it looks like we aren't going to be able to land and get men ashore, they are to reverse course and return to the fleet immediately."

Bomilcar nodded, turning to relay the orders. The deck sprang to life as men rushed to their stations, preparing for the assault.

The fleet began to shell the shoreline beyond the intended landing point, the thunder of dozens of cannons echoing across the water. Under the cover of the bombardment, two galleys broke from the formation, oars dropping down and pushing the ships in a straight course for the shore.

As the galleys drew closer, the Carthaginians responded with a barrage of their own. At first, it was only arrows and boulders hurled from catapults, all falling short. It seemed a waste. The arrows looked mostly to be coming from the civilians. A panicked move. The catapults were another thing. Operated by professionals, they should have known they didn't have the range.

It wasn't until the crude cannons started firing that Ky realized they had been gauging the range. The weapons sounded odd, deeper and more guttural with a much dirtier smoke drifting up from them, but they were still dangerous, based on the velocity readings Sophus was extrapolating.

"Look there!" one of the men shouted, pointing towards the shore.

Ky followed his gaze and saw, to his disbelief, Carthaginians throwing themselves into the sea. They swam towards the galleys, arrows plunging into the water behind them, shot by men in Carthaginian light armor. The galleys were a long way out and anyone who reached them would be so exhausted as to be unable to fight seriously, but it explained the arrows. They were sending their own civilians like lemmings, trying to overwhelm the galleys.

"They're mad," Bomilcar muttered. "They'll never reach the ships."

Ky wasn't so sure. There was a desperation to this whole defense that would make any landing costly. It was wild and unfocused, and could almost certainly be defeated, but not without a cost.

Suddenly, one of the enemy cannons found its mark. With a splintering crack, a section of railing was ripped away from the lead galley, sending legionaries tumbling into the sea. The ship listed heavily, oars faltering in their rhythm.

"Damn," Ky muttered before calling out to a signalman. "Order both galleys to pull back to the fleet."

There was a moment's hesitation, a pause that stretched for what seemed an eternity. Then the galleys began to turn, their oars straining against the water as they fought to reverse course. The Carthaginians redoubled their efforts, swimming frantically to close the distance, but the galleys were already pulling away.

Thankfully, there wasn't another hit from the cannon on shore, although several got close.

"All ships, focus fire on those cannons!" Bomilcar ordered as the galleys cleared out of the way.

Signalmen relayed the message, each ship letting off a barrage of fire as the word went down the line of the Britannian vessels. Wave after wave of fire pummeled the shoreline where the cannons had fired from, sending up geysers of sand and dirt.

There were a few well-placed, or at least lucky, shots, striking a handful of Carthaginian cannons, obliterating them and scattering their crews in a shower of limbs and debris. The rest, however, remained intact. The Carthaginians might have been many things, but incapable of learning from past battles wasn't one of those. They'd experienced Britannian shelling many times, had adapted to it, dragging the guns back to prepared positions with strong overhead cover.

"They're pulling back," Ky said. "Still close enough they can quickly roll them forward again to deploy, but protected enough that we'll need direct hits to take one out."

"We got a few before they pulled back," Bomilcar pointed out.

"True, but not enough. We'd burn through all of our powder and spend a week here, going back and forth, trying to whittle down their artillery, during which time they would be reinforcing and probably bringing up new pieces."

"That isn't going to work," Bomilcar said.

"No. It isn't. Halt the shelling."

"So we give up?"

"No, we're not giving up. They're just too well entrenched for us to dislodge them. We could probably still force a landing, but the losses would be heavy, and we're still going to need to fight once we get to Carthage itself. We'll have to move to an alternate landing site further down the coast. There aren't enough men and cannon in Carthage to cover the entire shoreline of North Africa, so they will have concentrated them within range of their capital. It'll mean a longer march to Carthage and allow them to concentrate more forces, but in the field we stand a better chance than we would in an amphibious assault."

"Won't they have people watching, consolidate forces wherever we land?"

"Probably, but they can only see so far out and we control the seas. We'll have to pull further out, well out of sight and avoid any civilian traffic, since some will undoubtedly be eyes for their emperor, but a day or two's sail down the coast will put us well beyond what they can cover. Send one of the messenger ships to order two caravels out of Kalb to begin shelling Carthage itself. They're to keep a good distance from the shore and don't need to be concerned with controlling the port, I just want to give the Carthaginians something for their attention to focus on. Send out the rest of our scout ships to begin looking for a secondary landing point. From there, it will be a long, dry march to Carthage."

"If we stick close to the shore, at least we won't have to work too hard to get supplies until we reach their capital."

"Precisely," Ky said. "No one said this was going to be easy."

Chapter 31

Carthage

The room, usually bustling with courtiers and petitioners, was eerily silent. Imilcar slouched against the gilded backrest, not even bothering to hide the lines of worry and fatigue any longer.

He could see the few courtiers and generals attending him looking concerned, but he didn't know if it even mattered. The recent landing attempts by Roman forces so close to his capital had dealt a devastating blow to his already waning confidence. He had always prided himself on his ability to maintain control and order, but now it seemed that everything was slipping through his fingers like sand.

"Gentlemen," he began, his voice low and somber, "it appears that our efforts to repel the Roman invaders have been ... insufficient. Only the forces we put along our coast kept them from landing directly on top of us. While they did an excellent job repelling their landings, we do not have enough men to cover the entire coast. It is now apparent that we will not keep them out of Africa."

The men shifted uncomfortably, avoiding eye contact with their emperor, as they usually did, waiting for his outburst. For the orders to execute whoever was in charge of the latest fiasco.

Instead, Imilcar said, "In light of this development, I have come to a difficult decision. We must withdraw all our forces from across the empire and consolidate our defenses around Carthage itself. I know most of the continent has been abandoned, but what forces there still are in Greece or anywhere else on the continent, as well as Asia, are to return home at once."

A wave of shock passed through everyone in the room.

General Hadar cleared his throat and said, "Your Excellency, does this include our vital regions in Persia and Egypt?"

"Yes, General. All regions."

"But, Your Eminence, Egypt is of strategic importance to us. It serves as the primary trade route for receiving shipments from the TianYou. This includes both the gunpowder and cannons. If we lose control over Egypt, we effectively cut off our supply of weaponry."

"And what do you suggest, General? That we spread our forces thin, trying to defend every corner of the empire while the Romans march on our capital?"

"No, Mighty One. Of course not. I just … I am not sure we can hold off the Romans without those weapons."

Imilcar wasn't sure they could hold off the Romans with them either, but the general had a point.

"Very well, General Hadar. We shall maintain our presence in Egypt to protect the trade route. But Persia and Anatolia must be abandoned. We cannot sustain our holdings there any longer, not with the Romans bearing down upon us."

"As you command, Your Excellency. But the forces currently stationed in those regions, by the time they reach us, the enemy will already have set foot on African soil."

"A good point," Imilcar said. "They are to consolidate their forces and engage the Romans directly, with orders to inflict as much damage and as many casualties as possible. They are to use their entire forces if they must, but I want the Romans utterly weakened before they reach our walls."

"Sire?" an advisor said, stepping forward. "These commands. Such a strategy … it would mean …"

"It would mean," Imilcar interrupted. "That we are no longer the empire we once were. We are now a power confined to Africa. Unless you have armies tucked away inside your robes, or the favor of the gods to bring the sun down and crush our enemies, I'm not sure what other option we have. Make no mistake, gentlemen. This is our last stand. We will make the Romans bleed for every inch of ground they take. We will fight them in the deserts, in the mountains, in the very streets of Carthage if we must, but we will not surrender. Not while a single one of us still draws breath."

The room fell silent as the gravity of Imilcar's words sank in. He wasn't done yet, however.

"To that end," he continued. "Any town, village, or people that could aid the Romans or provide them with supplies is to be destroyed as our forces withdraw."

"Your Excellency, are you suggesting we ... eliminate our own citizens?"

"I am ordering exactly that. The populace is to be either absorbed into the army or ... dealt with. We cannot risk leaving anything behind that the Romans could use to their advantage."

"But, Your Eminence," another general interjected, "many of these people have been loyal to Carthage for generations. To turn against them now ..."

"Loyalty means nothing if it leads to our downfall," Imilcar snapped. "I want the Romans starving and weakened by the time they reach the gates of Carthage. If that means sacrificing our own, then so be it."

"As you command, Your Excellency," Hadar said, before anyone else could offer new arguments. "We shall begin the preparations immediately."

"See that you do, General. And remember, failure is not an option. The survival of Carthage depends on the success of this plan."

Dismissed, the generals and advisors filed out of the room, leaving Imilcar with only a few attendants as he stared at the ornate map of the empire that dominated the far wall. The once-vibrant tapestry of colors representing Carthage's vast holdings now seemed to mock him, a reminder of all that he had lost and all that he stood to lose.

He wasn't going down without a fight. If his reign ended with him, he'd take as many of the damned Romans as he could with him and leave nothing of his vast empire but blood and sand.

North African Coast, West of Egypt

The darkened waves lapped at the longboats as they glided towards the North African coast. Unlike the last time, there was no artillery or horde of men forced into the ocean at arrow point. They were a days sail down from their last attempted landing, which Ky hoped was enough.

Already, half a legion was on shore, formed up and prepared to counter an attack, should it arise. Not that it seemed to Ky that they'd be surprised. While not exactly the Sahara, the land was flat and lightly covered in trees, allowing his enhanced vision to see well into the distance. Other than some herders and a few huts scattered about, there didn't seem to be much in the way of hostile soldiers to challenge them this time.

It had been a tough landing, with the lights covered or put out on the ships, and the men forbidden from using torches and lanterns after they landed, but Ky had been adamant in his orders. Even this far from Carthage, Ky didn't trust that the enemy didn't have mobile units, waiting to be signaled by scouts spread along the coast. He wanted enough time to get all of his men ashore before they were hit by whatever the Carthaginians had waiting for them.

"How's it coming?" Ky asked Aelius, whose small command detachment met them as he hopped from the longboat.

"We should have both legions ashore in the next hour," the legate said.

"Good. Very good. Once they're ashore, move the men inshore just a little bit, far enough that we can entrench and build a proper defensive position while still close enough for the ships offshore to offer some protective cover. Keep three cohorts on watch, one set up in each direction and have everyone else building a temporary camp. I know wood is at a premium here, so use what the ships unload. We'll have to waste time digging up the stakes and everything each morning, but in this kind of climate, there's not much of a choice. We'll have to set up a rotating schedule where those on the deconstruction detail in the morning get up first, tear down while the rest of the forces march, and then fall in the back of the line and can avoid new defensive work preparations that night. Get with Bomilcar's aide and work up a schedule that can be given out to the cohort commanders. Also, all legionaries, even those on construction, are to keep rifles with a minimum amount of ammunition on themselves at all times while in Carthaginian territory. I won't take any chances now that we're this close."

"I will see it done, Consul, but … is this wise?" Aelius asked. "We're a long march from Carthage. If we stop to build fortifications every night and take them down each day, it will increase our journey by weeks, opening us up to attacks."

"It's what we'll have to deal with. The Carthaginians have made it clear they are willing to throw every person capable of holding a spear at us, and this is their homeland. If you thought we faced problems in Italia, that is nothing compared to being in Africa itself. I will not let our men get whittled down each night by harrying attacks just to save a few days march."

"It will slow us down more than a few days march," Aelius pointed out.

"Still, my point stands. We are on the verge of winning this. I have looked at the histories of how they took down Scipio Africanus. I will not fall to the same mistake."

"As you command, Consul," Aelius said, and then paused, as if unsure about his next sentence. "I apologize if it seemed like I was questioning your …"

"Think nothing of it," Ky said, interrupting him. "I want my officers to feel free to offer their thoughts and opinions of my orders, as long as it happens at the appropriate time. I'm not a tyrant."

"Certainly not," Aelius said, smiling again. "I'll see to the disposition of the men."

"Good man," Ky said, staring out into the darkness. "Good man."

It took several hours to get the rest of the legions, along with their equipment, wagons, artillery, cavalry, and horses, and the tools of war off the ships bunched along the coast and onto shore. The men did him proud, moved with a quiet efficiency, unloading supplies and equipment from the ships in the dark with little complaint, and then setting to the task of constructing a temporary fortification for the night, in spite of the late hour and their exhaustion.

Under the guidance of their commanders, they dug trenches and erected wooden palisades around the perimeter. They even used it as a learning experience, with some of the more experienced soldiers demonstrating the proper techniques to their younger comrades, ensuring that the defenses were sturdy and well-constructed. Ky couldn't help but smile at that. Time may change, but soldiers learning in the field, in the midst of battle, how to be better soldiers from their lower officers and friends was something that never changed.

As the night wore on, Ky patrolled the camp, observing the progress and offering words of encouragement to his men.

"Keep up the good work, lads," he called out to a group of legionaries who were driving stakes into the ground. "Remember, these defenses could be the difference between life and death."

By midnight, the camp was finally complete and most of the men not on watch settled into their small tent groups to catch a few hours sleep before they had to be up and marching west. Ky had allowed torches to be lit once the palisades were up. By now, if there were scouts out there, they would know the Britannians had landed, lights or not. And his legionaries didn't have the same physical advantage he had.

Ky himself found it difficult to enter his normal rest state. After years of fighting, they'd finally made it to the heart of Carthaginian territory. The end of the war was so close he could taste it.

Just as he was beginning to finally settle, a shout of alarm jolted him back to focus. Ky bolted out of his tent, his hand instinctively grabbing his sword, before the rest of him was aware it had happened.

"Carthaginians to the south," a sentry cried out.

Ky dashed to the parapet wall to get a better look. He wasn't even sure how the sentry had seen them, as they were still several hundred yards away, but Ky could make them out clearly. Dozens, maybe even hundreds, of Carthaginian horsemen thundered toward the Britannian position. Already, a rifle spoke here or there, although Ky seriously doubted the men firing could see what they was shooting at.

"Form a firing line," Ky called out as more legionaries showed up, half-dressed and unarmored, but carrying their rifles and cartridge pouches. "Prepare to fire by volley."

The Carthaginian cavalry had already started to turn, flowing across the expanse in front of the Britannian fortification, letting arrows fly into the camp. Ky could hear cries from the men unlucky enough to be in the way of one of those blind-fired arrows.

The horses thundered around the camp, reversed themselves, and came back in the other direction. In a normal situation, pre-firearms, this would have worked well, as most archers needed room to fire and were trained in arched volley fire, which meant that moving horsemen, who changed direction randomly, would be harder to hit, giving the attackers more time to rain their own arrows into a stationary camp.

Rifles did not fire in arched volleys, and the Britannians had enough men and weapons to cover the entire perimeter of the fort. The time between a commander calling for a volley and that volley impacting was measured in fractions of a second.

"Fire," Ky called out as the horsemen came back across his section of the line.

His men reacted instantly, a crackling wave sweeping the side of the palisade, its fire lighting up the night. Dozens of saddles emptied as his men fired. Within seconds, his force was ready to fire again as the man in each spot was replaced by the man behind him, his weapon already loaded.

"Fire," Ky called out.

Again, horses and men crashed to the ground as fire raked through their numbers.

If charging the temporary fort manned by rifles had been foolhardy, what the enemy did next was even worse. Bunched up together, they tried to ride away from the defensive works toward some semblance of safety. Instead, they opened up enough range to allow the cannon, loaded with grapeshot, to take aim at them.

The artillerymen had been waiting until the horses were no longer so close to the fort. They could not depress their weapons enough to fire at such a close range, but they had orders to take shots as they saw fit.

As soon as the horses tore away from the palisades, the first cannon opened up, its deep baritone boom distinctive from the lighter, higher-pitched cracks of the rifles. For the horsemen, it was like the gods themselves had pulled a hand across the earth, smashing through men and animals. Entire ranks fell after the first blast. After the other cannons had their say, almost none of the attackers survived. Those that did were riding hell for leather to the horizon, away from the death behind them.

"And that," Ky said as Aelius joined him on the battlement, "is why we need fortification."

Four hours later, Ky was still awake in his command tent, listening to the sounds of activity across the camp. The first cohort of legionaries had already roused, eaten, and were preparing to file out to the west to begin the long march to Carthage. Meanwhile, the temporary fort itself was already being dismantled, piece by piece, ready to be loaded on carts that would accompany them to their next stop.

The few they'd lost in the battle were already wrapped for final rites and cremation, their personal effects given to comrades or put in a pouch with letters to be sent to their families back home.

Ky doubted this was the last night his men would go with little sleep, as the Carthaginians would almost certainly try that again, probably with gunpowder and cannons as they got closer, instead of horse archers. It had been a risk, not having enough patrols out the night before, but Ky didn't want tired men out in the dark. At the next stop, they would better fortify their position and set up a patrol schedule to give them time to prepare for an attack.

Ky knew they'd lose more men, but he wasn't going to let them falter. Not when they were this close.

Around him, his aides darted about, carefully packing maps, dispatches, and other vital documents. Ky's personal belongings, sparse and utilitarian, had already been secured in preparation for the day's march.

"Consul," Aelius said from the entrance of the tent, or rather the south-facing wall, which had already been rolled up in preparation for the entire tent to come down.

"Aelius, good," Ky said, picking up the last of his things and taking the legate by the arm, leading him away from the tent. "We should get out of their way before they bring the whole thing down."

"Consul, I wanted to apologize for questioning your decision regarding the fortifications last night. It was not my place, and clearly I was wrong."

"As I said last night, there's no reason to apologize. Your input is valuable to me."

"Thank you, Consul. I'm just glad we have you with us. I'm afraid my legion would have been decimated by the attack last night."

"I think you would have done better than you think. However, since you bring up your legion, that's what I wanted to talk to you about."

A flash of worry passed across the legate's face that caused Ky to laugh in spite of himself.

"No," Ky hastily said. "It's not like that. I meant that I have orders for you and your men."

"Ohh," Aelius said, clearly relieved. "We are, of course, yours to command."

"We captured a few of the injured Carthaginians from last night's skirmish. They didn't know much, but what they told us was alarming. It seems the Carthaginians have ordered all of their forces, save those in Egypt, to return home. That includes the armies in Persia, which are the largest not including the ones in Carthage itself."

"They're abandoning Persia? After all the blood they spilled to conquer it?" Aelius said.

"It seems the Carthaginians have finally realized the gravity of their situation. This is no longer a war of conquest for them, but a fight for their very survival."

"I assume this changes our strategy."

"It certainly does. We cannot allow the Carthaginian army in Persia to march in behind us, smashing our forces between their armies. Which is where your legion comes in. Bomilcar and I will continue west, pushing toward Carthage with the Seventh Legion. You will take the Ninth Legion and head east. Your mission is to block and, if possible, defeat the Persian forces before they can reach us. I'm not sure how long it will take them to disengage their forces and begin their march in this direction, but I want you to only go as far as Egypt, even if you beat them there. I don't want you venturing out into the desert. Establish a defensive position around the delta. Hold it if you can, but fall back rather than being destroyed. This isn't about conquering Egypt but keeping their army from preventing our attack on Carthage."

"In a strong position with cannon and rifle, I think I can defeat them," the legate said.

"Maybe, but you're going to be outnumbered and it's unclear what you will face regarding the local populace. Do not take any risks. If possible, you have leave to make any alliances necessary with the Egyptians, following the structure we've already established. What's important is that you remain in contact with us at all times. As you advance, have your men set up telegraph lines. I will split our supply fleet and send half with you, which you can also use to carry messages if need be."

"Consul, with my legion heading east, will the Seventh Legion be enough to take Carthage by itself?"

"I hope so," Ky said. "I'm not sure we have much choice. Both of our forces will be outnumbered, but at least we'll have seaboard support. If we stay together, we risk being smashed into a single group, attacked from all sides. This is the only option I see."

Aelius only nodded. Ky knew it was a tough position to put him in and it said good things for the man that he was already thinking of the larger strategic picture. It showed potential for leading larger scale forces in the future, not just units as part of a larger force.

"One last thing. Either in Egypt or, if you fall back along the coast further west, I suggest you maintain hold as long as you can on a port city, using it for your base of operations. It'll allow you easier resupply. That's just a suggestion, however, and I leave the specifics up to you. You know your men and their capabilities better than anyone."

"I won't let you down, Consul."

"I know you won't. Now, get with your tribunes and prepare for your march. And Legate … make sure you set up defensive positions at night."

"I absolutely will," Aelius said with a smile.

Chapter 32

The Red Sea

Valdar was pleased. It had been a long and difficult voyage, but they'd finally made it to what the Romans called Sinus Arabicus, although he'd heard others call it the Sea of Reeds.

As they'd entered into the southern part of the sea where the old Egyptian charts actually picked back up, at least enough for him to navigate, he'd pulled his fleet away from the coast of Africa, choosing to sail up the center of the sea itself. He couldn't see the Arabian Desert to his east, but he knew it was out there. Close enough that it was unlikely a Carthaginian fleet could pass by unnoticed.

It wasn't foolproof, but it was the best plan he had without more thorough scouting. It also paid off.

An hour after they entered the waters of the Sinus Arabicus, his lookout called out that there were sails on the horizon. They were still a distance out, but he could make out a grouping of sails to the north, closer to the African coast.

That had to be who he was looking for, or at least it was a Carthaginian fleet. No Britannian ships had made it this far, so any ships they did see either belonged to Carthage or one of their vassals.

It wasn't until they started to close the distance that Valdar noticed something unusual about this fleet. Most of the ships were Carthaginian-designed galleys carrying the Britannian-style rigging that most of their ships used now. Four, however, were different. Their hulls were taller and more robust than his own caravels, with high sides that set them well off the water. More bizarre were their sail plans. Unlike the familiar square sails of Britannian ships, these vessels bore a strange, ribbed design, with multiple sails arranged in a fan-like pattern.

Ornate carvings adorned their prows, and vibrant banners fluttered from their masts, bearing symbols and scripts that Valdar had never seen before. More alarming were the clearly seen gun ports along the vessels' sides, much like those on Valdar's own ships.

The enemy fleet had clearly spotted his ships and were already turning to close the distance.

"They have cannon, boys. Prepare for action," Valdar called out.

This would be interesting. So far, they'd only really fought more traditional-style ships, which had given them every advantage. This was the first time his fleet, or really any Britannian fleet, would face off against ships that looked, at least, to be of a similar build. They knew it was coming, and the Consul had even instructed him a bit on the difference between combat with cannon-armed ships against galleys versus two ships equipped roughly the same.

At the time, Valdar had thought it a waste of time, seeing as how no one was able to build something like the caravels he'd been gifted with.

Now, he wished he'd spent more time listening to those combat strategies.

Their ships might be different, but the Carthaginian tactics seemed like they always had been, with them arranging their galleys out front in a crescent shape, clearly intending to encircle his ships. Behind them, the four strange vessels hung back, following the enemy fleet but not directly part of its formation.

If they chose to sit it out, Valdar was more than happy to oblige them and deal with their captains after the battle.

"Signal the fleet," Valdar called out. "Form a line, caravels in the center, schooner at the rear. Galleys on the flanks."

A minute later, signal flags began to flutter as the orders were passed from ship to ship. His ships tightened up, having practiced this formation many times and fought together through multiple engagements in the Middle Sea.

The Carthaginian were attempting the classic ram and board method. Good against other ships that fought more as platforms for spear-armed soldiers, but a poor choice against cannon-armed vessels.

"Turn to port and prepare to broadside," Valdar ordered.

His ships wheeled as one, turning to present their broadsides to the oncoming Carthaginian galleys. Valdar watched, patiently, standing steady on the forecastle as the ships got into position. It was important for the men to see their leader unafraid and confident, and that is the air he projected.

The moment his ships finished their turn, the row of cannon across each one pointed at the enemy fleet, Valdar yelled, "Fire!"

The caravels' cannons erupted, sending a hail of iron spinning toward the enemy ships. Rounds tore through the Carthaginians, splintering oars and rails. Men screamed as wooden missiles erupted in all directions, rending flesh and bone.

Then the galleys sailing in his wake opened fire, their cannons finishing what the caravels had started. In moments, what had been eight galleys had become three, two of which were listing as their crews fought to maneuver them out of the way.

"Sir, those strange ships at the rear are not moving," his first mate said.

"I know. My hope is that they choose not to engage."

Valdar could taste the irony, feeling doubt about the ability of an enemy ship and its unknown firepower, something many Carthaginians must have felt when coming against his caravels for the first time.

Sadly, his wish was not granted. As if on cue, the four ships began to advance, their sails billowing in the wind as they drew closer.

"Turn the fleet north and prepare for a broadside engagement."

As they closed with the enemy ships, Valdar could see the simpler cannon he'd intercepted, which had sent him on this mission, rolling out of the gunports on the sides of those ships.

"Brace yourselves, lads!" he shouted.

Enemy shot slammed into Valdar's ships, the rounds crashing against the sturdy hulls. Some ricocheted off the reinforced planking, leaving deep gouges in their wake. Others found their mark, piercing through the wood and sending splinters flying across the decks.

Valdar felt the deck shuddering under his feet as rounds tore through the hull before smashing out the other side. All around him, men screamed and died, in a level of horror he'd never been on the receiving end of before. And his ship did not get the worst of it.

The schooner, positioned at the rear of the formation, took the brunt of the punishing fire. Rounds tore through its lighter construction, leaving gaping wounds in the side of the ship, flinging men into the sea.

"Return fire!" he bellowed, pitching his voice up to cut through the chaos.

In spite of the horror around them, his gunners leaped into action, their well-drilled movements a testament to their training. They swabbed the bores, rammed home the powder and shot, and ran out their guns with practiced efficiency. A heartbeat later, the Britannian broadsides erupted, sending a hail of iron hurtling towards the enemy ships.

The Britannian rounds smashed into the strange vessels, splintering wood and sending debris flying as their lines passed. More Britannian guns roared, tearing hole after hole in the enemy ships. One well-placed round nearly cut the main mast of the lead enemy boat in two, sending it crashing over the side a moment later.

Despite the intense cannon fire, the Britannian ships held their formation, the caravels providing covering fire for each other as the lines passed. The danger wasn't over. The three remaining Carthaginian galleys, seeing that the Britannian ships were injured, looked to be swinging around, trying to come in while they were occupied.

"Signal the galleys on the flanks!" Valdar shouted to his first mate. "Engage those Carthaginian ships. Don't let them through the line!"

The Britannian galleys surged forward, putting themselves between his larger ships and the oncoming enemy galleys. With only one or two cannons apiece, they weren't able to take down the enemy through weight of fire alone, the way his larger ships had. Their captains, clearly seeing the danger, put their own ships in harm's way, smashing into the enemy galleys, their battle becoming a free-for-all as men began to swarm onto each other's ships. Seeing their lead, more of his galleys piled on, until the enemy ships were completely surrounded, boarded from all directions.

He would suffer losses there, but it took those enemy ships out of the fight. Two of the enemy's larger ships were out of action. One listing hard to the side, already on its way to the bottom while another, the one with the smashed mast, veered out of line, traveling in an aimless line, a plume of dark black smoke billowing from one of the holes in its side.

His ships did no better, with the vessel behind his showing serious damage. Worse was his schooner, which was clearly in trouble, its movements sluggish and erratic, hampered by the damage it had sustained.

"Order her out of line," Valdar said, pointing at the schooner. "And see if there are any galleys to come to her aid. The rest of the fleet will swing around for another pass."

His ships swung around, preparing for another pass at the enemy vessels. The damaged schooner limped out of the line, listing heavily to one side as a pair of galleys moved to support her.

The remaining caravels, their decks slick with blood and debris, crossed the remaining two enemy ships. The enemy let loose a concentrated attack, piling all of their shot into the second of Valdar's ships, the one that had already sustained heavy damage. Round after round slammed into her hull, leaving gaping holes that exposed her innards. Men screamed as they were cut down, their bodies torn asunder by the relentless barrage.

To its credit, the crew never wavered. Even as their companions died, they continued to load and fire, sending their own answer into the enemy. His ships were giving more than they got. Seeing the enemy cannon in action, it was clear that not only did their shot not penetrate as well, they also fired at a much slower rate.

For every two shots the enemy managed, his crews delivered three in return. The difference was telling. The enemy ships were taking a terrible pounding.

"Maintain the pressure!" Valdar bellowed. "Don't let them breathe!"

It was hard, at times, to even see the enemy ships through the thick clouds of smoke being put out by the five vessels doing their level best to kill one another. The more his ships hammered the enemy, the slower their rate of fire got, showing the toll his barrage was having on them.

As the two lines cleared each other, Valdar saw the last two enemy ships founder, their hulls taking on water as they began to sink. A cheer went up from his crews, silenced by a massive explosion that ripped through the enemy ship that had drifted away earlier with smoke pouring out of it. The blast was tremendous, the shock wave hitting Valdar like a fist to the chest.

Two of his galleys, which had been closing on the drifting vessel, were caught in the blast. One had its mast sheared clean off, sending it crashing to the deck in a tangle of rigging and screaming men. The other was peppered with debris, its hull punctured in a dozen places.

The enemy fleet was gone, either captured or heading to the bottom of the sea, which was now littered with debris, the remnants of shattered ships and broken bodies. Even for Valdar, with all his experience, it was a shock. The first clash of cannon-armed ships against one another showed him a terrifying vision of what naval battles could someday be.

"Sir, the schooner is lost," his first mate said. "She's taking on too much water. We need to abandon her."

It was clear to tell by looking at her that he was right. The ship had already started to roll and would be on its side in another ten minutes.

"Transfer her crew to the other ships. We can't afford to lose any more men. If there's time, save what supplies we can."

It was unlikely they'd be able to get cannon off, but perhaps they could save some of the valuable gunpowder, a resource he was already running short on. Thankfully, that was the worst of his losses. None of the galleys had been sunk, but five were in bad shape with varying degrees of hurt. His own ship and another of the caravels were damaged but could be repaired underway. The third, the one that took the brunt of the enemy fire, was in bad shape.

"Order the Hrafn and the damaged galleys, along with two undamaged ones, to return to the port to the south for repairs. Reorganize the men from our losses among the surviving ships. I want to be ready to sail in two hours."

"Sir, with this level of damage ..." His first mate said, leaving the rest of the sentence unspoken.

"I know, but we don't know if this is all of them. I don't want to just float here, inviting another attack. Better to be on the move."

"Understood," the mate said, saluting and heading to the signalman to begin sending the orders.

Alexandria, Egypt

Aelius couldn't believe he was here. Even after centuries under Carthaginian rule, Alexandria was one of the most famous cities in the known world. He had grown up hearing tales of its wonders, the great lighthouse, its vast library that once held the entire world's knowledge, its bustling market that held goods from far-away lands. He'd pored over tales of Alexander the Great and the Ptolemaic dynasty that followed him, at least until the Carthaginians conquered them and ended Egypt's millennia of rule.

Aelius had dreamed of seeing this ancient wonder since he was a boy, but he'd never imagined that he'd actually make it here. While the lighthouse still stood in the harbor, towering above the landscape, the rest of the city was something less than he'd imagined. Even at far cannon range, where he had his legion deploying in preparation for taking the city from its Carthaginian defenders, he could see that it had not been maintained in the fashion its legacy should have demanded, with infrastructure that was in a sad state of disrepair. The aqueducts and walls were in poor shape, crumbling and cracked.

Even with the neglect, the city seemed almost a testament to the many empires that had fought over it, with an eclectic mix of Egyptian, Greek, and Carthaginian styles.

As Aelius sent forth a messenger under a flag of truce to give the Carthaginians a chance to surrender, as tradition demanded, the gates of the great city opened. Instead of a delegation of Carthaginians, however, a group of dignitaries emerged to meet them. It wasn't uncommon for the Carthaginians to send out a sacrificial lamb instead of their own commanders, who would deny the offer of peaceful surrender. That is where things usually ended.

That the messenger was coming back to his line with the delegation in tow meant that the city had accepted his offer to surrender. An unusual move for the Carthaginians.

Aelius waved his men to hold position and rode forward to meet the group, dismounting from his horse as they arrived.

"Greetings, Roman," their leader said, bowing his head slightly. "I am Tamasir, appointed mayor of Alexandria."

"Greetings. I am Legate Numerius Caesetius Aelius of the Britannic Empire," Aelius said, putting the emphasis on the name of the Empire. "We offer terms of surrender to your Carthaginian masters. If they lay down their arms and surrender peacefully, your city will be peaceably occupied, and no excess harm will come to its citizens. Should they refuse, we will have little choice but to take the city by force, in spite of the damage that will ensue. We urge your leader to take our offer seriously and make the best choice he can for the people of the city."

"An unnecessary offer. The Carthaginians have already withdrawn from Alexandria, taking all of their forces out of the city and traveling east. The great city of Alexandria is an open city and will not contest your control," the mayor said, finishing the formal-sounding pronouncement, and then pausing, looking at the men accompanying him to either side, almost nervously. "While I have no way to force any kind of concessions from you, I would ask, for my people's sake, your understanding and compassion as you take control of our city. Most of the young men in our city, and even most of the older ones, were taken by the Carthaginians to swell their ranks as they left. My people are mourning the loss of

374

their sons, fathers, and husbands. They are angry and hurt, and I cannot guarantee what kind of reception you will encounter from them."

"I understand. Your people's pain and anger is not uncommon. We have encountered it everywhere we have liberated a city from Carthaginian rule. We are not here to occupy Alexandria or add to your suffering. Our mission is to prevent the Carthaginians from regrouping and using Egypt as a base to continue their war."

"I'm glad to hear that. I know my people, and know how they might lash out. It is my hope that we avoid any incidents, if possible. Especially if they result in a backlash or reprisal to my city as a whole."

"We will, of course, try and avoid any such incidents, and will be reasonable if they occur, although the safety of my men always comes first. I am curious, however. Egypt has always been famed for its resilience and stubborn refusal to bow to foreign rule. If your people are so ready to fight their oppression, why have they not stood up to the Carthaginians before? Especially now that their rule is crumbling?"

Tamasir hesitated, glancing at his companions before responding cautiously. "There have been ... pockets of resistance over the years. Egyptians who refused to accept Carthaginian dominance. But their fight has been a difficult one, with limited resources and manpower."

"And most of those who might have joined them were just conscripted into the Carthaginian army," another official added bitterly.

"Are there any still in your city who want to fight for their freedom from Carthaginian rule? If there are, I imagine such people would make good intermediaries between ourselves and the rest of your populace, since we would share goals and they would be more able to deal with your people's reaction to a new occupation. If there are any left, I would very much like to meet them."

"There might be some still in the city, although I myself do not know of any. It would be ... difficult to convince them to expose themselves. They have fought long and hard against Carthaginian rule. The idea of aligning with another foreign power ..."

"I assure you, we have no intention of conquering Egypt," Aelius said firmly. "We have not, in any region we have fought, set up permanent rule for ourselves. Which is why our forces here are small, and our main army marches west to Carthage, not east. We are here solely to deal with the Carthaginian threat. Nothing more."

The men took a step back, bending their heads together, whispering frantically. Aelius waited. What he was asking for, that they convince rebels inside the city to come forward and deal directly with a new invading force, was a hard sell. He honestly didn't expect it to happen, but considered it worth a try before he moved forward with his directive, setting up defenses for the eventual Carthaginian counterattack.

"We can try to arrange a meeting with the resistance leaders, although it will take time, as none of us or anyone we know is in contact with them directly," Tamasir said as the group broke apart and he stepped forward again. "However, even if we can contact them, I cannot guarantee their cooperation."

"I understand. Any effort you can make would be appreciated. In the meantime, what I can do is establish my base of operations outside the city, instead of occupying your city directly. That should help keep frictions between our people at a minimum."

"That is amazingly reasonable of you," the Egyptian said, relief clear on his face.

"We will need to make use of your docks, buy supplies, and my men will want to have some access to your city. I will ensure they only arrive in small groups, stick together, and come only for necessary supplies and provisions. I would ask your permission to purchase what we need from your merchants."

"That can be arranged. We would welcome the business. As for your ships ..."

"That area I will, unfortunately, need more control over," Aelius said, interrupting the man before he could lay out terms. "I will have to leave a detachment at the docks to ensure their security, but I assure you, they will find an unused space to operate out of and will not interfere with the city's business."

Tamasir looked much less pleased with this pronouncement and said, "Very well. As long as your men remain confined to the docks and do not cause any disturbances, we will do our best to help keep conflict under control."

"You have my word," Aelius promised. "My men are disciplined and will respect your city's customs and laws."

"Thank you. My people were very worried, seeing your army approach. It is … unexpected, to find you so accommodating. I will send word to you when I have news of the resistance leaders."

"Excellent. I look forward to a productive partnership between our peoples, however temporary it may be." Aelius extended his hand, which Tamasir grasped firmly.

As the Egyptian delegation took their leave, Aelius returned to his mount, signaling his commanders to join him.

"Marcellus, take the Twelfth Cohort and secure the docks. Talk to the leaders there and find some place that's unoccupied, a warehouse or something. Pay for it if you need to, I don't want to be fighting the people in the city when the Carthaginians show up. Make sure we have security provided for any of our ships that enter the city while we're here."

"Yes, Sir," Marcellus replied.

"Good. The rest of us will pull back about a half hour's march. Once there, I want fortifications set up and the artillery mounted. I don't know how long we'll be here, but I don't trust that the Carthaginians have gone entirely. Dig trenches, erect palisades, and create clear lines of fire for our artillery. Ahenobarbus, take your cavalry and start conducting reconnaissance to the south and east. Get a sense of what the civilian population is doing, what obstacles the Carthaginians might have put in our way, and any idea of where they might have gone. If you see a contingent of the enemy, *pull back.* **Do not engage.** Once our fortifications are set up, I want to have the last of the telegraph line extended into them to establish communications back to the Consul. Alright, let's get moving."

As his tribunes moved to get their men back in line and headed in the direction of their temporary encampment, Aelius cast one glance back at the city. He'd come back and see it again, hopefully, while he didn't have to worry about keeping an eye on thousands of soldiers at the same time.

Chapter 33

Carthage

"Say that again," Imilcar demanded, staring down at General Hadar.

"I ... Great One ... I regret to inform you that we lost the latest shipment from the TianYou. All of it is gone."

"How did this happen? I thought we moved the path of these shipments to the Sea of Reeds specifically to avoid this situation."

"We don't know how the Romans learned of it, or got a fleet all the way around Africa, but their new ships and cannon appeared in the sea, sank the ships we recently built on that sea to protect the shipments, along with the larger TianYou ships carrying the goods. What's worse, the Romans have kept their fleet there, patrolling up and down the coasts, sinking any of our boats that set out, and shooting at forces that get within range of their cannon. I have not heard from the TianYou yet, but I believe that we will see no more shipments, Your Excellency."

"What about overland routes? They were slower, but ..."

Imilcar knew he was grasping at straws, but they were all he had left.

"I'm sorry, Great One, but that was difficult even before the Romans landed an army on Africa. The last report we were able to receive from the nomads in the northern desert suggested part of the Britannian force broke off and headed toward Egypt. Which means there is no way to get across from the Sinai without being intercepted. Perhaps if our Persian army is successful ..."

Hadar held out his hands, palms up in a 'maybe' gesture, but they both knew that was a forlorn hope. They had already been drawing off the army in Persia for almost a year, and the rebels there had stepped up attacks after the Britannians took control of the Middle Sea, seeing an opportunity to take advantage of the situation. It was unlikely that what remained of their forces there would be able to fight through the Romans. At best, they could do enough damage to weaken the Roman forces.

For more than a minute, Imilcar just stared off into space, thinking. It went on long enough that the nobles around the room began to shift from foot to foot, unsure of what was going to happen.

Just as General Hadar began to say something, the emperor said, "Withdraw all remaining cannon and gunpowder from the field and any ships. Reserve them for the defense of Carthage."

"But Your Excellency," a shocked Hadar said, almost uncontrollably. "If we pull those weapons back, we will have no way to protect our shores."

"And how have they done protecting our shores so far? That fleet you were so hopeful of, that would strike at the Roman capital and force them to capitulate? How did it fare? The observers my agents heard from say they did not even get a single shot off. All we managed was to send a dozen of our precariously acquired cannon and a large supply of gunpowder to the bottom of the ocean. Now that our supply is cut off, you think we can still afford those kinds of losses?"

"They were successful at the shore, Your Excellency. We managed to keep the Romans from landing."

"Which proved they can be effective if used correctly, and why I want them for the final defense of Carthage itself. Besides, the Romans have already landed their armies. I find it unlikely, with their forces splitting and going in two directions, that they would board their ships and re-land closer to us. Assuming they even know we've removed our cannon. Or do you think I'm wrong?"

Imilcar glared down at the general, daring him to argue again.

"Of course not, Excellency. Your clear thinking is, as always, correct. I will begin the transfer of weapons at once," Hadar said, bowing low.

"While that is being done, I want you to prepare a rapid training program. The Romans are moving closer every day, and I want a massive army prepared to greet them. Over the next week, you will begin receiving thousands of new recruits for our armies. I know there isn't time to train proper phalanxes, but teach them which end the sword to drive into the enemy and make sure they understand the full scope of their duties."

"Your Majesty, I was not aware of a large number of new recruits?"

"Which is why I'm telling you about it. You will need to begin building intake centers for these recruits now. Not all will be willing, so have some of your more trusted men guard the camps to keep these recruits from escaping before they can join the army."

"Yes, Great One," Hadar said, bowing again before backing away from the throne and scurrying out of the room.

Imilcar ignored him, turning his attention to one of the acolytes of Hexitas standing along a far wall. The black-robed men with their skull masks didn't speak or interact as part of the daily routine of governance but were always around. Lurking.

"You," Imilcar said, pointing at one of them, deep red lines across the cheeks of his mask marking him as a senior brother of the order. "Come forward."

The acolyte stepped out from the shadows, bowing slightly as he approached the throne.

"How may I serve, Great One?" the man asked, his voice muffled by the mask.

"I want your acolytes to begin rounding up every able-bodied man not engaged in efforts critical to the operation of the city or the army, and begin putting them in the intake centers General Hadar will be setting up. By essential, I mean those in fields such as farming, foundry work, and smithing should remain in those professions. Everyone else old enough to pick up a sword and not too old to fall down holding it is to be drafted into the army. There will be no exception for station or wealth. In fact, you can start with the leeches gathered here."

Imilcar swept his arm across the nobles who lined one wall of the audience chamber, hoping to curry favor or grift wealth from the empire. The men looked at each other, their shock evident.

"Yes, Great One," the acolyte said, bowing once more, deeper this time. "We shall begin at once."

With a gesture, several of the other black-robed men emerged from the shadows, moving swiftly toward the nobles. Some attempted to flee, their expensive robes and ornamentation slowing their escape. Not that it would have mattered. The acolytes were upon them in an instant, grabbing them and dragging them out of the chamber.

"You can't do this!" one noble shouted as he was pulled out of the large, gilded doors. "I am a member of the High Council!"

Imilcar ignored him and the cries from the others. This was going to be the end of his empire, the empire his ancestors built. The gods had played him for a fool. He could see that now. See their efforts against him.

He wouldn't go down easily. If this was going to be the end of Carthage, then it would be the end of all things. Better the world destroyed in fire than left to be ruled by the Romans.

Britannian Camp, Outside Alexandria

"Legate. Legate?" a voice called from outside Aelius's tent.

It had been almost a week since they arrived in Alexandria, and Aelius had been waiting for this moment. Things had been running smoothly, almost too smoothly, and in his experience, that meant he was due for the other hand to show itself. He knew it wouldn't be the Carthaginian army. He'd sent scouts out in all directions, and that movement would be too large to hide.

Perhaps a small raiding party of some kind, like the one that hit them when the legions first arrived in Africa, or something going wrong in the port.

"What is it?" Aelius said, stepping out of his command tent, sword belt in hand.

"A large group of men just arrived at the front gate. Maybe forty in number."

"Hostile?"

"Unarmed. They stopped short of the gate, and Tribune Priscus, who had the watch, has a full century surrounding them. They say they want to speak to the commander."

"Then let's not keep them waiting," Aelius said, walking past the messenger toward the front gate of the temporary fort. The man's description had been accurate. At the gate, Aelius saw a crowd of between forty and fifty men, unarmored in well-made civilian clothes. Not laborers or farmers by any means. These were merchants or men of means.

Aelius signaled to the guards to stand down, then stepped forward to address the assembly.

"I was told you wished to speak to me," he said, getting to the point.

Next to him, their interpreter began passing the message along in their dialect of Egyptian.

Before he finished translating, one of the men stepped forward and said, "I am Ahmose, descendant of the Ptolemaic dynasty and rightful ruler of Egypt. I speak your language. We lead the resistance against the Carthaginians in this region. The leaders of Alexandria told us you wished to speak with us."

Aelius was stunned for a moment. When he'd asked about some kind of resistance, he'd been expecting merchants or the like, not a member of the ruling family that, from what he'd always heard, had died out when the Carthaginians captured and subjugated the kingdom.

This was well beyond his experience as a legate. He was a soldier, not a diplomat. And yet, the Consul's directives had been clear.

"Then I bid you greetings in the name of Flavia Lucilla Germanicus, Empress of Britannia and Rome."

That must have been the right thing to say because Ahmose bowed his head slightly in acknowledgment.

"We were told your offer was to help remove the Carthaginians, then leave. Is this true?"

Aelius nodded. "It is. My orders are clear. We're here to defeat the Carthaginians and then rejoin the main body of our force. I was given no mandate to stay and rule Egypt."

"And after? What does Britannia want?" one of the other men asked.

"My government seeks to establish diplomatic relations with whatever leadership arises here after the Carthaginians are gone," Aelius said. "But we have no intention of controlling that government or maintaining a permanent military presence."

"You would truly leave the governing of Egypt to the Egyptians?" another man asked.

"That is the plan."

"We would be the leadership in Egypt after the Carthaginians are gone," Ahmose said flatly. "Aside from the fact that the Ptolemaic dynasty was the last rightful heir to Egypt, it will be our people and preparation that will see this through. We appreciate what support you can lend us, but we have been in this fight for generations while you are newcomers."

Aelius didn't point out that Romans had been fighting the Carthaginians much longer than the Egyptians, nor that the reason they were the 'last rightful' heir was that their ancestors conquered the dynasty that was already there and set themselves up as rulers after Alexander died. Not that much different than what happened when the Carthaginians arrived.

Instead, he said, "We can accept that. Before we sent the first of our legionaries from our islands and onto the continent, our Empress declared that Britannia was only interested in direct control of Britannia itself. We had to come here to fully defeat the Carthaginians, but beyond that, our only goal is to establish a network of allies, not to conquer and rule distant lands. As such, we have made alliances with tribal groups in Gaul, Germania, and Hispania. After the war, they will maintain control of their regions, with trading and diplomatic relations and an alliance with the Britannians. Which is their choice to maintain or not, although we would welcome a working relationship and have both new weapons and tools for civilian use that I'm sure your people would greatly benefit from trading for."

"And what would this alliance entail, exactly? We've seen the weapons your legions carry. Would you be willing to share such technology with us?" Ahmose asked.

"Within reason, yes. We're prepared to supply muskets to our allies, which are a form of these weapons here," Aelius said, pointing to one of the weapons. "Along with gunpowder, the substance that makes them work, and training in their use and maintenance. But it goes beyond just weapons. We have other advanced materials and techniques that could greatly benefit Egypt, such as improved agricultural tools, materials that help plants grow stronger and faster, irrigation technology to expand what you already do and offset some of the uncertainty caused by the flooding seasons along the Nile, along with better materials such as higher quality steel."

Several of the Egyptians began talking to one another in their language. They had an interpreter hired from the city, and one of their men who was good with languages had been studying with him, to at least cross-check some of what the man said, but Aelius didn't need them now. He'd seen this response in Germania and some of the villages of Italia, and knew what they were discussing.

Ahmose held up a hand for silence. "And in exchange for all of this, what would Britannia expect of us?"

"In the short term, assistance in our efforts against the Carthaginians here in Africa. But looking ahead, we seek treaties to ensure ongoing peace and cooperation between Britannia and our allies. We also hope to open new markets for the goods produced by our allies, to everyone's benefit."

Ahmose was quiet for a moment, considering. Aelius waited him out. In negotiations like this, the first person to speak almost always came out weaker.

"These are fair terms. Egypt has languished too long under the Carthaginian yoke. If removing that threat, alone, was what we got in exchange, we would gladly help. Much of our negotiations will have to remain for after, but if you hold to what you said, I see no reason our peoples can't have a long and profitable future."

"I am glad we can come to an agreement. However, before we can fully realize this future, the Carthaginians must first be defeated. Their presence in Egypt remains a threat to both our peoples."

"You are correct, Legate. But know that we are not without resources of our own. The Ptolemaic dynasty still commands the loyalty of a significant number of Egyptians. We can provide thousands of men to aid in the fight against the Carthaginians. But understand, our priority is Egypt. We will defend our land, but we cannot promise to venture beyond our borders."

"I would not ask you to. In fact, I believe Egypt is where we must make our stand. My scouts have reported a Carthaginian army marching here from Persia. They will likely arrive within the week."

"How large is this force?"

"Fifty-thousand men, maybe more."

"We have allies among the nomads and friends further east. We will send word to get more detailed information about their army and where they will attack."

"Good. If you and your commanders will come with me, we can discuss what we have available and what our people know already. If I might suggest sending some of these men back to begin rounding up recruits who can help. We are prepared to arm some of them with weapons similar to what we carry, but they will have to spend the time while we prepare for the attack learning to use them."

With a wave of his hand, Ahmose sent all but five of the men back in the direction of Alexandria. Clearly a man who commanded their obedience, Aelius thought.

"Then let us begin our partnership," Ahmose said, smiling for the first time since he arrived at the Britannian gates.

Devnum

"... unacceptable. The Empire cannot function without a steady flow of raw materials from Caledonia, and you and Hortensius promised this would solve all of our problems in that area. Instead, not a single weight of ore has made it to the foundries in Factorium."

The engineer shifted uncomfortably, "Regent, I understand your concerns, but the terrain in the mountains is treacherous. We've never built through such challenging geography before. The construction weakened the mountainside, which allowed for rockslides when the weather turned, that damaged the tracks extensively. We have made note of the error and are working on ways to correct this problem in future iterations."

"Which helps us not at all now. I don't care about reasons and excuses, I care about results. The Empress left me with the responsibility of keeping our weapons shipments and goods flowing to both the legions and our allies, and I will not allow you to keep me from fulfilling my obligations."

Ramirus, standing beside the throne, cleared his throat softly and said, "Perhaps we could ..."

Medb silenced him with a sharp look before turning back to Aemilius. "You have one week. One week to restore the supply line and ensure the trains are running smoothly. If you cannot manage that, I will find someone who can."

"Yes, Regent. I will do everything in my power to resolve the issue within the given timeframe," Aemilius said, bowing and backing away from the regent before scurrying out.

As the man walked out, Ramirus leaned over and began to say, "Regent, if I may suggest ..."

His suggestion, and Medb had a strong guess as to what it would have been, died on his lips as another figure burst into the audience chamber, walking quickly toward the raised dais.

"Speak," Ramirus commanded the man as he dropped to one knee, his head bowed.

"I am from the fleet that sailed around Africa to the Mare Rubrum, to intercept a shipment of weapons on the way to the

Carthaginians. We were dispatched home to let the Empire know what was happening. The fleet met the enemy and defeated them, including four unknown vessels of unusual design bearing cannons, which damaged several of our vessels, sinking several galleys and one of the schooners. All of the strange enemy vessels were sunk along with most of the Carthaginian galleys, although several were captured. The admiral has also begun setting up a second port on the coast of Africa, this one well south of the Mare Rubrum on Africa's eastern shore."

"What are his plans now?" Ramirus asked.

"He is concerned about these strange, well-armed vessels, which would have defeated our own galleys, if not for our superior caravels," the messenger said. "He intends to hold the Red Sea, until the fleet can be reinforced and provided with sufficient supplies to maintain a permanent presence along the entire coast."

"The damaged ships will require significant repairs and supplies," Ramirus said. "Especially if they are to be repaired afloat, as opposed to returning here to be put into a dock. If this other power is out there and capable of sailing ships able to sink our own, it seems wise to maintain a strong presence in that region."

Medb didn't look to Ramirus as he spoke but nodded as he finished. "It would. Check with Lucan. I want the next several ships coming off the docks not allocated to private factors to be loaded with supplies and sent to this port the admiral has established. Include both supplies to repair the ships, material to help build and fortify the new port, and additional cannon and gunpowder for the fort's defense and to resupply of the ships. You, return to your ship and rest your crew until you hear from us. You will need to travel back with them and show them the way."

"Yes, Regent," the man said.

"A good decision," Ramirus said as the man left.

This time Medb did look at him.

"I live for your approval," she said flatly. "In addition to the supplies, I want three centuries of our newly trained legionaries sent with the ships. They will reinforce both the new port and the one previously established by Valdar on the coast of Africa. I leave it to him to determine where they are best assigned, but include a high enough leader, a tribune or whatever you people call them, to see to the command of both ports."

"I will see orders sent out."

"Wait," Medb said as Ramirus turned to leave.

"Regent?"

For a moment, Medb said nothing, tapping her fingers on the arm of the throne, thinking.

"Send a message to the Scandi merchants we have good relationships with," she finally said. "Invite them here for a meeting to discuss a potential business opportunity."

"What should I tell them this 'opportunity' entails, when they ask?"

"The ports Valdar is establishing along the coast of Africa will need regular shipments of supplies and trade goods. I believe the Scandi captains would be interested in providing those shipments."

"And what would be in it for them, beyond the usual profits from transport?"

"Access to the natural resources of Africa. Ivory, gold, exotic woods. The ability to trade with the locals for spices, textiles, and other valuable commodities. And," she paused for effect, "the possibility of opening up sea-borne trade with the civilizations at the other end of the eastern trade routes. Those have been controlled by the Carthaginians for a long time, and the Scandians still have to go through Parthia and Persia. Thus their access remains limited. This could solve that."

"Assuming those civilizations are friendly. We know someone far to the east has been aiding the Carthaginians."

"Selling weapons, which is a very different than being allies. Another reason to convince the Scandi to make those contacts. As a third party not directly involved in the war, they wouldn't have to worry about who is friendly to us or not. It would also be a way for information about those civilizations to make its way back to us."

"Clever. Very clever. That is an excellent idea, actually."

"You aren't the only one who's good at their job, you know," Medb said. "Maybe you should stop thinking of me as a novice when it comes to this."

"I apologize. While I know you are very smart and you have long experience ruling a kingdom, that is very different from strategic diplomacy and statecraft. I think, perhaps, when this is all over and the Empress has returned to her throne, you should consider how much further these skills can get you in the Empire than merely ruling. Speaking from personal experience, I suspect you might find it more stimulating than simply hearing audiences and making decisions on governance."

"I just might," Medb said, for once not sounding annoyed by the Roman's suggestions.

Chapter 34

North Africa

The army was a bustling whirl of chaos around Ky and the other commanders. As they had every night for weeks, they stood in the center of the madness, in the open air, going over the day's events and confirming the next day's plan, not that there was much variety in their agonizingly slow march west toward Carthage.

As with Italy, they had been harassed the entire way, except these attacks had been more spread out, in the way of ambushes, than attacks on small garrisons. In fact, there hadn't been much in the way of anything to garrison on their entire trip. Every town, village, and settlement between their landing and Carthage had been burned to the ground by the time they arrived at it. Ky was surprised that the Carthaginians were willing to go in for such a scorched earth policy, a term that wouldn't arrive in history for almost two thousand years, but that described a tactic as old as civilizations.

If they did win, it would take the Carthaginians generations to repair the damage they were doing to themselves, not that Ky planned on letting that outcome get anywhere close to happening.

Worse than Italy, the attacks never let up, with small groups harassing the fortified works each day. Just to dig in, he had to surround the temporary works with three full cohorts, to keep the nomads that had been shadowing them far enough away to let the work progress. By the time they did reach the enemy, he was a little concerned the men might be too tired to actually fight.

"...another burned-out settlement, their wells spiked with salt and sulfur."

"We still have enough supplies from the ships, right?" Ky asked.

"Yes, Consul," Dexippus said. "Although our initial plan assumed we would be able to get some basic supplies from the locals. Having to keep completely supplied off the fleet is starting to severely tax the fleet's capabilities. I'm told they had to pull fleets from Kalb to have enough boats to ferry the needed supplies."

"Fine, whatever they have to do. We're too close now, we can't allow this campaign to fail for lack of water."

"Yes, Consul."

"We have other news," Bomilcar said. "The scouts reported in just as we made a stop for the night. The Carthaginians have finally begun to move out of their city to meet us."

"I wondered how long that would take them. With their number superiority, allowing themselves to be hemmed up behind walls with tens of thousands of mouths to feed would be suicide."

"I think they were just buying as much time as possible to rally troops, which explains the harassing attacks. And it seems to have worked. The enemy greatly outnumbers us. This might be the largest army we've ever faced. Our men couldn't get a good look at their force composition, but from rumors they've been able to pick up from refugees fleeing the burned-out cities, I'm told it is made of a very large number of new recruits, many of whom will be fighting with swords at their back."

"That might actually work in their favor. The Carthaginians will certainly use them as human shields in front of their better-trained units, to absorb our bullets until they can get to melee range with us, after which it's all over."

"That was my thought. Still, it means while they may have a hundred thousand men to our ten thousand, two-thirds of those will be minimally effective once they close," Bomilcar said.

"Which only leaves us thirty thousand trained soldiers to fight hand-to-hand three-to-one."

"That about sums it up."

"There's more, actually," Viridius, the seventy-fifth cohort tribune said. "I know the Legate didn't want to bring up details not confirmed, but ... I thought this important."

The look Bomilcar gave Viridius as he spoke suggested the two would be having a lengthy conversation later, but Ky wasn't one for shutting down subordinates.

"Do tell," Ky said.

"Some of the refugees coming east from Carthage say they are running from conscription gangs, who are pulling every able-bodied man on the street into their armies."

"Which explains the size of their force," Ky said, not sure why Bomilcar had an issue with something that seemed so obvious. "I'm not sure that's particularly news."

"No, I mention it just to say these people come from the capital itself. They also told us that it had been announced that the emperor himself was going to lead this army."

"Really?" Ky said, eyebrows shooting up in surprise.

If the Carthaginian emperor was willing to lead this army, it would change things significantly. Carthaginian society was an absolute monarchy in the most brutal of terms. Civilizations like that did not usually hold up well to even the most prepared leadership change, let alone a sudden one in the middle of a war. Should he fall, it could cause the rest of Carthage to fall with him.

"We don't know how accurate that information is," Bomilcar said, giving another glance to Viridius.

"I understand, and it doesn't change our plans one way or another. We're going to have to face them if we want to bring this to an end, and whether in Carthage itself or at the head of an army. This doesn't end until he does. Which leads us to the obvious question, what do we know now that we know what we're facing?"

"There are really only two options, right?" Brangh, the Ulaid tribune in command of the 4th Cohort, said. "We either fortify and let them come to us, or we attack them in the field."

"If we meet them in the field," Bomilcar said, "we risk being overwhelmed by sheer numbers. The Carthaginians may be willing to sacrifice their conscripts to secure victory. Our rifles and cannons can only do so much against a tide of bodies. If they are willing to accept the casualties, I'm not sure we can stop them."

"Wouldn't the same be true if we built up fortifications?" Dexippus asked. "Anything we could build would be hasty at best. There are no settlements we could build up, so we'd only have the supplies we've been fortifying with every night, much of which is starting to see significant wear. I'm not sure it would stand up to a sustained attack. Even if it does, they also have well more than enough men to surround us. We've been almost completely supplied by our fleet, which we would be cut off from. They could just sit out there and wait until we all die of thirst. It would be a death sentence."

"We could do both," Viridius suggested. "Fortify our position here, or wherever, as best we can and then send out smaller units to harass the enemy, disrupt their supply lines, whatever."

"No. That would be the worst opinion we could choose," Bomilcar said. "We would do little damage to them and would lose men on every outing. When we do end up behind our fortifications, we would be in the same place as Dexippus just described."

"Okay," Ky said, ending the conversation. "I think our options are clear. There's nothing for us to fall back on out here, and if we try to fortify, we'll just be surrounded. With their cannon, that could be fatal. At least in open battle, we'll have room to maneuver. We should reach the enemy army in a few days. Prepare your units. Make sure if you need additional supplies, ammunition, gunpowder, whatever, you request it now so we can get it from the supply ships. I should have a more detailed breakdown of our battle strategy and your assignments before we make contact."

The meeting broke up, and the commanders headed off to their various duties, leaving Ky standing alone in the middle of the camp. His tent almost set up, so he'd turned to head toward it when he saw a figure moving through the bustling activity towards him. When she broke through the crowd of soldiers and he saw who it was, Ky stopped dead in his tracks, shocked.

Lucilla had acquired a small crowd following her as she made her way through the camp, soldiers dropping what they were doing to find out why their Empress had suddenly appeared in their midst.

"Lucilla," Ky said, grabbing her by the elbows and stopping her as she ran up to him and started to throw her arms around him. "What are you doing here?"

"I came to support our legions in this final push against the enemy."

Ky looked past her, glaring at the men gathering around, watching them, all of whom seemed to collectively realize they had work to do at the same moment. As they started to disperse back across the camp, Ky took Lucilla by the elbow and led her a little away, to the emptiest spot he could find.

They weren't alone, but it was as good as he was going to get in a bustling military encampment.

"You shouldn't be here. It's too dangerous."

"It's dangerous no matter where I go. If the legions fall now, Carthage will be on Britannia's shores within a year. It would be the end of me and the empire either way. At least now, the men know their empress stands with them."

"Battle is a chaotic place, Lucilla. We could win, but a stray bullet or arrow or even a wrong step could cause us to lose you. The empire couldn't survive that. I couldn't."

"This isn't the first time I've been in the field with the legions, Ky. And now, at the end of it, I have to be here. These people are fighting for me. For my family. I will not let them do it alone."

"Why didn't you even tell me you were coming."

"Because I knew how you would react exactly like this. I'm pretty sure, had you known I was coming, you would have sent half the ships in the fleet to intercept me, tie me up, and cart me back to Devnum under guard."

Ky was considering doing exactly that, except he knew as much as his men were loyal to him, they loved their empress more. All she had to do was counter his command, and they would cheer as they untied her.

"Sophus should have..."

"I told Sophus to keep its mouth shut, and if it did say anything, I would take this thing out of my ear and crush it."

"*She left me little choice, Commander,*" Sophus's voice rang out.

Ky didn't blame the AI. It had been showing more and more attachment-like behavior, and he knew it also had a special preference for Lucilla. It seemed everyone in his life loved her the most. Not that he blamed them, as he felt the same himself.

"I don't like this, Lucilla. The battlefield is no place for an empress."

"The battlefield is wherever I need to be," Lucilla said. She stepped closer, placing a hand on Ky's chest. "I'm not some delicate flower, Ky. I'm the Empress of Britannia. If my empire is at war, then so am I."

Ky covered her hand with his own, feeling the warmth of her skin. He knew her. The most stubborn woman in the world. Once she made her mind up, there was no arguing with her.

"Very well, you can stay. *But,* you will remain in the rear, with the reserve cohorts. I will not have you on the front lines."

"Of course," Lucilla said. "I'm here to inspire the men, not lead a charge. It's your legion, you're in charge."

"We both know that isn't true," Ky said, putting his hands on his hips.

"Maybe," she said, stepping close to him on her tiptoes, and kissing him.

He returned the kiss with vigor. In spite of how angry she made him, putting herself in danger like this, he was happy to see her.

East of Giza, Egypt

In spite of it still being early fall, the sun still beat mercilessly down on Aelius and his men, who stood in well-lined rows, facing the desert expanse stretching before them. He was proud of them. Even with the heat and dry air, they had maintained good discipline all morning.

That was all the more impressive as most of that morning had been spent watching the approaching cloud of dust close on them, heralding the approach of the Carthaginian army. From his scouts, their force was at least four times the size of his whole legion, and eight times the force he had with him at the moment.

"Are you sure we shouldn't prepare defensive works?" Hirrus, his second in command, asked, watching the enemy force continue to grow in size as it closed, stretching endlessly in either direction.

"I am, but make sure the men are prepared to move. Any units that stop or slow down are going to get swamped."

"Yes, legate," Hirrus said, giving one last look to the wall of Carthaginians before turning to relay the orders to the signalman.

Minutes ticked by as the enemy closed. Aelius could feel the tension in his men as the seemingly endless wave of enemy soldiers. Of course, it wasn't endless. They had faced larger armies than this several times, but rarely with so few men on their side.

"Steady, men," Aelius called out as the enemy passed an imaginary line Aelius had placed on the battlefield. "Rifles at the ready."

His timing was good. Almost as soon as the order was given, the Carthaginian cavalry on either flank began to surge forward, closing ground with frightening speed.

"Focus fire on the cavalry!" Aelius ordered. "Volley fire... now!"

A thunderous crack split the air as hundreds of rifles discharged in unison. Smoke billowed from the line as the deadly hail of lead tore into the Carthaginian cavalry. Horses and men tumbled, the charge faltering under the withering fire.

"Reload!" Hirrus bellowed. "Second rank, ready!"

The front rank knelt, ramrods clattering as they reloaded. The second rank stepped forward, leveling their rifles.

"Fire!"

Another volley erupted, the close range devastating the Carthaginian horsemen. The charge crumbled, horses veering away or collapsing in the sand. Not all of them, however. Some made it through the barrage, closing the last span between them and his men.

His officers were diligent in their duty. Before he could utter another command, bayonet-tipped rifles sprang up along the threatened section of the line just as the enemy horses slammed into them. Ben screamed, metal clashed, and a few rifles discharged in the melee, but his men stood firm, a bristling hedge of steel driving back the remnants of the charge.

About half the cavalry that had made the initial charge returned to their lines while the enemy infantry continued to march unstoppably forward, having hardly been touched by his initial volleys, which had been almost completely aimed at the cavalry.

"Begin falling back," Aelius commanded. "By cohorts, leapfrogging. Twelfth and Twenty-Second, withdraw. Twenty-Third, Fifty-Fourth, and Nineteenth, cover them. Maintain volley fire from the covering cohorts."

Seeing the Britannians starting to withdraw, the Carthaginian phalanxes surged forward, only to be met with a hail of bullets from the three covering cohorts, which sent them reeling back.

For hours, they repeated the pattern, each cohort taking its turn to fire and fall back. Both armies were tired, Aelius knew that much. His scouts had tracked the Carthaginians' march for days, and they'd started out early in the morning and marched through the desert sun for four hours before making contact. Now they'd spent hours more in a brutal advance, leaving a string of bodies in their wake as hundreds fell with each charge.

It was a series of engagements and disengagements rather than one long, prolonged battle. Aelius held his men's fire, waiting until the enemy caught up and tried to surge forward again, in order to conserve ammunition. The Pyramids, which had never been fully out of sight, now loomed high overhead as the light started to dim, alerting them to the last few hours of the day.

If Aelius had been in charge of the other side, he would have broken off long ago. They had lost almost a third of their entire number, maybe fifteen thousand men, a butcher's bill that was beyond compare. Especially when considering that Aelius had lost under two hundred, mostly to the handful of cavalry charges that had enough momentum to at least make contact before scattering. That had been early in the engagement, their commander allowing his cavalry to be whittled down until it didn't exist anymore, for all practical purposes.

He could only guess that the Britannians' continued retreat gave them hope that each time, they were on the verge of breaking. Or maybe just that all they had to do was catch up and they would crush the Britannians. Either way, Aelius was happy to let them continue. The worst thing that could happen, from his point of view, was that the enemy decided to disengage and come at him at a different time or from a different direction.

It wasn't until his men passed the pyramids themselves and split to either side of a long line of men, with prepared positions of stone, wood, and dug trenches designed to slow and break up enemy attacks, with one of the consul's 'hot air balloons', it's long trailing cable going to the rear of his formation, that the enemy seemed to waver for a moment, realize that they might have fallen into a trap themselves.

Along the line of fresh cohorts were lines of artillery, which opened up as soon as the Carthaginians, who funneled in between the pyramids, made their appearance. The weight of cannon and rifle fire smashed into the enemy, entire formations disintegrating in an instant.

For a moment, the Carthaginians wavered, and Aelius thought, again, they might do the smart thing and withdraw. Now, not only were they outgunned, but they were in the worst possible position for that. Thankfully, from his point of view, they still had not learned enough about fighting a force with superior technology. Worse, this army had spent the entire war, so far, in Persia and had not really experienced this kind of warfare before. They'd clearly been prepared for it, since they didn't run at the first crack of a rifle, but they didn't really understand it.

So they did what every Carthaginian army had been trained to do. They charged and tried to steamroll over their opponent, relying on weight of number and willingness to spend lives with abandon.

And it was working, after a fashion. The death toll was gruesome, but they were closing ground, step after brutal step.

"Legate, the enemy is getting close. Should we prepare to withdraw?" Hirrus asked, casting a worried look at the ever-closing distance between them.

Hirrus was a good man, but he tended to the cautious side of things. It was true that, as good as their weapons were, once those phalanxes got into melee, his men would fare badly. But this was the plan, and it was going to work. If they withdrew, it would all fall apart. The enemy was so close to complete destruction, and they didn't even know it. According ot the reports coming down the telegraph wire from the balloon soaring above them, they were exactly where they needed to be.

"No. Hold steady. Just a little longer."

"But, Legate..."

"I said hold." Aelius's tone firm. "They're right where we want them. We will not give it up now."

Aelius watched them closely. Closer and closer. They were now in arrow range, and his men were starting to fall. Not a lot, at least in comparison, but he was taking losses. His men held strong.

"Steady," he called out as one century near the front looked to waver, seeing the wall of men coming toward them. "Pour it on, boys. Keep the fire up. Get ready."

The enemy was now close enough; they were pushing into a massed, all-out charge. The tide stemmed for a moment, as canister shot shredded row after row of men, but it did not let up. They could see their tormentors, the people that had been killing their friends with abandon for hours, now within arm's reach.

Still, Aelius waited. Held his men firm.

"Brace," he yelled as the enemy closed the last gap, their spears slamming into his men.

The front rank had shields up, but this was a different style of battle than legion against phalanx. His front rank buckled as men fell, some taking up the fallen shields, others stabbing furiously back with bayonets or pushing spears out of the way with rifle butts. If this went on for very long, his lines would buckle and rout.

Thankfully, that had never been the plan.

Aelius barked an order which sent a large red banner trailing up the cable that led to the balloon floating over his forces, allowing its brightly dyed fabric to be seen far and wide. For a moment, Aelius wondered if the Carthaginians had any idea what that large strip of cloth meant.

They didn't need to wait long. As soon as the signal crested above the line of Britannians and made its way skyward, thousands of Egyptians, armed with swords, muskets, and an assortment of other weapons, swarmed out from the ancient pyramids and surrounding buildings like a vengeful tide. They slammed into the Carthaginian flanks, catching them completely off guard. The enemy had been so focused on their target they hadn't even looked to the phalanxes. So focused on the Britannians ahead, the phalanxes had no defense against this sudden onslaught.

"By the gods," Hirrus breathed, his eyes wide with astonishment.

He wasn't wrong. They had set the plan up, knew it was coming, but seeing it in practice, it was still astonishing. It was like ants swarming a wounded animal, devouring it.

The Carthaginian formation began to crumble under the relentless Egyptian assault. Men screamed as they were cut down, their blood staining the sand. The once orderly phalanxes disintegrated into a chaotic melee of clashing swords and desperate struggles.

His men slowed their fire, taking aimed shots now instead of massed volleys, to avoid hitting their new allies. Except for the ranks already engaged with his men, the Carthaginians didn't seem worried about the Britannians anymore. Without the rest of the phalanx at their back, pushing them, the lead elements that had made contact with his men fell quickly. Fueled by years of oppression and hatred, the Egyptians tore into the Carthaginians with a savagery he had rarely witnessed. It was as if the very desert had come alive to exact its vengeance.

The enemy was crumbling. All they needed was a push, and they would fall apart. Aelius was all too happy to give them that push.

Raising his sword arm, Aelius bellowed, "Charge!"

Chapter 35

North Africa

"Consul, my analysis indicates nearly one hundred thousand soldiers in the Carthaginian army," Sophus said.

Ky had been watching the Carthaginians approach for almost an hour as his men set up defensive works as best they could. His scouts had come in contact with theirs the night before, and it was clear to everyone that this battle would happen today. Ky let the enemy come to them, having his men dig in, putting in pits and trenches to slow cavalry as best they could.

He wished he was still in Germania, where rivers and hills gave him more opportunity to funnel the enemy and counter the advantage of the numbers they had. The desert gave them too much room to maneuver. True, they weren't in the desert proper, but the rocky ground wasn't much better. There were a few narrow spots between the crest behind them and the sea, but the way they were laid out, he could hold maybe a few hundred men in them, and they funneled in the wrong direction. Even if he set up on the other side, he wouldn't be able to get enough guns in position to stop them, with the slope and drop off was on the other side.

Sure, he could force their troops through the narrows before they got to melee range, but they could wheel cannons and position archers up the slope and shoot down the cliff edge on his men. There were a few other passes, but they were even smaller. Besides, past that cliff was open beach and the sea, not giving him very much room to work with.

So here he sat, lined up, his forces horseshoed back slightly to lower the chance that the enemy would wrap around and surround him, even though it made his volley fire slightly more ineffectual.

"Most of them aren't soldiers," he replied to Sophus. "No armor, a lot of crude and makeshift weapons, just like we were told. It looks like they're all up front, set to take the brunt of our fire, keeping their 'real' troops safe for when they come into contact with ours. Smart. Brutal, but smart."

Before he could sub-vocalize anything else, Bomilcar rode up and said, "They should be in range in a few minutes."

"Nothing fancy," Ky ordered. "Have the artillery open up as soon as they are in range. We're not going to trick our way out of this one. We need to pound them hard and keep it up until we break them."

"Consul, with all due respect, with those numbers ..."

"I know, but we don't have many other choices. The men are ready, and we have the firepower. Let's use it."

"As you order, Consul," Bomilcar said, saluting and riding off again to hand out orders.

They watched and waited as the Carthaginians drew nearer and nearer. Finally, they crossed an invisible line, bringing all of the Britannian artillery to life. Cannon across their line roared, sending a hail of iron and smoke into the Carthaginian ranks. The ground shook with each volley.

It did not stop the coming onslaught, but it did provoke a response. While their infantry was still outside of acceptable rifle range, a cascade of horns sounded across the enemy line, unleashing their heavy cavalry.

"Rifle volleys, now!" Ky shouted. "Concentrate fire on the cavalry!"

The Britannian soldiers responded as a rippling crack of rifles sounded along the line. They were moving fast, too fast to get his artillery reloaded before they connected. Despite the withering fire, the Carthaginian cavalry crashed into the Britannians, their initial impact sending their horses deep into his lines. While the ones that did penetrate didn't last long, learning the lesson of why cavalry charges against bayonet-wielding soldiers didn't last long, the impact did its damage.

They were also a distraction as the huge main body marched on. Ky kept his artillery fixed on them, trying to thin the massive horde out as much as possible, and focusing on the catapults and cannon being pulled by teams of horses.

"Increase fire on their artillery. Focus on those," Ky called out as the Carthaginian artillery stopped and began setting up. "All cohorts, volley fire."

He wasn't sure how powerful their cannon were going to be, but the exploding gunpowder was going to be devastating. They'd been experimenting with fuse-equipped charges of their own, to enable shells that exploded on impact, but they were still in the initial stages of development. More testing was needed for a proper fuse. Ky had known it wouldn't be ready before the war was finished when he'd given the plans to Hortensius, but he dearly wished he'd had them now.

Carthaginian cannon opened fire, their shells, while underpowered, still wreaking havoc as they smashed into his lines. Their gunpowder pots opening holes in his formation as the fire and shrapnel from their containers ripped into his men.

And finally, the Carthaginian line connected. They had taken unfathomable losses, but the sheer number of men was so great they could absorb them. His men fought valiantly, the front-rank shield bearers and the men with bayonets behind them fighting not that differently than the legions had when he'd first arrived. While they had trained for it, this kind of combat lost them almost all of their advantage.

"Hold the line!" Ky bellowed. "Stand your ground!"

He was glad that, at least this time, Lucilla had listened to him and was with the ships just offshore a few miles in their rear.

"Consul!" a messenger cried as he rode up, his face streaked with sweat and grime. "Our flanks are bending back! The enemy is trying to pour around our edges!"

"Send in the reserve cohort, half going to each flank. Reinforce the faltering lines. We must hold!"

He'd hoped to use the single cohort he held in reserve for reinforcing the center, which was getting hammered painfully, but if the enemy got around him, he would be surrounded and crushed, as he'd done to them several times.

The death toll along the line was brutal. The conscripts were not fighting well, and dying by the dozen, but they did their job, taking down men, pushing back his line, creating gaps. In this kind of fight, weight of men alone was a powerful advantage.

"Consul, we're taking heavy losses," the Tribune Euan from the 26th Cohort in the center said, blood dripping from a gash on his forehead. "What are your orders?"

For a moment he just looked around the battlefield, seeing the chaos and death all around him. He knew this was going to be bad, but he'd held out some hope that they could continue to counter the manpower disparity with more firepower alone. He'd seen the massive number of enemy soldiers and hoped that, since so many were untrained conscripts, their numbers wouldn't hold up under fire.

He'd been wrong.

The estimated counter Sophus kept in a section of his vision, based on the feed from the drone far above, suggested that both forces had lost maybe ten percent of their men. For him, that was devastating, amounting to almost a full cohort. For the enemy, that was as many men as he'd brought into combat all together. They still had nine times what he'd brought into the battle and didn't look to be slowing.

"Sound the retreat," Ky ordered. "We need to get back to the beach and regroup."

"Consul, if we disengage now, they'll overrun us before we can form back up," Bomilcar said next to him.

Tribune Antonius, who'd been nearby since his cohort was in the dead center of the line, stepped forward. "Consul, let me take three centuries. That narrow pass through the cliff behind us can be used to funnel them. If I place my men right, with a few cannons, we can make a stand; buy you time to pull back."

Ky looked at him. It would work, at least to slow them down, but there was no way any man assigned to that duty would survive.

"You understand what you're asking?"

"I do, Consul."

"Take what cannon you need. Find good cover. Make them pay for every inch."

A grim-faced Antonius, saluted, fist hitting his chest hard enough it seemed to hurt his hand. "I will Consul. For Britannia."

"For Britannia," Ky echoed.

It took time for his men to pull back, as actual disengagement was not possible, the enemy pushing forward with each step his people took back. The losses continued to mount.

The cavalry peeled back first, followed by the artillery crews, who needed to limber their guns, costing more time that his men had to keep the enemy horde back. Ten guns and precious munitions broke off in the pass, allowing them time to dig their weapons in. Their teams were sent with the rest. None of the men left to man them had any illusion that they would leave that place.

Finally, the infantry began their gradual withdrawal, the shield line holding the enemy back as riflemen kept up a steady fire aimed just behind the enemy front line, to keep them from pushing too hard. His force collapsed through the narrows, pulling back on itself into a tighter and tighter coil, units managing to disengage as they backed into the cliffs.

For now, the enemy had only infantry up front, so there wasn't a danger of them shooting down on his men, although that would change as more and more of his forces got through and moved off to the beach. He had chosen the terrain carefully for the battle. He might not have known this would exactly be the plan, but it had been a possibility, and he'd made sure to pick a section where the cliffs were just high enough that any men trying to jump off would almost certainly break limbs in doing so, taking them out of the fight as effectively as a bullet or bayonet.

"Keep it steady, boys!" Bomilcar shouted, riding up and down the line. "Don't let them break through!"

The general was everywhere and already had two horses take arrows, forcing him to switch animals.

As the bulk of the Britannian force made their way through the narrows, Antonius and his three centuries took up position in a series of caves and crevices along the narrows. It looked as if the path was open, but any who tried to get through would find themselves riddled with case and shot. This was made worse by the way it funneled in as it narrowed, helping avoid crossfire while opening up the largest section of the enemy to them. The design would make it harder for his men to escape, but that wasn't part of the plan anyway.

Ky made it through with one of the last cohorts, holding back long enough to see his men make the break. He ordered an additional century to hold at the neck itself, on this side, to help keep them bottled up. Once Antonius's men fell, they wouldn't be able to cap it for long, especially as cannon were brought up on the cliff above, which is why Ky ordered them to pull back as soon as things got too hot.

They were good men and they'd do their job.

Ky continued to watch the battle in the narrows as he pulled back to the beach. The enemy seemed to sense victory, watching the Britannians fall back, running for their ships. They surged forward and were met with a hail of bullets. The land in the narrows became a killing ground. When the Carthaginians entered the narrows it was as if they had kicked an angry nest of hornets. His men were well dug in, and difficult to dislodge.

Wave after wave of enemy soldiers crashed against the Britannian position, only to be cut down by rifle fire and cannon blasts. The ground between the forces became a charnel house of mangled bodies and shattered weapons. The Carthaginians responded, bringing up their own artillery. They rolled their cannon forward, blasting the cliff face at nearly point-blank range. It wasn't shot, and his men killed many of the Carthaginians working the heavy, oversized tubes, but their huge shot smashed into their defenses, pulverizing man and stone alike.

Still, the men fought on. They would not hold forever. Finally, the bottleneck he'd left behind was forced to retreat, running flat out for the beach a mile behind them. Surprisingly, the Carthaginians did not immediately follow. Maybe because they didn't realize the path ahead was clear or maybe just out of rage at the hurt those three hundred men had caused them.

They charged them again and again, throwing conscripts and trained soldiers alike. And then time ran out. Trying to rally his men to keep fighting, Antonius wielded two gladiuses with an expertise that impressed even Ky, the enemy finally found an opening, a long spear punching through his chest.

Antonius's last words were to command his men to keep fighting. The firing trickled off as, one by one, his men fell, until the entire rearguard was gone.

They did their job, however. They had bought him time to get his men back to the beach. Broken units reformed, and a new line just off the soft beach sand was ready to fight again.

"Is it over?" Bomilcar asked.

The general had long ago figured out Ky could see things from far off perspectives. He could have even sent a message up to one of the balloons, moored to the largest galley, that would have had a view of the fighting, but he didn't. His question was as much prayer as anything else.

"Yes. They did their duty. The enemy's casualties are very high. If he took less than ten or fifteen of them for every one of his killed, I would be shocked."

"So, they've resumed their march."

"Not yet. They have to reform and are waiting until the majority of their force is on the other side. I give them thirty minutes to an hour before they march. Have the men rest in line. Eat something if they can. Drink water. Signal all of the ships to pull shoreward as close as they can and prepare to provide support. Have the supply ships send us more gunpowder and ammunition."

"I'll see to it."

As Bomilcar walked off, a longboat skidded into the sand not far away, Lucilla jumping out of it.

"No," Ky said, the word coming out angry and clipped. "You said you'd stay on the ship."

Ignoring him, she asked, "How is the battle faring?"

"Terribly. Our losses have been very high. We've inflicted far greater casualties on the enemy, a staggering number, but they still outnumber us significantly. If the losses continue at the same rate, we will run out of men before they do."

"Do you think we can hold out?"

"I don't know. There's nowhere for us to run. The enemy will smash us into the sea, and there's little we can do about it. The added weight of firepower from the ships will help, but I'm not sure it will be enough to turn the tide. I think it's time to consider that you and a few others get to the ships, prepare to flee if it goes bad."

"I'm not leaving. If you fall, I fall with you. If you want me safe, figure out how to win this fight."

Ky glared at her a moment, furious, but didn't argue. There wasn't any point and he didn't have time for it.

"We hold here and pound them hard with the ships. I've ordered everything afloat with cannon to move forward as close as they can and prepare to fire on the enemy. That should triple my artillery, and it can't be overrun. I'm hoping it accelerates their losses enough to change the balance."

"There's something else we can do," Lucilla said. "The cavalry are practically useless here, and there's that smaller pass to the west. While the enemy regroups, I can take the remaining cavalry and a cohort or even a few centuries. We can circle around and hit the enemy from the rear. Phalanxes struggle when attacked from two sides. And to answer us, they'll have to push through those narrows again, while I can put my men up on the cliff. If they try to ignore us, I hit them with the cavalry. They'll be forced to fight in two directions."

"That's not a terrible idea, but there is no way I'd let you lead it. Anyone in that rear force would be exposed and if the enemy decides to turn around and focus on you ..."

"Then he'd open himself up to your smashing into him, letting his army be pushed between the cliff and you, which also works for us," she said, and then gestured to the battle-weary soldiers around them. "Look at the men. They're shaken. They haven't seen losses this bad since we fought outside Devnum four years ago. I need to be with them. Don't make me make it an order."

For a long time, Ky didn't answer. He could see the enemy was getting assembled through his drone feed. They'd start marching soon. She wasn't going to back down, and if he tried to set it up and go around her, she'd just order her way into leading it anyway. Any tribune Ky tried to put in charge wouldn't dare ignore his Empress. Short of tying her up himself and carrying her to the ship, there was no way to stop her.

And he didn't have time for this.

"This is a terrible idea. Fine. Take a cohort and get moving. You have maybe thirty minutes before they attack us, forty-five at most. Be careful."

"I will." Lucilla turned to start gathering the men, then paused. "Ky, if I don't ..."

"Don't say it."

Ky pulled her into a fierce embrace.

"I love you," she said into his chest.

"I love you, too."

Letting her go, he watched as she walked off, already calling out orders and assembling her men. He spared one last look before turning his attention back to his own men. They were now one cohort down, making this all the harder.

It took almost an hour, but finally, the enemy finished shuffling around, getting their forces reorganized, and started moving forward again. If he'd been in their place, Ky would have pressed his men forward as soon as they got through the narrows. Instead, they had their soldiers and conscripts in the heat, after hours of desperate battle, constantly being moved around and yelled at, with only the food and water they had on them for sustenance.

In comparison, his men had an hour to sit on the ground, drink the water and food they brought up, and have a moment's peace. They all knew the fighting was coming again, but it would help shore up morale and give his men the energy to fight again.

Their rest was now over.

It didn't take long for the Carthaginians to come into view, although they could hear the army almost as soon as it started moving. Only the slight rise and falling off the about halfway between their forces kept them out of view.

That rise also made the perfect marker for when to start firing. Even with volley fire, they would need to cross at least another four hundred yards before they could hope to cause any number of casualties. His artillery didn't have those limitations, however.

As soon as the Carthaginians crested the rise, his artillery and all of the cannons on the ships began firing.

So far, the only ranks that had made their appearance were conscripts, which were getting hammered hard by the now greatly augmented Britannian artillery which pounded into their ranks again and again, tearing men in half and leaving craters in the rocky ground.

Behind every few rows of conscripts, were officers and armored soldiers, pushing the men ahead of them forward. A group of conscripts, no more than a dozen men, broke ranks and tried to run. They made it no more than a few paces before the soldiers behind them cut them down. The only way out of the hell they were facing was forward, so on the Carthaginians pushed in spite of the damage being done, as row after row of Carthaginians followed behind, a seemingly endless stream cresting over the small rise and into view.

For every man that fell, two more seemed to take his place, stepping over the bodies of their comrades. In spite of the heavy price they were paying, the Carthaginians continued their advance. As they reached the four-hundred-yard mark, the Britannian rifles joined the battle, volley after volley adding to the cacophony of fire, tearing into the oncoming men. Where men had been falling by the handful, they now fell by the dozen. The ground was littered with so many bodies that it slowed the advance, allowing more death to be dealt to them, and still the Carthaginians moved forward.

As their men crossed the three-hundred-yard mark, the Carthaginian artillery made its appearance, cresting over the hill and stopping, their crews setting the weapons up. Their cannons were much lower quality, but at this range, they were good enough to hit they're targets. The ships were too far for them, most likely, but they seemed to be happy ignoring that source of danger anyway.

They began to do their damage. Many shots missed, falling short or flying out into the water, but just as many hit, landing amongst his men, tearing them apart or peppering them with shards from the containers thrown by the catapults.

They were inaccurate enough that they weren't likely to cause the same causalities as their infantry would, when they finally connected, but they were tearing holes in his line. A badly placed, or probably well placed, from the enemy's point of view, shot could open a gap in his line, allowing the Carthaginians to spill through, splitting his forces in two.

Which would be the end of his army.

"Have the ships redirect their fire toward that artillery," Ky ordered. "Keep on them till every piece of siege equipment is gone.

By Sophus's estimate, the Carthaginians had taken another fifteen thousand casualties as his men tore into them again and again. But they never stopped. They pressed forward, over the dead, until they finally crossed the last few feet and their lines met with a clash of steel. Again, the tide started to turn, with the weight of numbers and armed for hand-to-hand combat, the Carthaginians had the edge once the battle closed. His men were making the Carthaginians pay the price for their success, but they just didn't have enough firepower to end it.

Several times, Ky began to rush forward, to put himself with the men, and each time his lictore and officers pulled him back. One time even Sophus turned against him, using his muscle assist to freeze up his legs as he tried to run forward. They were right to do it. Ky, even with his augmented abilities and the assistance of Sophus, was still only human. If he'd had his old flight suit with its kinetic shielding, maybe he could have made the difference, but that was lost two years ago.

There were just too many men coming at them. So instead, he watched. Watched his men fight and die, knowing that soon, he'd have to fight anyway, as the enemy pushed them back into the surf.

Ky had avoided using the few rounds he had in his sidearm, since he had a very poor shot from where he stood, needing to go either to the front line or onto one of the ships to have enough of an angle to fire it. That wait was about to end, and Ky reached down, gripping the weapon. Soon the front line would come to him and he would show them they still had teeth.

"New contact on the drone feed, Commander," Sophus said, breaking Ky's single-minded concentration on the battle.

He'd been so focused, he'd stopped looking at the drone almost entirely.

At first, he wasn't sure what was happening, other than the rear of the enemy formation was in chaos. Instead of pushing forward, some had begun to reverse their direction. Ky would have thought it a retreat, except that armies didn't retreat starting with the rear, especially when those elements had yet to engage.

411

Then he saw men flung about as something smashed into them, tearing through the rear of their ranks. Pulling the drone feedback, Ky shifted, following the trajectory of the shot. There, on the ridge where the Carthaginians had pushed his army back through was Lucilla's detachment, lined on the cliff. She'd apparently dug out the artillery he'd given to Antonius, wheeled them up to the ridge line and was using them to hammer the rear of the enemy force.

A ripple started to spread through the Carthaginians as they realized they were being attacked from behind, with men dying who were still on the other side of the ridge, where Ky's own fire shouldn't have been able to reach. As the rear force of the enemy began to react, retracing its steps to deal with the threat behind it, the pressure on Ky's men eased off. Men, even those close to the front lines, seemed confused, unsure of what was happening.

"Signal 'press the attack!'" Ky commanded.

"Consul, our men are almost to the surf. There's no ..." Bomilcar started to say, his surprise at the order evident.

"Lucilla has begun to attack their rear. She's set up on the cliff edge we passed through and has several centuries blocking the narrows itself. Look to the ridge line."

Bomilcar, whose attention was focused on the men in the front line, making sure no hole in the line lasted long enough to break his men, looked amazed. A Carthaginian who had been on this side of the rise turned and ran in the other direction. Every minute, more and more of the Carthaginian army, realizing they were suddenly the end of the line, joined him. They were turning around to address the threat behind them. The Carthaginians had convinced the soldiers in the center of their line it was some kind of retreat.

Worse, a lot of those turning and running were the soldiers keeping the conscripts in the battle. The few that remained, mostly black-clad figures wearing some kind of mask, were being swarmed by their own men as the conscripts turned their weapons on the men making them fight.

The rest of the conscripts, at least those not directly in contact with the Britannians, began dropping their weapons and running, both to the rear, pressing into the forces trying to attack Lucilla's position, but also east and west down the beach.

The Carthaginian army was in complete chaos.

Which is when Ky saw it. A group of men with a litter on their backs were pushed back onto the ridge by soldiers spilling around them, making a run for the rear. Kneeling on that litter, shouting at everyone around him, was a rotund man in deep purple robes.

"Hand me a rifle," Ky said.

"Consul?" Strabo, the lictore closest to him, asked, seeming confused.

"Quickly, hand me your rifle."

Although not understanding what was happening, his guard didn't have to be told twice, extending the loaded weapon to his commander.

Ky swung it around and hefted the weapon to his shoulder, squinting down the barrel. The Carthaginian emperor was at very long range for this weapon, or it would have been for anyone other than Ky. The former pilot, following a targeting display presented across his vision, lifted the weapon slightly, aiming over the head of where the emperor was.

He stopped breathing entirely, the weapon pressed into his shoulder with unnatural stability, as he pulled the trigger. There was a long delay for those around him, still trying to figure out who he was shooting at as Sophus projected the bullet's path as it flew.

One moment, the emperor was shouting commands, pointing this way and that, and then his head all but exploded as the large, fifty-two caliber bullet smashed into the side of his head.

His position allowed nearly the entire Carthaginian army to see him die. What had been almost like a rout as the Carthaginians turned to take on Lucilla's forces, now turned into an actual one. Men pressed for the rear, trying to get away, only to find the narrow entrance into the pass through the cliff blocked by hundreds of Roman soldiers, who had spent the time waiting for the Carthaginians to attack them rolling rocks and even bodies in the way, forming a barricade. As the enemy tried to break through, the barricade grew as men died by the dozen from concentrated blasts of fire from above them on the cliff as hundreds more fired down on them. It was a slaughter.

"Push the men forward," Ky ordered. "Let's end this."

Chapter 36

Carthage

Ky walked through the ruined halls of the Carthaginian Emperor's palace, amazed by its sheer opulence. After a lifetime growing up in the spartan and utilitarian barracks and space stations, he'd always considered the Roman palaces and temples to be the most extravagant places in all of existence. Seeing this, he realized he was very wrong.

Thanks to the Carthaginian Emperor's decision to conscript nearly every adult male in the city and across the countryside, they'd managed to take Carthage itself without a fight, sparing it from the devastation that the rest of the Western world experienced from this war.

"How is it?" Lucilla asked him as he entered the emperor's massive personal rooms, which they had begun to turn into a headquarters for the legions.

"So far so good. After what happened in Sicilia, I'm still having squads go door to door, spiraling out from here to the rest of the city, just in case. I've cordoned off several blocks in all directions around this building as a safe zone for our men to operate out of until reinforcements begin to arrive. The priests are outraged about being ousted, but they were the only ones who worked in this region. Or at least the only ones still living. Once we get more men, we'll start pulling back the martial law and letting people operate a little more freely."

"And the hospital?"

"Set up. I already sent a message back home requesting some of the Imperial physicians be sent with whatever chemicals Sorantius can spare to begin setting up something more proper, but the medics with the legions have enough for now."

"Good," Lucilla said, and then did a slow turn, looking around the room. "It's hard to believe it's really over."

"I know. The cost was high, but we managed to end it once and for all. Britannia is safe."

"The cost was high," she said. "Two thousand dead. Twice that many injured. We've managed to kill a generation of our most loyal men. It'll take us decades to recover."

"I think you'll be surprised by how fast we rebuild," Ky said, thinking of some of the images from the nineteenth and twentieth centuries Sophus had showed him when Ky had expressed a similar sentiment.

"I hope you're right."

"I'm not saying it will be easy. We'll need to occupy this region for an extended period. The people here are still hostile. Even if they had no love for their emperor, there isn't a person here that didn't lose someone."

"There is some good news, at least."

"Yeah?" Ky asked.

"Yes. The last supply ship had messages from Medb. We've received reports from our allies, who are equally thrilled to learn the war is over. Most of the major regions have begun to coalesce into more stable political entities. She and Ramirus are already putting together a large meeting of all of our allies to begin discussing what things should look like now. From what they're saying, I believe the alliances we have now, or at least partnerships, have a good chance of not only holding, but becoming something more in the future. The kind of alliance we can really build from, like what you described to me."

"Those parallels weren't exactly close. Most of those were nations with an inherent identity when they formed their alliance. I know Gaul, Germania and the like are starting to set up something like that, but they're still not particularly centralized, which will make any kind of large scale, region or multi-region wide alliance difficult to maintain."

"We can at least try," Lucilla said. "We have the model we set up which, at least for now, is working."

"That doesn't even include Persia, Italia and Greece. Considering their proximity to Germania and Gaul and their position in the Middle Sea, we can keep men in Italia for some time, but Greece and Persia will both be in chaos for a long while, and I'm not sure how anyone would feel about us becoming involved in another large scale project like that, especially so far from home."

"No. We'll leave them to their own devices, aside from maybe having Ramirus make enough contacts to keep an eye on them and continuing to have Valdar's ships patrolling the region. I think, eventually, they will stabilize. The only region that I'm really concerned about is Egypt. They got away more or less intact, and have made agreements for us to sell them equipment, but have been very cagey as to what they're willing to agree to. Ramirus will have to keep an especially close eye on them. But ... I still think this all bodes well for the future. With so many allies and no major enemies outside of bandits and whatever warlords set up in Persia or Greece, it seems likely we'll manage to have security and peace. Finally."

"Maybe. There's still the people who were supplying weapons to the Carthaginians. We've only been able to find a handful of witnesses who saw the envoys and messengers. The emperor's entire noble class and inner circle were wiped out by the emperor's religious zealots after his death, and any military leaders mostly died in the battle."

"You said they were very far away, further than even Alexander conquered, beyond mountains and deserts," Lucilla said.

"They are, but they've managed to send a lot of supplies this way. With the new sailing ships, which according to Valdar they have also more or less built, the world is much smaller than it once was. Beyond the fact that they openly chose a side to support, since they never contacted us or our allies to sell supplies, their level of technology is very concerning to me. The cannons they supplied to Carthage were far ahead of what they should have been able to produce. I don't understand how they managed to develop such advanced weapons, and that could be a problem."

"I thought they reverse-engineered our designs."

"It seems unlikely, Your Majesty," Sophus said. "Having an opportunity to examine what was left of the Carthaginian stores, it seems clear the designs and construction techniques used in their weapons are different from ours. They exhibit elements that we chose to skip over in favor of more advanced models."

"Then we'll deal with that when we have to. As you said, their construction methods were inferior to ours, right?"

"For now. Just because these weapons weren't reverse-engineered doesn't mean they can't still do that. Actually, since they could get this far on their own, it's more likely. We lost enough weapons over the last several years of fighting that, considering how close their relationship with the Carthaginians was, they might already be doing that."

"None of us ever believed that defeating Carthage would end all conflict in the world. We'll figure out the mystery of their suppliers, but for now, our focus should be on patrolling our region and recovering from the war. The death toll across the Carthaginians, Britannians, allies, and civilians numbers in the millions. It will take a long time to overcome that loss. Aside from that, many of our allies are still operating at the same technological level that Rome was at when you first arrived. There's much work to be done before we need to worry about external threats."

"True," Ky said. "I just don't want us to ignore a possible threat by assuming we solved everything by defeating Carthage."

"And we won't. But for now, we focus on rebuilding and strengthening our alliances. We share our knowledge and technology with those who are willing to learn and adapt. We establish trade routes and encourage cultural exchange. Strengthening the West and our alliances is the best thing we can do to counter any potential Eastern threat. In the meantime, we keep an eye out for any new information. Ramirus and his network will continue to investigate, but our priority should be the stability and prosperity of our people."

"And if they come for us before we've recovered?"

"Then we'll handle it like we've handled everything else the last few years," Lucilla said, crossing the distance between them and putting her hands on his chest. "We'll deal with it together."

"I can work with that," Ky said, leaning down and kissing her.

The End
(until Imperium, Volume II)

About the author

Travis writes science fiction, fantasy, and thriller novels (and the occasional coming-of-age story), with the hope of transporting and enthralling readers. Publishing novels since 2015, Travis's passion is creating worlds and characters that live and breathe, and experiencing the joy of those stories with his readers.

When not writing, Travis enjoys connecting with readers and other writers, managing the popular Complete Marvel Reading Order website, where he works on his other passion for comics and graphic novels, and spending time with his family.

If you have enjoyed this book, please consider taking a moment to rate or review it wherever you found your copy, as it helps new readers find my works and ensures I can continue writing book into the future.

Find out more at:
amazon.com/TravisStarnes/e/B072YBDC3S/

Or visit
https://tstarnes.com

Maps available at

https://tstarnes.com/book-series/imperium/

Signup to get free previews and notifications of upcoming books at

http://tstarnes.com/preview-notification-newsletter/

Other Books

John Taylor Stories

Rebirth
False Signs
The Wrong Girl
Burying the Past
Family Ties
Election Day
Danger Close
Extraction
Designated Target
Border Crossed
Desperate Rendition

Country Roads Series

Playing by Ear
Fanfare
Dissonance
Elegy
From the Top
Center Stage

Imperium Series

Volume 1
The Sword of Jupiter
The Trumpets of Mars
The Sands of Saturn
The Depths of Neptune
The Fires of Vulcan
The Triumph of Venus
Volume 2
The Wings of Mercury
The Plains of Pluto

Shattered Lands Series

In the Shadow of Lions
An Ending of Oaths

False Start Series

Second Down

The Veilguard Saga

Threads of Destiny

Stand Alone

Going Home

www.ingramcontent.com/pod-product-compliance
Lightning Source LLC
Chambersburg PA
CBHW070834260626
47170CB00007B/2361